BABYLON

CAMILLA CEDER

Translated by Marlaine Delargy

ISIS

LARGE PRINT

Oxford

First published in Great Britain 2012
by
Weidenfeld & Nicholson
an imprint of the Orion Publishing Group Ltd.

Published in Large Print 2013 by ISIS Publishing Ltd.,
7 Centremead, Osney Mead, Oxford OX2 0ES
by arrangement with
Orion Publishing Group Ltd.

CIP data is available for this title from the British Library

ISBN 978–0–7531–9188–0 (hb)
ISBN 978–0–7531–9189–7 (pb)

Printed and bound in Great Britain by
T. J. International Ltd., Padstow, Cornwall

BABYLON

"It is important to distinguish between envy, jealousy and greed. Envy is the spiteful feeling that someone else owns and enjoys something desirable — the envious impulse is to take it away or destroy it [. . .] Jealousy is based on envy, but affects at least two other people; it concerns principally the love to which the subject believes he has a right, but which has been taken from him [. . .] Greed is a violent and insatiable desire to possess something, above and beyond what the subject needs and what the object can or wishes to give. On the unconscious plane, the main aim of greed is to hollow out the breast completely, to suck it dry and eat it up."

Melanie Klein, *Love, Guilt and Reparation*

CHAPTER
ONE

Gothenburg

"I didn't plan it all in advance. Somewhere in my mind I had a picture of his new Volvo covered in bird shit. But I didn't think it through: *If I tip a bucket of prawn shells over the car, it will be worth significantly less in the morning. The paintwork will be scratched. The dried-on shit will be almost impossible to remove.* I didn't think like that. I just did it. I just tipped the shells over the car."

"The window on the driver's side wasn't properly closed."

"Sorry?"

"You told me the window wasn't completely —"

"Yes, I pushed some prawn shells through the gap too. I've told you that already."

Rebecca Nykvist fiddled irritably with a feather she had pulled out of the armchair. Birger Warberg followed her movements as she extended her arm and allowed the feather to drift slowly to the floor, where it disappeared into the carpet's pattern.

"You were the one who brought this up again, Rebecca."

"Of course I knew I wasn't doing him a favour. The whole point was to make life difficult for him. But it

1

wasn't *planned*. I'd had a couple of girlfriends round. We'd eaten prawns. I'd been talking about Magnus and how he'd let me down, I'd drunk a fair amount of wine and . . . I was bloody furious. I did it on impulse, I've told you so. I've said it over and over again, and it was a long time ago. I don't see the point in digging it all up now."

"I thought it sounded like something you'd described before, in some way."

"Something? In some way?"

"Now you sound annoyed."

"Sorry. So what are you getting at?"

"You behave impulsively when you feel under pressure. You're jealous. I think it's significant that you've brought up the business of Magnus's car in relation to your fears about Henrik's fidelity. And that you are possibly . . . how can I put this . . . underplaying your own part in the story."

"I am not underplaying anything!"

Rebecca raised her voice. "How could I? I had to spend hours going over the whole thing with the police; it was like a murder inquiry. And besides, the little bastard got the whole fucking car resprayed at my expense."

"I still believe I can see a connection. You talk about your fear of being treated badly by Henrik, just as you felt you were treated badly by Magnus . . ."

"Was. Just as I *was* treated badly by Magnus."

". . . and at the same time you are trying to work through your fear. To deal with your insecurities. But recently you have gone from acknowledging that your

2

jealousy is a significant problem to questioning whether what you did to Magnus and Georg was in fact wrong. Whether Magnus and Georg had done something to deserve your rage."

"It's cruel of you to bring up what happened with Georg. That was ten years ago, Birger. It's old news. I'll say it again: how could I underplay the situation? I was barely allowed to keep my job, and I had to give up everything I found fulfilling."

"Old news, then?"

"Isn't our time up soon?"

Rebecca glanced over her shoulder. A wry smile crossed her freckled face.

"I see you still have that clock. I thought we'd agreed that it's not healthy in a therapeutic environment. You know I find it distracting."

"I might be wrong, but I think you're afraid of your own volatility. Of your impulsiveness. I think you're afraid that your anger will bring destruction. Figuratively speaking."

"Oh, figuratively speaking. Thank you very much. I am a psychologist as well, you know."

Rebecca got to her feet.

"Three minutes left. I don't think we're going to make any more progress today."

Rebecca ran her hand through her curly red hair and headed for the door, her high heels tapping loudly as she walked.

CHAPTER
TWO

She still hadn't fitted a new lock on her mountain bike.
Having lost the key and cut off the old lock, she didn't
dare leave the bike in front of her house. They were like
magpies, whoever *they* were. Instead she pushed the
bike into the passage between the wall and the tool
shed; it was going to be fenced in, but at the moment it
was cluttered with rubbish: broken kitchen chairs, a
garden hose, old pots. The washing machine that had
broken last year; nobody had got round to taking it to
the tip.

Rebecca swore as she banged her shin on the rotting
stepladder, which was hidden in tall grass.

Henrik was sitting at the computer in the study,
concentrating hard. She could see his back through the
window. A second later he got up and went into the
kitchen.

Even though her shin was throbbing and walking was
painful, she still took the longer route around the fence
and garden path up to the porch. Having bought the
house quite recently, she loved looking at its façade
from the street. She imagined she was seeing it for the
first time: the narrow, pale-green house in a row of
equally lovely, pastel-coloured homes; a picture

postcard street in the middle of the city She loved the expensive paving stones, the way the path cut through charmingly overgrown flowerbeds and led up to the red door.

The first thing they did when they moved in was to buy a red door and a knocker in the shape of a lion's head. Rebecca knew she wanted to live in a house with a red door and a doorknocker; she had always thought of herself as a homemaker. She had grown up in a fairly large house, and had been spoiled by having so much space. Even though the apartments she used to rent had been airy and attractive, she was never at ease with the fact that other people were living and breathing under the same roof. Sometimes she would lie in bed at night imagining a stranger in the darkness, separated from her by just a thin wall. She had never been entirely comfortable with the thought.

Unsurprisingly, she was the driving force when they started talking about houses and they finally settled on the terraced property in Kungsladugård. The area lay to the west of the city; it was comparatively central and not far from the sea, just like the street in Billdal where she grew up.

She was pleased with how things had worked out. She could walk to work easily, through Slottsskogen Park and across Linnéstaden into the city centre. During their first year in the house she often went down to Röda Sten at the weekends, and would read on the jetties there before gathering her strength and taking the long way home via Nya Varvet and Kungsten. On a hot day she could cycle to the naturist beach at Saltholmen; they could manage perfectly well without a car and still enjoy the best the city had to offer.

Unfortunately they hadn't been the only ones to see the advantages of the house. She had had palpitations all day while the bidding process was going on. Henrik had remained silent and tense. Since Rebecca already had a well-paid job as staff welfare coordinator at what was then one of Sweden's largest companies, it was taken as read that she held the purse strings. Now, her post was restricted to an administrative role.

When Rebecca had met Henrik six years earlier, she had realised her ex-boyfriends were almost interchangeable. Like Rebecca, they had all grown up in well-off families and they had all followed in Daddy's footsteps, training to become doctors or lawyers, with a sense of purpose but also a sense of anxiety. Some of them had been very easy to get on with. Some she had really liked. But when she met Henrik, she fell head over heels in love; he made every other man seem dull. He was proud and quick and excitingly charismatic; artistic and sensitive to a fault. She fell for him, and they moved in together.

They had a good life. Henrik was attuned to the feelings of others. He exuded love, warmth and positive energy. Women loved him for it, as did Rebecca, and a classic situation developed: the thing she loved most about Henrik quickly became one of their major stumbling blocks. His charm made her jealous and this, in turn, made him evasive.

6

Their friends usually claimed the gender divide didn't kick in until children came along. The house had been Henrik and Rebecca's child; it was only when they had an attic, a cellar and a garden on their hands that Rebecca realised Henrik didn't match up to *The Husband* she had imagined since she was a child. Her father had always managed to look after both the large house in Billdal and the summer cottage in Mollösund while doing a responsible and well-paid job.

It was clear, she thought, as she gritted her teeth and avoided the loose third step, that the same rights and obligations should apply to both men and women, at work and behind closed doors. From that point of view she was a feminist. But, in recent years she had experienced a creeping irritation at Henrik's way of shirking traditional male responsibilities.

"Hello?"

Rebecca kicked off her boots in the hallway and went into the kitchen. An open packet of cheese and half a loaf caught her eye. From the shiny surface of the cheese, she guessed it was a while since he'd eaten.

"Hello?"

Henrik appeared in the doorway with a smile on his lips which immediately made her suspicious. He looked irresolute for a moment but, she thought, obviously aware of her scrutiny. He blew his long fringe from his face, a gesture so well practised that he owned it. He was wearing a tight T-shirt, no doubt deliberately a little too short, which emphasised his muscular body; given that he never set foot in a gym, he clearly had good genes. Perhaps no one else would call Henrik vain, but

Rebecca sometimes thought he had a coquettishness about him.

"I thought you were going to study today?"

She immediately regretted the underlying reproach. She was still glad to see him. In theory, her criticisms were justified, which was why she still made them, but the feeling remained that she wanted to be with him. That, right now, she was happy to be the one he wrapped his arms around, and no one else. But that feeling didn't last. As soon as they parted, doubt crept in.

In recent months she had thought he seemed more distant, physically and emotionally. He had been revising in the university library for a couple of evenings each week, and when they were together he either appeared distracted or overcompensated by being particularly nice. Sometimes he simply switched off his mobile when she rang.

He passed her on his way to the sink, where he quickly rinsed out his mug, filled it with water and took a couple of gulps before pouring the rest away.

"I'm just off. Axel's waiting, we're going to work at his place."

"When's the exam?"

"Monday. But I've got an assignment to hand in as well."

He cut a large piece of the rapidly drying out cheese and popped it in his mouth. She watched his jaws work, feeling her disappointment grow.

"And I thought you might like a bit of time to yourself."

His casualness seemed forced. The voice of her therapist echoed in Rebecca's head. *See if you can ignore the signals. Can you decide not to act on a particular feeling immediately?*

"Actually, I've had a bloody awful day."

His eyes darted round the kitchen; he couldn't meet her gaze.

Rebecca's problem was that the signals were clear. They were real enough to fuel her jealousy. The other night she dreamt Henrik stubbed her out beneath his boot like a cigarette butt. Yet she knew she had overreacted many times before.

"Is it method and theory, or whatever it's called?"

"*Method and Theory in Classical Archaeology*. It's a doorstop of a book. I'd be lying if I said I'd read it from cover to cover, but it does go on. It tells you stuff that's obvious. I'll pass the exam, don't you worry."

It hadn't taken long to work out that Henrik was good at starting things but not at following them through. But he had managed to complete half of his modules. Perhaps this was a sign that, after living a semi-adult life of casual jobs and daydreams, disorganised studies and half-hearted efforts to become a jazz musician, he had finally found his vocation. It was only natural that he couldn't quite go the distance. Rebecca knew, more than anyone, that the road to hell was paved with good intentions.

You couldn't live other people's lives for them, but Henrik's enthusiasm a couple of years ago had been infectious. It had given her hope that one day they would be financial equals.

"That old saying that someone whispers in your ear before you're even born and tells you what your role in life will be — I believe in that more than ever," Henrik had said after his first module in archaeology. "If you're lucky you find out what it is early in life, but whenever it happens, it feels fantastic."

Henrik could live by his wits, duping others into *believing* him. It wasn't that he was stupid. Or lazy. He still devoured piles of books that weren't on the reading list, which proved that his passion was real. Unfortunately this passion didn't cure his deep-rooted problems with authority. He overslept, missed tutorials and seminars, handed in assignments answering different questions from the ones his tutor had set. He complained to Rebecca about the syllabus, the staff (with just a few exceptions), and the faculty as a whole. He made up excuses as though she were his mother, and his aim was to pull the wool over her eyes and not his own. She was all too familiar with the process. He was clearly beginning to tire of the whole thing.

Rebecca turned her back to him and started to put the food away in the fridge.

"You're meeting up this late?" She deliberately kept her voice neutral.

"I told you, I'm just leaving."

Henrik fetched Rebecca's big Marimekko bag from the bedroom. With deliberately purposeful gestures (or so she thought), he placed the book in the bag along with a couple of other reference books and a notepad.

"I've bought a bottle of red," she couldn't help saying. "If you're not too late back, I mean."

Was he avoiding her gaze?

He paused. "I'm not sure. I've still got loads to write. And Axel's asked me to help him with a couple of things he doesn't understand. I wouldn't wait up if I were you. I think we're really going to get stuck in tonight. Get everything out of the way."

He went into the hallway and opened the cloakroom door. Rebecca hated herself for following him.

"By the way, have you heard back about your student loan? I can barely afford to pay the mortgage on top of everything else. And I'm sure it's going to cost a fortune to get the boiler fixed, or whatever we have to do . . . I thought I might watch that film you rented yesterday."

She was saying anything just to keep him there. Instead of answering, he leant over and planted a cool kiss on her lips, then put his hands on her shoulders and held her away from him.

"Rebecca . . ."

She sighed.

"Do we have to talk about this now? Everything will turn out just fine. Trust me."

"What are you talking about?"

"I've got to go. But if the worst comes to the worst, I can always earn a bit extra a couple of nights a week. A couple of gigs now and then and we'll be fine. No problemo, baby!"

The door closed behind him.

Fuck. She walked upstairs slowly, flopped onto the bed and switched on the TV. The window was ajar, and she could hear noise from the street below. Voices and laughter rose and fell; there were footsteps on the pavement. Suddenly she heard the front door open.

She rolled onto her side and put one foot on the floor. "Hello?"

"Sorry, only me. Forgot something."

She heard Henrik rummaging around in the hallway, then he swore loudly as something fell on the floor and smashed.

"I hope that wasn't my grandmother's vase," she shouted, just as she caught sight of her reflection in the mirror. The sinews in her neck were fully extended, making her look grotesque.

"No . . . fuck. No, it was just a glass some idiot had left on the stairs. Me no doubt. Shit . . . Listen, sweetheart, I'm horribly late, I'm going to leave you to clean this up. I'll wash up for the rest of the week, promise. Love you!"

He left for the second time. Rebecca turned up the volume so she wouldn't have to hear him setting off towards Mariaplan, where Axel lived alone. She pulled a blanket over her legs and made a nest of pillows. In the ad break she would go down and fetch a glass of wine.

CHAPTER
THREE

Henrik was in a hurry. He almost came off his bike outside the ICA supermarket when his wheel got stuck in a tram line. Luckily, he managed to put one foot on the ground, suffering a severe blow in the solar plexus but emerging otherwise unscathed. He reflected on the fact that he was the only person who cycled without a helmet these days, the last rebel in a circle of acquaintances who were mostly the weary parents of small children. Even Rebecca had fallen in line. When she was in a rush in the mornings, she would slip her contact lenses into her pocket and put on her thick glasses and shiny red helmet. He didn't even recognise her then.

He carried on along the cycle track at a more measured pace, down Bragebacken to the car park on the edge of Slottsskogen Park. In the past this spot had been rumoured to be a haunt of rent boys, and all manner of shady dealings were supposed to go on. He hurried on when he saw a black van parked behind the deserted ice-cream kiosk.

But the kiosk would be opening up soon. The long winter was over. The demonstration that had taken place the previous day was usually the first sign of spring. The weather was always good on May Day.

Henrik was in his usual state: hungover but content.

Today outdoor types were hunting for the best spot for a barbecue. The May evening was the warmest of the year so far — no doubt the festivities would continue well into the small hours. Just as he was passing the Domen College of Art, his mobile beeped: *c u wknd 4 revision. nd 2 wrk hrd.*

Axel. Should he tell him the official version of events? Axel wouldn't ask questions; Henrik's relationship with Ann-Marie Karpov was hardly news to him.

Sometimes Henrik had the feeling that the knowledge bothered his friend. Perhaps it had something to do with the firm convictions Axel held, even though he rarely made a big deal of them. Axel had only brought the affair up once, and had been blunt: *And what the hell does she see in you?* Even if that sort of comment wasn't good for Henrik's self-confidence, at least it was honest. Henrik valued directness.

They hadn't been friends for very long, although they had passed in and out of each other's circles for several years now. They first met at the Nefertiti, back in the good old days; Henrik played regularly at the jazz club and Axel seemed out of place — but then again he did everywhere. Henrik took pity and bought him a couple of beers out of his fee. Later, they had kept on choosing the same courses. When they both enrolled for archaeology, they couldn't help exchanging a wry smile: "Fancy seeing you here . . ."

14

But it had taken a week in the creative chaos of Istanbul for Henrik and Axel to become close. Before the study visit they had never spent time together one on one. Axel was regarded by fellow students as the slightly eccentric country bumpkin, whose defining feature was his fanatical opposition to computers. He and Henrik were both independent when it came to their work, and in any case it was rare to strike up close friendships in adulthood. But it just so happened that on the trip to Istanbul they both wanted to experience the feeling of being in one of the world's most fascinating cities; they weren't interested in downing shots, going to noisy bars or even to the techno clubs with belly dancers at the top of the Galata Tower, where the dry air was dotted with nesting swallows. And, as a result, they unexpectedly found each other.

Axel had become the person Henrik spent most time with, apart from Rebecca.

And Ann-Marie.

Because it was during this trip that Henrik and Ann-Marie Karpov, researcher and tutor in the Department of Archaeology and Ancient Civilisations, had also found each other.

Afterwards, Henrik found it difficult to understand how it had all happened. The triumphant scale of the city, the bewitching blend of the past and the future — Henrik at least was overwhelmed by the countless museums he visited, by the hustle and bustle of Beyoglu at night. Everyday life had begun to seem distant, irrelevant.

Their hotel lay between the historic Sultanahmet Mosque and the point at which the waters of the Bosphorus flowed into the Golden Horn and Lake Marmara. In its salons the raki and sweet Turkish wine had flowed in a most un-Swedish manner during the trip's spontaneous seminars. He remembered Ann-Marie watching him through the curtains of mist. His sense of reality had diminished; he had thought: *Go with the flow*.

What she had thought was less clear, but so far he had chosen not to speculate on her reasons. She was an authority in the subject he wanted to master more than any other. Her self-confidence made her attractive, in fact she was positively beautiful for a woman in her fifties, with a steel-grey bob exposing her long neck and defined facial features.

She saw something in him that he sometimes, though not often, doubted was really there. Admittedly he wasn't bad-looking, even if he had to admit in moments of self-doubt that a shaggy pageboy haircut was more charming on the twenty-four-year-old musician he had once been than the rather too mature student he had become. And his leather jacket, which he alternated with 1950s jackets, had been around since his youth and was threatening to fall apart.

He was definitely one of the more gifted students in the class. Their first conversation had arisen from his studies, which was only to be expected. Karpov had admired the way he challenged the limitations of the syllabus and asked for advice on the areas he wanted to pursue further. She had given him encouragement, and on one occasion they had conducted a long and remarkably relaxed conversation over coffee.

She intrigued him. Those who knew Henrik could have seen it in the very first week: he wanted Ann-Marie Karpov. And Ann-Marie Karpov had fallen for him — not immediately, but later, in Istanbul. Since then they had been a couple, albeit only to a limited group within the thick stone walls of the archaeology department. Their relationship was a secret from the rest of the world.

He just had to take the chance. Not to seize the opportunity when Ann-Marie Karpov offered him the post as her lover would have been just as absurd as Alice deliberately ignoring the key to Wonderland, just as stupid as those cowards on game shows who answer quits when they should have said double. You had to believe that double is better than quits. Perhaps this was what all those who were unfaithful claimed, but surely there was a kind of logic there that balanced out his guilt.

OK was his only response to Axel's message. There were limits to how dishonest a person could be. Forcing others to lie for him was definitely overstepping the mark. *If* Rebecca should ring Axel, against all the odds, and if Axel was stupid enough not to realise what was going on, then the entire house of cards would come tumbling down. In which case, so be it. At least it would mean an end to all the lies. *Inshallah.*

He thought about Rebecca with a pang of conscience as he cycled out of the park and down Rosengatan; his guilt was partly genuine, partly liberating. Rebecca's pathological jealousy had been a constant source of problems in their relationship. She had started seeing a therapist again, ironically after an ultimatum on his part. This might seem particularly heartless, given that he was now acting out her worst fears. But he still wasn't ready to end the affair.

He needed it.

He tried to rationalise the situation. Rebecca had driven him to infidelity with her constant suspicions; we become as others see us and so on. Qualified nonsense, but it was still true. He had enjoyed feeling appreciated and acknowledged by a woman who didn't use him only to vent her displeasure. He was sick and tired of hearing that he disappointed Rebecca on every level — sexually, emotionally, and not least financially. For several years now he had been forced to constantly justify himself, insisting that his finances would soon take a turn for the better.

He had decided to put his jazz career on the back burner and go back to his studies. Get a proper job — it was impossible to make a living as a musician in Gothenburg. Rebecca had been happy with that idea until she realised that his student loan would hardly cover his share of their outgoings, and that was when she had resigned herself to her fate. She had thrown in her lot with a pauper. These days she hardly seemed to have the energy to talk about the injustice of it all; their arguments had given way to a muted air of discontent which came to a head at the end of each month when the bills had to be paid. It was a time neither of them looked forward to.

Their relationship wasn't sustainable in the long term; there weren't enough reasons to stay with Rebecca, and he'd been thinking that way for a while.

But Henrik had major plans for himself and Ann-Marie. All he had to do was set the ball rolling. Things had gone wrong lately, he couldn't deny that, but today they would talk. Ann-Marie would listen and she would understand.

Because he needed her.

He braked outside the house on Linnégatan, then stood there for a while catching his breath. He took out his phone and called Axel.

"We're revising tonight," he informed his friend, and as he said that he made his decision once and for all. "Sorry to drag you into this, but soon there'll be no more lies. I want to be with Ann-Marie, and the whole world is going to know that. I've got a plan, but I have to carry it out in my own time. And I want to tell Rebecca myself. If she calls you, I want you to lie for me."

Axel said he understood.

After their conversation Henrik felt more exhilarated than he had done for a long time.

The city centre was full of life and movement. He loved how the streets were lined with restaurants. When he met up with his old friends they would usually stay around Järntorget: Jazzå or Solrosen, Pusterviks Theatre. He particularly liked the cosmopolitan atmosphere surrounding Andra Långgatan, where the porn shops and adult cinemas rubbed shoulders with Asian restaurants, cellar bars and specialist music shops. And yet he was usually glad to leave the party at the end of the evening. The group would disperse, as they had dispersed a few years ago because of career choices or the decision to start a family. Some would get in a taxi and head off to Munkebäck or Fiskebäck. One would take the night bus into the centre to wait for the first train to Lerum. Henrik would cycle home through the park as dawn broke.

But now he was pushing his bike along the short path that led from the street to the main door; slender trees trimmed into topiary spheres and chunky, low wrought-iron fences lined the path. Suddenly he felt like a man in his prime again, on his way to a passionate encounter with a fiercely intelligent, sexy woman, having an affair that was a secret for the moment, but would soon be clear for all the world to see, instead of a cowardly, lying little shit who was not only sponging off his girlfriend but also two-timing her; that thought had passed through his head without really registering. But now the winds of change were blowing.

He walked into the courtyard which never ceased to leave him dumbstruck. It was the result of ambition on a large scale in days gone by, but the secret was time. Only time could give a city garden such authority and dignity: enormous shrubs and roses scrambling around arches and up the hundred-year-old stone walls.

Karpov enforced a strict smoking ban in her six-room apartment, so Henrik rolled a cigarette before he went upstairs. His hands fumbled, and he realised he was nervous. It had been a while since they had seen each other one on one, after their last disastrous encounter. A series of tiresome conversations about their future together had inevitably culminated in conflict. A shabby, grudge-filled quarrel, as if they were a married couple. And that wasn't right. Their relationship wasn't meant to be like that. They should be above that kind of destructive sniping. Otherwise, what was the point?

Tonight he had decided that if Ann-Marie wanted to talk and sort things out, he would hold up his hands and take his share of the blame. He would accept that he had been pretty bad-tempered lately. He would explain why: everything at home. Constantly being told that he was irresponsible, incapable of acting his age. But it had still been wrong of him to flare up. Wrong of him to hurl an ornament onto the floor, that was a pathetic thing to do. Raising his voice, that was wrong too. Perhaps it was because he was stressed. There was a great deal at stake, and more than anything he wanted her with him.

And she would be his, as soon as she'd calmed down.

It was only natural really that tensions should arise between them. The situation was difficult. There was Rebecca, their different stations in life. The secrecy. The gossip that sometimes reached them by a circuitous route. But no relationship was static, after all; that was a well-known fact.

He could see a light in the fourth-floor window. Ann-Marie was waiting for him. She had probably cooked a meal which they would eat at the big dining table before withdrawing to the bedroom.

Henrik would be lying if he said he didn't feel a frisson when he stepped into this unfamiliar world of chandeliers and red carpets. Compared with a wordly, middle-aged woman, he was like a chimney sweep's lad. He smiled and decided to share the thought with Ann-Marie; it would probably amuse her. Or, with a bit of luck, it might inspire them to try some entertaining role-play later on.

The image made him laugh out loud as he ran a hand over his slicked-back hair, stubbed out his cigarette and pulled open the door.

"Henrik?" Ann-Marie Karpov's voice echoed between the stone walls. "Is that you?"

He set off up the stairs.

"Yes," he called back. "I'm just wondering whether to step into your minuscule, rattling cage of a lift, which stopped the last time, or risk a heart attack walking up eight flights of stairs. I think I'll go for the heart attack. Call the ambulance!"

The syllables bounced off one another; a discordant muddle of echoes which fell silent only when he reached her door.

CHAPTER
FOUR

It had been the perfect bag: large and practical, with compartments that could hold everything from files to spare clothes and make-up. And it looked good. Rebecca had a soft spot for simple but assured design. She had used the bag day after day for several years; now the fabric was beginning to fray and the seams were ragged. Since she didn't feel she could go to work looking scruffy — it was the kind of workplace that demanded a certain standard of dress — Henrik had taken over the dark-green bag to carry his books.

Rebecca's resolve had weakened after that first glass of wine. The TV programme came to an end and she crept down to the hallway and started rifling through Henrik's pockets. It had been a while; the therapy must have done some good. But now endorphins were coursing through her blood as if she were about to start a race as she examined his receipts and flicked through college notebooks, searching for unfamiliar phone numbers, women's names, coded messages concealed in dry lecture notes. Searching for anything that might reveal something. Anything at all.

She found the bag right at the back of the hallway cupboard, underneath a jacket which had fallen or been yanked from the hanger above. It was heavy. Inside she found *Method and Theory in Classical Archaeology*, a couple of reference books and two notepads. Before the realisation hit home, she weighed her find in her hands as if she sensed that it would have an important role to play in how her life panned out.

He hadn't taken his books. She turned towards the door and dropped what she was holding; it landed at her feet with a thud. And he hadn't come back to pick them up. He should have realised long ago that he'd left them behind. Which meant he hadn't forgotten them, he'd left them on purpose. Which in turn meant that he'd lied. People don't lie without a reason, so the question was: why had he lied? The answer was obvious: Henrik had not been going to Axel's flat to revise.

She took a few tentative steps; she needed to sit down and think. The leather seat creaked as she sank down numbly; the sound of the television upstairs faded away. Selective deafness, she thought. It affects people in shock. Then she pulled herself together and tried to look at the situation rationally.

Henrik hadn't even gone to the trouble of fully concealing his lies. Packing the bag right in front of her, that was good. But he hadn't been able to follow his plan to its pathetic conclusion. Presumably the bag had been too heavy. Too heavy to drag around unnecessarily, so he'd hidden it in the cupboard, where he thought she would never look. All a bit slapdash, which was just typical; he couldn't do anything properly. He wasn't all that clever, really. Particularly given that he knew she went through his pockets, knew that she was sometimes unable to resist the urge, even if she gave in less frequently these days. They had discussed the matter countless times, they'd even gone for relationship counselling. Nowadays her snooping wasn't generally the result of anger. It was more of an eccentric hobby, something that she did to calm herself down, and she always felt significantly better once the endorphin rush had subsided, and she had established that there was nothing suspicious among Henrik's things.

Her condition had improved so much that she no longer seriously expected to find anything. It was just nice to cover herself. To keep the possibility in mind, and so be ready for the worst.

And now the worst had happened.

She tried to think logically. She had to admit that on every previous occasion when jealousy had overcome her, the signs had seemed obvious, the signals impossible to misinterpret. There always seemed to be evidence that the man in question was letting her down, was betraying her. And a number of men really had.

She tried to push that thought from her mind.

She thought of her therapist, and wondered whether she could be exaggerating the signs in her mind. Had she been under too much stress lately? The sound of the television returned at full volume, adverts booming down the stairs, and she covered her ears with her hands.

The first time she rang Axel it was getting on for half-past ten, by which time she had spent over two hours pacing the room. Two voices were arguing in her head, the first alternating between a measured, conciliatory approach and a more severe tone: *It doesn't necessarily mean anything, there could be an innocent explanation, there always is, Rebecca! Don't treat Henrik the way you've treated the others. Don't crush him with your suspicions!*

The second voice was manic, and determined to wind her up: *There's still time to prevent the ultimate humiliation.*

She had the upper hand: Henrik didn't know that she knew. She clung to this fact like a drowning man to a lifebelt.

There was no reply from Axel. *They might have switched off their phones so they wouldn't be disturbed.* The conciliatory voice. *Obviously nobody's studying round at Axel's this evening,* said the manic voice.

After listening to Axel's answering machine three times without leaving a message, Rebecca just couldn't help herself. She found a list of telephone numbers for the University of Gothenburg and started ringing around. It was bordering on insanity, given the lateness of the hour. But if anyone was annoyed, they didn't mention it. Rebecca said she was Henrik's sister, and explained that they were supposed to be picking up their parents from the airport in the early hours of the morning. She was beginning to worry that he'd forgotten the whole thing — he was so distracted these days, poor soul.

Nobody had seen him.

"Maybe he's with Ann-Marie?" one of the women ventured. She had a shrill, slightly breathless voice. She sounded secretly triumphant, as if she knew everything.

Rebecca froze.

"Ann-Marie?"

"She's one of our tutors. She —"

"Yes, I know. Henrik's mentioned her. Karpov, isn't it?"

Henrik *had* mentioned Ann-Marie Karpov; she was one of the tutors he thought highly of. In the beginning Rebecca had got irritated with Henrik's obvious hero-worship; he talked about the woman the way a teenage girl talks about her favourite pop star; the way a five-year-old boy talks about his father. Rebecca had learnt to switch off when Henrik talked about what Karpov thought of this or that, what she had written and which debates she had been involved in. Now it struck her that, after the first year, Henrik had spoken less and less about Karpov. For Rebecca it had been something of a relief not to have to listen to his drivel, and if she had given it any thought, she had probably assumed the honeymoon was over, just as Henrik's enthusiasm for every project had a beginning and an end.

She had never, ever imagined that Henrik would have an affair with his tutor. The age difference had blinded Rebecca to the possibility. As if it were the first time a powerful woman had snared a younger man.

"They've been hanging out together quite a bit lately — there's a chance he might be with her."

Everything went black. Rebecca heard herself say, "Ann-Marie Karpov. You don't happen to know how I can get in touch . . .?"

She glanced at the telephone list in her hand, then hung up on the gossiping bitch. Her hands were shaking. She needed to calm down.

She took a sleeping tablet from the bathroom cabinet. She lay on top of the sheets, clasping the list to her body and just had time to think: *This is pointless, I won't be able to get to sleep anyway.* Her heart was beating in time with the rise and fall of her chest and she could hear her heart pounding in her ears as she drifted into a state which had very little to do with sleep. When she awoke two and a half hours later, she had the feeling she had dreamt something nasty but couldn't remember what. The pillow was wet with sweat or saliva or both. She swung her legs over the edge of the bed and poured herself another glass of wine from the open bottle. With the glass in her hand, she wandered around the house several times before picking up the phone again.

"Oh . . . hello . . ."

Axel answered this time; he sounded as if she'd woken him up.

"Sorry, Axel, it's Rebecca. I know what time it is, but I'm just so worried about Henrik. He hasn't come home yet. I'm afraid something might have happened to him."

"Er . . . I . . ."

"Come on, Axel. There's no point in lying. You're too tired to come up with anything good."

At first she thought he'd hung up in sheer terror. Then he cleared his throat, sounding troubled.

"Sorry, Rebecca. I don't know anything."

She gave up, put her coat on and went out.

Linnégatan was never completely deserted at night. Several bars had just closed and small clusters of people were still chatting in the street as reggae music poured from a restaurant kitchen. Occasionally, a nocturnal dog-walker would wander past.

The entrance Rebecca was looking for was tucked between the bar and a small English-language bookshop. She saw a courtyard that resembled a park. Wrought-iron benches were arranged around a disused fountain, with tall street lamps glowing between them. Along the sides of the courtyard she could make out roses and lilac. Rebecca had walked up and down this street ever since she was a child, and she had never known there was a garden behind the old stone buildings. She almost forgot why she was there. Then it struck her with full force.

She chose a door at random and tugged on it, but wasn't surprised to find it locked; of course the outside doors would be locked. And it was the middle of the night so there was little chance of following someone in.

She stood absolutely still, allowing her gaze to roam over the buildings' façades. They really were beautiful, and curiously silent. Were the buildings just as reluctant

29

to let in strangers as the people who inhabited them? *How the other half live,* she thought uncharitably. Lights were on in a small number of apartments. At one window, she caught sight of a figure behind a curtain. Rebecca allowed the shadows to swallow her up.

That was when she spotted his navy-blue mountain bike. It was almost invisible in a stand among several others. At least, she was sure that it was his at the time, even if it didn't have any particular distinguishing features. After a moment's hesitation she picked up a sharp stone and made a scratch along the frame. If she couldn't catch him red-handed, the scratch would provide proof when he rolled home in a few hours. She realised with growing frustration that she couldn't do much more. But if there was one thing that amazed Rebecca, it was how God had a tendency to hear the prayers of desperate people. She walked up to Karpov's door and found that it wasn't properly closed, or perhaps the lock was broken.

She let herself in, and tiptoed quickly up the stairs.

The turn-of-the-century panelled door was beautiful, but it was also thin; breaking it open would be a piece of cake.

She could hear footsteps from the apartment on the other side of the landing; she pulled up her hood over her red hair and slowly pushed the letterbox inwards. The hallway was dark and silent. She could smell food: curry, cumin and something else, something sweet.

CHAPTER
FIVE

Ann-Marie was lying in the bath. He was sure she'd gone in there simply to avoid him, even though their time together was precious. He could hear the sound of rushing water behind the door. Henrik sat on the sofa as the TV flickered silently a few metres away. He leafed through a magazine, but was too agitated to read.

She had turned off the tap; she must just be lying there now. A small green alarm clock, which looked totally out of place, ticked away on the mantelpiece, as if to remind him that every minute was a minute they would not get back. It was the middle of the night. He had covered himself by mentioning Axel, and telling her it would be a late one, but you never knew with Rebecca. She might suddenly get an idea in her head. He ought to go home.

Henrik had outlined his plans for a shared future to Ann-Marie; in the end he had talked himself into a dead end, and he ought to go home before he made the situation worse. But he didn't want to leave just yet. This was no note to leave things on.

Henrik really wished Ann-Marie hadn't gone into the bathroom with such an air of weary resignation. He wished she hadn't been so distant, as if her mind were

the two of them, but on something else entirely.
t she was going to do at the weekend, when Henrik
Rebecca were visiting mutual friends outside
ungsbacka, eating shrimps and tiramisu.

She seemed distracted, but was she actually afraid?

Earlier that evening he had been appalled by how much he had upset her. He had been frightened by the fact that he had scared her when he raised his voice and shouted in frustration: *I don't see what we have to gain by keeping our relationship a secret! I have no intention of doing so any longer!* When she accused him of threatening and blackmailing her, he had thought: I shouldn't be upsetting and frightening her.

He had apologised.

He had stopped laying out their future. Realised that he had to take a different tack, talk about love. Of course! She was a woman, after all. Like other women, she needed to feel wanted. She needed to know what he had always assumed was understood: that he was choosing her. *He* wanted *her*. He couldn't offer her much in the way of financial security or social standing, but then she was pretty well off anyway.

He had to be tender now and rational later. Henrik wasn't a calculating person, but this was what his relationship with Rebecca had done to him.

"*I want you, Ann-Marie. I'm ready to make a commitment. I'm by no means perfect, but . . . Blah, blah, blah . . .*"

He'd really gone for it tonight, cut straight to the chase. In his mind it had sounded honest. Disarming. Like someone who has learnt what he wants and is

32

ready to fight for it. In Henrik's mind, his words had sounded really good, almost like a film script.

As the words "I'm by no means perfect" came out, it did indeed sound like a film. A film with a banal, clichéd script, dashed off on a Monday morning. A script written by a spotty intern. He was suddenly painfully aware of how he must have looked in her eyes. The charming, scatty boy was beginning to look pathetic. He was trapped. Trapped in his relationship with Rebecca. Trapped in the person he had gradually become: the person who, compared with the oh-so-capable Rebecca . . .

"What's to say you wouldn't feel the same about me?" Ann-Marie had broken in, her voice thin, already weak. "What's to say that you wouldn't start comparing yourself to me and my achievements, and that you'd end up feeling inferior again? What if you didn't like that either?"

And he had forced himself to laugh, as if to suggest that her comment had been meant as a joke. Said that of course he had no interest whatsoever in measuring achievements within a relationship. It was Rebecca who weighed every success and failure along the way, to his detriment.

"I'm not afraid of strong women," he had said firmly. "In fact, I'm clearly drawn to them."

And this might have been demonstrably true, but it was wrong, and it was doubly wrong to start talking about Rebecca, even if it was Ann-Marie who brought her up. *What's Rebecca got to do with this?* He'd fallen, head-first, into the trap with his sad clichés. *My partner doesn't understand me, boohoo, she's so perfect, she castrates me with her perfection . . .*

He wasn't pleased with how his declaration had gone. And, on this occasion, Ann-Marie hadn't really argued with him, in spite of the fact that he was taking her for granted in what he was saying. And he didn't believe for a moment that it was because she accepted him as he was, warts and all.

No. She was withdrawing from him; when he touched her she flinched.

He thought it had a lot to do with all the gossip, the talk. It didn't particularly bother him. In some twisted way it made him feel important. And it was something of a turn-on, forbidden fruit and so on. But Ann-Marie worried about what people thought. Whispers and giggles had given way to frowns and moral outrage. He could see that she was beginning to wonder whether it was worth it. Whether *he* was worth it.

Well, he would just have to make sure that it was worth it for Ann-Marie.

He had to turn the situation around. He needed her, after all.

The bathroom lock clicked — why the hell had she locked it? OK. He stretched his legs out in front of him. It was time to win or to disappear. He would round things off, tidy things up before he went home. Make everything right for their next meeting; he would play his trump card. The only thing his relative youth enabled him to offer that her successful academic contemporaries couldn't: better sex.

"I thought you were leaving," said Ann-Marie.

She wouldn't meet his eye. Her body must still have been wet when she pulled on her T-shirt; there were darker patches and her short, straight hair was still dripping. She put on a dressing gown as if she wanted to cover herself up. She rubbed a towel over her hair half-heartedly.

"Let me help you with that."

"No."

Ann-Marie hesitated, or at least that was how it seemed to him, before squatting down with her back resting against the sofa. Henrik wrapped the towel around her hair and pressed against the fabric with his palms and fingertips, then he removed the towel and continued to stroke her wet head.

She sighed heavily, her body trembling. He gently pulled her head backwards. She let it happen, but he could feel that her neck was stiff and reluctant.

"Listen," she said after a while. "I . . ."

He was surprised to hear a sob as her body contracted and convulsed beneath his hands, her shoulders quivering and tense. He didn't know what to do as the storm of weeping passed, but it only lasted a few seconds.

"We need to talk," she said eventually, as if her tears had given her a sense of resolve. "Everything has to come to an end."

We need to talk. Words that seldom boded well; frustration was making his jaw muscles clench. He would have liked to be able to see the expression on her face. Suddenly every utterance, every action seemed horribly crucial. He would have liked more time, but realised that maybe that was just the way things were, and that their time had come.

A second later, the doorbell rang.

The doorbell?

"Is that my doorbell?"

Henrik shrugged, even though she couldn't see him. They waited for a moment in silence. Henrik had an unpleasant feeling in his throat. It was rare, perhaps unheard of, for Ann-Marie to have unexpected visitors.

He should have cycled home a long time ago. Every thought he had entertained about Rebecca soured the taste in his mouth.

The doorbell rang again, and Ann-Marie got to her feet. She wiped her eyes with a corner of her dressing gown and quickly cleared her throat. She didn't look at him.

"Yes, it's definitely my door."

"Are you expecting anyone?"

"No, but . . ."

If she had opened the door between the living room and the hallway, Henrik would have been able to see down the darkened hallway, and he would have been visible to the person standing at the door, silhouetted against the light pouring in from the stairwell.

Instead she went through the kitchen.

She was already in the hallway.

Henrik felt distinctly uneasy; he began to feel afraid. He wanted to call out as he imagined the safety catch being flicked up, perhaps he tried, but his words didn't come out. She wouldn't hear him anyway. Or didn't he want to make himself heard? Did he want to remain invisible to the unknown for as long as possible, coward that he was? All he really knew was that *something* was about to kick off, and that he was afraid of the consequences.

"Oh . . . hello?"

The tiny muscles in Henrik's body, which had been as taut as piano strings for the past two minutes, relaxed slightly as he waited for what came next. Ann-Marie hadn't sounded panic-stricken. But nor had she sounded completely normal. Surprised, more than anything.

He lowered his eyes, still listening. The door closed with a loud bang.

CHAPTER
SIX

The car was being taken to the garage via Linnéplatsen to have its gearbox looked at; the officer at the wheel had reported that first and second were difficult to engage. But first it was redirected to an apartment block occupied by one Anna-Klara Stenius. The call had come in during the night.

"Ann-Marie Karpov. Noise reported by a neighbour in the early hours of the morning," Granberg explained to Andersson. "There was a scream and the sound of something heavy falling on the floor, then loud bangs, and a while later nobody answered when she rang the doorbell although she knew someone was in. A patrol was sent out, but of course it was as silent as the grave when they got there. For goodness sake, it could have been anything!"

"Karpov, that sounds Russian. Domestic violence?" said Andersson, turning left up by Sveaplan.

Granberg shrugged irritably. Sometimes it was best to ignore such comments, even if the prejudice behind them still perturbed him. Besides, he'd just got used to the idea of an unexpected break in the garage — he had landed badly during a squash game the night before, and could feel his foot swelling by the hour. He might have to sign himself off for a few days.

"I don't understand why we have to go back," said Andersson.

"Because now the old woman's insisting she's seen something in her neighbour's hallway. She's in a state."

"I thought the door was locked?"

"She's seen something that looks like blood . . . and something that looks like a person's foot."

"Seriously?"

"That's what she said."

Andersson parked in a loading bay outside the building. "It'll only take a couple of minutes. Stay in the car if you like, give your foot a rest. I'll be back in no time."

Granberg tried putting his foot on the ground. He grimaced as the pain shot up his leg.

That decided the matter. Andersson slammed her door. "You're no use at the moment, anyway. You're a hindrance, in fact."

She slipped the radio into her pocket. "If the worst comes to the worst, I'll call you."

Granberg looked at his colleague with gratitude as she keyed in the entry code fru Stenius had given her, pushed open the heavy wooden door and disappeared into the courtyard.

Only a moment later, he was regretting the decision. They weren't supposed to respond to calls alone; if anything happened, however unlikely that might be, it wouldn't look good. He gritted his teeth and gathered his things before limping after Andersson, but he hadn't even got to the doorway when he picked up her call on his radio.

Her voice sounded faint, and he could sense immediately that something was wrong.

"We need to go in."

He half ran the remaining few steps to the doorway. Afterwards, Andersson would describe the smell seeping out through the letterbox: the sickly smell of blood suddenly hitting her nostrils. And what she'd seen through the gap.

CHAPTER
SEVEN

Christian Tell could just as easily have not bothered going into work. Since the department was quiet for once, and the crisis was over for now, there was no reason to sit there twiddling his thumbs. Besides, when he was at his desk there was always the risk that something would come up, a case that would swallow him whole and refuse to spit him out for days on end.

On the insistence of his girlfriend, Seja Lundberg, he had written one and a half day's leave into his diary. Tell suspected she was keeping note of how long it had been since they'd done anything together that could be described as fun. It had been about six weeks, a period of neglect that required a decent level of compensation, which was why he had requested a few days' leave later in the summer.

This time they were planning a full day in the southern archipelago. The boat from Saltholmen left at twenty to two; they would sit for a while in the garden at Café Öbergska on Styrsö. Perhaps they would go for a walk. Seja would no doubt want to swim; she swam all year round in every kind of weather. That evening they would go for dinner with Tell's former colleague, Josef Palmlöf, and his new girlfriend. Tell had started looking forward to the trip once he managed to get over his first, instinctive reluctance to break from his routine. When it came down to it, his routine consisted more or less entirely of work and the diffuse state that followed: the magical magnetic pull of the sofa in front of the TV.

He shut down his computer and glanced at the clock. He had plenty of time. Perhaps he would stroll down through Haga and buy something for Seja: absurdly expensive olive oil, gift-wrapped and placed in a rustling paper bag. Loose-leaf tea in a little retro tin from the health food shop. Almond butter face cream. Jewellery? There were endless possibilities, so many things she loved to receive but would never buy for herself.

He also wanted to make up for the previous day's exchange of words, which had ended in strained silence, even if he didn't really understand why.

They had been on the way home from his father's birthday celebration. Seja's first meeting with her future father-in-law had gone more or less as Christian had expected; she had charmed him by being sharp and funny and appearing to be perfectly relaxed, unlike his elder sister Ingrid who, true to form, fussed and tried to act as hostess when none was needed. It was unlikely that anyone apart from Christian had noticed the slight twitch at the corner of Seja's mouth that appeared when she was nervous.

On the way home they had joked about his father's not particularly discreet flirting with the staff. When they had almost reached Seja's cottage, Christian had asked, on the subject of family gatherings, why she hardly ever saw her parents. If his eyes hadn't been on the road he would no doubt have seen her body language change, her arms folding across her chest, as she glanced restlessly through the window.

"I do see them," she answered curtly. "But not very often, that's all."

"You've only seen them once since we got together, as far as I know."

"You don't know everything."

At which point, when he really should have withdrawn, he decided to smooth things over with a jokey remark about how she always said *he* was the one who set boundaries. Now she was the one who . . .

It had ended with Seja slinging her rucksack over her shoulder and marching down the slope towards the cottage on her own. He waited until she had crossed the footbridge and was heading up the other side. In the autumn and winter it was possible to see the house from the lay-by on the track, but yesterday she had been quickly swallowed up by the trees and was gone. He sat there sulking for a while with the engine idling, wondering if he ought to run after her and try to make amends. He decided to let things be.

They hadn't actually discussed whether he would spend the night with her; he had just taken it for granted. And if there was one thing he had learnt in his dealings with women, it was not to take anything for granted.

When Seja rang later in the evening, it was with a casual request to bring her trainers the following day;

she'd left them in his apartment. The matter was resolved.

They had been a couple since falling for each other eighteen months earlier in an unholy mess of mixed-up roles: she had been a witness in a murder inquiry, and a journalist into the bargain, while he was a police officer. He had resisted and tried to behave professionally. She had stuck it out and waited. In the end, he had given in and admitted that he was hopelessly in love. He couldn't really claim any credit for that; he hadn't had any choice. And it was probably this realisation that made the times when he imagined he missed his uncomplicated bachelor life both short-lived and rare: he needed her.

For reasons which completely escaped him, the feeling seemed to be mutual.

Christian Tell was dazzled by a bright light when he looked out of the window. Behind him someone tapped on the doorframe.

The figure spoke before Tell had time to blink away his sunblindness. "Thinking of leaving, were you?"

Detective Inspector Bengt Bärneflod was stroking his bald head with an unmistakable expression of schadenfreude as he leaned his corpulent frame against the wall.

"Grankvist and a colleague of his came across a pretty unpleasant scene this morning. Quite strange, in fact."

Tell took out the fresh shirt which he had been keeping in his cupboard.

44

"I presume you mean Granberg." Tell was not indispensable and his colleagues were perfectly competent. But still, he had a sense of foreboding.

"A man and a woman, shot at close quarters. He'd been shot in the head. She'd been shot in the chest. Incredibly cold-blooded."

"And what's so strange about that? That sounds like a gangland execution. No tag?"

"Well, that's just it; the odd thing is the context. An upmarket apartment on Linnégatan, nobody famous at that address. A single woman, a teacher, according to the neighbour."

Tell picked up the phone. "Who's in?"

"Beckman, and Karlberg's on his way from Biskopsgården. He should be here at any moment."

"They don't all need to go."

"I'm not doing anything."

"OK, you and Beckman go on ahead and take a look. I'll be there shortly."

Bärneflod patted Tell on the shoulder and smiled. Tell sat quietly with the receiver a few inches from his ear as he keyed in Seja's number.

CHAPTER
EIGHT

When Andreas Karlberg found Bengt Bärneflod, he was checking the courtyard for alternative points of entry and exit.

"Have you been inside?"

"Not yet. But Tell's spoken to the technicians; we can go in and have a look."

In the sunshine that flooded through the stairwell's leaded windows, Bärneflod's pale cotton jacket took on an orangey hue. They reached the fourth floor, huffing and puffing, and found the red panelled door marked Karpov.

Karlberg nodded to the constable on duty, stepped inside and stopped in his tracks. Karin Beckman was just emerging from the apartment next door. She didn't look in the mood for talking.

The murdered woman was lying just inside the door, in the corner formed by the wall and a wardrobe. Her body was lying in an unnatural position, with her knees and feet pressed together at one side and her arm and the fingers of the other hand pointing pathetically up to the shelves. She had bled copiously.

Karlberg sighed.

They could hear the lift complaining as it struggled upwards; it stopped and Tell pulled the creaking metal grille to one side, clocking the people assembled in the doorway. Bärneflod pushed his way into the apartment and crouched down next to the woman, carefully avoiding the blood that was seeping into the red carpet.

"Shall I hide inside the wardrobe or under it?" he muttered in an affected voice. He bent down and peered under the wardrobe. "As if she had a chance either way."

"Logic goes out of the window when you're faced with a deranged murderer," Tell retorted, placing his briefcase on the floor, unbuttoning his jacket and adjusting his shoe protectors. His tolerance levels were always significantly lower when it came to Bengt Bärneflod. His irritation would attach itself firmly to his spine, before overriding everything that his mature, rational self wanted to say. However he only gave in to his frustration in extreme cases. Most of the time it ate its way inwards, causing him stress.

But they had worked together for many years. They'd had their ups and downs. Sometimes Tell even valued Bärneflod's competence; if experience and competence could be equated. He had a lot of years in the job under his belt; nobody could deny that. He had seen everything at least once, as he himself was fond of saying. And no doubt it was true. The criminals of Gothenburg could do little to surprise Bärneflod.

"Have you been inside, Beckman?"

"Only briefly. But I've spoken to the neighbour who made the call, and picked up quite a bit of information about the woman in there; we can safely assume she is Ann-Marie Karpov. Fifty-one years old, researcher or lecturer in archaeology at Gothenburg University. She's the only person registered at this address — it seems she's divorced from a professor in the same subject, who is currently attached either to the Department of Archaeology in Copenhagen or to a museum called Glyptoteket. She didn't know for sure. Ann-Marie Karpov has lived here for years."

"Good," said Tell. "Pass all that on to Gonzales and he can start work on it straight away."

A white-clad figure was moving around at the far end of the passageway: Magnus Johansson, the forensic technician. Tell had worked with him on several cases, and thought very highly of him.

"Who's in there?" Tell asked without looking at Beckman.

"So far just Granberg and his colleague, a young woman. Johansson and some of his team."

"Which is more than necessary." Tell ran a hand through his hair. "But we might as well take a look inside before it gets too messy, don't you think? Where can we start?"

Beckman, who had already checked with the technicians, led the way. They passed through a suite of two rooms to reach a third which had a bay window facing onto Linnégatan. The room was a good size, with a high ceiling and an imposing open fireplace.

Bärneflod greeted Granberg, his old trainee, in a subdued voice, then stopped dead in the middle of what was apparently the dining room.

"So this is how the other half lives. Stucco and fancy skirting boards and God knows what else."

He walked through to the next room. "There's another one in here."

The man's body was propped at an angle, his legs outstretched and his head resting against the back of the sofa. What made the sight absurd was the expression on the dead man's face. His eyes and mouth were wide open; he looked like a child who was completely amazed. On closer inspection, other things looked out of place: he seemed to be bracing himself against the sofa cushions with his fingers spread wide, as if his body had been pressed or thrown against the piece of furniture.

Tell leant forward cautiously and flicked a lock of hair from the man's temple with his ballpoint pen. The entry wound. He went round to the other side.

"Straight in through the temple. No exit wound."

"The bullet's still lodged. Explains the lack of blood," said Bärneflod.

He took a couple of steps back and looked at the scene, lost in thought. The man on the sofa was wearing only a T-shirt and shorts, which suggested that he and the murdered woman were somehow intimate. Or perhaps they were related.

"Can I borrow him for a minute? I need to take a couple of photos."

Tell nodded mutely to the woman with the camera.

He went into the kitchen, which was large and could have come straight from a feature on French country living in a glossy magazine. One of the walls curved inwards; it was painted a striking burgundy and was fitted with bespoke shelves, which showcased objects from around the world: masks, tapestries and carved wooden figures. A generous oak table stood in the middle of the floor, cluttered with everything from cookery books to candle holders and used mugs. Photocopied material bearing the University of Gothenburg logo lay in surprisingly neat piles. The person who lived here liked order in the midst of chaos.

The doorbell rang. The sound was strangely distant, giving a sense of how large the apartment was.

Someone cleared his throat right behind Tell. "Not exactly a fan of minimalism, I see."

It was Karlberg.

"No. She likes her bits and bobs. And she clearly travels a lot."

"They've found the man's wallet," said Beckman. "Henrik Samuelsson, thirty-five years old."

She clamped her mobile to her ear and tried to make notes in her black book at the same time, holding her palm up to Bärneflod and Tell. "OK . . . yes, I'll be in soon. Yes."

She slipped the notebook in her pocket. "Henrik Samuelsson. His registered address is in Majorna. Kungsladugårdsgatan. One Rebecca Nykvist is registered at the same address."

"Is that Samuelsson?"

"Definitely. The photo on his ID card seems fairly recent."

"Tell . . ."

"Gonzales has everything he needs. I'm going to join him and go back to the station, unless of course you want an on-the-spot report from the door-to-door inquiries."

"If nothing jumps out, we can leave that until later," Tell decided without any great enthusiasm. "We need to pay a visit to Kungsladugårdsgatan first. I'll take that."

Turning up on someone's doorstep to announce the death of a loved one was an awful task; it was impossible to predict what would happen.

"I'll come with you," Beckman said quickly, "but I just need to call in at the station first. I'll meet you there in a couple of hours, if that's OK? And before I forget: the neighbour just told us she'd forgotten to mention that Ann-Marie Karpov had a *gentleman caller* last night. But we knew that already. Apparently it happened from time to time."

They walked through the passageway connecting the kitchen and the old servants' bedroom with the rest of the apartment and went into the living room.

"If she heard them talking, then presumably she heard the shots as well," said Tell. "What time?"

They stopped in front of Samuelsson's parody of a surprised expression. It was obvious he had been caught unawares in front of the TV.

"Around one o'clock in the morning," said Beckman, flicking through her notebook. "She heard screams, loud thuds, as if something had fallen over, and a while later she decided to ring Karpov. She got worried when no one answered and called the police. A

51

patrol car came out, but everything was quiet when they got here, and no one answered the door, so —"

"It must have been the woman who screamed and fell over," said Bärneflod after glancing around the tidy room. "There's no sign of a struggle anywhere else."

"I think it's strange," said Karlberg. "It's obvious that the woman was surprised by the murderer. She opens the door to a known or unknown attacker and *bang*. But the guy on the sofa — why didn't he try to get away?"

"We should work on the assumption that the assailant used a silencer," said Tell. "But I don't know . . . the man doesn't realise what's happening at first, he gets up and turns towards the doorway, it might only have been a matter of seconds before the killer was there, he's shot and thrown back down onto the sofa."

They shook their heads in mutual agreement, suddenly moved by the horror of it all. Karlberg was the first to break the silence.

"So there's an ex-husband; we'd better get in touch with him as soon as possible. We need someone to ID the body, if nothing else."

CHAPTER
NINE

"Rebecca Nykvist?"

"Yes?"

The woman on the stairs was rigid with impatience and her voice didn't sound as if it had been used that day. She was half-clad in a very short, not particularly clean silk dressing gown and her curly red hair was tousled around her puffy face. She had been crying.

Tell was momentarily confused. Had she already found out? That was impossible; only a few hours had passed since the bodies had been discovered. Imperceptibly he shifted his weight to the other foot.

Rebecca Nykvist had a strong aura of integrity. Neither Tell nor Beckman stepped forward to give her shoulder a reassuring squeeze, which was often the best response they could muster at moments like these. No situation made Tell feel more powerless. And, of course, the current situation was more complicated still. It seemed likely that this woman's husband or partner had been deceiving her, and this was how she would find out.

"Detective Inspector Christian Tell. This is my colleague, Karin Beckman. May we come in?"

Rebecca suddenly looked afraid. She tugged at the hem of her dressing gown. A single tear slid out of the corner of her eye.

"I don't know," she said. "I'm ill. I've got a splitting headache."

Her voice was no more than a whisper. What was going on inside her head?

Beckman moved quickly up the stairs to the door. "I'm afraid we do need to come inside, Rebecca," she said, leading the woman gently by the arm.

Tell followed them into the messy hallway. Shoes had been piled up along the walls and outdoor clothes dumped on the nearest piece of furniture. He noticed that a pale-reddish liquid, which might have been red wine, had soaked into the floorboards at the bottom of the stairs. Shards of glass had been brushed over towards the wall and crunched beneath his shoes. A succession of darker red stains led into the kitchen, where Rebecca had been persuaded to sit down at the table.

Beckman discreetly moved a half-full bottle of wine to one side and looked in the cupboard, where she found a packet of painkillers and a litre of lemonade. Rebecca Nykvist was sitting with her chin pressed to her chest, shaking her head almost imperceptibly.

"I'm so tired . . ."

Dark-red stains were spreading around her feet.

"You're bleeding," Tell said. He went into the bathroom and rummaged in the cupboards for something to wrap around her feet. Rebecca seemed completely at a loss as he bandaged her stiff legs. Tiny shards of glass had lacerated the soles of her feet and she was bleeding profusely. He pulled a thin shard out of her heel.

"I think you need to get this looked at by a professional," he said eventually.

Beckman poured a glass of lemonade. They waited in silence as Rebecca took it and drank.

"So," Tell began. "We . . ."

He paused before he had even begun what he had to say. Then he tried again, with fresh determination.

"What is your relationship with Henrik Samuelsson?"

She looked at him over the rim of her glass, her eyes cloudy.

"Have you found him?" Her voice was completely expressionless.

"I'm sorry?"

"He's my partner."

"When did you last see him?"

"Last night." She shook her head slowly. "I . . . I thought he was with another woman, he'd said he was going to do some revision with a friend, and . . . Sorry, I . . ."

She blinked several times, as if she'd just realised that the police officers in her kitchen must be there for a reason.

"I'm afraid we have some bad news." Beckman sought Rebecca's gaze. "We've found a murder victim, and we have reason to believe that this man is your partner, Henrik Samuelsson. I'm very sorry."

She reached out and grasped Rebecca's hand firmly. Her eyes were darting all over the kitchen; Tell and

Beckman both thought she was about to faint. Then she appeared to pull herself together.

"Where did you find him?"

"In an apartment on Linnégatan. We —"

Rebecca interrupted her with a thoughtful "Hmm", and no longer seemed particularly surprised. The shock was making her act irrationally, Tell thought. She hadn't asked what her partner was doing in Linnégatan in the middle of the night.

"We're going to need your help with this," he said. "As soon as you feel up to it. But first of all I want you to get these cuts looked at. And I'd like someone to come over and stay with you for the next day or so. We can make arrangements for you to see a psychologist or a doctor."

He waited a few seconds, then went on: "I'm sorry to have to ask you this, but I need to know where you were when your partner was murdered. You can answer now or later, but the sooner the better."

Rebecca got to her feet abruptly and went over to the worktop, where she stood with her back to Beckman and Tell. She wiped her eyes and nose with a piece of kitchen paper and twisted her red hair up into a knot.

"I was at home last night."

"You didn't leave the house?"

"No."

"Were you upset?"

"I rang the friend Henrik was supposed to be revising with. Axel Donner. And I rang a couple of other people on his course." Rebecca Nykvist turned her head and surprised Tell by looking him straight in

56

the eye. "You can check that, I made the calls from here, round about eleven o'clock. No, I rang Axel later as well."

"Is there someone we can ask to come over?" he asked.

"No. I have a friend who's a nurse. I'd prefer to ring her myself."

Tell and Beckman exchanged glances. Rebecca's demeanour had changed considerably. Neither was particularly keen to leave, but she didn't seem like the kind of person who would be easily swayed.

"OK," Tell said eventually. "DS Beckman will be in touch, probably this evening or tomorrow. And of course you can call us when you feel up to talking. We'll just wait outside for a while until your friend arrives."

"I'd like to be alone now."

They settled down to wait in the car. Tell picked up the phone to ring Seja, weighed down with guilt, but before he had the chance to key in her number, Gonzales called. Henrik Samuelsson had a record: violence against police officers and resisting arrest during an anti-racism demonstration some years ago. Samuelsson had spent the last few years at university, reading a wide range of subjects: literature, religion, social anthropology, history. Rebecca Nykvist worked as an administrator. Gonzales had tried to run a search on her, but had encountered difficulties, he would check with Renée, the team administrator, to see why it was taking such a long time, whether it was just the computer playing up, or . . .

57

"Thanks," Tell interrupted Gonzales' diatribe just as Nykvist's friend, after some twenty minutes, clambered over the low garden fence with a horrified expression on her face and went into the house without knocking.

Tell suspected Rebecca had only called her friend to get rid of them.

CHAPTER
TEN

Karlberg blew his nose on the same tissue for the third time. With a feeling of revulsion, he pushed it into an empty sweet packet, which he screwed up and tucked into his pocket.

He tried to perk himself up a bit before ringing the doorbell; the sign said K. von Dewall in ornate script.

"I'm sorry to disturb you, I'm a police officer. Andreas Karlberg."

"What's this about?"

"May I come in?" Karlberg showed his ID. The man was convinced, and pushed the door shut to remove the security chain.

"You can't be too careful these days."

"We're asking people in this building whether they saw or heard anything unusual last night," said Karlberg. "If I could come in for a few minutes, I'll explain."

"What's this about?" von Dewall asked again.

Karlberg was seized with a childish desire to ask the man if his ears were blocked.

"Ann-Marie Karpov, your neighbour, has been murdered."

At last the man looked more amenable. "Oh my God. I . . . But I didn't really know her all that well."

"Perhaps you could answer the question anyway. Did you notice anything unusual last night?"

"I just need to get my head around this first." Von Dewall placed a hand over his heart and took several deep breaths.

"Do you need to sit down?" Karlberg said. "Put your head between your knees, maybe?"

"No . . . I was sitting working until two, half-past two in the morning . . . The thing is, I did see someone in the courtyard. A woman. I noticed her because she spent quite a long time shuffling around down there. And it was an odd time. She . . . she seemed to be looking for something. She tried to get in. I think she spotted me at the window, because she moved out of the light. I didn't give it much thought until I was on my way to bed. I heard something on the stairs. I peeped out, only because it was the middle of the night, and . . . There was someone standing outside Ann-Marie Karpov's door, kind of . . . lifting up the flap of the letterbox. I thought it was strange, at that time of night."

"Hang on . . . Was this the same woman you saw in the courtyard?"

Von Dewall shook his head frantically. "I couldn't possibly say. This person was standing sort of at an angle with their back to me, almost as if they knew they were being watched, and besides, they were wearing a hood. I mean, it could just as easily have been a man.

Then the light on the stairs went out, and nobody switched it on again."

"Can you give me the exact time? Or a description of the woman you saw downstairs — was she tall, short? What was she wearing? A hooded jacket?"

"Well . . . it was definitely late. Maybe two, half two as I said. I was absorbed in my work. Unfortunately I didn't notice what she was wearing, but the woman in the courtyard definitely had red curly hair. It was glowing in the lamplight."

In the stairwell a while later, Karlberg glanced anxiously at his watch. He was well on the way to being late for the team meeting back at the station. Tell got really annoyed when someone was late. With a headache pounding behind his eyes, he ran down the stairs, across the courtyard and out into the street. He had forgotten to display his police parking permit and found a ticket tucked behind the windscreen wipers. He put it in his pocket and was just about to get in the car when something occurred to him. He went back inside. He went up to the first floor, hoping the residents of the apartment he had chosen weren't in as he tried peering through the letterbox in the way von Dewall had just described. He bent down, conscious of every movement, trying to push the flap inwards with his knuckle or the side of his index finger while holding the external flap open with his thumb and index finger in order to get the clearest possible view.

On the way back outside he rang Tell to explain that he would be late, to report on what von Dewall had said and to share his recently gained experience of peering through an old-fashioned letterbox.

"Shouldn't we get the letterbox dusted for prints?"

"That must have been done already," said Tell.

"Yes," Karlberg persisted, clamping his mobile between his ear and his shoulder as he pulled out and changed gear, "but I'm thinking about the *inside*. The *back* of the flap, the bit that opens inwards into the apartment. Maybe we could take a closer look at that."

"I have no idea what you're talking about. But I'm sure we could."

On the way to the station Karlberg went over what he had learnt from that afternoon's door-to-door enquiries.

Most of the time, people had neither heard nor seen a thing, something that had ceased to surprise him a long time ago. People tended to be blind and deaf, and disinclined to spy on each other. However this time they had both von Dewall and fru Stenius and, through their fragmentary accounts, a decent picture of events was beginning to emerge. He was pleased with his contribution.

They had worked out a preliminary allocation of tasks and got the investigation under way. When Tell rang Magnus Johansson after the first team meeting, Johansson was stressed and on his way home.

Tell explained that he realised the forensic examination of the scene had been completed, but he had just learnt that Karpov's neighbour had seen someone peering in through the letterbox. They didn't yet know whether this sighting matched the time of death, but would it be possible . . . preferably straight away . . .

"To check the letterbox for prints?"

"On the inside."

"I can ring Berggren and ask her to do it."

The last fifteen minutes had given them a breakthrough, and if the fingerprints did match someone who already had a record, then they were at least well on the way, if not home and dry. The neighbour who had seen the hooded figure fumbling with the door — *Had that person been trying to get in?* — didn't see that same individual going into the flat to commit murder, but it was undeniably suspicious behaviour, peering in through someone's letterbox in the middle of the night. If nothing else, perhaps the person in the hood could provide some information relevant to the case. Had the red-haired woman — *Rebecca* — been wearing a jacket with a hood?

Tell kept on coming back to Rebecca Nykvist. He doodled absent-mindedly on the back of a statement, forming a vague plan in his head before dialling the direct line to Forensics. He got Strömberg's assistant.

"He's told me to tell you he won't know anything until tomorrow. But hang on a minute . . . Hello? He says the cause of death was probably the bullet wounds in both cases. He can't identify the weapon yet, but he thinks . . ."

She disappeared again, and Tell could hear Strömberg mumbling in the background.

". . . no, no, OK. We don't know the type of weapon yet. But they probably died around midnight, give or take an hour either way."

Tell flicked through the notes on the desk in front of him. The first call from Anna-Klara Stenius had come in at 01.58. She said she'd heard the noise coming from Karpov's apartment at around one o'clock. That would fit. However, according to von Dewall, the hooded figure had been creeping around in the stairwell at two o'clock or half-past two in the morning, although he hadn't been absolutely sure of the time. Give or take an hour, Strömberg had said, but what else could have caused the noise?

Outside his office someone switched off a light, and shadows glided across the newly polished floor. Further down the corridor a door opened and closed.

He leant forward and shut down the computer.

CHAPTER
ELEVEN

The woman on the other end of the line had relented after listening to Seja Lundberg's heart-rending tale. Hadn't she also once been left in the lurch by a coward whose preferred method of cancelling a much longed-for break was via the answer machine?

"Perhaps you could come and stay some other time, when it suits you better?"

The woman's voice was now kind and gentle, perhaps because Seja had managed to inject a faint tremor in her own. But she *was* upset. More about the way he had done it than the fact that their visit to the archipelago had gone down the pan, and what irritated her most was what the situation said about her. She understood perfectly that Christian had a job to do; she just wished she was more absorbed in her own career so that their relationship was on more of an equal footing.

"I'm just not comfortable being The Girlfriend," she said to her friend Hanna when she called her a couple of minutes later. "Even if I do like having Christian as my boyfriend."

"But you're happy that he *has* a job, aren't you?" Hanna countered. "I think you're making something out of nothing. My blokes are always unemployed and generally useless. I can promise you that's no picnic either."

Seja took the phone into the stable with her. The warm straw stank of urine, and needed mucking out.

She didn't want to ring Christian and end up talking to his bloody answerphone.

As soon as her eyes grew accustomed to the semi-darkness, she spotted a shapeless lump on top of the mousetrap.

"Shit, there's another one."

Hanna made sympathetic noises as Seja picked up the trap between her thumb and forefinger and carried it out into the unforgiving light. Turning her face away she freed the limp, brown body and dropped it into a bank of ferns at the bottom of the garden.

"What the hell are they doing in the stable when it's so warm outside?"

"They prefer to wallow in a manger of oats rather than searching out titbits for themselves."

Seja was distracted by a fir needle that had found its way in between her bare toes. She stood on one leg and dug it out before going back to sit on the bench by the stable wall.

"I suppose it's just pride, really. I mean, I know he has the kind of job that has to take priority. And precisely *because* I know he has a job that has to take priority, I always put him first. And that annoys me. If I were busy too, then at least I could get my revenge by cancelling on him sometimes. I hate the feeling of being at his beck and call. And I hate talking about *priorities*."

"I'm sure you're not at his beck and call. Anyway, what about going out tonight? By way of consolation, plus you'd be cheering me up as well?"

"What about Markus?"

"I'm a free woman! Markus is at a sleepover tonight."

Seja felt much better by the time she hung up, so much so that she rang Christian's friend Jonas right away to tell him the trip was postponed. But perhaps Jonas and his girlfriend would like to meet up with Seja and Hanna later?

It was rare for Hanna to have a child-free night and Seja always had to think about night buses or make arrangements for the animals if she stayed away overnight. As a result they usually met at Hanna's house. After Markus had gone to sleep, they would sit and chat while stuffing themselves with over-salted popcorn. And that was fine. But Seja still liked the opportunity to go into town, particularly as she spent most of her time working and studying at home.

Järntorget had been regenerated so thoroughly that it was difficult to believe it had ever looked any different, that it hadn't always been an airy cobbled piazza. Sitting outside the old Customs House was a perfect spot to watch the world go by. The perfect place to see people getting on and off buses and trams, waiting for each other, meeting and parting, hurrying past with sunglasses pushed up on top of their heads and their hands full of shopping, or cutting across the square on their way from Majorna and Masthugget towards Vasastaden and the city centre.

As soon as the sun had gone down, the air had lost its mildness and they were sitting wrapped in blankets, chatting about the fact that Järntorget used to be a sprawling roundabout before the tunnel was built.

"Here's to the Göta tunnel," said Hanna, clinking her glass against Seja's. "But everybody still used to arrange to meet here, in the days before mobiles. See you in Järntorget, we'd say. I remember we used to eat falafels at Grand Burger. After Solrosen and Gillestugan, but before the terminus."

"The Red Room? Or that illegal club . . . the French club?"

They laughed at the memory.

"We'd better stop talking about the past, it's making me feel ancient," said Hanna. "These days we'd never cope if we stayed out till five in the morning."

"No, but back then we used to sleep all day," said Seja.

That phase of Seja's life had only lasted a year. Before she was forced — or persuaded — to go back into education at the age of nineteen. But if she looked back, it seemed as if the whole of her youth had been spent in dive bars or in illegal clubs where underground bands played. She remembered dragging herself through her apartment from her stuffy room to the toilet. Blinking sleepily at her mother and father as they sat at the kitchen table like beings from another planet.

"Sometimes I think it's amazing they didn't go completely crazy," she said to Hanna. "I mean, they

68

never told me off. I suppose they had no idea what I got up to at night."

"They probably realised there was no point in having a go at you. My mum and I fought non-stop for ten years. I didn't take any more notice of her just because she was yelling and screaming."

They fell silent. Hanna's mother had taken her own life a few years earlier. Seja didn't want to make Hanna talk about that if she didn't want to but, just at that moment, Christian's former colleague and friend Jonas Palmlöf appeared with his girlfriend Sofia Frisk, weaving their way between the tables.

Seja just had time to explain: "These are the friends we were supposed to be going to the archipelago with. I hope it was OK to say they could meet us here?"

Hanna allowed the blanket to slip from her shoulders onto the chair and straightened her back. She was wearing a tight cerise top with a striking pearl necklace nestling in her generous décolletage. She flicked her hair back from her shoulders in a smooth, practised movement. Hanna was almost certainly unaware of it, but Seja noticed that her friend changed as soon as a man approached. Particularly if he was good-looking, like Jonas Palmlöf. As soon as Jonas and Sofia had disappeared in the direction of the bar, Hanna whispered her verdict in Seja's ear: he was totally gorgeous.

"Pack it in, you trollop," Seja laughed. "He's here with his girlfriend!"

"So?" said Hanna, vaguely offended. "I'm allowed to say what I think. Do you know how rare it is for me to get out the door without a child in tow? And besides, it's not often you see such a —"

She stopped as Sofia came towards them with a glass in each hand.

"I'm just kidding," she hissed.

"Yeah, right."

This is how it feels, thought Seja, to let go. To lose yourself.

This is how it feels, lying by the water and drying off, while Lukas grazes on birch leaves and whinnies, the sound travelling across the inlet and bouncing off the rock face on the far side.

They had left the Bishop's Arms and strolled along to Skål, which had got busier and busier as the night went on. Hanna had met an old boyfriend in the bar and was sitting very close to him, their shoulders touching. They were deep in conversation; every time Seja glanced in their direction, Hanna's head was leaning even closer to the man's.

Jonas had come with them to the Vasastan area of the city after Sofia had taken her leave. Seja liked how easy-going he was, even if he had had a little too much to drink by this stage.

He returned to a conversation they had had earlier in the evening. They had been talking about work, about priorities in general, and about the abruptly postponed mini-break in particular. When Seja explained what had happened, and told him how upset she had been, Jonas didn't seem that surprised.

70

"I don't think you necessarily have to buy into the idea that the job takes up all your time. I mean, it's true that if you're in the CID you have to be a bit flexible with your working hours, and of course there are emergencies from time to time, and so on. But these things also come down to your personality and how you handle things. There's always back-up. Nobody's expected to work non-stop."

He took a swig of his beer, aware that Seja was waiting for him to go on. "Christian is a friend of mine, as you know. But Christian is — to put it diplomatically — a complete control freak. He's never really happy until everyone else is being as obsessive as he is."

"That wasn't tremendously diplomatic."

"Believe me, it was." He laughed gleefully. "Don't get me wrong, I love the guy." He thumped his breast pocket dramatically, just over his heart, a macho gesture which almost made Seja blush. "He's one of the most morally upright people I know. He'd take a bullet for anybody. Well, perhaps not for anybody, but for a colleague, a friend. What I mean is, I think maybe he just can't understand that other people might want something different out of life. It might be that he demands way too much from everybody else. But he allows himself even fewer concessions. You know, I actually think . . ."

He banged his glass down on the table. A girl smiled and raised her eyebrows as she walked past. Jonas waved theatrically. "I think Christian is harder on himself than anyone else I know. It'll finish him off one of these days."

Seja didn't know how to respond to that. The Christian Jonas was talking about didn't sound like the Christian she knew.

"I don't really know," she said eventually. "I don't see him as a police officer when he's with me. I see a completely different side of him."

"Rubbish!" shouted Jonas.

Seja gave what sounded even to her like a slightly strangled laugh. "What do you mean, rubbish? What do you know about our relationship?"

The light from above was reflected in his eyes, making them glint.

"You do *not* see a different side of him. There is no other side to Christian Tell. That's what I mean!"

Seja leant forward, her expression challenging as she met his gaze. "What do you want me to say to that?"

"I'm just telling it like it is. Someone needs to save Christian from himself."

"If I'm to believe what you say, it sounds as though it would be a better idea to dump him straight away."

"Well, if you get fed up, *you'll* have to dump *him*. Because he'll never leave you. Do you understand? Deep down, he's incredibly loyal. He might mess everything up, he might *act* in a way that makes you think he's leaving you, but . . . He'll hang onto you like a bloody lifebuoy."

He fell silent. Seja didn't speak either. She felt surprisingly embarrassed. A bell rang behind the bar. Last orders.

"Hang in there. He really needs you."

72

Seja groaned and covered her face with her hands. "Enough, Jonas. You really are embarrassing me!"

Jonas grinned as he suddenly realised how soppy he'd been sounding. He took Seja's hand and shook it vigorously.

"Does it embarrass you to be told that you're an exciting and very beautiful woman, Seja? I thought you knew that! Hello! Earth to Seja! The old sod's been very lucky, and he knows it."

"As I said, you're embarrassing me."

"Really? Brilliant."

Seja contemplated Christian's friend in profile as he got out his wallet. Yes. It was probably best if the evening came to an end at this point. She was invited to her neighbours for dinner the following day, and she had no wish to turn up with a hangover. Besides, she needed some time to go over what had been said this evening. Had she heard genuine insight or simply drunken ramblings?

She stood up.

It was illogical, but she was suddenly desperate to see Christian. Only a few hours earlier she had been upset and disappointed. She considered going round to his apartment. Actually, she didn't have a choice. The last bus to Stenared had already gone.

She saw Hanna leaving the bar with her ex, just as her mobile beeped. She had a good idea what the message was about.

CHAPTER
TWELVE

Tell had been driving with the window wound down and his elbow resting on the door, a position that encapsulated freedom precisely because it was such a cliché. He wasn't the kind of person whose day was dictated by the weather. If anything, he was inspired to achieve as much as possible on warm, sticky summer days, when you shouldn't really be indoors working. Conversely, days that were heavy with rain sometimes felt positively liberating: a slight feeling of depression meant you were normal after all. Nevertheless, when the first warm days of the year cooled off towards dusk, even Tell was filled with a quiet sense of solemnity. He felt as if the world around him were softening, its scents and smells fading. Heat lingered in the fabric of buildings. As he got out of the car on Mariagatan, the cold night air came rolling in and bumped against the hot walls around him; perhaps it was this contrast that perked him up.

He was struck by how quiet this part of the city was compared with where he lived. He could just about make out the noise of a party from an open window further down the street, and the sound of the odd car or siren broke the relative quiet. But then all was silent once more.

The entrance to Axel's block wasn't locked. Tell did his best not to thunder up the lino-covered stairs to the first floor; he raised his hand to knock on the door and thought of Seja, as had happened so often lately when his mind should have been on the job. Sometimes the feel of her skin was like a memory on his hands. A fleeting reminder that she existed. Usually this made him feel warm and happy; occasionally he felt guilty, as he did now, but then he was annoyed at the very idea of feeling guilty.

The man's face was pale beneath his stubble and he plucked constantly at his shirt.

He was in shock.

"I can't get my head round this," Axel Donner repeated.

"First of all, I'd like to thank you for agreeing to see me at this late hour," said Tell.

It really was an ungodly hour. Tell had been heading in the direction of home when a feeling of restlessness had made him choose between letting off steam with a couple of drinks and trying to work for a couple more hours. He hadn't called Seja since he'd left that cowardly message asking her to cancel the booking. She hadn't called back, which didn't bode well. And now she was probably asleep.

According to Rebecca Nykvist, Donner was an eccentric bachelor, a slapdash character who seemed all over the place, and Tell was banking on the fact that this lack of structure applied to his sleeping habits. His

visit wasn't ideal from a security point of view —
current guidelines warned against conducting even
preliminary interviews alone. But here he was. Alone.

And Axel Donner was indeed still up. The paused
image on the TV screen indicated that he'd been
watching a DVD.

"I won't take up very much of your time," Tell
repeated, but Donner didn't seem to hear him.

Slapdash wasn't the first word that occurred to Tell
when he stepped inside the tiny one-room apartment.
Two simple bookshelves were well filled, and apart
from that there were just four pieces of furniture.
Sparse would be a more appropriate word under the
circumstances.

"I don't understand . . . she rang me," said Donner.
"Rebecca. Henrik's girlfriend. She rang me last night,
really late. She woke me up and asked about Henrik."

Tell pricked up his ears. "Go on."

"It was clear he'd told her — I might as well say it
now — he'd told her we were going to revise together.
But he wasn't here, and she —"

"Got upset?"

"Yes, I think so."

"You knew about his affair with your tutor?"

Axel Donner nodded. "I think a lot of her students
knew but then again, maybe they didn't. The ones who
were on the study trip knew, though."

"Study trip?"

"To Istanbul. Last September. That was when they
got together — you couldn't really miss it."

He leant back against the wall, his head thudding as it made contact.

"Do you know what time it was when she rang?"

"It was in the middle of the night, I don't know exactly. Definitely after midnight."

That would be easy enough to verify. Tell tried another tack. "What do you know about Henrik's relationship with Rebecca?"

"She was a very jealous person," he said without skipping a beat. "Henrik used to talk about it — it was a real problem. I don't know if he'd fallen out of love with her, but I think he was tired of her . . . how shall I put it . . . hysteria. I think he was on the verge of calling the whole thing off. Otherwise he'd never have gone with another woman. Henrik was really . . . ethical. A good bloke, kind of."

There was a glimmer of sorrow in Donner's eyes and Tell gave him a few seconds to collect himself.

"Did you know Henrik well?"

"Yes."

"Rebecca?"

"No, not at all. She was never with us, she was . . . she wasn't with us."

"And Ann-Marie Karpov?"

"Did I know her personally, you mean? No, only as a tutor. She and Henrik didn't really meet openly, or when other people were around. She was quite . . . she had integrity and . . . authority."

"Hmm . . . You don't know if Henrik felt threatened in any way? Or to put it more accurately, was there anything odd about Henrik's behaviour recently?

Anything that seemed strange? Did his behaviour alter ...? I'm sure you understand what I'm getting at."

Axel Donner gave the matter some thought. "Well ... after he started seeing Ann-Marie Karpov, he pretended to be cool with everything, but I know he was stressed out by all the lies he had to tell. He was afraid Rebecca would find out. I think he was getting a bit tired of it all."

"Did he seem afraid of Rebecca?"

Now I'm putting words in his mouth.

"No, not exactly, but ... maybe he was stressed about other stuff too. I think he might have been thinking of dropping out of uni altogether. He wasn't really keeping up, but at the same time he was doing his own research, going beyond the syllabus. It was ... I don't know. He didn't do anything he didn't want to do, if you know what I mean. He was a free spirit."

"So you don't recall Henrik being worried about anything specific? What was the situation with Karpov's ex-husband, for example?"

Donner shrugged. "What situation? She'd been divorced for years, hadn't she? I don't really think I can help you in terms of evidence or anything ... But if you want my opinion, I think you should concentrate on Ann-Marie Karpov more than Henrik. She was an important figure, a person who commanded respect. Henrik was ... Henrik was a good friend, but ... I mean, he was a nobody in the grand scheme of things, just like me."

Donner took a deep breath. "And maybe that's a good thing. No one bothers to murder a nobody. Unless he falls in with the wrong crowd."

Half an hour later, Tell was standing in his living room with the lights off, looking down at the deserted street. He suddenly realised how tired he was; he couldn't even think straight. Even his plan to make himself something to eat — he was definitely in need of food — seemed completely beyond him, so he made do with a few spoonfuls of yoghurt and a slice of crispbread.

Seja was fast asleep, her breathing deep and even. He didn't know where she'd spent the evening, but if she'd been really angry she would have gone back to the cottage. The thought cheered him up.

He slid in carefully beside her. Close, so he could smell the scent of her hair. The morning would give him the chance to explain what had happened, and she would understand. She usually did, but he really wished he didn't have to catch a glimpse of that expression, that unspoken disappointment. Let her be angry instead, absolutely furious for ten minutes. Then she would point out what a depressing sight he was, and they would laugh together and everything would be all right.

The following morning he overslept. When Seja stretched like a cat in the tangled sheets, he pushed aside thoughts of work. Instead he devoted his attention to re-establishing his position as a Very Important Person in Seja Lundberg's life, a person who deserved her love and care. An hour later, he had almost convinced her. He had even agreed to join her for dinner — her elderly neighbours had invited her round. He promised in a particularly weak moment.

Seja was resting on his arm. Her breath smelled faintly of the previous evening's outing, and her dark hair fanned out messily on the pillow. She reached up to the shelf above the bed for her tin of chewing tobacco, which lay on top of his. He felt a rush of warmth, just like when he found a moisturiser in the bathroom cabinet and realised she hadn't bothered to take it home. Or when she dropped her loose change in his box above the stove, as though they were saving towards a common goal, a holiday, perhaps. These everyday signs of closeness amazed Tell. He didn't want the sense of amazement to disappear, to be replaced by a familiar feeling of entrapment. For the first time in many years he felt . . . yes, a kind of harmony, but that very feeling brought with it the fear of losing what he had.

It was ironic, he thought; *It's as if I can't allow myself to be happy.*

"Do you know what would make this morning even more perfect?"

She kicked the covers down to the bottom of the bed and turned her back to him. He lifted her thick mane of hair and blew on the nape of her neck, which was slightly damp; she pulled him close, moving the palm of his hand up to her cheek.

"No, what would make this morning even more perfect?"

"A strong espresso with hot milk. Freshly squeezed orange juice. Croissants, the ones with chocolate inside . . . No, actually, that would be excessive. Plain croissants, but fresh and dripping with butter."

He laughed and rolled onto his back. "Such pretentions! Well, if a day-old croissant isn't good enough for you, I don't know where to shop."

"For God's sake, we're in the most chi-chi part of Gothenburg, among the most pretentious people in the entire city! You could get a proper French breakfast on every street corner around here. Off you go. It's the least you can do after yesterday. And besides, do you know how much crawling I had to do over the phone so that we wouldn't have to pay the full amount at the B&B?"

"You didn't have to do that," Christian ventured, even though he knew the discussion would get him nowhere. At the moment he couldn't work out whether there was a serious undertone, or whether Seja was joking. "I would have paid, obviously. And this is blackmail, by the way."

He went over to the wardrobe. "Is it OK if I have a shower before I go?"

"No, and in any case it would be a waste of time. You're going to get all sticky with jam and chocolate if we're to have breakfast in bed."

"Chocolate? I thought you said you wanted plain."

"Get both."

Tell pulled on yesterday's clothes. In the back of his mind he knew perfectly well that he should have been at work hours ago. He glanced at Seja, lying on her back with her arms above her head, her eyes closed and a gentle smile playing on her lips. His decision was made.

"Hey," she said with laughter in her voice just as he was about to leave. "I was only joking, you know that, don't you? Go if you have to. I'll see you at Åke and Kristina's tonight, if not before."

"I do have to go, but I'll nip over to the café first and buy breakfast. You deserve it."

CHAPTER
THIRTEEN

Istanbul, September 2007

Ann-Marie Karpov tipped back her head. The greenery formed a vault over the walkway, the interwoven branches forming walls and a ceiling, overrun by skinny feral cats. One of the cats got its claws caught and let out a loud shriek. The men sitting on stools around a table by the kitchen door laughed quietly as cat pee trickled down through the branches and splashed the paving below. Marie Hjalmarsson quickly backed away. The cat tore itself free and scampered over to the next roof.

Marie, Henrik, Axel, Annelie and Helena, all students at the Department of Archaeology and Ancient Civilisations, were on a study trip with their tutor and guide Ann-Marie Karpov and had almost finished their kebabs, koftas and stews. The owner of the bar pulled up a chair and told them that he had visited Sweden as a young man. Somewhere near Stockholm, with his football team; two nights in Sweden and two in Norway. He remembered a tunnel, a long, long . . . ?

He told them he'd spent eleven years working in Germany, *long time ago*.

"Building cars. Nine men in a small apartment, no furniture. I sent all my money home."

No, he didn't remember what the tunnel was called. *It was more than twenty years ago!*

When he came back from Germany he had opened his restaurant.

Henrik Samuelsson thought the whole thing was fantastic. He wanted to go back to the restaurant the following day. Said he'd never eaten such a perfect lamb stew, and tucked the man's card away in his wallet.

They moved on, heading down towards the harbour. The smell of fried fish hung over the square in Eminönu. In the twilight the ground was covered with blankets displaying the goods on offer — belts, toys, clothes, sandals. Bargaining was done under cover of darkness; the party was left dizzied by the combination of heat and poor street lighting in some areas, which lay in soft, warm darkness as night fell.

Marie wanted to buy a top for her daughter and they stopped at the end of the bridge. She had just paid the hawker when a signal passed through the sea of people.

Plain-clothes police. Blankets were gathered up, turning the displays of goods into big, unwieldy bundles. The men were gone in seconds, dispersing at lightning speed. The group had seen this happen in daylight too, in the large square in front of the University of Istanbul which they had attended as part of their visit. The pigeons instinctively rose up en masse.

Marie stuffed her purchase into her handbag. "Can't we sit down and rest somewhere around here?"

"I think we should go over to the new part of the city," said Ann-Marie. "If we're going to see something of the nightlife."

Helena Svanström looked dubiously at her watch. "It's rather late and we've got to get up early. It'll be a long walk back to the hotel so I don't want to stay out too much longer. Is there anybody who'll walk back with me in a while?"

"I'll come with you," said Marie. "Besides, we've all got to get up early. None of us is likely to stay out all night."

"We're all adults," Henrik brought the discussion to a close. "Everybody can do as they please."

"Absolutely," said Ann-Marie. Henrik and Ann-Marie: they always seemed to agree. Ann-Marie smiled.

As they strolled along the wide pavements of Galata Bridge, men of all ages jostled as they fished over the side. The loud cries from the restaurants beneath echoed through the night. "Sir! Madam! Just one second, take a look at the menu. Best fish in town!"

Narrow, winding streets lined with dilapidated grey houses and scruffy courtyards climbed the hill on the other side of the bridge. They were out of breath by the time they reached the top, and the square in Beyoglu. They sat down in the first suitable spot, resting their aching feet while flapping their sweaty clothes and trying to calm their breathing after the rapid climb in the heat.

"That was hard work. But what a contrast," said Ann-Marie, nodding to a group of long-legged models at the bottom of the Galata Tower, posing in silky evening dresses in front of a white screen.

The waiter came out with six glasses of foaming beer.

Henrik murmured his approval. He was tapping his foot in time to a blues track blaring from a music shop.

They carried on talking about contrasts. Henrik ventured that their own city, Gothenburg, had been held up as the most segregated in Europe. They chatted about the cities they had visited. Henrik and Ann-Marie were the most well travelled and compared their experiences. Annelie Swerin talked about the time she had spent in Goa; Henrik maintained that Goa wasn't really India, but a hotchpotch of Western influences. Annelie thought he was being self-important, and protested as much.

They made plans for the following day.

A couple of hours later, Marie and Helena had said goodnight and gone back to the hotel. Ann-Marie, Henrik, Axel and Annelie had moved on to a street in Istiklal Caddesi, and were drinking raki. Axel went off to the toilet.

Ann-Marie was chain-smoking. She stretched her strong, slender arms above her head and her face broke into a smile. "I'm going to stay out all night!" Henrik, who had been watching her, smiled too. The world around them faded away. "In that case, I'm staying with you."

"OK. You stay with me."

Henrik threw caution to the wind — the little of it that remained — and reached out for Ann-Marie's hand under the table. She responded, hesitantly at first, but oh, the joy of it, when she let her fingertips brush against his.

A tidal wave surged through Henrik's body, his brain was electrified, his heart almost stopped. All he could do was laugh, an exhilarated, hysterical laugh, and Ann-Marie joined in, it was a laugh that said: Yes, of course! Why not? Life is too short to let things slip by! Too short to let differences get in the way, to think about consequences all the time. They had wordlessly agreed on a mission, and they were prepared to fulfil their part by following an impulse governed by lust.

With the tips of Ann-Marie's fingers touching his, with her happy, surprised, slightly rebellious gaze fixed on his, on the moment, he allowed himself everything. He allowed himself to hope and believe that this was the beginning of something he only now realised he had wanted for a long time. He was daring, reckless as he caressed his tutor's knee and she let him. He felt all the blood in his body flow into his groin.

His thoughts were disrupted when Axel flopped down on the chair beside him. Henrik was also vaguely aware of Annelie's searching expression, but he couldn't care less whether she realised what was going on under the table.

Annelie tried to turn away, struggling with the chair, which had got its legs entangled with another; suddenly she hid her face in her hands and began to cry.

Reluctantly Henrik floated back up to the surface.

Ann-Marie also turned to Annelie, who helplessly waved away their concern.

"Sorry, sorry. It's not you. It's got nothing to do with you, it's OK . . . I'm just a bit of a mess right now."

Henrik nodded. She had talked about her problems before, and he had been surprised by her openness. She'd told them she'd been having an affair with a married man for quite a while. It was the time-honoured story. She loved him. She was waiting for him to leave his wife. He said he would, but that he felt guilty about his son.

Henrik explained this discreetly as Annelie went off to rinse her face.

"Tricky," was Ann-Marie's only response.

Axel nodded and seemed distant. But when Annelie came back, he leant across the table and caught her eye.

"How about you and I go back to the hotel?" he said. "We can talk on the way. I think you could do with some rest."

Annelie thought for a moment, then shook her head. "No. There's no need. I'm fine. The feelings come and go. I keep thinking about what I ought to do. And then something reminds me . . . No. It's fine. But thanks anyway, Axel. It was sweet of you to offer."

From where they were sitting, they had a perfect view of a huge vintage store. It was on the opposite side of the narrow street, and it boasted a powerful stereo system. From the basement Jefferson Airplane was turned up to full volume and people all around them raised their voices to be heard above the noise.

Ann-Marie moved closer to Henrik so that she could hear what he was saying. Their faces were close, close enough to kiss. And Axel leaned closer to Annelie, so close that she could make out the pores on his nose. She withdrew.

"So what is it you're thinking about?" Axel asked.

"Thinking about?"

"You said you keep thinking about what you ought to do?"

She had talked so much about David. David who was married, David whom she loved so shamelessly. She talked about him till she was blue in the face. She didn't know if she had the strength to go through it all again with Axel. But at the same time, every time she opened her mouth to speak, there was the faint hope that in the repetition she might find a solution she hadn't thought of so far.

So she talked to Axel, while Ann-Marie and Henrik sank deeper into one another. She told Axel how she had been forced to give up her part-time job — although that was the least of her worries — because she'd got together with her boss. Plus she had to walk past his shop every single time she left the house.

If she finished the relationship, she would be reminded, day after day, of everything that had existed between them, all the promises and betrayals, all the hopes that had come to nothing. And yet she had never been with a man who had given her so much. She said she could talk to David about anything.

Annelie was so close that Axel's eyes looked slightly green; she had thought they were blue-grey. His eyelids drooped a little, narrowing his gaze. He listened, nodding as his irises moved back and forth.

CHAPTER
FOURTEEN

Stenared

Christian, Seja and her neighbours, Kristina and Åke Melkersson, had just finished their filet mignon; throughout the meal Kristina had reproached herself for putting too much salt in the potato gratin. Christian, Seja and Kristina then moved into the living room, Åke refusing their offer of help with clearing away and disappearing into the kitchen.

Seja was sitting in the armchair to which she had been shown, a whisky and soda in her hand. She was full to bursting. Both she and Christian had had seconds, although that didn't stop Kristina complaining that they ate like birds.

Åke and Kristina were positively gushing, as she had known they would be. After all, this was the first time they'd had the opportunity to talk to Christian properly and, God knows, they'd been curious about him. Kristina complimented him on his suit, which was the one he wore for work; she'd always thought a man looked wonderful in a suit. Then she began interrogating him about his job, dropping in the names of the crime series she watched on television.

Seja listened distractedly, wondering why they had been invited. She very rarely set foot inside the inner sanctum of the Melkersson residence. If she did have cause to call round, the conversation was usually conducted on the patio, or at the dining table in the room next door. Otherwise, Seja and Åke met virtually every morning on the way to pick up their post. This had become something of a routine, an accepted part of everyday life. They would exchange a few words, and Åke would mention anything with which he might need Seja's help. This happened more rarely these days, but before Åke retired he had been grateful for the fact that Seja was willing to help Kristina, whose aches and pains meant that she rarely left the house.

Seja, in turn, was happy to know that she could rely on Åke to look after her animals if she wanted to be away from home. This had been invaluable since she met Christian and sometimes stayed over at his apartment. It meant the animals were less of a burden, although she was careful not to exploit the elderly couple. She was glad they were there, and she liked the feeling of being part of a small community. A grove of trees lay between Seja's cottage and her neighbours; she could see nothing but those trees from her window. But her fear of the dark was allayed by the knowledge that she could ring the Melkerssons if she needed to.

Seja swirled the amber liquid in her glass, still slightly preoccupied by the as yet unspoken reason behind the invitation.

★ ★ ★

When she moved into the cottage in the Glade with Martin, her partner at the time, she had been a typical city girl. She barely knew the other people who lived in her apartment block; she was quite clear in her head about the fact that you chose your friends carefully, based on age, shared interests and outlook. She never thought life would turn out this way; that she would end up spending most of her time with her retired neighbours — and Christian, of course.

Perhaps her need for the Melkerssons' company had something to do with the fact she spent a great deal of time alone now, or with her animals. Occasionally she wondered whether she was turning into an eccentric as she wandered around her garden talking to her horse and cat.

She was happy with her life. But sometimes she worried about the future.

She had almost completed her training as a journalist, and already had a small number of freelance jobs. She was good at her job when she really got involved in a story, but the competitiveness of the industry scared her. She loved the slow passage of time in the Glade, although she sometimes worried it gave her too much opportunity for navel-gazing.

And yet, things had mostly turned out well, after hanging in the balance for a while. They had only just moved in when Martin left her, and everything was turned upside down. Back then, she still missed the lights and noise of the city; the desolation of the forest was palpable when she realised she was alone there. Alone in a cottage that needed renovating, alone at the end of the world, which was how it felt, and at night it really *was* dark, darker than it ever was in the city.

But every morning Åke Melkersson set off on the short walk towards the letterboxes to collect his paper, *Göteborgsposten*, and post, as did Seja. That was how they met for the first time. He walked slowly, his hands behind his back and a contented expression on his face. He carefully avoided the hollows and potholes, and liked to complain about frost damage to the road surface, and overhanging weeds. He would talk about the weather: *Going to be a lovely day today. Seems as if they've got the forecast right.*

At first, Seja hadn't encouraged him, thinking he was just a garrulous old man. Then the time came when she had neither the desire nor the energy to talk. It was easy to avoid human contact after Martin had disappeared; not many people lived up at the top of the hill, and Seja's cottage was some distance from the road. Only Åke seemed incapable of taking the hint that Seja wanted to be left alone with her broken heart. Only Åke carried on making small talk, even though she answered evasively or simply shook her head. Afterwards, she began to suspect that he hadn't been quite so clueless all the times he had gone on about the weather or asked random questions: *So when did Gren have the roof redone, had she asked him? Was the outhouse properly insulated for the winter?*

He hadn't known what to say, so he had simply kept on talking.

Åke and Kristina had bewailed the fact that such a young girl should be living all alone in Gren's old, dilapidated cottage. Nowadays, their relationship was more like the one she could have had with her parents and she had gradually realised that the small errands she carried out for Åke and Kristina marked the beginning of a change for the better. She often found Åke and Kristina irritating, but it felt good to know that they cared about her. That they had her best interests at heart.

But it felt odd to sit in their living room with a whisky and soda after eating filet mignon. And there was something afoot, she was sure of it. Åke had phoned and invited her to dinner several days ago. And Christian was welcome too, of course. He had sounded slightly too formal, somehow ill at ease.

"It's your birthday, isn't it?" he'd said.

"No, it isn't."

"But you'll come anyway? Kristina will be so pleased to see you."

Christian's mobile rang. Kristina immediately fell silent, looking on with excitement as he picked up the phone and went out onto the patio to talk. When he came back a few minutes later, his expression was noticeably more strained. He apologised briefly, explaining that he had to make a number of calls that couldn't wait. His mind was clearly already elsewhere as he shook Kristina's hand. "Thank you so much, it was a lovely evening. No, don't get up — I'll see myself out. You stay a while, Seja. I presume your place is open?"

She nodded mutely.

He went into the kitchen to thank Åke, then the door banged shut.

Kristina cleared her throat.

Seja felt embarrassed by Christian's abrupt departure. She smoothed down her skirt, which had crept up above her knees, trying discreetly to cover a swollen cut. Since she had never been invited to the Melkerssons formally, she hadn't had a clue what to wear. Kristina gasped: a circle of purple bruises on Seja's leg didn't make the cut look any better.

"For goodness sake, Seja! What on earth have you been doing to yourself?"

Seja had to laugh. "I'm trying to build a new shelter for Lukas and I got in the way of the hammer!"

She didn't want to prolong what was sure to turn into a conversation about her life choices. She already knew that Kristina couldn't understand how anyone could choose to live all year round in a cottage with no indoor shower and toilet.

"It looks worse than it is," she said.

"But can't you get someone in to do it? Or what about him?" said Kristina, gesturing towards the dining room and the door through which Christian had disappeared. "Can't he help you? I mean, what's the point of having a man around if you have to do everything yourself?"

"He's really busy." Seja could hear how defensive she sounded. "With work. Besides, it's my house. It's not as though we live together."

"Nonsense. If you love each other, you help each other out. Any sensible man knows that. And if it's serious, you'll be moving in together, surely? If he doesn't want to, he's not worth having. Don't get me wrong, he seems really lovely. Although I can understand how it might be difficult for the two of you to live in your little cottage. Might be a bit cramped. And maybe he doesn't like showering outdoors when the temperature is below freezing, and —"

"I'm not sure I'm ready to live with Christian. As long as we want different things, and he works such long hours while I'm tied to this place because of the horse, it's perfect just the way it is. People can have a good relationship without moving in together. We see each other when we really want to, and in between times we make our own decisions and do what we like."

"I see. Right. Yes."

Seja could see that Kristina was slightly put out. But she didn't want to discuss her relationship with Christian. It was enough that she allowed it to occupy her thoughts so often.

A gentle breeze drifted in through the door leading to the veranda at the back of the house, bringing with it the fresh smell of pine needles and a faint hint of moss, just like the scents in her own garden. It was a mild evening. If she'd been at home she might have sat outside.

Kristina called to Åke, "Seja wants coffee."

Seja protested. "I don't want coffee this late."

"Late?" Kristina exclaimed. "It's not late at all!"

"It's late for me."

"Nonsense." Kristina sounded impatient. "Anyway, you can have a mouthful or leave it, it's up to you. What are you doing, Åke? Where's our coffee?"

Åke came in with a tray on which he was balancing some kind of gateau and three small dark-blue cups and saucers.

"It's strong, Seja, just the way you like it."

"Goodness," said Seja. "Cake as well. Are you sure it isn't somebody's birthday?"

She took the plate Åke was holding out to her. "If I didn't know you better, I'd think you were up to something."

Kristina gave Åke what surely had to be a meaningful look: *Out with it, Åke!*

"Come on then," said Seja. "*Are* you up to something?"

No one spoke. They sipped their coffee; it was good, completely different from the thin liquid Seja drank at home.

"No, it's nothing to make a big fuss about," Åke went on hesitantly. "But there was something we wanted to talk to you about."

"Oh? That sounds serious."

"No, no, nothing serious," he reassured her with a sudden laugh. "It's about selling the house."

"This house," Kristina added.

"This house?" Seja almost choked. "You're moving?"

Kristina coughed. It seemed to have been agreed that Åke would break the news. Now he'd done his job, the baton had clearly been passed to Kristina. "We're not getting any younger, Seja, and Åke won't be able to manage the house and garden for much longer."

"I can manage," Åke objected. "But I'm not sure I want to."

"No," Kristina agreed. "We're going to have to move to a more practical apartment eventually. And it's more fun to do that while we're reasonably fit and well."

Seja was lost for words. "I have to say I'm really surprised," she managed eventually.

"Anyway," Åke went on, "the thing about this house is that, unlike yours, it's completely modern and everything works perfectly."

Seja was bewildered.

"You'd better explain to Seja," Kristina chipped in.

"Yes," Seja said, totally lost. "I think you'd better."

"Explain? There's not much to explain, is there?"

"We thought you and Christian could buy it," Kristina clarified. "It's a good house, and we'll keep the price down because we'd really like to see someone we know take it on. Someone who cares about it."

"The idea was," Åke went on, "that we, or I, would keep the cellar for storage. If we move to an apartment in town, I won't have room for all the stuff I've collected over the years. You know how it is."

"I'm still not sure I completely understand this."

"Don't get us wrong," Åke added quickly. "That's not a deal-breaker. If you need the cellar, I can do without it."

"You want us . . . me to buy your house? But . . . what about your son? Doesn't he want it?"

"He already has a house, Seja. He doesn't want another one, and definitely not out in the wilds. In any case, he'll get a share of whatever we make, which he's very pleased about."

"I buy your house and you keep the cellar to store your stuff?"

Åke looked uncertain, as if he were just beginning to have his doubts about the whole thing.

"Well, I mean, I wouldn't be popping in and out all the time. I'd ring first."

Kristina leant forward and placed her hand on Seja's. "Seja, my dear. You must surely realise that you can't possibly spend another winter in that cottage. It's not good for your health, it's cold and damp with no inside toilet."

"Cold and damp? You've hardly ever set foot inside my house, Kristina." Seja pulled herself together. "Right. Listen. It's very sweet of you to think of me. Of course it is. But this isn't on."

"What?"

"The idea of me buying your house. And it's got nothing to do with you wanting to keep stuff in the cellar, Åke. I don't want to move, that's all. And as far as Christian is concerned, nothing would persuade him to leave the city."

"We could talk to the bank about the financial side . . ."

"This isn't about money. I'm happy in my house. But I am very sorry that you're thinking of moving. It will feel very empty up here without you."

100

Kristina sat back, pursing her lips. She wasn't happy. "I can see that."

Seja controlled herself. She really didn't want to upset them, it was just so . . . unnecessary.

"I shall be very sorry to see you go, Kristina, but I'll be fine. And you should get an agent and sell the house for as much as you can get. Obviously."

"We weren't planning to give you the house for free, you know." Åke clapped his hands. "But never mind! That's that. Would anyone like another piece of cake? Seja?"

Seja nodded.

Then she said, "You know what? I promise I'll give it some thought, OK?"

"Excellent." Åke took her sticky plate and shovelled on a second helping.

Kristina watched his movements pensively, then put her plate next to Seja's. "I'll have another piece too. And a drop more coffee."

"Well, there we are," she said eventually. "We've asked you, anyway. And you've promised to give it some thought. We won't mention it any more."

Kristina ate her second piece of cake with obvious pleasure and seemed to forget both Åke and Seja, along with all thoughts of selling houses or storing things in cellars.

CHAPTER
FIFTEEN

Gothenburg

Gonzales began the briefing: "About ten years ago Rebecca Nykvist was reported to the police by her then boyfriend. Several times."

A hush descended on the meeting room.

"Actual bodily harm, threatening behaviour, a death threat on one occasion. Harassment. Illegal entry, damage to personal property, you name it."

Beckman whistled. "Well, that's . . ."

"Wait," said Gonzales. "Forensics have sent in their initial report. Tell asked Johansson to prioritise the fingerprints inside the letterbox. Guess who they belong to?"

"Rebecca?

"Bingo."

"And inside the apartment?"

"Nothing. We've run the prints that were found inside, but there's no match. She, or whoever committed the murder, was wearing gloves. Either that, or they're not on our records."

"Or she didn't touch anything," said Bärneflod. "She might have just shot them and left."

"You look doubtful, Tell," said Beckman.

"Doubtful?"

Bärneflod banged the table. "It could hardly be clearer: the girl is pathologically jealous and has a history of violent behaviour. The boyfriend was playing away, that much we know. We also know from Karlberg's witness that she was there, creeping around, behaving suspiciously. We know she got inside the building, we even have her fingerprints on the door. Besides which, she lied about going out that night."

Tell waved vaguely in Bärneflod's direction.

"Yes, yes, I hear what you're saying. But think about it this way: we're looking for someone who has access to a weapon and is prepared and able to use it. Would Rebecca have been able to get her hands on a gun? Did she kill her lover's mistress, then walk into the next room to kill him in cold blood?"

"Can't most people get hold of a gun these days?" Beckman chipped in. "And it doesn't take great marksmanship to fire a bullet into someone standing a metre away."

"They picked the lock without damaging the door or the lock." Tell chipped in. "Is that something someone like Rebecca would know how to do?"

"I've been wondering about that," said Gonzales. "The door was locked when the bodies were found. Granberg and Andersson had to force the lock."

"My point exactly."

Tell leant forward, picked up some paperclips from the middle of the table and started to straighten one out. He was desperate for a cigarette. Sometimes he wondered about his decision to give up smoking. Was it really worth it?

"The perpetrator opened the door, went inside, shot Ann-Marie Karpov and Henrik Samuelsson dead, left the apartment, closed the door and locked it behind him or her."

Bärneflod said in a resigned voice, "Let me refer you to lesson one of any criminology course you'd care to name. Motive: yes. Opportunity: yes. Evidence . . . Oh, hang on a minute. Ah, yes, her fingerprints are at the scene of the crime! A witness saw her and her curly red hair — how many girls have curly red hair? The fingerprints are enough to bring her in for questioning; we know she's unpredictable and she could well decide to do a runner, I mean it's just —"

"I'm not arguing with that," Tell said sharply. "We'll bring her in and I think you should be the one to talk to her, Beckman. I'll ring the duty prosecutor right away. In the meantime, Gonzales will do more research into her record of threatening behaviour and violence. I want to know who she is. And what she's capable of."

"I'm suspected of murder and this is a formal interrogation?"

Rebecca Nykvist's eyes were green with pinprick pupils.

"You're being held as a suspect, as I explained earlier. You have the right to wait for your solicitor."

"So why bother asking me how I am? It's hardly relevant, is it?"

Beckman held Rebecca's gaze without faltering for a moment before replying: "I merely asked whether you're getting any help."

"Help with what?"

"With your jealousy. This isn't the first time it's caused you problems."

"No doubt you've got all the paperwork. You know exactly what I got in terms of punishment, care, help, whatever you want to call it. You know what I was accused of. But you don't know what really happened, or why. That's not on file."

"That's why I'm asking you."

"I've fulfilled my part of the care plan. The episode you're talking about was years and years ago. It has nothing to do with the tragedy that has hit me now: my partner has been murdered. My life is in tatters and I'm being accused of killing him. It's scandalous, its absolutely insane."

She put her hand down on the table, a couple of inches from Beckman's forearm, visibly struggling to compose herself. Breathing deeply, she leant back in her chair.

"It's ancient history. It has nothing to do with any of this."

"I'll bear that in mind," Beckman said calmly. "As I said, you have the opportunity to talk to me now, to give me your version of events."

Rebecca Nykvist's chin dropped to her chest. "There's no point," she said.

A knock on the door from the duty officer announced the arrival of Nykvist's solicitor. Viktoria

Ekholm walked into the room with a perfunctory nod. She slid into a chair next to her client and signalled that the interview could proceed.

"14.35, Viktoria Ekholm enters the room. OK, since you claim there's no point in going through your version of events, I'll give you mine first; this is what I think happened last time. You attacked, threatened and harassed your then boyfriend Georg Broberg due to uncontrollable jealousy. An affair, imagined or real —"

"You don't have to respond to this, Rebecca."

Viktoria Ekholm made a point of turning away from Beckman. "It's not a question, it's an assertion which, furthermore, has no relevance to the crime of which you are currently suspected."

"If your client is guilty of the crime of which she is suspected, there is in fact a great deal of common ground with the previous crime," said Beckman. "I am merely trying to understand how it all came about."

"So far my client is a suspect for reasons I have yet to hear you explain. I think it would be best to use those as your starting point."

"OK. One," Beckman started to count on the fingers of her left hand. "You said yourself that on the night when Ann-Marie Karpov and your partner Henrik Samuelsson were murdered you'd just found out that he'd been having an affair. You also found out that it had been going on for some time, behind your back, and that several other people knew about it."

"I don't see the relevance of that."

"Two. You were seen by a witness at the location where the murder took place; you were creeping around and trying to enter the building."

"Stop!" Viktoria Ekholm's cheeks flushed. "The witness saw a woman with red hair. My client is not the only woman in the world with red hair."

Beckman was secretly impressed by the way Ekholm had assimilated every detail of the case so quickly. She raised her voice. "Three. Whether the red-head seen behaving suspiciously in the courtyard was you or not is irrelevant. We found your fingerprints on the inside of Ann-Marie Karpov's letterbox. We know you were inside the apartment block. You were wearing a dark hooded top and you pushed open the letterbox. You were definitely at the scene. So why did you lie about it?"

Rebecca closed her eyes and joined her hands in her lap. Beckman didn't think she was praying; Rebecca didn't look the sort to rely on others, not even a higher power. But maybe she *was* praying; appearances could be deceptive.

Ekholm sat there in uncomfortable silence. This was a question her client couldn't dodge.

Rebecca looked up at the ceiling. "I was there. I was there for the reason you think."

"When?"

"At about two o'clock, maybe a bit later. I'd found out that . . . I didn't go there to kill them, I just wanted . . . I don't know."

Her face crumpled, but tears didn't come. Beckman waited, then pushed a couple of packets of tissues across the table. Rebecca didn't touch them.

"Well, what did you want to do?"

"I suppose I wanted to confront them."

"And?"

"I didn't murder them!"

"You looked through the letterbox. If the time you have stated is correct, and you're not lying about anything else, then you must have seen Ann-Marie Karpov lying just inside the door, as her neighbour did in the morning. So why didn't you call the police?"

"No!" Rebecca shouted. "I didn't see a thing, it was the middle of the night. It was pitch black in the hallway. I thought . . . I went back home. What could I do? What else could I do?"

"You just went home? Did anyone see you? Did you speak to anyone?"

She shrugged helplessly. "No. I don't know, I cycled through the park, through Slottsskogen. As I said, it was the middle of the night."

"And when you got home?"

"I drank more wine. Eventually I fell asleep."

Rebecca began to wail. Beckman grabbed hold of her upper arm. "Rebecca."

The shock brought Rebecca back to her senses. She tore her arm free and buried her face in her hands. Her breathing became a series of long drawn-out sobs.

To Beckman's surprise, she felt a sudden surge of sympathy. "Rebecca."

"My client needs a break."

Beckman switched off the tape with a sense of relief. She too needed some air. Those dry sobs were hard to bear.

CHAPTER
SIXTEEN

The house in question turned out to be a terraced house with a red front door and Samuelsson-Nykvist on the letterbox. That fitted. Preparation was the key; the difference between a job well done and a job botched. Between success and a cock-up. Torsen would have sold his mother for the cash this job could bring in. And it would put an old ghost to rest. Knud's ghost.

Knud had been clean for many years. He'd sorted his life out. Got a job in a museum. None of the new lot even knew who he was. And it was far more about who you knew than what you knew in this business. Knud should have understood that himself. In this situation, the fact that they'd spent a short time together inside meant nothing. OK, they'd got on well and done a few things together afterwards. Before Knud decided to stick to the straight and narrow. It was all so long ago.

Torsen could write a fucking book about everything that had happened since then. He still carried the marks of it; marks on his skin and marks deep inside. It was stupid of Knud to think he could ring up after years of silence, just like that — "A little job for me, for old times' sake" — coldly counting on Torsen's help.

Knud had hardly any contacts left. What he did have was attitude. It shone through his mates-from-the-old-days chat. As if he had just touched a pile of shit, Knud had discreetly wiped his hand on his trousers after shaking Torsen's hand.

What bothered Torsen was the companion Knud had forced on him. Young, moody, annoying. He had a crazed look in his eyes, as if he was on something. He was off-hand and way too mouthy.

"Just like you in the old days," Knud had said, but that was bullshit.

Before his body let him down and the bigger jobs dried up, Torsen had always known how important it was to cover your tracks.

"Fucking idiot," he hissed as the lad blundered inside, running a hand through his spiky hair. Shedding two or three hairs on the carpet, no doubt.

Torsen swayed in the doorway as he pulled on his gloves. He wasn't a hundred per cent today, definitely not. But so far, the job seemed straightforward. In and out. There was no one home. They'd parked the car a few streets away. They knew what they were looking for. They wouldn't have the usual hassle of several journeys to the car.

The lad was a risk. But he hadn't a clue what was going on, beyond the fact that he would get a few thousand for a quick job. He knew they were in a house in Sweden where some guy had hidden a number of items Knud wanted to get his hands on. And Knud had been very specific: Don't touch anything else. Don't waste time on mobile phones or any of that crap. Get in, pick up the stuff, get out.

Torsen felt slightly better. He resisted the urge to give the lad a slap. The more methodically they went to work, the quicker they would find what they had come for.

Then he would need a fix. And a lie down.

"I'll take the attic. You take the cellar."

"Aye aye."

Aye aye. Still, he was in no state to do the job on his own. It was age, it was the dope, it was the other thing clawing at his body. Of course he could go to the doctor about the other thing, but he'd never liked doctors. Doctors did tests and discovered things that didn't belong in the human body. He had a feeling that he was beyond the point of no return. It was only a matter of time until he had done his last job, conned his last punter. In some strange way, he was almost relieved.

The attic was a dusty hellhole. His body ached even though he'd taken his pills. The boy should have been the one crawling around up here, but Torsen couldn't trust him to be thorough.

If he had wanted to hide something important, would he have chosen the attic? Perhaps in the alcoves below the sloping roof, behind boxes of junk. Or in the utility room, behind the tumble drier. Maybe under the fridge. No, not under the fridge, that was too much of a cliché. In the air-con system. Or stitched inside a piece of furniture. No, they would slice open every single thing in the house.

Torsen didn't know why he lost control. It might have been his bitterness at being saddled with a twenty-two-year-old. Or the fact that he was beginning to think Knud had got it wrong, that they were wasting their time searching every nook and cranny of the house. Or it might have been his treacherous body, the fact that he lacked that extra bit of strength. But, whatever the cause, he abandoned his systematic approach and fell into a desperate frenzy, smashing open the stud wall and hurling the contents of the wardrobe onto the floor.

When he finally found what he was looking for, it was only one item, hidden in a box behind the books on a shelf in the bedroom. A clay figure. He weighed it in his hand.

His rage subsiding, he searched the attic and upstairs one more time. Went through the kitchen and the living room again, the hallway and the downstairs bedroom. The cellar this time. In his peripheral vision he could see that the lad was a little calmer, as if his own carelessness had been subdued by seeing someone else who was equally reckless — or perhaps he was just afraid. Torsen was having an attack of the shakes and he felt as if he was using up the last of his strength. When they finally came to a standstill, it looked as though a hurricane had passed through the house. There was a pervasive smell of desperation secreted through their skin. They had been in there for hours.

As a car backed onto the drive next door and the outside lights came on, Torsen's bloodshot eyes met the lad's suspicious gaze. He thought: *Got to keep the lad quiet, he won't like the idea that we've been conned, he's already getting ideas.* They wordlessly established that the job was over. It was time to go.

CHAPTER
SEVENTEEN

Istanbul, September 2007

The area between the Hagia Sophia and Sultan Ahmed Camii could have offered coolness and shade, with its fountain and neatly clipped trees. But all the spots in the shade had been taken. Henrik had at least managed to find a vacant place among the hundred square, backless benches in front of the Blue Mosque. He sat down to rest his aching feet, grimacing with pain as he pulled off his Converse trainers to expose the burst, fleshy blisters on his heels. It was the heat that made the body vulnerable. His feet weren't the only part suffering. For the first two days his stomach had been unsettled — along with some of the others, he had found it difficult to adjust to the strongly flavoured food and the sweet Turkish wine. They had been constantly on the lookout for the nearest public toilet, joking amongst themselves: *Here we go again.*

He put on the leather sandals which he had just bought from a street trader. They were well made and looked good, although they did press slightly on his big toe when he slipped them on his feet — if it wasn't one thing, it was another. But they were still his best bet; the heels of the trainers were stiff with dried blood. He

115

perched them on top of an overflowing bin, and immediately a boy appeared from nowhere and grabbed them, clutching them defiantly to his stomach as he disappeared into the crowd.

The trader, whose goods were spread out on a blanket in front of him, spun around as if he had eyes in the back of his head. He gesticulated wildly, shouting at the boy.

"It's OK," Henrik said. "I'd thrown them away."

He took his water bottle out of his shoulder bag, in case it was dehydration that was making everything flicker in front of his eyes. He had learnt to drink water with his raki now; in the beginning he had refused. *As it comes*, he had said the first evening; he never drank water with red wine, nor put ice in his whisky. The waiters had smiled condescendingly. No doubt they knew all about the iron band that would slowly tighten around his head in a few hours' time.

It was the worst hangover Henrik had ever endured. The only thing that helped was a quick hair of the dog in the hotel lobby before the others came down. He consoled himself with the thought that he was on holiday; he was usually much more careful when it came to spirits.

Henrik emptied the bottle thirstily. A young woman immediately appeared by his side. She was strikingly beautiful, dressed in a sequinned shawl that dazzled when it caught the sun. She was holding out bottles of water in different sizes. He didn't even need to get up; he simply picked a couple of coins out of his wallet.

"You American?"

116

The usual polite phrases to butter him up, giving the impression that she actually cared who he was and where he came from.

"No, no, absolutely not. I'm from Sweden. A town called Göteborg, Gothenburg."

As soon as he had paid, she lost interest in him. He watched her disappear into the crowd, her thin body stooped under the weight of the water. Anyone could disappear into that throng and never be seen again.

He gazed over towards Alemdar Caddesi, looking for Ann-Marie; if she finished early at the museum she would come that way. He couldn't see her sky-blue suit anywhere. His stomach somersaulted at the thought of her.

Henrik knew that if he went to look for her at the Museum of Archaeology, he would find the upstanding, learned professional who had been the object of his admiration for so long. He felt a tremor of doubt: perhaps he had imagined the moments they had shared.

He pushed his doubt aside. The nights had been real, they had belonged to them.

Their days were spent as a group. Annelie fell in love with the old, handwritten books and the objects made of stone, wood, metal and ceramics, in particular the hand-woven kelims. They were determined to take home some examples of Turkish handicrafts. Even though Henrik wasn't exactly a fan of shopping, he had gone with them to the Egyptian market and had been amazed by the array of goods on offer. He had pottered among mounds of piled-up herbs and spices, but then he reached his limit. When the others went on to the Grand Bazaar, he had returned to the Archaeological Museum on his own. He loved its collections and the building that housed them. He wandered through the echoing exhibition halls more or less alone, gazing at the three-thousand-year-old remains of buildings and Roman sarcophagi. He spent hours sitting in the inner courtyard, enjoying being surrounded by ancient Greek columns and statues. The feel of the museum particularly appealed to him. In contrast to its Swedish equivalent, the institution seemed completely lacking in educational aims. There was no sense of curation; the artefacts were displayed in no particular order and only occasionally had the sparse lines of text been translated from Turkish.

At this time of day the historic Sultan Ahmed was packed with people. Henrik amused himself for a while trying to guess the nationality of those who were clearly tourists. Towards evening the crowds would thin out. There were many mosques in this area, which made the nightlife quieter, and revellers tended to disappear by midnight. But you only needed to go down to the harbour or Eminönus Square, or cross Galata Bridge, and the night seemed young at any time.

Henrik wondered whether to go back to the museum. Or should he go and look for Ann-Marie? God, no. He must never get clingy. And it was important to show that he respected her work.

They had dedicated three whole days to the collections before exploring the rest of the city. They had travelled by boat across the Bosphorus to the Asiatic side, to its promenade and holes in the walls serving raki or hot, sweet tea in tinted glasses. And then back to the European side. The city silhouettes on both sides of the water, scrambling up the hillsides, looked as if they were carrying thirty metres of smog, like a dark-grey mist covering the buildings, the domes of the mosques, the pointed minarets, palace towers and pinnacles.

Late at night, when the others had headed back to the hotel — Axel Donner was usually the last to throw in the towel — Henrik and Ann-Marie would stay out. They were both night owls, egging each other on until the first light of dawn crept over the city like a gentle caress, before the traffic made their eardrums tremble and the heat arrived. Before the first call to prayer echoed across the rooftops. The nights had followed a quickly established ritual. They would start off at a courtyard restaurant high up in a narrow street behind the Hagia Sophia, with its lights shining on their laps. Or they would go to the place opposite, a more modest bar with kelim-covered sofas, tucked below the high wall of the Topkapi Palace park. A number of artists wearing paint-spattered white coats frequented the courtyard next door, their abstract paintings hung up to dry in the sun.

The first evening they talked about art and architecture, drawing on what they had seen that day. But it wasn't long before they were teasing out a deeper connection. Gradually, they shed the inhibitions of being teacher and pupil. The city was instrumental in

119

this. It pulled and tugged in every direction, refusing to respect boundaries, refusing to keep itself in check.

Henrik told Ann-Marie about the stirrings he had felt on the way from the airport. As their yellow taxi zig-zagged among hundreds of others, with thousands of cars revving their engines and sounding their horns. There were traffic jams as far as the eye could see, the smog was suffocating, making his eyes smart and his lungs burn, and Henrik had thought: I can't breathe. *I can't breathe*, just as he had thought on his way into Cairo. As he had thought on his way into Bombay and Bangkok, New Mexico and countless other cities. He had been terrified at first, then exhilarated. And after that, he wanted nothing else other than to be in the city, to be nowhere else for the rest of his life.

Ann-Marie had smiled at the fact that they were so alike. And that it had taken them so long to find out.

CHAPTER
EIGHTEEN

Gothenburg

"What were we talking about?" asked Karin Beckman.

"Rebecca's employer."

"That's it," Tell replied. "She said Rebecca used to work with patients, short-term therapy and so on, but that she was barred from direct contact when the offences against her ex-boyfriend came to light. If I understand correctly, it was some kind of compromise allowing her to keep working there after she'd completed her punishment. At the moment she has some kind of administrative role. I also discovered that our new chief constable is a bureaucrat right to his fingertips, an absolute master at digging out sensitive information. Thanks to him, I've been in touch with a psychiatrist who saw Rebecca back then. From what he said, I could easily imagine that . . ."

She fell silent suddenly to concentrate on the traffic, muttering about the one-way system. A man battled his way across the crossing with a Monkshood plant in an ornate pot. They watched him in silence as they waited for the lights to change.

"I still think it's peculiar that she's trusted to work in a place where they're dealing with people's psychiatric problems, given her history . . ."

"Admin duties could just mean she spends all day writing invoices," Beckman replied. "And, to be fair, it appears that her aggression is linked to whatever man she happens to be living with, or at least to people with whom she has a close relationship. She's not a danger to the public. And if you've completed your punishment, surely you deserve a second chance, don't you?"

"I take your point. But is that argument ever going to be watertight? Can a person be aggressive, extremely aggressive I mean, to one particular person or in one situation, and behave completely normally to everyone else? In my opinion, if you're crazy in that way you're a liability. A time bomb. Surely all it would take would be for someone to piss you off one day when you've got out of bed on the wrong side?"

The corner of Beckman's mouth twitched almost imperceptibly.

"Hmm . . . No, actually, I think that a person could function perfectly normally and do their job and have friends but still lose it over and over again in one specific context. After all, it's not particularly unusual to have hang-ups about infidelity. It's only human."

"And what's behind it? In the case of Rebecca Nykvist?"

He opened his door to help as Beckman tried to squeeze their Hyundai into a parking space which looked smaller than the car itself.

122

"Shall we?"

The letterbox was marked Samuelsson-Nykvist. But Samuelsson wouldn't be coming back and Nykvist might not see her front door for a while, Beckman thought, with a sudden, surprising feeling of melancholy. She had no relationship with Rebecca Nykvist. Or her problems. She thought back to her earlier conversation with Tell.

"You asked what's behind it? Well, I don't really know, but it could be that any situation that evokes a fear of abandonment acts as a trigger. Her aggression is a survival instinct."

The lupins on either side of the path made her think of Österlen, where her family used to have a summer cottage. *Just imagine lying down in the flowers and forgetting everything else.*

She was getting annoyed with Tell, who was now on the street, chatting on his mobile. She didn't usually get annoyed with Tell and she wasn't usually tired. There was a connection. The tiredness meant that she was constantly on edge and she was conscious of the fact; it made her uncharacteristically cheerful until her defences came crashing down, when she would shout at people who let a door close in her face, were walking their dogs without a lead, or who simply happened to be nearby. She felt unreliable.

She shoved a handful of peanuts into her mouth and blinked away a tear as she swallowed too soon and felt the sharp nuts scratching her throat. She shouldn't be too hard on herself, she thought. She had just ended a ten-year relationship that had been anything but restful, and she had yet to develop a new routine as a working single mother. She really didn't want to think about her feelings. But she knew deep down that the separation was for the best, and that was all she could focus on for the present.

When you were young, you thought breaking up would get easier. Perhaps it did, in a way. After all, she was a master of suppressing her emotions. She simply put certain matters to one side, tackling them when there was the time and space to do so. And it was only four weeks since she had left Göran. Four weeks, that was no time at all. She wasn't stupid; she realised that at some point she would have to face up to the grief. But not today.

Then she noticed something. She raised her arm and gestured to Tell without turning around.

"Tell! Come here!"

She heard him end the call.

"The door. It's unlocked. Or has someone broken in?"

Beckman withdrew her hand instinctively and fumbled in her bag for latex gloves and shoe protectors.

"You can never be too careful . . ."

"There's no reason for the door to be open," Tell agreed, automatically lowering his voice. "When Rebecca was brought in for questioning she must have known that it could be some time before she came home. Be careful until we're sure the house is empty."

The red door opened slowly. It took them a couple of seconds to establish that the hallway was in a considerably worse state than on their previous visit.

124

The cloakroom and wardrobe doors were wide open, and the floor was covered with clothes, bags and shoes.

Beckman listened intently at the foot of the stairs before going up to check the landing and bedrooms. Judging by her response, things were much the same upstairs. Tell walked around the ground floor taking care not to touch a thing, a grim expression on his face. Whoever was responsible for this devastation had done a thorough job.

They met up in the living room five minutes later. The sofa had been ripped open and its stuffing was spread all over the floor along with shards of glass from a painting. The poster that had been in the frame had been torn out and had slid under the table. Even the pot plants had been turned upside down, and compost had fallen between the floorboards.

"Look." A vase had been knocked over. Tell crouched down beside the broken glass, taking care not to step in the pool of muddy soil and water. He found the long-stemmed gerbera halfway under the piano stool.

"How long does a cut flower like this stay fresh without water?"

The fat stem exuded a foamy liquid when he squeezed it between his thumb and index finger.

"Not very long, I should think."

"So the disturbance probably happened less than twenty-four hours ago?"

"What do you think about the marks on the floor? They're not footprints."

"No, I noticed that too. It almost looks as if the person made a conscious effort to remove all traces. What's your take on it?"

"I think whoever did this knew what they were doing. I don't think this is the work of kids."

Beckman walked slowly to the kitchen, resisting the impulse to flop into one of the chairs and rest her head on the table. Instead she tried to marshal her thoughts. *You can always read a crime scene.* The perpetrator will always give away something of himself — or herself. Who they are, what they want, and what they are planning to do next.

The kitchen sofa had been dragged away from the wall, and the drawer beneath it had been emptied. Photographs of different sizes lay in drifts around the dresser, having been tipped out of a shoe box that now lay upside down. Many of them showed Rebecca and Henrik on holiday, striking fun poses. There were several arty pictures of Rebecca, taken in black and white. They were pictures of a happy life together, just what you'd expect. Nobody wanted to capture their misery for posterity. And yet the tragedy was palpable, given that one of these smiles had been mercilessly taken away.

"But this puts Rebecca Nykvist's involvement in a completely different light," she muttered. "Because it doesn't look like a straightforward burglary. The house appears to have been searched. Perhaps it's not a crime of passion after all."

"What did you say?"

"Nothing," said Beckman, shaking her head. "So what do you make of it?"

"Well . . ." Tell's laugh was somewhat strained. "I don't think we can rule out a connection to the murder of Henrik Samuelsson. Given that the evidence against Rebecca is unsatisfactory in some ways, I think we need to reconsider whether she is our prime suspect. I'm not sure we can hold her."

"What about the witness?"

"The witness statements don't tally. Rebecca's fingerprints were found on the letterbox, there's no doubt she was there, but they weren't found anywhere inside the apartment. Her calls on the night of the murder have been verified. The woman who reported the disturbance said it happened at around one o'clock. The next-door neighbour's account puts Rebecca at the scene closer to half-past two."

"In which case Henrik and Ann-Marie were already dead by the time Rebecca got there," said Beckman. "She said she didn't see anything when she looked through the letterbox, presumably because it was dark outside and the hallway lights were switched off. The neighbour who called looked in after it got light."

"Plus, do we think Rebecca is a danger to the public? Do we think she's planning to do a runner or continue her life of crime? No, we don't. We don't have enough evidence to arrest her. And now this. I'm beginning to think we need to cast the net wider."

Beckman pointed her toe at a sewing kit — even that had been searched. Reels of cotton and packets of needles had spilled onto the kitchen floor.

"The burglars were after something very specific, wouldn't you say? Something they expected to find which wasn't here. Or which was so well hidden that they couldn't find it. Or they didn't find it until they'd searched the entire house. It *could* be that Rebecca Nykvist is unlucky enough to be the victim of a break-in while she just happens to be in police custody. But it doesn't look to me as if this house was chosen at random. It looks as though this particular house was searched."

Tell agreed. "Do you know what confuses me most?"

"No."

"If we believe the two crimes were linked, why hadn't the apartment on Linnégatan been searched?"

Beckman shrugged. "Perhaps they knew that whatever they were looking for was here. Perhaps Ann-Marie Karpov and Henrik Samuelsson needed to be silenced, because they knew something about . . . about whatever the murderers were looking for?"

Tell bent down and examined a black imitation-leather case which contained an iPod.

"They don't appear to have taken any valuables."

"So what do you think they were looking for?" Beckman persisted. "Off the top of your head?"

Tell looked exhausted. He had absolutely no idea. "Something small; the bubble bath has been poured out in the bathroom, the jewellery box has been searched. Something that would fit inside a jewellery box."

"More than one person?"

"Yes, it's an incredibly thorough job even for two people."

Tell took the snuff tin out of his breast pocket, inhaled, then tucked a pinch under his top lip.

Beckman's expression was now one of amusement. "So is it working? No cigarettes hidden in your desk drawer?"

"Not so far. But, as you know, it all depends on how the case goes."

She patted him on the shoulder. "I wish you were joking. But I'll be the first one to snatch the cigarette out of your hand. You might not believe it yet, but it's definitely worth the trouble. You'll think so the first time you walk up those stairs at home without getting out of breath."

"I have a lift," said Tell.

Beckman clapped her hands. "So, what now? We can't touch anything here, the place needs to be gone over properly. By the way, did we hear any more from Forensics about Linnégatan?"

Without replying, Tell walked over to the window and parted the curtains. A middle-aged man was getting out of a Renault Mégane on the other side of the low fence between the gardens.

"Here come the neighbours. You ring the station. I'll go over and ask if they happened to see a gang of masked men turning this place upside down."

CHAPTER
NINETEEN

Karlberg was interviewing students and members of staff in the archaeology department. The interviews he had conducted so far hadn't yielded much information beyond what they already knew. Nothing about the lives of the two victims seemed unusual at first glance. That was to be expected; shady goings-on generally took place behind closed doors. Everybody had something to hide, a skeleton in the cupboard. Or at least dirt swept under the carpet. And people really did make an effort to hide whatever they were ashamed of, regardless of whether this had anything to do with an ongoing police investigation. Sometimes police officers felt that their authority was being eroded, but the fact remained that Joe Public wanted to appear irreproachable in the eyes of the law. Of course this could send the police in completely the wrong direction.

Of the four members of Henrik Samuelsson's study group that Karlberg had managed to speak to so far, one hadn't seemed very clear on who Samuelsson was, while another had tried to be a gentleman and drew a veil over his affair. When Karlberg tartly pointed out that the police were well aware of what had been going on, the young man insisted he had acted with the best of intentions. He just wanted to protect Henrik Samuelsson's partner from the knowledge that her recently deceased boyfriend had been unfaithful.

The woman who came in next, Marie Hjalmarsson, had already heard about the "tragedy". It was undeniably a tragedy, but her choice of word also seemed to be a way of keeping violent death at arm's length. Refusing to use the word murder. Or killing.

She was the first to mention the study trip.

"The main people who knew that Ann-Marie had started a relationship with a student were on the study trip. There was lots of gossip, of course. We weren't a very big group, and we grew quite close."

"Gossip?"

"Yes, on the trip. It became very obvious that there was something going on between them."

"In what way?"

Marie Hjalmarsson looked doubtfully at Karlberg. "Well . . . in the usual way? The way they looked at each other. The way they kept trying to slip away from the rest of the group. They stayed out until everybody else had gone home. There were a few instances of inappropriate touching by the end of the week. It almost seemed as if they didn't care if other people knew."

"Did anyone react badly to this?"

"I think we were all influenced by the fact we were in a foreign country. There was a kind of rebellious, un-Swedish spirit pervading the whole trip. We sat outside drinking wine. We went out every night. I think the atmosphere made us more tolerant. Because

131

actually, if you ask me, it's not OK for a tutor to get together with a student. Ann-Marie was a respected member of the university staff. Besides which, Henrik had a partner. And Ann-Marie was a good deal older than him."

She hesitated. "A teacher is supposed to set a good example, even if he or she works at a university, don't you think?"

"OK," said Karlberg. "So you didn't approve?"

"People can do as they please. But I was the only one, apart from maybe Axel Donner, who questioned the relationship, or . . . saw it as a problem. Axel was Henrik's friend, and I don't think he liked what was going on. Although it could just have been because he'd lost an ally. I might have hinted at what several of the others were thinking, or wanted to think, but didn't quite have the nerve. They were afraid of being called narrow-minded."

"It sounds like there was bit of a conflict going on."

"Not really; it wasn't an argument, more a matter of discussion."

"Discussion about what precisely?"

Marie squirmed. "I don't really like the idea that everything I say is being written down."

"But there's a risk that I'll misinterpret what you say if you just drop hints."

"Surely you're not allowed to do that?"

"I'm only human. Hints and things you don't say could well influence what I take from this interview. By the way, who would you say knew Henrik best among your fellow students?"

"Axel Donner and Annelie Swerin, definitely. Axel was like a fly buzzing around Henrik. OK, I'll tell you. Annelie had an affair with her former boss."

"Was he on the trip as well?"

"No. But she talked about it, she said it was hard. He was married, and . . . There were a number of tensions within the group. I said something about infidelity which she misinterpreted and took as a personal criticism. This business with Henrik and Ann-Marie had happened. There was a peculiar atmosphere between Annelie and Axel. I don't think Annelie particularly likes Axel. He's a fairly quiet person, but he can be quite difficult, and with her he was even trickier, somehow. Perhaps he had a bit of a thing for her and didn't know how to show it. Or she didn't know how to handle it. Oh no, this is all getting too messy. I don't know what happened in Istanbul, just that Axel somehow overstepped the mark. It wasn't just him, they were all pretty drunk. They made a joke of it later, but I think Annelie was upset."

"And you don't know what actually happened?"

"No. I'd already gone back to the hotel that night."

Nothing but a vague stream of information. "Axel and Annelie," said Karlberg. "They're on the group list, are they?"

Hjalmarsson nodded. "I'm sure they are. But there's no point trying to get hold of Annelie at the moment. She's gone to some place in India to volunteer on a dig. I don't think she'll be back for a while. Anyway: I can understand why Ann-Marie Karpov was attracted to Henrik. It's not that I begrudged her good sex or

Henrik *even more* female attention, but . . . If it had been a male lecturer carrying on with a twenty-two-year-old girl, there would have been an outcry, wouldn't there? People would have called him a dirty old man."

Henrik Samuelsson was no twenty-two-year-old, thought Karlberg, and started wondering why tutors — male or female — started relationships with their students. Was it out of the question that these two really had fallen in love?

As if Marie Hjalmarsson could read his mind, she said, "It all comes down to power. Even in a relationship between two people who are in love and believe themselves to be equals. And if you think the word power is too strong, then you could say instead that in *any* social interaction, all parties are aware of their status. Like you and me, just now."

Karlberg couldn't help himself: "You don't think it's rather cynical to assume that everything comes down to sex and power?"

"All I'm saying is that you can't suddenly change your status, just because you happen to be in love. But being with Henrik must have made Ann-Marie feel young. In the end it comes down to whether you think people can consciously *allow* themselves to be exploited. Is that OK, as long as they get something out of it too?"

"Otherwise every relationship would be doomed," said Karlberg.

She tilted her head to one side. Karlberg suddenly realised her smile was quite appreciative, because his ears began to burn; those reddening ears were the last vestige of an agonising teenage tendency to blush. He went back to his script.

"Did you know Henrik Samuelsson well?"

The answer came quickly. "Not well."

"How would you describe him?"

She squirmed again. "Hmm. Most people liked him. He was good at making other people feel as if he was really paying attention to them, whether it was true or not. He was charismatic and committed and he knew a lot, but perhaps not always as much as he liked to suggest. He seemed to need to stand out, to show how special he was. He was one of those people who always has to express an opinion, preferably one which goes against what everybody else thinks. He could be a bit of a know-all sometimes. Vain. And maybe he was also a bit . . . no."

Marie Hjalmarsson waved away what she had been about to say.

"Go on, tell me what you were thinking," Karlberg leaned forward as if he wanted to draw the words out of her.

"His style seemed to work, on the whole. You know, the jazz musician thing: pretty laid-back, left-wing of course . . . but he still wore expensive designer 1950s suits. He was popular with the girls, but . . . It's all a matter of taste and opinion. I thought he could be a bit sleazy sometimes. One of those 'handsome' guys with long hair who doesn't quite get the fact that he's not so young any more, and is still on the prowl for twenty-something girls."

"You mean he tried it on with you?"

"No, no! Heavens, no, I knew I should never have mentioned it. He never did anything, it was just the way he looked at me. As if he was kind of thinking things."

Marie Hjalmarsson started rummaging in her bag, obviously embarrassed. As Karlberg scratched the back of his neck, he realised he needed a haircut. His encouraging smile gradually faded.

CHAPTER
TWENTY

Rebecca Nykvist had almost been dreading the moment she was to be released. Suddenly she was no longer in custody but free to go. One hundred and twenty-nine square metres of chaos and emptiness just a short taxi-ride away.

She had been warned that the house had been turned upside down, but she was still shocked when she walked through the door. The cold fury discernible in every room: someone had searched her home.

She stood there quietly, contemplating the dirt that had appeared, the dust from hidden corners that had been disturbed and was now visible on the floor. The clothes that had been touched and strewn everywhere.

She would need to wash those.

Private papers and letters, tossed all over the place.

When the telephone rang, she had just started to tackle the mess. It was Henrik's mother; Rebecca wished she hadn't answered.

She turned down the invitation to her in-laws' house in Vänersborg. Görel Samuelsson's voice intoned empty phrases such as "there is no strength in being alone", and insisted that they ought to, they *must*, share their grief. Be there for each other.

"We're all here. Everyone came as soon as they found out. Lennart's ordered food so we don't have to bother with anything. We don't have the strength, it's all been so ghastly. The police came and spoke to us, it was almost like an interrogation, but we felt so helpless, after all we don't know anything about . . ."

Rebecca didn't know how things stood. Did Görel know that her daughter-in-law had been held in custody on suspicion of the murder of her son, and subsequently released due to lack of evidence? It was best not to say anything — in any case, Rebecca had no idea what to say.

She could hear a tissue rustling and held the phone a little further from her ear. In the background she could hear the low hum of voices. Should she hire a car? The thought of a long drive with the wind in her hair was tempting, but the sobbing at the other end of the line disrupted her thoughts.

"We'd like everybody to gather here before the funeral. We have plenty of room, you can stay as long as you like."

Görel's sobbing was making Rebecca feel ill. It reminded her of the grief she didn't dare give way to.

"After all, you were his partner."

After all . . .

"I just don't feel I can leave here at the moment because of work. Going to work is a good thing; it helps . . . take my mind off things."

Rebecca knew this sounded harsh and false, but her brain couldn't keep up. And she was probably doing the Samuelsson household a favour. At least now they'd have something to talk about between the outbursts of weeping. Rebecca would be someone they could talk about, their words sounding kind enough on the surface, but everyone would know they held an undertone of reproach for her coldness, her exaggerated sense of purpose.

"She's difficult to get close to," Görel would say. Görel was never openly hostile. But everyone would know exactly what she meant.

And of course they had never married. Perhaps Görel didn't know that Henrik was the one who didn't want to. Nor did she seem to know that bottomless grief sometimes leads to a bewildered sense of despair that leaves you paralysed and mute. Rebecca put the phone down.

It was Thursday in the normal world. She had an appointment with her therapist at five o'clock in the afternoon. Rebecca had always regarded her relationship with Birger Warberg as rock solid. He knew exactly what to ask. When to keep quiet, when to speak. She could see herself reflected in his gestures, his neutral yet understanding expressions. But would she see a freshly sown seed of doubt there today?

Would he be sure that she hadn't murdered Henrik? If he wasn't sure, would he manage to hide that fact? Would he steal glances at her when he thought she wouldn't notice before his face closed down once more?

That was what she feared.

She sat there twice a week, head down. Sometimes resigned, sometimes defensive. Rebecca had noticed how keen Warberg was to expose the areas she didn't dare to touch upon. They talked about her fear of abandonment, her lack of trust.

But she had been abandoned. Henrik *had* been unfaithful. Now she knew that reality was much uglier than she could possibly have imagined. And Rebecca realised that, deep down, she had known all along. Even though Henrik had tried to blame her for all their problems, even though he had maintained they were caused by her unhealthy suspicions and the fact she was a control freak, they had been there all along.

CHAPTER
TWENTY-ONE

They were in Pelle Höije's office, the only place apart from the conference room that could accommodate the whole team. This was largely irrelevant at the moment because the number of those present was significantly reduced. Karlberg had prioritised his interviews with the archaeology students. Beckman was caught in traffic on the way back from Vänersborg, where she had been to visit Henrik Samuelsson's parents and sister.

Tell was extremely annoyed, and hoped to God she actually was stuck in traffic. He made a mental note to stress the importance of full attendance at briefings, otherwise they were fairly pointless. The aim was to piece together the results of everyone's efforts; only then could they gain an overview of the investigation so far.

He couldn't help feeling even more irritated by the fact that his team must have looked slapdash to the chief constable. Höije was new, and all he knew of his colleagues came from daily progress reports. Tell felt a strong sense of responsibility when his team appeared in a negative light, as if he had somehow failed to create structure and efficient working practices. He couldn't remember feeling this way under his former boss.

Ann-Christine Östergren had taken early retirement the previous year due to illness; she and Tell went back a long way.

Perhaps it was just a matter of time. No doubt Höije would grow into his role. Perhaps a mutual respect would develop as they got to know each other.

Höije was listening politely to Bärneflod's diatribe on law and order. "The police need to have the powers to act. Organised crime, youth gangs, everybody in fact — they all see us as a doddery, bureaucratic joke. Do you see what I'm getting at? We have no power these days, and that means no respect, no authority."

Christian Tell chose to distract himself with thoughts of breakfast in bed with Seja.

Höije was nodding; either he was actually interested in what Bärneflod had to say, or he was a good actor. But his little finger was tapping silently on the mouse mat, a sign of impatience that Tell noted with some satisfaction.

The young, blond chief constable, who according to some women in the building was quite good-looking, had started in the new year. He wasn't a career police officer, which was enough to upset some people. Tell hadn't yet formed an opinion. So far Höije hadn't been given the opportunity to show his true colours. He had been optimistic, diplomatic and well organised, albeit in a slightly self-conscious way. As if he had read about the importance of being clear and direct on some leadership blog. And he was too young to be a chief constable, but if Tell held this against him he would be hoist by his own petard.

Höije had discreetly tidied the piles of papers adorned with pie charts from his desk. There were still a couple of weeks to go until the budget submission, but Höije was conscientious and probably highly competent in this area. Didn't he have some advanced qualification in economics? Tell was certain this was behind Bärneflod's ridiculous lecture.

"Gonzales, you're from Gårdsten, you know what I'm talking about . . ."

Tell groaned inwardly, but Gonzales was polite enough to simply murmur that he actually lived in Hammarkullen.

Höije's response was measured; he still wore that thoughtful, interested expression. I bet he learnt that on a leadership course too, Tell thought.

"You've raised a number of interesting points, Bengt. I agree that it's important to make good use of the high level of competence among our more experienced colleagues. The problem as I see it is that every concession to individual capriciousness — if you'll forgive me for putting it like that — involves a legal risk. It's a balancing act. As you say, an organisation which is too bureaucratic becomes noticeably inefficient."

By now, even Gonzales was looking at his watch. Tell leant forward and read Gonzales's notes over his shoulder. He had been interviewing individuals found in Rebecca Nykvist and Henrik Samuelsson's address book. Gonzales had also gone through Samuelsson's hard drive with Karen Stenhammar, their data expert. *Programs: Word, QuarkXPress, Photoshop, Limewire . . .* Everything was neatly logged on a page of A4 which slipped out of view as Gonzales coughed and crossed his legs.

Tell had had enough. "Stuff this. I've got loads to do. I'm going to my office — you can come and get me when you've finished chatting."

He met a surprised Karlberg in the doorway. "Have you finished already?"

"No, we haven't started yet."

"Tell!"

Tell turned around and met Höije's gaze, which was steady and significantly chillier than it had been.

"Sit down."

It was unmistakably an order.

"Rebecca Nykvist is no longer in custody. She has been released since we are unable to establish that she actually entered the apartment which was the scene of the crime. We know that she was creeping around, we know that she lied. We are aware of her background. I think this is a borderline case. We will be keeping her under surveillance for the time being. Tell, get that sorted please. We will continue to work with no preconceptions and will review the situation so far. Do you wish to organise your presentation in any particular way?"

"No."

Tell, still smarting from being put in his place, had no special way of delivering reports or conducting feedback sessions with the team; everybody simply went through anything new they had discovered.

"Right then," Höije said when Tell failed to expand on his answer. "In that case we'll start with you, Gonzales. You've been working with Stenhammar, haven't you? Were there any particular reasons why the computer was password protected? Anything Henrik wanted to hide? Feel free to use the whiteboard if you wish."

Höije gestured invitingly at the board. Gonzales nodded and swallowed. He suddenly felt as though he were back at school.

"I can't see any reason why he chose to protect the contents of the computer hard drive." He started to go through his papers. "The programs were standard: text and image manipulation, music and film downloads. A statistics program. Lots of games, mainly with a medieval theme, good versus evil — you know the kind of thing I mean."

Nobody moved a muscle.

"The hard drive is divided into Henrik's folders and Rebecca's folders. I haven't had time to go through hers yet. He has an extensive music collection stored on the computer. And a number of documents linked to his studies: essays and so on. Nothing out of the ordinary, apart from —"

"Apart from what?"

"Well, there is one document I don't really understand. It's just one page, with a whole lot of names and numbers. I've managed to identify some of them. But there are several that neither Rebecca nor

Henrik's parents can help with. We're talking about a dozen names and numbers. It's as if each person has a number. And it's not a telephone number."

"So what is it?"

Gonzales frowned and passed a print-out of the document to Tell, who read it aloud.

"Ma . . . 4500. Roger . . . 3000. Jessica A . . . 1500. Jerry . . . 2000."

"Have you tried his email contacts?"

"I've gone through them and tried to match names with the other lists of people known to Henrik that we've compiled so far. Certain names recur on several lists, Annelie Swerin, for example. Axel Donner. Marie Hjalmarsson."

"And? Have you spoken to her?"

"I've spoken to Hjalmarsson," Karlberg chipped in. "She seemed very sensible."

"Are you checking alibis?"

"Yes, but several have yet to be confirmed."

"OK. Carry on, Gonzales."

"Hang on." Karlberg again. "Could it be a list of people Henrik owes money to?"

"That seems like a possibility," said Tell. "All the information we have so far indicates that he had financial problems. Check with Rebecca whether he was a gambler. If that's a list of debts, it's worth thinking about it in terms of motive. Although the sums involved aren't exactly significant."

Höije turned to Tell. "Could I ask whether there was any sign that items might be missing from the apartment on Linnégatan?"

146

"Whether anything had been stolen, you mean? Hard to say. It didn't look as if the place had been searched. There were valuable items on show: jewellery, a mobile phone, that type of thing."

"The computer," said Karlberg.

"You mean . . ."

"There was no computer. What sort of academic doesn't own a computer?"

Höije nodded thoughtfully. "Check this out. See if it might be somewhere else, try her office at the university as your first port of call. Otherwise it might be worth considering whether Ann-Marie Karpov's computer could be the motive for the intrusion. Something on that computer."

"Speaking of searches, I would like to work from the hypothesis that the break-in at Samuelsson's house could be linked to the murders."

Höije gazed at Tell for a few seconds without speaking. "On what basis?" he said eventually.

"This wasn't any old break-in. Every inch of the place seems to have been searched, but nothing of value was stolen. And the sofa cushions had been slit open, which indicates that they were looking for something specific. The break-in happened just after Henrik Samuelsson was murdered, and while Rebecca Nykvist was still in custody. There are a lot of coincidences."

Höije nodded. "Indeed. In that case we will treat the link between the murders and the break-in as a line of inquiry. But we must not exclude other possibilities. As I said, we are not ruling Rebecca Nykvist out of our inquiries. Have we checked for possible witnesses to the break-in?"

"No luck so far."

Höije removed his glasses and placed them on the desk. "Who's contacted Telia and the mobile phone operator?"

That had been Beckman's job. Tell must remember to ring her after the meeting.

"We're still working on that."

"OK. When are we speaking to Karpov's ex in Copenhagen?"

"I'm going there myself," said Tell. "Tomorrow."

"Just for the day?"

"I'll catch an early train back the day after."

Tell thought Höije had raised his eyebrow.

"I can pay for the bloody room myself."

He regretted his words as soon as they had come out, and he regretted ever thinking that an evening in Copenhagen would put Seja in a better mood. It wasn't her style to reproach him, but he thought she'd been looking down lately. He might be in the habit of neglecting his women, but he wasn't completely incapable of reading signals. He was just useless at doing anything about it.

It wasn't long since he had promised himself not to let it happen again. Not to let Seja slip through his fingers. He might be up to his eyes in work, but a trip that combined business and pleasure had seemed like a good compromise. Now the whole thing would have to be pointlessly chewed over at length.

"There's absolutely no need to sound so . . ." Höije began as he put on his glasses and took them off again, just as Beckman tended to when she was about to analyse what she presumed were Tell's innermost thoughts.

"Oh, so you're taking the opportunity to have a few Carlsbergs on Strøget?" Bärneflod had managed to make the whole thing even worse.

Tell groaned. "I've got a couple of meetings arranged in Copenhagen in the afternoon. I was intending to catch the 06.28 back to Gothenburg. But of course I will rebook that immediately."

"For fuck's sake, Tell. Nobody is questioning your arrangements." Höije's voice was still calm, but now he had colour in his cheeks. "Perhaps we should discuss this. We're new to each other, we don't seem to have found a way of working together yet."

Tell wished the last five minutes of his life had never happened, mainly because he didn't have the energy for the conversation his boss had suggested. Nor did he have the time. And it was so bloody unnecessary.

"This is neither the time nor the place for that discussion," he said.

Gonzales and Karlberg looked uncomfortable and gazed out of the window; only Bärneflod appeared completely unmoved.

"No, perhaps you're right. But I'd still like to say that I'm fully aware of how highly you all valued Ann-Christine Östergren. It won't be easy for me to fill those shoes."

Höije fell silent for a moment, allowing his words to sink in.

Then he continued, "I am in no doubt with regard to your competence, and I have the utmost respect for you all."

"Thanks," said Bärneflod.

Tell wished he was miles away from this drivel.

"For me, respect is all about communication," Höije went on, earnestly. "Talking and listening. I expect the same from you in return."

Höije met each pair of eyes in the room — Karlberg and Gonzales nodded obediently — and allowed his gaze to linger on Tell for a long time.

"And, with that, I wish you good hunting. Tell, enjoy your trip to Copenhagen."

Tell left the car at work and walked home. Given the fine weather, Vasagatan was unusually quiet. It was hard to believe this was the same place that had been filled with demonstrators just a few days ago, but a pamphlet stuck to the sole of his shoe, and the lamp posts were still plastered with posters.

From his living-room window, Tell had been able to hear the shouts of protestors.

He had never regarded himself as a political animal; he was always more certain of what he was against than what he stood for. The idea of joining a march, and so identifying himself with the idea of the worker, didn't strike a chord with him. For Seja it was important to take a stand, for or against. And she had demonstrated every single year, ever since she was a toddler on her mother's shoulders.

Nor did Tell feel an affinity with his neighbours, owners of fine apartments and summer cottages in the archipelago. He had lived in his little two-room apartment for as long as he could remember, one of the few rental properties still available in that part of town. And if he hadn't been born in the area, he would hardly have been living there today.

He suddenly felt hungry and went over to the kiosk; he ate meatballs with mashed potato and lingonberry sauce as he walked home. The exposed parts of the street were chilly; all that remained of the light and warmth of the day were patches where the sunbeams melted into shades of red, soon to disappear.

The apartment was empty when he got home.

His first thought was that it had all been a dream. It was an irrational thought, but one he had often. Seja and that blissful, tense closeness, a feeling connected to the love-hate feelings he had about living on his own. The feelings of both freedom and loathing. The stuffiness, the smell of over-filled rubbish bags left in the hallway. Late nights eating pizza straight out of the box, the flickering blue tones of the television the only source of light. No one to share with. And no one to answer to.

These days there were still signs of Seja even when she wasn't there, small outposts of her that dispelled his doubts. Her hair slide on the kitchen worktop. An item of clothing left on the bedroom armchair. Her

151

toothbrush in the bathroom. She was part of the fabric of his life.

Once he had reassured himself of this fact, he welcomed the chance to be alone. He flicked through the newspaper without finding anything to engage his limited attention span. He picked up a carton of yoghurt and carried it into the living room.

He stood there at a loss.

If Seja had been home, she would probably have been sitting at the desk in the corner, bent over her laptop. If she was tired, she would be stretched out on the sofa under a blanket, perhaps lulled to sleep by a sitcom.

Reluctantly, he thought back to his conversation with Höije. It had gone badly wrong. He had felt backed into a corner, incapable of a decent response. He could have highlighted his dedication to the job by calmly mentioning the number of cases he had solved over the years, or the countless hours of overtime he had put in. The unclaimed holidays, so numerous that he would soon be able to take early retirement. He could have gone further and talked about his private life; the way it had been so completely absorbed by work that these days he felt insecure in any situation where he wasn't first and foremost a police officer. Sometimes this was a mere inconvenience, sometimes it was utterly debilitating.

The last time it had happened was when he met Seja. He thought about the sudden awkwardness her presence brought out in him. The way he felt naked when his professional identity was of no interest, and the sudden dizzying terror about what else he had to offer in life.

Christian hadn't responded to Höije's ridiculous speech on respect, simply because any possible response would have fanned the flames. He would have come across as being defensive.

The phone rang. He considered letting it ring until the answerphone kicked in, but he thought it was probably Seja, and picked up. The sound of her voice made him realise that his exchange with Höije had spoiled the pleasure he would take in bringing up the trip to Copenhagen. That annoyed him all over again.

Tell had been accustomed to Ann-Christine Östergren's unquestioning trust in her colleagues; her reassuring blend of empathy and directness. He realised that he missed her, more than he had thought he would. He didn't know to what extent Höije had intended to disarm him, to back him into a corner and step over him. He didn't know whether it was a demonstration of power or not.

Until he knew, he would remain alert. He would be more careful about how he presented his work to his boss.

When he did mention Copenhagen, Seja sounded pleased.

"What fun! I haven't been to Copenhagen for . . . Ooh, it must be ten years! But how come . . . I thought you said the other day you had a lot on at the moment?"

"It does involve a certain amount of work."

"That's fine! I'm happy to spend an evening in Copenhagen with or without you. But preferably with you, of course."

"Thank you very much."

Neither of them spoke. Tell went over to the window and looked down at the street.

"Christian? Is something wrong?"

He shook his head, even though she couldn't see him. Perhaps because she couldn't see him. He thought about an episode of *Seinfeld* where George, the guy who gets everything wrong, decides to do exactly the opposite of what his instincts tell him.

"It's nothing," he said. "Just work . . . work stuff."

Seja remained silent at the other end of the line, just as he did when he was waiting for the silence to oppress the other person, waiting for them to talk out of sheer frustration.

He told Seja what had happened with Höije. Her laugh surprised him; it seeped out of the receiver like a muted rumble.

"You don't think you might be overreacting slightly?" she said eventually.

"You don't think you might be finding this a bit too funny?" he said sourly, but somewhere inside he knew she was right. He was feeling the strain, as he always did at the beginning of a murder inquiry.

Before Seja had burst into his neat bachelor life, many things had been a lot simpler: the job took up his time, and nobody but himself would suffer if anything happened. These days it wasn't just that he often found himself at work mentally, when he was sitting at home;

154

he was also distracted by thoughts of Seja when he was at work. He kept thinking about what all the time she spent alone might be doing to her, what all the broken promises and cancelled plans were doing to their relationship. It was a paradox in itself: his constant feelings of guilt made him even more fiery and unreasonable.

But just hearing her voice . . . the walls of resistance he had built up came crashing down: she wasn't angry, disappointed, upset, about to leave him.

It's as though you walk around with some kind of imagined guilt; you don't really know what it consists of or where it comes from, you just know you have to fix it, Beckman had once said. Perhaps she was right. She had added that she found it incredibly tiresome.

"Where are we staying?"

Christian took the phone into the kitchen; he had stuck the address of the hotel on his fridge door.

"A small hotel in Christianshavn."

"How appropriate."

"The tourist office recommended it."

"In that case it must be close to Christiania too. Years ago I always used to go to a place near Pusher Street to buy the most wonderful hand-woven cloths for next to nothing. I wonder if it's still there."

"I really, really hope you're joking."

Seja laughed. "Of course I am. It's not as though you'd let anyone forget you're a police officer. Although I have to admit that you're unusually good company for a policeman."

He read out the train times and heard the start-up tones of her computer.

"Sweetheart, I really have to go now — things to do. Shall we meet at the station first thing tomorrow?"

"OK," he said.

A line from a song by Lars Winnerbäck had stuck in his mind for some reason, and Christian thought about it now: *I would get trapped in my loneliness again, if you left me now.*

He ended the call and, to his surprise, realised that he was disappointed that she wasn't coming over to stay the night.

CHAPTER
TWENTY-TWO

Copenhagen

People's reactions to the loss of a family member never ceased to amaze Tell. All the indications were that Alexandr Karpov had already been informed of the violent circumstances surrounding his ex-wife's death, and yet it seemed as if it were only now, while talking to Tell, that he was able to absorb what had happened.

He rubbed his forehead, then sat down to pull himself together. When he took off his glasses, exposing the dark, lined skin around his eyes, he suddenly looked ten years older.

"I just can't . . . I haven't been able to believe it. This couldn't have happened to Ann-Marie. It's impossible . . ."

"Sadly that isn't the case."

Tell had given the man a little time to compose himself. The Karpovs had been divorced for a long time, but that didn't mean the thought of never seeing her again was painless.

"Who would want to murder her? It's absurd."

"As part of the ongoing investigation, I do need to ask you some questions, including the matter you've

157

just raised. Can you think of anyone who would want Ann-Marie dead?"

Alexandr Karpov stroked his sparse beard. The distant look in his eyes suggested that he was still reluctant to accept the facts.

Tell tried a different approach. "What was she like? Can you describe her?"

Karpov gave a violent start, as if he had been woken by a loud noise. "I'm sorry. But it's all still so difficult to understand."

"I realise that."

"What was she like? Well . . . she was a passionate person, I would say."

"About what?"

"About . . . a great many things. She was very dynamic. She was passionate about beauty, art . . . Have you visited Glyptoteket before, Inspector?"

"No, I've never been here."

"And you're not particularly well informed on the subject of ancient art?"

"No."

Karpov had got to his feet; although his legs were clearly still shaky, he seemed to gain strength from his latest idea as he guided Tell out of his office, ignoring the policeman's feeble protests.

"You asked me who Ann-Marie was. If you're going to understand her, then I have to give you an idea of what she did."

So Tell allowed himself to be steered around several of the museum's exhibition halls, starting in the basement with the Ancient Art of the Middle East.

Closely woven mesh covered every source of light, leaving the underground rooms in darkness punctuated by small pinpricks of light.

Karpov talked about his fascination with finding out how people created societies at different times and in different places.

"Many of these cultures were enlightened and influential. This area, for example, has been referred to as the cradle of civilisation," he said, running his hand over a map on the wall. "Mesopotamia — 'the land between the two rivers'. This is where the first urban societies were formed. The wheel was invented, the measurement of time, written language or cuneiform script. Man began to document his reflections on his relationship with the world and with higher powers."

The museum was still open to the public, and it wasn't long before Christian spotted Seja, who had taken the opportunity to look around. He felt obliged to introduce her.

Karpov smiled. "How nice — you're combining business with pleasure. Have you seen anything exciting? Perhaps you'd like to join us on our tour, Seja?"

"That would be very interesting."

Tell carefully avoided Seja's teasing glance. He had briefly explained the reason behind their visit when she asked during the journey down. There was no point in letting her get too involved in his work. The last time their professional roles had collided, she had written several articles linked to his investigation. It wasn't an episode he looked back on with any fondness.

★ ★ ★

As Karpov sank down into his armchair after their tour, it struck Tell that the man was nowhere near as conservatively dressed as an academic in a position of authority at a major museum would presumably have to be. But his appearance did tally with the cliché of the absent-minded professor: the scraggly, ill-kempt beard, spectacles perched so close to the end of his nose that they looked as if they might tumble to the floor at any moment. The white hair, half-heartedly combed over his bald pate. The dark-blue corduroy trousers which bore witness to the fact that Karpov had once been much more robustly built. Now they were flapping around his legs, drawn tight around his waist with a belt, the end of which dangled down over his flies. He must have been at least ten years older than his ex-wife.

When Karpov rested his forehead on his hand, Tell thought he was going to burst into tears. But he didn't make a sound. Tell waited. The surprising enthusiasm Karpov had summoned up during the tour had no doubt been a way of distracting himself, a way of pushing aside the powerful emotions that were overwhelming him once more.

"I've got so much on at the moment . . ." Karpov murmured. "But I'd still like to show you some of the work Ann-Marie was involved in over the past few years. She'd begun to develop an interest in —"

"Alexandr."

Tell let his hand fall slowly to his thigh. "I'm sure I will need your help with matters relating to Ann-Marie's work, but right now I need to ask my questions in the order that I choose. I'd be grateful if you could just try to answer as honestly and fully as possible."

"Of course."

"You and Ann-Marie had been divorced for seven years, is that right? You seem upset about her death."

"*Too* upset, you mean? I don't think I heard anything resembling a question there."

"My question is: what kind of contact did you and Ann-Marie have over the past seven years."

"We had ended our marriage in every legal and practical respect. I moved out of the apartment in 2001 and came to Copenhagen. This was a more convenient arrangement anyway, since the majority of my work is based here. We haven't seen each other very often since then. Occasionally we would have dinner when Ann-Marie was visiting the archaeology department here, or when I happened to be in Gothenburg. We spoke on the telephone from time to time. We were good friends. We got on well."

"Did you draw the short straw?"

"I'm sorry?"

"Was she the one who wanted a divorce?"

"Is that important?"

"I don't know. But as I said, I would appreciate it if you could simply answer my questions. Please assume that everything I ask is important."

Karpov sighed. "Well, I suppose she was the one who brought it up. It's such a long time ago, I hardly remember how it began."

"I'm sure you do."

"I didn't want our marriage to end, no. But there was never any conflict — I must emphasise that. I gave her the apartment and the things that were important to her. I wished her no harm."

It was as if Karpov had only just realised that he could be under suspicion. Bewilderment was writ large on his face.

With striking agility he leapt out of the deep armchair and went over to a grey display cabinet with frosted glass doors. Tell heard clinking and thought perhaps the man was in need of a strong drink, but Karpov returned with two glasses of sparkling water.

"I'm sorry if I sounded a little abrupt just now," he said, offering Tell one of the glasses. He took a couple of sips and briefly closed his eyes. "To be honest, I've been surprised at my reaction over the past few days, Inspector. Naturally I'm shocked that she's dead, who wouldn't be? She was an innocuous person — no, that's the wrong word — but she was a good person. Well-liked, hard-working. I'm sure you're right; my feelings for Ann-Marie haven't faded entirely over the years. I haven't remarried. It took me a couple of years to grasp the fact that we were never going to be together again, that this business with the divorce wasn't just some whim on Ann-Marie's part. And by that time I had got used to being alone, I suppose. I'd got used to a different life, where work comes first. And we didn't have any children."

Tell nodded; he could empathise. "And you knew she'd met someone new?" he asked gently. "The man who was murdered in her flat."

162

Karpov was silent.

"Did you hear the question?"

"Yes . . ." he was still reluctant to answer. "I sensed it at quite an early stage."

"What, that she'd met Henrik Samuelsson? How did you sense that?"

"Henrik Samuelsson, so that was his name."

Tell tried to suppress his impatience. "You met him?"

"He came to an event; it was the unveiling of an Egyptian sculpture donated to us by a French collector called . . . Well, that doesn't really matter — anyway, it wasn't open to members of the public. Ann-Marie was here at my personal invitation, and she brought this young man as her guest. She mentioned that he was on the foundation course — he was one of her students."

"She didn't give any further explanation of why he'd come?"

"She said it was some kind of study visit."

Tell noticed Karpov's cynical smile.

"But you didn't believe that?"

"For God's sake, they were staying . . ."

His voice died away. A strand of white hair flopped down over his forehead and his chin sank towards his chest. Tell couldn't help but feel sorry for him.

"They were staying . . .?"

"I don't know."

"They were staying together? At a hotel? You checked whether they were staying at the same hotel, or even in the same room?"

Karpov let out a shrill laugh, temporarily robbed of the dignity he had earlier possessed. Now he was just another jealous ex-husband who had spied on his former wife. He pulled himself together. "I must admit I did check on where they were staying, and they'd booked a double room. But there was really no need. It was obvious they were together."

"Henrik lived with his partner, Rebecca. Their house was broken into three days ago. We believe the burglars were searching for something specific, and that this could be related to the murder in a way we don't yet understand. What's your view on that?"

"I know nothing about it."

Beneath the comb-over, Alexandr Karpov's scalp was shining in the glare of the ceiling spotlight.

"Did you let Ann-Marie and Henrik know what you thought about their affair?"

Tell had overstepped the mark. A chill passed through the room as Karpov peered over the top of his glasses, like a disapproving headmaster.

"You are talking to me about my ex-wife in order to find out more about what kind of person she was. You said that was the purpose of this conversation. So why do I suddenly feel as though I am being interrogated? Because if you are intending to interrogate me, I insist on being informed of this in advance. And if that is the case, I wish to contact my solicitor."

"If I regard you as a suspect, I'll certainly let you know." Tell loosened his tie as discreetly as he could. "I apologise if you feel under attack. However, I would still like to know where you were on the night of the second of May. This is a purely routine question."

"At home, in my apartment. In bed. Asleep."

"Is there anyone who could confirm that?"

"Of course not."

Karpov's rapid change of demeanour had made Tell lose his train of thought. "You can't think of anything else in your ex-wife's behaviour that struck you as strange?"

"No. As I said, we had very little contact. The last time I saw her was at the event I just mentioned. That was last winter, about six months ago. And before that . . . we had dinner in Gothenburg after I'd given a lecture, so a year ago. Hos Pelle, that was the name of the restaurant. Good, traditional food."

Karpov reached across the desk and grabbed a pack of tissues from the windowsill. He wiped his nose carefully, as if he needed something to do with his hands.

It was time to call a halt. Tell tucked his pen into his top pocket, a signal which made Karpov stand up quickly, holding out his hand. "I'm here if you think of anything else."

"Thank you."

Tell ran down the stairs, and was soon out in the street. The siren of a passing ambulance mirrored his growing sense of urgency.

The demonstration was slowly disbanding as Seja and Tell arrived. The drum still echoed rhythmically, but the cluttered trucks that had made up the procession were rumbling slowly down towards Nyhavn and protestors were drifting away. A banner had been left behind, propped up against the statue of Kristian V in Kongens Nytorv: *Don't panic — it's organic.*

"I'm perfectly happy doing touristy things. But I feel no compulsion whatsoever to go to Christiana," Tell said firmly, keeping one eye out for the Italian restaurant he had visited on his last trip.

Seja burst out laughing. "Oh, for goodness' sake! You sound like a retired bureaucrat . . . a Social Democrat."

"Because I want to sit and have a beer in the peace and quiet of Strøget instead of racing off to rub shoulders with drug addicts and losers? I get enough of that at work. I do vote Social Democrat, if you really want to know. And I'm not ashamed of that."

Tell's smile was strained; he certainly wasn't feeling cheerful. Something about Seja's naive, woolly liberalism bothered him a great deal. And now they were standing in Rådhuspladsen with an entire afternoon and evening at their disposal. Well on the way to wasting it all in petty bickering.

"I don't know why you've got such a problem!" Seja crossly began to follow the stream of people heading for Strøget, even though she had just made it clear she had no intention of allowing herself to be carried into the commercial heart of the city along with thousands of other tourists. "Why have you got such a thing about Christiania — we don't have to go there! I was just curious about what had happened there after all that talk of evictions. When I was seventeen or eighteen, my friends and I often went there. We used to sit in Månefiskeren, drinking Hof and eating chocolate pastries."

"That thought doesn't exactly fill me with pleasure."

"You're so uptight, Christian!"

Seja stopped to look at a jewellery stall, so abruptly that he almost walked into her.

"How much is this?"

She picked up a ring with a large, transparent stone and held it up to the light, but put it down when she heard the price.

"Listen. I know your job makes you look at things in a certain way, and I respect that. But sometimes you're not very good at seeing things from different perspectives. There is more than one truth."

"Is there?"

"My friends and I didn't go to Christiana to smoke weed. We went to gigs. There was a terrific music scene back then. The father of one of my friends lived there."

"If you run, you might catch up with the demo," Tell snapped, suddenly tired of pointless arguments.

Irritation gave way to resignation. Seja noticed his change of mood, took his wrist and drew him close.

"Hey. Let's not quarrel. We've got the whole day ahead of us for once. And night."

He squeezed her hand in return. "You're right. Let's drop it."

"Can't we go up here? There are lots of lovely little shops and cafés."

She chose a winding street at random, and she was right: the atmosphere was very different just a few metres away from the main street. Brightly coloured paint was flaking off the roughly plastered walls. In places it looked as if the buildings were leaning over the

167

narrow pavements. The shops offered everything from macrobiotic food to office supplies and vinyl records, all competing for the limited space.

When Seja disappeared down a flight of steps to look at skin creams in a health shop, Tell sat down on a bench outside a tobacconist's and inhaled the aroma of a cigar being smoked by a bearded man. He went inside and bought himself one too — treating himself to a cigar while on a trip wasn't the same thing as starting smoking again — and tucked the slender packet into his jacket pocket.

He longed for a cold beer.

They continued along narrow streets towards Gråbrsødretorv, where Tell was intent on sitting down with his cigar. They found a spot near the square in the cool shade of a tree and bought beer.

Seja stretched out her legs and took a deep draught of her Hof.

"This the kind of place I was talking about. Something outside the mainstream; you can walk past an H&M just as easily in Gothenburg. And as for Christiana, I think it's simply glorious out there in the summer. There's such a contrast to the frantic tempo of city life, sitting on the grass by the river and . . ."

Just leave it, for God's sake. Tell didn't want to let their differences of opinion spoil the moment as he took big gulps of the cold beer, snipped the end of his cigar and lit it. It tasted wonderful; he inhaled deeply, even though he should have known better. He coughed and offered it to Seja.

168

"Sadly it's not hallucinogenic." He couldn't stop himself. She kicked him hard on the shin under the table.

"You're being absurd. You know perfectly well that I'm not interested in smoking hash — that's not what this is about. But to be perfectly honest, a joint would do you good. You're just so uptight and narrow-minded."

He couldn't help being bothered by that comment; he wasn't sure to what extent she was joking.

"Narrow-minded?" he said in the same casual tone of voice.

"Don't you think you should at least have tried things before you decide you're dead set against them? Then you'd know what you were talking about."

"I think that's the stupidest thing I've ever heard you say."

"Oh yes?"

"So, by the same token, you could say I ought to take heroin just to be sure it's not a good idea, or chuck myself off a roof, or shoot someone in the stomach, to earn the right to think it's wrong?"

"Have you ever shot someone? As part of your job, I mean."

"That's not what we were talking about."

He knocked back the rest of his Pilsner and waved to the waitress. Seja gazed at him, deep in thought.

At times like this she almost found his indignation amusing. "So when we have kids you'll be telling them that one single puff will send them psychotic and kill them, just like we were told in school? And you think that'll keep them off it?"

"Speak for yourself. I'm much older than you. We didn't learn anything about hash in school. And besides . . ."

He lost the thread as a chill ran through him. Kids? He suddenly felt raw, worn down by this never-ending discussion about drugs. And the fact that the word kids came so naturally to Seja's lips frightened the shit out of him.

Not *if*. *When* we have kids. As if he had no say on the subject. They'd never even talked about having kids. He had no desire whatsoever to have kids, although he was bright enough to realise that if he kept hooking up with childless women, the subject was bound to come up.

He just hadn't thought it would come up so early. They'd only been together for a year or so. They didn't even live together.

"You know what Åke and Kristina asked me the other day?" said Seja, changing the subject; Christian thought she sounded irritatingly blasé. "When we went round for dinner — after you left. They offered me — well, us really — the chance to buy their house. At a reduced price, on the understanding that Åke could keep some of his stuff in the cellar. What do you think about that? They've decided it's time for you and me to put our relationship on a more serious footing, start living together." She imitated Kristina's voice. "And when we do, their house is *much more modern and practical, of course.*" She waved away a man selling roses.

170

Christian shook his head, feeling as if his brain had come away from his skull. When the waitress arrived with his beer, he dug out a couple of notes and placed them on the table.

"Shall we go?"

Already on the move.

"But we've just sat down. I thought we were going to eat?"

She got up and ran after him, grabbing his sleeve.

"What the fuck's the matter with you? You're the one who's been going on all day about just sitting down and chilling. If something's bothering you, then let's have it out. I've got no desire to sit around second guessing you, for fuck's sake."

Seja had raised her voice rather more than he would have liked on the crowded street. A passing group of men in suits grinned at them.

"Could you tone it down a bit?"

"Do you know what this is? It's a fucking power game, that's what this is!"

"What are you talking about? Could you calm down, please?"

"What you did, what you're doing right now! We're chatting, I think everything's fine. Suddenly I happen to say the wrong thing. I tread on one of your fucking sore toes, and bang! You're sulky, you're angry. The switch flicks and you clam up! You're punishing me for something I don't even know I've done."

"I am not sulking! Look! Here we are, walking along together, everything's absolutely fine! I just didn't want to sit there any more, we could . . . we could . . ."

He spread his arms wide.

She stopped. "Yes, what shall we do? What do *you* want to do?"

His brain stopped working. "We could . . . Shall we go to Tivoli?"

Seja set off, but he didn't move. He gazed after her as she stomped off, heading back down towards Strøget against the flow of the crowds. Part of him wanted to see her disappear into the crowd. He wanted these pointless discussions to go away, along with the suffocating feeling that was overwhelming him.

It was a familiar sensation, he realised now. When he had found Seja's things in his chest of drawers, he had felt happy because she still wanted him, in spite of his unreasonable behaviour and bad habits and the fact that he was often vile first thing in the morning. But another feeling had been lurking just below the surface: the feeling that he needed an escape route. He had felt an uncomfortable pang last Christmas when she had started talking about their summer holiday.

Several other situations came to mind now. Just a couple of weeks ago he had arrived home to find her friend Hanna in his kitchen, with her wild gestures, wine-stained teeth and long purple nails. Hanna was only supposed to be calling round to pick Seja up, but instead she had stayed there with her wine box and her chatter and her cigarette stubs. He had felt trapped and had withdrawn to the living room. *If there's no escape route, I'll kick my way out.*

If you had kids, you nailed every escape route shut.

He set off towards Rådhuspladsen and the hotel; it was far too early to go back, but he had no idea what else to do. He couldn't see Seja anywhere, nor was it likely that she would return to the spot where they had parted company. Because she was too proud. She was just as proud as he was.

But then he was overcome by a wave of tenderness when he thought of her patience, the way she was always battling with her pride. Of the strength of character it took to be with someone who always made things difficult, always having to compromise her own needs and desires. And yet she still managed to stick to her guns. Seja never went for the easy option. That was why she lived in her little cottage in the forest, with her horse and her cat.

He laughed out loud. A woman in front of him turned around and smiled.

His sudden change of heart made Seja reappear. She was sitting on the far side of a church he didn't know the name of, at a pavement café. She had switched on the palmtop she always carried and was absorbed in the screen. She had a steaming cup of something in front of her, a cappuccino perhaps, and a frothy little moustache on her upper lip.

He was close enough to see the moustache. And the Danish pastry; she took a bite, then crumbled a piece under the table for the pigeons.

That's what she looks like when I'm not with her, that's Seja when she doesn't know I'm looking at her. He hadn't the faintest idea why this felt significant.

He sat down at the edge of the steps leading up to the church door. He didn't want the moment to end.

She stretched her back without taking her eyes off the screen. Lifted the hair from the nape of her neck, as she usually did in the heat. She had small, dark patches of sweat under her arms; she screwed up her eyes as she looked into the last glimmers of the evening sun, then put on her sunglasses. When she turned her face towards him he couldn't work out whether she was looking at him or not. Not until her expression lightened and she sang, just loudly enough for him to pick up Stefan Sundström's classic: *It was almost like an advert, la la la la . . . Like some handsome stranger, but the same . . .*

He smiled back and felt overcome by warmth. He got up and walked slowly to her table.

When he leant over her, the pigeons took off with a cacophony of flapping wings.

"Shall we go back to the hotel?" he whispered against her mouth.

When she shook her head, his rough cheek gently scratched her face. "The night is young. In fact, it's only just begun."

CHAPTER
TWENTY-THREE

Gothenburg

It wasn't going to be a pleasurable visit. Even Beckman had moments when she was tempted to apologise for the job she had to do. When Rebecca opened the red door, her expression couldn't have made her thoughts any clearer.

"Haven't you people done enough?"

"Well, you could say that."

"I really don't have time for this."

"No?"

"I'm working from home today, I've got loads to do."

Beckman cleared her throat. The fact that Rebecca Nykvist had been taken into custody and subsequently released gave her the upper hand, and she was making the most of this. Or perhaps she really was busy. Beckman was surprised that she hadn't signed herself off work, but perhaps she needed to work to keep her anguish at bay.

It was as if Rebecca had read her mind: "It feels better if I keep going. I'll go crazy if I'm just pottering around the house."

It was a start. Self-awareness? Beckman asked if Rebecca would prefer her to come back some other time. There was no reason to engage in an unnecessary trial of strength. In any case, she wasn't really sure what she was looking for.

"I don't really need you," she said. "If you want to carry on working, I can look around on my own."

Rebecca peered distrustfully at Beckman and the officer standing behind her on the steps.

"Isn't spying on me 24/7 enough for you people? You mean you want to poke around the house as well? I thought you'd already searched the place?"

"I'll be looking around on my own. My colleague will wait outside. Or in the hallway." Beckman was getting tired of standing on the steps. "Unfortunately, looking around is part of the process in a murder investigation. And I'm not searching for anything in particular. I just want to take a look around."

Rebecca stepped aside. "I'll be in my study. But if you take anything away — evidence or whatever you call it — I want to be informed."

"Of course."

Beckman removed her shoes. The hallway was still in disarray. Perhaps Rebecca was depressed. Beckman knew that she saw a psychologist on a regular basis, which was reassuring. However, as Rebecca pointedly disappeared into the room beyond the kitchen, Beckman couldn't help remembering that she had abused her ex-boyfriend and threatened to kill him. Several times.

She went upstairs and stood on the landing, contemplating her non-existent plan. She heard the floor creak downstairs, then silence. No doubt Rebecca was listening to her every move.

She was searching for Henrik's secrets, because Henrik had definitely had secrets. This was true of most people who were murdered without an obvious reason.

There were two alternatives: firstly, that Rebecca knew about these secrets and was lying. Beckman was in no doubt that she was a skilful liar, that wasn't the issue. And yet she was leaning towards the other option: that Rebecca's confusion under interrogation had been genuine; that she knew nothing about her partner's secret life. Or was she afraid? Perhaps. She had a good poker face.

Beckman thought for a while. Where would Henrik hide things he didn't want Rebecca to find? Was the study his private space? No. Henrik would choose a much better hiding place than that.

She went into the bedroom. There was a cabinet on either side of the double bed; the one on the right had obviously been Henrik's. *The Land of Ur* could well have been on his reading list, even if it looked old. As she flicked through it, a bookmark fell out. She put it back between the pages. She looked at the next book: Åke Jönsson's *Football — the Development of the Greatest Sport in the World*. So Henrik had been a football fan.

Camorra — the Mafia in Naples. Beckman had heard of that. Tomas Lappalainen. She read the back cover before opening the first page and scanning a couple of paragraphs.

A clattering sound from downstairs made her put the book back; there was nothing else in the dark recesses of the cupboard apart from a half-empty packet of painkillers. It sounded as if Rebecca were rummaging through the kitchen cupboards. Beckman went through the storage space under the bed and the little room leading off the bedroom, her eyes stinging in the dust as she rooted among things that had been packed away long ago. Under the mattress of the spare bed she found a DVD in a blank case. Deciding that someone could have hidden it there deliberately, she took it with her.

The musty smell of the wardrobes made her feel ill. Her back creaked as she stood up. Perhaps this was a waste of time. She had to assume the burglars had found whatever they were looking for; they had certainly been thorough. Signs of their activities were everywhere, but she could also see traces of the police search. She wondered how long Rebecca would wait before sorting out Henrik's possessions, his clothes, his books. The smells, the immediate reminders. People handled that kind of thing differently. Beckman had always imagined it would be easier if memories didn't confront you everywhere you looked. But then what did she know?

There was no light in the loft, just two small windows at each end casting a small amount of daylight across the wooden floor. Beckman considered going out to the car to fetch her flashlight, or asking Rebecca if she could borrow a torch, but decided against it.

178

She was on her way down the stairs when a sudden thought sent her back to the bedroom. She picked up *The Land of Ur* and turned it upside down. The bookmark — or had the picture in fact been hidden between the pages? — was a photograph of a necklace and a clay statuette, perhaps in the form of a person. It was difficult to tell how big it might be in real life. The photograph was amateur and, judging by the things just visible in the background, it had probably been taken in that very room.

There was nothing written on the back. Tell had called to tell her about his conversation with Karpov, and the man's ill-timed lecture on ancient artefacts. Something was niggling at the back of her mind.

When Beckman walked into the kitchen, Rebecca was on the phone. She waited by the sink, close to the door of the study, which was ajar.

". . . it has to go. The new system has already been installed . . . Yes, I can hold. Thank you."

Beckman hadn't heard Rebecca's formal voice before; presumably that was how she addressed her colleagues. Her professional voice. Her private voice was more defensive. Tense, reserved and ready to attack.

This was how Beckman usually walked into people's lives: straight into their grief, their vulnerability, their fear. No introductions, no getting-to-know-you. In that way it was a peculiar job. In many ways it was a peculiar job.

It sounded as if Rebecca was talking to a workman.

"I just want it dismantled. No, you'll need metal-cutting equipment. That's right, in the cellar. There's a door at the back and it's three steps below ground level."

Beckman moved so that Rebecca could see her; Rebecca mimed that she would be another minute, then spun the chair around so that she had her back to Beckman.

"When was the boiler made? I have no idea. Does it matter?" She rubbed her eyes. "I'll check and call you back." She slammed the phone down. As she spun around to face Beckman she looked tired, with dark shadows forming hollows under her eyes.

"The boiler's bust. I bet it wasn't half as much trouble having it installed as getting rid of it appears to be."

Beckman made appropriately sympathetic noises. She knew nothing about boilers, but was surprised by Rebecca's friendly tone of voice. This woman was certainly unstable. Was she even aware of the confusion she inspired in other people?

"I'm taking these with me," Beckman said, showing her the DVD and the photograph. "Have you any idea what the photograph is of?"

A shadow passed over Rebecca's face. "No," she said. "But I suppose it might have something to do with Henrik's course; why are you taking it?"

"I don't actually know," Beckman said honestly. "But you'll get it back."

CHAPTER
TWENTY-FOUR

Gothenburg

Torsen needed to be on his guard. He had been in pain the night before, but had taken very little medication. He had made sure he stayed awake. He needed to think, to make decisions. Stay in Gothenburg and see what happened. Await new orders from Knud. Or say sod the lot of it. Sell the figure he'd kept hidden from the lad. He deserved the money. Go back to Copenhagen and forget the whole bloody thing.

The fact that they hadn't found ancient gold from the Middle East, as they'd been promised, was something the boy found as difficult to understand as Torsen. The lad thought they'd been conned, and he didn't like it. His face rarely showed emotion, but suspicion and discontent had filled his narrowed eyes.

Torsen should have taken control of the situation yesterday, but it was all he could do to stay on his feet. And now he had no money. He only had enough smack for a small fix. But he needed more than that.

When day broke, he finally decided to leave the sinking ship. The lad's purple, veiny eyelids twitched as Torsen passed the alcove in the hallway, where their

181

rucksacks and a couple of blankets formed a temporary camp.

He went out the back way, moving as quickly as he could in the direction of the tram depot because the car belonged to the lad, and he watched over the keys like a hawk. As Torsen headed for the city centre, he was already beginning to have doubts. For the second time he broke his resolve not to contact Knud while he was in Gothenburg.

After the break-in, he had left a message out of sheer frustration. It was cryptic, but Knud would understand: only one object that matched the pictures he had been shown. Now he rang again to issue a warning. The clay figure they had found would barely cover his costs. He had taken risks. For twenty-four hours, no more and no less, he would lie low and wait for new orders.

The number you have called is not available at present.

The cops were hanging around down by the stop at Gamlestadstorget. Two of them, leaning on their patrol cars.

His stomach turned. If they searched him, he would go down both for the break-in and for possession. He was sweating. Without arousing too much suspicion he had to dig a couple of tablets out of the nylon pouch he wore around one calf. His mouth was powder-dry, saliva a distant memory. The tablets scratched his throat as he swallowed them. The revolting taste would last for hours.

He jumped off at the central station and headed straight for Nordstan. There, he searched out a dealer he knew only by sight; it was a crazy idea and he had to pay over the odds, but Torsen had neither the time nor the energy to look further. Having spent the last of his money, he stuffed the goods in his pouch and said he'd be back in a couple of hours with more cash.

The figure was burning a hole in his pocket. Brunnsparken was swimming with cops too; he wanted to get rid of it as quickly as he could.

Knud had told him that many antique dealers didn't give a fuck who was buying or selling. Private individuals, buyers within the trade and even museums would irresponsibly purchase artefacts which had been smuggled or stolen from graves. Those in the business would usually pay up for exclusive items, no questions asked. If the figure was as valuable as Knud had said, Torsen hoped he would be able to shift it pretty quickly. Cash in hand, no names, no receipts. When he walked into one of the three shops he had found via Directory Enquiries, he tried to hide his shaking hands.

"How may I help you?"

The man behind the desk was elderly, slim, dressed from head to foot in beige, and wizened. Along his hairline the wrinkled skin of his forehead gave way to a crusty landscape of yellowish-brown flakes. Torsen focused his gaze on something else; he would be out of here in twenty minutes max and would find somewhere safe. He rummaged inside his jacket and imagined that he was gaining strength from the object pressing against his chest.

Before he went in, he had decided to say as little as possible. He placed the figure, which looked like a woman, carefully on the desk and asked in only slightly accented Swedish: "How much will you give me for this?"

Beneath the eczema the antique dealer's skin had turned pale. At first it seemed as if he didn't dare touch it, but then he picked up the figure and looked at the base, scraped it gently with his nail and shook his head, murmuring something Torsen didn't catch. The man looked shyly up at Torsen, as if he were unsure what to do next. Torsen broke out in a sweat. It smelt bitter from the tablets he had taken for the pain in his back. A drop fell from his forehead onto his dry, cracked hand.

A couple who had been conducting a muted discussion in the corner fell silent and edged towards the door. Torsen realised he had jumped the gun. His decision to keep the lad in the dark would no doubt bring a whole heap of trouble on his head.

He wasn't well enough for trouble. As he tucked the clay figure back in his pocket, the antique dealer started, then groped under his desk — did he have an alarm down there?

Torsen backed away, spun around and was back on the street once more. He had the feeling he was being followed, and kept looking over his shoulder. His fix was burning against his calf. He needed to get away from these busy streets.

With one more glance over his shoulder, he rounded the corner. His heart was pounding. The whole thing had been a mistake. He couldn't think clearly. He could see a church, greenery and trees in his peripheral vision. Up ahead lay narrow cobbled streets and old buildings. In between were the tram lines; the ground came closer and he had to rest for a moment. He covered his eyes with his hand and breathed. He was still on his feet, it was just the sun dazzling him. It was spring and the sun was bright.

The shrubbery in the churchyard was sparse; there was nowhere to hide. He walked past a dark door set back in a stone porch, then another. He could feel his knees giving way and turned back to the porch. This would have to do. He saw shadows in the corners of his eyes, groped for support to keep his balance.

By the time the lad hurled himself at him, Torsen was already numb with pain. He took a kick in the guts and another in the ribs. He stopped breathing briefly, a pure reflex, but when the lad smashed his head against the stone wall, he felt nothing.

Torsen was unable to place the pictures that came to him in the minutes before he came round. They had no connection with his life, or maybe the blonde woman with the troubled expression reminded him of the adults when he was a kid; they were worried and soft-hearted and cross all at the same time. *Mads, what have you been up to now?*

Far away he heard a woman's voice; she seemed to be on the phone. "Hello? The other guy's run off . . . He's lying in a funny position and he's bleeding quite heavily from his head. Either he's unconscious or . . . No, nobody here knows who he is. I was just walking past and I saw what happened. I didn't have a phone on me so I ran into Holmström's, the antique shop next door, and . . . hang on a minute."

Although he was drifting in and out of consciousness, he was aware of someone crouching down beside him, uncertain and keeping as far away as possible while still able to reach his neck. He thought he ought to defend himself, but his body didn't react. He felt a faint tickle beneath his skin for a few seconds after her fingertips had touched him.

"I think he might still be alive," the woman said. "Wait a minute, he might have some ID on him. Yes, there's a driving licence."

His body jerked. A stab of pain ebbed away as he floated into the mist once more.

When he vaguely regained consciousness, he heard an anxious man saying something about the recovery position, and that the ambulance would be here any minute. The man's voice was shrill and somehow familiar; Torsen opened one eye a fraction and saw that it was the antiques dealer. Feeling returned to his body in fits and starts, along with fear and the realisation of what had happened, what was happening. He moved almost imperceptibly. Yes, he could still feel the figure rubbing against his aching ribs.

The lad had taken his revenge, but had been interrupted.

Torsen's eyelids twitched; they were swollen and stuck together, but through his bloodied eyelashes he could see glimmers of light, and the blurred outlines of people standing over him. The ambulance was on its

186

way, they reassured him again, the ambulance and the police.

If it was the last thing he did, he had to get back on his feet. He had to get out of there. Soon it would be too late. Torsen gritted his teeth.

With a rattling in his throat, he hurled himself upright. The pain made bile surge into his throat. He was dizzy, whimpering, and he crashed into the wall. The blonde woman cried out and jumped to one side to avoid his flailing arms; he managed a feeble blow to the antiques dealer's midriff, enough to make him double over in shock and sink to the ground.

Torsen summoned up every last scrap of strength and ran.

CHAPTER
TWENTY-FIVE

Istanbul, September 2007

Henrik closed his eyes and tipped back his head. Even the sky looked different in Istanbul. A veil of smog coloured the woolly clouds a dirty brown, as if someone had slipped a nylon stocking over the sky.

He didn't want to accept that it would all be over soon. Three more days and he would be back in Sweden. Standing in front of his red door, suitcases in hand, then putting them down in the hallway with a thud. He would begin to feel guilty towards Rebecca, and realise quite how badly he had betrayed her. The smell of incense and cherry tobacco would quickly evaporate from his clothes, disappearing along with the image of himself and Ann-Marie Karpov between crisp hotel sheets. Everyday life would drop down like a lid, pushing them both back into their former roles. The memory would slowly fade.

It was a humid day, and his scalp felt itchy. In a sudden, pointless rage, he scratched his head furiously. Then he contemplated his nails: damp and lined with dirt. And yet it was only a couple of hours since he had scrubbed his hands clean back at the hotel, and had a shave. Washed his hair and slicked it back with gel. The exhaust fumes had turned his white Eton shirt grey, and after a day out on the streets a black mess emerged when he blew his nose.

The heat really was unbearable. Henrik looked around. There was no shade in sight.

Ann-Marie had gone to a meeting with the head of the archaeology department and someone from the Museum of Archaeology to discuss a future exchange between the universities. She had arranged to meet Henrik afterwards at the entrance to Gulhane Park, at the bottom of the hill leading up to the museum. Like two giggling teenagers they had planned to steal an hour in each other's company before rejoining the rest of the group later that afternoon.

There was quite a while left until he was due to meet Ann-Marie.

He got up, his legs wobbly, without any real plan. The main thing was to get out of the sun. The shade of a balcony, even of a tree, anything but this exposed, crowded square where his brain would begin to boil at any second.

He passed the queue for the Hagia Sophia, pushing through a group of Americans who were fanning themselves with maps and brochures. One of the guards, who had been on duty at the entrance to the nearby Blue Mosque earlier that week, reluctantly acknowledged him. It was a sign that they had shared a less than pleasant experience.

Axel, thought Henrik, his fucking integrity and those bloody shoes.

On the plane from Amsterdam to Istanbul they had discussed fingerprints and the new regulations surrounding passport applications. Both Henrik and Axel had been united in their determination never to supply their fingerprints as long as it was voluntary. It was a question of principle. But when Axel decided to apply his libertarianism to the Blue Mosque's ban on shoes and expressly refused to cooperate with the guards, Henrik had been forced to intervene.

"Don't piss about when they're carrying sub-machine guns. Take your fucking shoes off, OK?" Axel had eventually come to his senses, sulkily removing his trainers and walking on the oriental carpets in his socks, just like everyone else.

Henrik began thinking about Ann-Marie again and a foolish smile spread involuntarily across his face. He decided to go for a walk before heading towards the park entrance. Beyond the open square it was both cooler and quieter: fewer tourists, fewer persistent hawkers. Even the smell of half-charred corn on the cob was less intrusive here.

Contentedly, he groped for his cigarettes.

"Mister."

Henrik deliberately didn't turn towards the rasping male voice. It had taken a couple of days to learn how to avoid the worst of the hassle from street vendors, and from then on the response became a kind of reflex. How to appear uninterested through a total lack of body language, when the tiniest misguided hint of politeness could lead to devastating consequences, bringing a surge of other hawkers. And they sold everything. From keyrings and jewellery to silver cutlery and socks, a little bit of everything packed into a box or spread out on a piece of cloth on the ground.

The voice belonged to a man with neither a box nor a blanket. He didn't look like a typical street vendor either; he was wearing a loose brown shirt and grey waistcoat. His feet were brown and dry, spreading over the soles of his flip-flops.

"Mister," he said again. He looked around warily before coming closer. Henrik felt uncomfortable. Even if the man probably wasn't intending to rob him — he would hardly have made the effort to attract his attention if that were the case — no doubt he would try begging for money. Henrik found it difficult enough to ignore beggars on the street, where he was just one of hundreds of tourists. It was much worse now he was away from the crowds. It was so clear-cut: a rich man, a poor man.

He searched his trouser pockets for spare coins, rattling them in some embarrassment when the man didn't seem to understand. He wanted to explain that he wasn't rich at all. That, by Swedish standards, he was poverty-stricken, up to his ears in debt, and that he'd had to borrow the money for this trip.

The man shook his head in horror, no, he didn't want money.

"You're selling something?"

He nodded, and gestured that Henrik should follow him.

Henrik hesitated. Maybe he was hiding stolen goods somewhere nearby. But Henrik was curious. If there was any trouble, he was still not too far from the crowd outside the Blue Mosque, he could shout for help. Besides which, the man wasn't young, he must be about twice Henrik's age. Henrik could beat him in a fight.

He followed the man but didn't speak, afraid of committing himself to something if he gave any verbal encouragement. The man limped across the car park.

"Come now," he said from time to time, waving his hand.

This is what travelling is all about, Henrik thought as he kept up with the man. Taking a chance, having the courage to let yourself be challenged, questioned. Throwing caution to the winds occasionally and going with the flow.

They didn't go very far; just beyond the main tourist drag. The city was still beautiful, but strikingly poor and much the worse for wear. Henrik soon lost his bearings.

The man stopped by an ancient pick-up truck, falling apart with rust, in a yard full of overflowing dustbins. For a moment Henrik gave in to his instincts, allowing himself to be both nauseated and fascinated by the rats scrabbling among the garbage, as big as cats with their swollen bellies dragging on the ground.

A boy emerged from the shadows of the yard. He seemed to have been doing something for Henrik's guide, because as soon as they appeared he vanished silently around the corner. The man held up a finger indicating that Henrik should wait, then hurried around the vehicle as he fished a key out of his waistcoat pocket. The driver's door opened and he leant in across the seat.

Henrik observed the man more carefully, and with a growing sense of unease. He had very little idea of where he was. The few people visible on the other side of the passage leading to the yard looked incredibly shady. They would feel no solidarity with him. They wouldn't come to his rescue. He ought to take the opportunity to do a runner. But he didn't. His curiosity outweighed his fear.

Perhaps the man was younger than he had first thought. The limp made his posture resemble that of an old man, but although the dry skin on his face was deeply lined, his physique and the sharpness of his eyes told another story. He had only the faintest shadow of a beard on his chin, but he had a splendid moustache, grey just like the hair on his head.

He held out his hand to Henrik.

"Come now!"

Henrik slowly moved closer, his eyes fixed on the pale bundle in the man's arms. The man squatted down and opened it out on his lap.

Henrik had been unconsciously holding his breath, and what first met his gaze was a conglomeration of varied objects. They looked scruffy. Disappointment washed over him. He didn't know what he'd expected but his fear, combined with his pride at having gone off the beaten track, had created a sense of anticipation.

The man poked the objects with his dirty hands. Just to be polite, Henrik moved closer to have a look.

"Is it bone and . . . metal?"

The man held up the items one after another: collar-like necklaces, hair slides and boat-shaped earrings, all ingrained with dirt and mud. Henrik touched something shapeless and cream-coloured that looked like a dog's bone.

"I don't suppose any of it's gold?"

"No . . . yes, gold," the man said quickly. "Ceramic. Different materials."

He doesn't know, thought Henrik. But he certainly doesn't think it's gold.

There were small figures made of clay, depicting animals and people; perhaps some thirty items including the cylindrical seals at the bottom of the bundle.

Suddenly Henrik's interest was reawakened. Something about these items seemed familiar. He picked up a necklace and tried to blow sand and earth off the intricate leaves. Turning it over and over, he weighed it in his hand: what he realised almost made him topple forwards.

His voice wasn't entirely steady. "May I see it in daylight?"

The man kept his eyes fixed on Henrik the whole time, his expression tense.

"A hundred dollars," he said, gripping Henrik's wrist tightly.

"What are these things? Where did you get them?"

The man didn't reply, but seemed intensely aware of Henrik's movements.

194

I need to pull myself together, he thought. Act calmly — think. I mustn't let him see . . . If these are what I think they are . . .

"I must get them valued before I know if I want to buy them."

One hundred dollars. I ought to buy them anyway, take the chance. It was a once-in-a-lifetime opportunity; he was almost certain the objects were worth a fortune. He must make sure the man didn't get away before the deal was done.

"I want to buy them as a gift for my wife," Henrik said cunningly. "All of them."

The man held up nine fingers. "Nine hundred dollars."

Then he bundled up the sheet and stood up, impatient for something to happen. Did he think Henrik was about to produce the money from his back pocket?

"Yes, but of course I don't have the money on me," Henrik said.

The man backed away a couple of steps, no doubt to indicate that he could easily tire of this game. Desperation caught up with Henrik. He tried a placatory tone.

"Listen. I'm staying at a hotel near here, this is the card." Eagerly he dug the card out of his pocket. "I'll take one of the sculptures or a necklace with me . . ."

Henrik hesitated for a second, then threw caution to the winds. What the hell. "You can take my passport as a guarantee."

If the worst came to the worst, he could always go to the embassy.

"Then you come to the hotel in the morning. I get the chance to value the things, and to get your money."

A minute or so passed without the man saying anything, and just when Henrik began to think that the man's English wasn't up to processing so much information all at once, he opened his mouth.

"You go hotel, get money. We meet tomorrow, and you buy."

"But how can I be sure I'll get to buy them, that you really will come?"

"You must trust me. I come."

He lifted the bottom of his long shirt and began to bind the bundle of objects around his hips and against his chest.

Adrenaline sent Henrik's blood racing through his veins like a herd of wild horses. *Can't let him disappear, got to keep him talking. Got to find out what he's got in that bundle.*

"Where do you come from?" he began hesitantly, moving imperceptibly so that he was in the way if the man tried to climb into the rusting heap of metal and drive off. He tried to keep his voice calm.

"You a salesman?" He noticed he was following the man's speech patterns.

The man slid away. "Farmer. Other things too."

"OK, like me. Doing different things for a living. In the countryside?"

"Up mountain, little village."

196

"What's it called, this village?" said Henrik, instantly aware that he wasn't going to get an answer to that question.

"You don't know it," the man said curtly, pushing past Henrik to get in the truck.

He had to work fast now.

"OK, friend. I will get you your money right away. But you have to follow me. Not far, just back to the museum."

The man squinted up at him, his expression suspicious. Henrik spread his arms wide, as if to show that he had neither concealed weapons nor intentions.

He's realised he asked for too little, now I've shown that I'm keen. But he's already set a price, we've got a verbal agreement. But Henrik was well aware that traditional rules didn't apply in this situation.

Ann-Marie, he thought suddenly. Ann-Marie would be able to carry out a valuation.

The man clutched at his chest, reassuring himself that the items were in safe keeping next to his heart. He stared at Henrik, assessing him one last time. Then he nodded.

CHAPTER
TWENTY-SIX

Istanbul, September 2007

"Stop moving them like that!"

Ann-Marie Karpov grabbed the man's wrist and held on tight for a couple of seconds, but she was looking at Henrik.

"Do you have any idea what this is?"

She turned her head and gazed towards the museums on the hill, as though she were expecting someone to rush in to rescue her, or possibly arrest her. Then she slowly lowered her arm and pondered deeply for a few seconds.

"Arto Suleyman came here with me after our meeting, he's up there now . . . I'll go and get him. He has to see this." There was a severity in her voice that Henrik had never heard before. "And you make sure he stays here!"

"Ann-Marie, for God's sake!"

Henrik's brain was working overtime. It had been a miscalculation to drag the man here, but it was too late to change his mind. Ann-Marie knew what was going on, and he had to make sure she didn't ruin everything. It hadn't occurred to him that, by bringing the man to Ann-Marie, the treasures might slip out of his grasp.

As soon as the artefacts landed in the hands of Suleyman, head of the archaeology department, they would be no more than a distant memory.

Fuck. A naive series of images had scrolled through his mind: he and Ann-Marie together; a life of freedom. Without debts or limitations, obligations or traps. But he hadn't thought it through; he'd moved too quickly. And now he had to act again.

First and foremost, he needed money, quickly, and Ann-Marie was the only one who had any. In a few rapid strides he caught up with her.

"Listen to me."

He kept his voice low, even though the risk of anyone nearby understanding Swedish was minimal. "I realise it's stolen property, for fuck's sake. But can't you wait a minute before you . . . Can't we just think about this together? Decide what to do?"

She stopped dead and stared at him. Her throat was shining in the heat.

"What exactly is it you want to discuss, Henrik? This man is a criminal, he's offered you stolen goods for next to nothing."

"He said he was a farmer, he could just as easily have dug them up on his land, and he's trying to get rid of them because he doesn't realise how valuable they are. In which case, in what way would it be unethical to —"

"For pity's sake, Henrik! Don't pretend to be stupid, you understand as well as I do that if these items have a cultural and historical value, then they belong to the state, and not to the first greedy, immoral tourist who comes along. Do you mean you're happy to be a part of this, to finance the continuation of these ravages? I'm not even going to have this discussion. I'm going to fetch Suleyman. Make sure that man doesn't disappear."

She moved a step backwards and waved to the man, who had sat down for a smoke by a tree trunk a little way off.

"One second! I'll be back soon, just wait for me!" She tottered as her heel caught in a hole in the tarmac, but managed to regain her balance. She had put on her best strappy sandals for the meeting with Suleyman.

Just before she disappeared from Henrik's view, she turned around. Her expression was affectionate once more. "It looks as though about half of those artefacts carry an inventory number from the Iraqi Museum. The rest are unmarked. What amazing fieldwork — it will be so exciting to be involved in identifying and dating them. And to help make sure a small percentage of a cultural heritage ends up in the right place!"

She waved and disappeared over the brow of the hill.

Henrik's hands were shaking as he took a cigarette out of the packet. He braced himself. In his head a plan was rapidly taking shape. By the time he stubbed out the cigarette beneath his new sandals, an icy calm had spread through his body.

The man stood up and greeted him with an outstretched hand. "We have deal?"

"We have a deal."

They arranged to meet later. The man limped off in the direction of the yard where his truck was parked. Henrik watched him go. He couldn't help worrying that the man might be robbed in the time it would take to get hold of the money; it was a lot of money, after all. But it could be done.

In a way it felt wrong to go behind Ann-Marie's back. He wanted honesty to be a key part of their relationship. But he consoled himself with the thought that he wouldn't keep the secret to himself for ever. She would gradually come round to the idea. All he had to do was choose his moment, put things to her in the right way.

He quickly tried phoning home, then Rebecca's mobile, but there was no reply. He bit his nails. Sometimes she didn't answer, and sometimes she didn't call back. He thought about calling his parents and asking them to transfer some money into his account, but it went against the grain and, anyway, how long would that take? He could try his fellow students, but he was well aware that none of them had much money with them. Besides, what would Ann-Marie make of his sudden desperate need for cash?

He splashed out on a taxi. From the back seat he called Ann-Marie and left a voicemail explaining with considerable agitation that the man had conned him, disappearing with both the money and the artefacts.

"You were right, he wasn't to be trusted. It looks as if he realised he was sitting on a gold mine when we started to look really keen. But I'm OK," he said, his voice breaking. "It was horrible, but I've just ended up with a bloody nose. And, of course, I've lost all my money. I don't know what I'm going to do about that, but at least I'm alive. Maybe I could borrow some cash, just until we get home."

He said he was going to go back to the hotel to lie down for a while, to have a rest after the shock.

Then he leant forward so that the driver couldn't see him in the rear-view mirror and pushed his nasal bone upwards with his knuckles in one sharp thrust. Tears blinded him. He thanked his lucky stars that he'd always had weak blood vessels in his nose. Just to be on the safe side he let the blood drip onto his chest, staining the expensive shirt — it had to be worth it.

None of the other students were on the street outside the hotel or in the lobby. He wiped his face clean as best he could with an old receipt.

It was almost evening by the time Henrik turned up in Arto Suleyman's office. Two hours earlier he had rung Ann-Marie and said that he felt dizzy from the blow and needed to sleep.

"Why haven't you been answering your phone, I've rung you a thousand times!" she said agitatedly. "I've been trying to explain that to Suleyman, but I only saw the artefacts for a few moments, you were the one who had the chance to look at them properly. He really wants you to come over here, Henrik. I know it must have been terrible to be robbed like that, and don't worry about your money, we can sort that out later. But I think it would be a really good idea for you to come over and tell Suleyman what happened yourself."

She lowered her voice at the last sentence, softening her tone; he knew that she was manipulating him, but he melted all the same. And what did it matter? He had already put down a hefty deposit on the treasures — all the money he had, plus what he had been able to scrape together from the other students. Within the next few hours the rest of the deal would be done.

Suleyman's room at Ordu Caddesi had nothing in common with Ann-Marie's poky little office back in Gothenburg. Where she had linoleum on the floor and faded blinds, he had a chequered stone floor and deeply recessed windows. Seats were grouped around the tiled stove, which was beautifully decorated with a mosaic in shades of green and blue.

There were no lights on; the room appeared gloomy and hazy. Henrik had dried blood in his nostrils and was still wearing the stained shirt. He made sure he looked completely disorientated, as if he had just woken up.

Suleyman came towards him.

"What can I say?" he exclaimed, pressing Henrik's outstretched hand between both of his, then apologising for the city and his countrymen, for the state of the government and the resulting poverty, for the immorality that afflicted both the rich and the poor, before eventually drawing breath and pushing his small, round glasses up on top of his head.

He was a slender man, middle-aged and anaemic-looking. The yellowish colour of his skin contrasted sharply with the wine-red pullover he wore neatly over his shirt.

"Are you in a lot of pain?" he asked anxiously; his English was heavily accented but grammatically correct.

Henrik shook his head. "It's OK, actually. I just needed a couple of hours' rest. Sorry I didn't get round to changing my clothes."

The last remark was addressed to Ann-Marie. She waved away his apology; she still seemed anxious.

Suleyman clapped his hands, which made Henrik jump. As Henrik had expected, he was a man who quickly dispensed with small talk. Suleyman walked over to a round table at one end of the large room.

"And you are a student, yes, Henrik? You find the subject interesting?"

He smiled to himself as he poured hot water from a flask into three glasses. "In that case, I can promise that you will find what I am about to show you very interesting indeed."

He kept his eyes firmly fixed on Henrik. Just as Ann-Marie got to her feet, Henrik took a couple of steps into the room.

"I wish I could have stopped him."

Suleyman pursed his lips, shushing Henrik. "You've got a bloody nose. I'm sure you did what you could. Please sit down, both of you."

The tea glass was almost unbearably hot in spite of the starched serviette wound around its base.

"I also wish you could have stopped him, of course. But I am wondering about the figures — you saw them, didn't you, Henrik? The jewellery, the other artefacts? Perhaps you remember certain things about them?"

Henrik nodded, raising the glass to his mouth. His tongue was quickly scalded into numbness. He felt as though he would never be capable of speech again.

"Good. In that case I am wondering whether you have heard of The Red List, Henrik?"

Henrik didn't reply, his mouth still paralysed.

"Naturally you know what I am talking about, Ann-Marie. Perhaps you would be kind enough to explain to Henrik?"

Ann-Marie Karpov nodded and stood up.

CHAPTER
TWENTY-SEVEN

Gothenburg

"Isn't there a psychological term for that, Beckman?" Karlberg joked. "It affects burnt-out detectives. The classic symptom is seeing connections everywhere. A double murder in academic circles somehow relates to one drugged-up tourist having a go at another out on the street."

A telephone was ringing persistently somewhere down the corridor. Tell tipped his chair back and slammed the door.

A pile of coloured copies of a photograph Beckman had brought along to the last briefing was lying in the middle of the table. He grabbed one and held it up.

"Listen to me. You know Beckman went round to Rebecca Nykvist's the other day, with nothing particular in mind, just to get a feeling for Henrik's secrets. An excellent idea, by the way. She was looking for something, anything, that we might have missed. She found a porn film under a mattress — not very exciting — and this photograph of a clay figure and a necklace. An amateur photo that Henrik may or may not have been trying to hide. She has shown a copy not only to the archaeology department at the university, but also to the staff at an antique shop who made a call to the police the day before yesterday. Over to you, Beckman."

"Holmström's Antiques is a shop not far from the cathedral. They had a Danish customer in the day before yesterday. Apparently it was all very odd. He seemed to be drunk, or under the influence of something else, he looked like a junkie. He wanted an object valued, the atmosphere got a bit strange and he took off. The thing is, just after he left the shop, he was attacked in a doorway just around the corner. All hell breaks loose and a girl comes running into the shop to ask the antiques dealer to call the police."

"A Dane who wanted something valued?" Gonzales said. "Give me a break . . . are we supposed to start looking at everybody who's interested in antiques now? Because if so, the whole of the archaeology department has to be under suspicion . . ."

"The whole of the archaeology department *is* under suspicion, Gonzales, since it's our primary link between the victims," Tell pointed out.

"Well yes, but there could be hundreds of other links. Henrik Samuelsson and Ann-Marie Karpov were having a relationship. They might have had mutual friends. And their relationship seems to have aroused interest, people were talking about it. What about her ex-husband? He has an obvious motive if anyone does. And no alibi whatsoever, as I understand it."

"I haven't finished," said Beckman. "This Danish guy was knocked out. The owner of Holmström's Antiques, the person who rang in, found the man's driving licence in his jacket pocket, but when they tried to put him in the recovery position while they were waiting for the ambulance, he came round and went crazy. He punched the antiques dealer and took off."

"He did a runner?"

"He did a runner."

"But we've got ID? And what about the attacker?"

"No. Unfortunately the witness who ran into the shop gave a description that could fit any number of people; she was afraid to get too close. But we might be able to use her later for identification, if we bring someone in."

"But there must be several witnesses if this happened in town in the middle of the day," Karlberg chipped in.

"Let's go back to the guy who actually *was* identified," said Beckman. "We managed to do a little bit of research on him straight away. Mads Torsen, well known to the Copenhagen police."

"A junkie," Tell took over. "He's been in and out of prison for the past ten years. He was a higher class of conman in the nineties, but he ended up on heroin and has mostly stuck to burglaries ever since. He went down for robbery the last time, but came out nine months ago."

"Going back to where Tell started," Beckman went on. "This morning I went to the antiques shop to show them the photo, and discovered that the clay figure is almost certainly the one the Danish guy had taken in. It's really old, apparently, and was stolen from some museum in Iraq."

"How could they be sure it was the same one?" asked Karlberg.

"It was marked in some way."

Karlberg looked thoughtful. He tapped his biro pensively on the table.

"OK. So we suddenly have three parallel cases. The murders in Linnégatan, the break-in at Rebecca Nykvist's house and an attack on a Danish junkie?"

He thought for a moment, then went on: "I'm thinking this guy is a well-known burglar. He's high, he gets confused and tries to get something valued that he's been hanging on to since his last job . . ."

"You're still not getting it — think about where he went," Tell interrupted. "Remember, the figure matches the photo Beckman found in Henrik Samuelsson's bedside cabinet. Look at the background: this figure had been in Henrik's home. We're talking about a unique object here. And don't forget: the Danish guy could have gone to any pawn shop, but he goes to Holmström's Antiques."

"And a guy like that knows about that kind of thing?"

"He knew the object was old and valuable. He wanted to find out *how* valuable. And he probably wanted to get rid of it."

"And how valuable is it?"

"It's valuable in many different respects. It's an artefact, after all."

Beckman leant back in her chair with an amused expression as Gonzales put his hand up.

Tell sighed. "Yes, Gonzales? We're not still at school, you know."

"Thanks. This Mads Torsen. Where is he now?"

"If I knew that I would have told you. We're looking for him; both Gothenburg and Copenhagen are working on it."

"But it gets even odder," Beckman continued. "We were alerted to the incident at Holmström's Antiques by one Tom Svensén, a tutor in the archaeology department. He reacted when I showed him the photograph. He knew the figure, because he and Evert Holmström are part of some kind of body involved in the protection of cultural treasures."

"And Svensén did well to work it out," said Tell. "But what's our next move, apart from trying to identify the lad who beat up Mads Torsen — can you keep an eye on that, Beckman? What do the rest of you think? He's been in Gothenburg, so we need to start looking for clues. We also need to look for the figure — where's that gone? Where's Mads Torsen been? — we're checking all known addresses. There was a receipt in his wallet from a tobacconist's in Angered. Speak to the drugs squad and see if they know anything about what's been going on in the dodgy parts of Angered. We'll start with that. To be on the safe side we'll check rooms as well — cheap hotel rooms, hostels. Hospitals too, since he'd been beaten up. I'll contact the Danish police to see if I can get a bit more information, and I'll send the picture of the figure to Alexandr Karpov. According to Svensén, he's one of the few experts on

210

this particular type of artefact. We'll see what he has to say."

"Sorry if I'm being a bit slow here," Bárneflod said. "But . . . are you thinking that Mads Torsen, this junkie, is the one who murdered Henrik and Ann-Marie and broke into Rebecca's house?"

"That's not what I'm saying. I'm saying that we have a number of leads that need to be followed up."

Gonzales stuck his index finger in the air once more. Tell waved it away.

"Yes, we are going to check the fingerprints from Linnégatan and Kungsladugården against Danish records."

Gonzales stood up. "Are we done, guv? Only I've got someone waiting for me downstairs."

Tell nodded and gathered up his papers. "Yes, I reckon we're done."

Gonzales patted Beckman and Tell affectionately on the shoulder as he passed.

"I get the whole connection thing. It's as clear as day."

"Good," said Tell. "You just keep on working."

CHAPTER
TWENTY-EIGHT

Gothenburg

They were sitting in the kitchen, curled up on Hanna's day bed by the window, the city spread out before them: the hill and Masthugget Church in the foreground, the roofs below, the harbour, the outline of cranes, all set against a darkening late spring sky. Seja hadn't intended to stay so long. She had a morning shift at the care home and would have to set her alarm for six-thirty when she got home.

The thought of the car parked not far away was comforting; she wouldn't have to worry about catching the last bus out to Stenared. She was grateful; she was starting to feel tired, her limbs and thoughts slow and heavy.

"I saw Sally the other day at one of those family events at the House of Music," Hanna said. "You know the kind of thing, *Drum your way to Africa*, the kids get to borrow instruments and the parents pretend to let it all hang out and dance . . . Remember Sally, from Year Nine?"

"I'm not sure I do."

"It doesn't matter. Anyway, she was telling me about her house in Långedrag and her husband who runs a building company; these days, when I see faces from the past I always feel so . . . immature. Like the eternal teenager, with my little apartment in Masthugget and no plan and no . . . savings. The idea that I could speculate in stocks and shares feels absurd."

"Why are you thinking about savings?"

Hanna gave a theatrical sigh. "Well, I don't have any. Everyone tells me I ought to have at least one savings account. Give myself a safety net."

"I don't have any savings either. Then again, I haven't really got much in the way of an income, or of outgoings. Sometimes it feels as if I've started to live outside society since I moved to Stenared. As if the pressure to be part of it all has eased."

"And what do you do instead? Instead of being part of it all?"

"Kick back!" Seja laughed and took a sip of her tea, which was getting cold. "Sometimes I wonder if I've missed out on something too. Those years when everybody else was becoming so responsible. I was studying drama and women's history and hanging out in the pub while others were getting ahead with their careers and saving up to buy a place of their own. At least you're a mum. I haven't got round to that either."

"I should think that's the least of your problems. I mean, you have a man and everything."

Seja hoped her expression didn't reveal what she was thinking, and quickly returned to the topic of conversation that had occupied most of the evening.

"So doesn't Markus want to know more about his dad?"

"No. Yes. Sort of. The thing is, I try to remember that I need to look at it from Markus' point of view — Peter hasn't been around for five years. For the whole of Markus's life he's been absent, uninterested. And now, all of a sudden, he pops up like a jack-in-the-box, wanting joint custody and insisting that Markus should spend half his time with him, talking about rights and . . . Oh, just thinking about it drives me crazy!"

Hanna pretended to tear at her hair. "Markus doesn't even know him, for God's sake!"

"Was Peter around even at the beginning?"

Hanna let her hands drop to her lap again. "No. We weren't together, we only did it once and I got pregnant. I rang and told him a few weeks later. He just said it was my choice, but that he had neither the time nor the inclination to be a father. He's spent a fair amount of time abroad since then."

"But now he's come home?"

"It would seem so."

The bedroom floor creaked as small bare feet moved across the parquet.

Seja leant on the window ledge, resting her chin on her hand. Outside, the silhouettes of the city were fading. She couldn't help thinking about what Hanna had said — that she had a man. Sometimes she still caught herself blushing at the thought of Christian, at the idea that they belonged together, in spite of the fact that they had been together for over a year now. It was as though she expected to be punished as soon as she took things for granted.

214

Across the hallway, Hanna slowly closed the bedroom door, pulling a face as it squeaked.

"Did he go back to sleep?"

"Mm. He's got a temperature. I hope it's not his ears again, I don't fancy spending tomorrow in a waiting room."

"Speaking of tomorrow, I'd better go. My shift starts at half past seven."

"Are you still at the care home?"

"Yes. It's OK. I get time to read, especially when I'm on nights. And I need the money."

Hanna opened the window and lit a cigarette. "You didn't answer my question."

"What question?"

"About you and Christian. About kids and . . . your plans."

"I didn't realise it was a question." Seja smiled. The fact that they had revived their friendship as adults after a ten-year pause was largely due to Hanna's insatiable curiosity. Seja had contacted Hanna — her former best friend — eighteen months previously, when it became clear that she had witnessed, as a teenager, events linked to one of Christian's more famous cases.

She hadn't expected Hanna to get so involved. Together they had opened a window on the past and picked up their friendship where it had broken off, without diminishing the significance of the years that had elapsed in between. Seja would probably never really know where the darkness in Hanna came from; perhaps it had been there all along. That was the way it was: you only ever knew what other people wanted you to know.

Her thoughts drifted back to Copenhagen.

"This is as good as it gets," Christian had said as she lay in his arms after making love in their hotel room. And she knew perfectly well that he was talking about the moment: the good food, their stroll, the conversation, the closeness. And yet she had felt a pang. It was a perverse, crazy reaction, but she wished he hadn't said it. *This is as good as it gets*. As if he didn't want anything more from her. From them. As if he didn't want their relationship to develop.

"Earth to Seja." Hanna rapped on the table.

"I was just thinking about what you said, about kids. But I didn't get anywhere."

"You mean you don't know if you want to have kids with Christian?"

"No, but then at the same time I don't know how it would feel if I did know. What the difference would be. I mean, I know how I feel about him. I know I want to be with him."

Seja stared into the cloud of cigarette smoke.

"And what about him — what does he want?"

"That's the problem — it's so bloody difficult to know! Sometimes I get the impression he's afraid because he thinks . . . I want more than he does. That I want the whole package, but I'm playing a strategic game and biding my time — which is true in a way. But it's as though he's lumping me in with all the other women he's known and assuming he knows what I want without asking."

216

"That doesn't sound great."

"No, but . . . I don't know what I mean. Sometimes it's just so hard to talk. It's as if he's not there. He shuts down as soon as he thinks it might get difficult, and he acts . . ."

She scratched furiously at a bite on her ankle; the skin grew flaky and red. "Like I said. He acts as though he already knows what I'm thinking, what I'm going to do, and he forgets to listen. Anyway, I really must go." Seja got to her feet. "Come over soon with Markus."

Hanna followed her into the hallway with the cardigan Seja had left behind on the sofa.

"OK, or I can come out during the day when Markus is at pre-school. It's nice to meet up without him sometimes. Although it might be the day after tomorrow, I've got to go to the advice bureau."

"Advice bureau?"

"For single parents in custody disputes, that kind of thing. But after that . . . Oh no. I'm going to the doctor on Friday." She sighed. "I'll get out to Stenared one of these days."

"Are you ill?"

"I just need to extend my sick leave, particularly with all this stuff that's going on with Peter."

Seja nodded and refrained from commenting on the fact that Hanna had been off sick ever since they had got back in touch, except for a very brief period. Sometimes it was because she was in pain somewhere or other, sometimes she thought she was susceptible to stress. Sometimes Hanna insisted on her right to concentrate on being a parent, particularly as she was bringing up Markus alone. Seja was aware that new regulations had made it more difficult to avoid work, so it was lucky she had *such a good doctor*. And the more time that passed, the more convincing Hanna's argument that she was unfit to work became.

Seja really wanted to understand. But she had grown up believing that no one was above paying their own way. She might have hated that attitude, but it was ingrained in her, and it kept her on the straight and narrow, made her determined to be a useful member of society, to grit her teeth and battle on just like everyone else. The fact that Hanna chose to play the martyr to avoid getting to grips with her life was hard to accept.

I know nothing, Seja reminded herself, and it was a relief to let go of her irritation. I don't actually know what Hanna's reasons are, and we have no right to sit in judgement unless we do.

Hanna passed her the cardigan. "I'll be in touch."

By the time the door closed, Hanna had disappeared into the apartment.

She's funny about goodbyes, Seja thought as she walked down the stairs, even casual ones. As if every small goodbye reminds her of a big one.

The darkness had seemed more intense looking out from the inside. In fact, only a grey-blue shadow fell on the empty street.

It was only when she turned off the main road that the car crept into the sort of blackness that never exists in the city. It was some time now since her fear of the dark went away.

She parked by the mailboxes. The slam of the car door echoed desolately in the silence. She was used to that too, and the thick trunks of the fir trees on either side of the gravel track; she knew there was life beyond them, other people. The Melkerssons. She had trained herself to think that way during those first trembling months alone in the cottage: there is nothing evil here. There is only good in this place.

It might sound stupid, but it had worked.

The warmth of the moss was evaporating in the cooling night air, which was noticeable as a faint dampness on her hands. Where the forest opened up, the night sky was visible high above the trees; there was no moon, just a summer twilight. She could make out both the cottage and the stable.

It took Lukas a while to register the sound of the grass rustling beneath her trainers; Seja had almost reached the door by the time he whinnied.

She unlocked the cottage, reached in and switched on the outside lights before going out to give him his evening feed.

CHAPTER
TWENTY-NINE

Gothenburg

Behind Linnéplatsen a group of early risers had laid out colourful mats to practise some martial art. It was going to be another warm day. The first rays of sun filtered through the leaves. The patrol car cruised among dog-walkers and joggers; there was no rush. The woman who rang in had explained that she was a trained nurse and that the man was dead. He was also hidden from public view.

"I should think he's been dead a while."

When she was asked about the location, she wasn't quite as clear. "Opposite the pond, the little pond, and that play area . . ."

"Plikta?"

"That might be the name of it. There's a kind of hill . . . he's lying on a stone bench."

They parked at the bottom of Pliktabacken. In the play area a mother was robotically pushing her child on a swing; she looked as if she had her eyes closed, or perhaps she was squinting in the sun.

"I've spent a fair amount of time here," said Markus Ekvall, whose sons had now reached school age. He pointed to the sandpit, which was usually teeming with children and their parents, but not at this early hour. His colleague nodded without interest; he didn't have children. Instead his attention was fixed on a person halfway up the slope, which was used as a sledge run in the winter. She raised a hand and pulled her thin trench coat more tightly around her body.

"How's it going?"

The woman didn't respond to his less than successful opening remark. She was far too caught up in what had just happened; she was pale, and swallowed with some effort.

"How are you?" Ekvall tried again.

"OK."

She seemed to relax.

"What were you doing up the hill?" his colleague asked, less gently.

"I . . . I . . ."

It was as though she had forgotten everything that happened before she saw the dead body. That could be the case: a traumatic experience can form a clear division between then and now.

"I was out for a walk, I usually go for a walk in the mornings before work."

"OK." Ekvall nodded, his expression kind. "So shall we take a look?"

The sound of a waterfall grew louder as they approached the brow of the hill: water cascaded down the other side from a pond carved from rough stone blocks. Perhaps it flowed into the duck pond down below, but Ekvall couldn't work out where the source might be. Nor could he name the rare fir with thick needles that formed the grotto-like enclosure, along with an impressively tall and mature bank of rhododendrons.

The man was lying face down. The back of his head was a tangled mess above the hood of his jacket. His upper body had slumped forward from a sitting position, his feet firmly planted on the ground.

"Overdose," Ekvall's colleague said confidently, nodding towards the man's rolled-up sleeve, the needle still inserted just above the wrist.

"How could you be certain he was dead and not just unconscious?"

Ekvall turned to the nurse, who was holding back; she didn't look very well.

"I felt his pulse," she said quietly, and looked away.

His colleague nodded with satisfaction: *Brave girl*.

"Well, there's not much more to say. Poor sod," he said, suitably subdued. "Shall we turn him over, just to be on the safe side?"

They took a firm hold of the dead man to turn him onto his back, but the stiff body tipped over the edge of the bench and almost fell on the ground. They were taken aback by the sight of his face.

"Bloody hell, he's taken some beating," said Ekvall. He keyed a number into his phone and moved away slightly in order to talk.

The man's glassy eyes were proof enough, but still Ekvall cupped a hand in front of the battered face to check for any signs of breathing, placed two fingers against the purple throat, then shook his head.

222

Shortly afterwards, two more cars pulled up at the bottom of the hill. A man carrying a medical bag got out of one, and a young, dark-skinned man in a red sweater got out of the other.

Ekvall's colleague kept talking as they waited for the doctor to confirm the obvious, and for someone to acknowledge that their task was done.

"Violent Crimes will want to look at those strangulation marks."

Ekvall nodded. It wasn't long before the guy in the red sweater came towards them, holding up his ID. Was he from the Violent Crimes squad?

"OK, we'll take it from here."

If he was, they were bloody quick off the mark. Ekvall's colleague straightened up and went to meet him.

CHAPTER
THIRTY

Gothenburg

Karin Beckman hadn't chosen the colour of the walls: they were pale green. Institutional green. The furniture was lined up against the walls any old how. Piles of cardboard boxes in the bedroom overlooking the garden contained her winter clothes and shoes. The only room she had put any effort into was the children's room. As soon as they had moved in, she had arranged Barbie dolls, cuddly toys and books on the shelves, unpacked the pink night lights and put Disney posters on the walls.

The living room was dominated by a flashy imitation leather sofa, not her own bright-red corduroy suite, which she had left behind. As soon as she found somewhere permanent to live, she would go and get it. She was the one who'd paid for it, after all.

As far as she knew, Göran was intending to stay on in the house. He had inherited it when he was young; the mortgage had been paid off, so he had only the day-to-day running costs to contend with. When property prices started to rise, he talked about selling up and buying a place in town to free some capital. But he would probably never get around to it. That house was everything he owned, his security and his lifeline, and he had been extremely protective of it in the marriage settlement. At the time, the terms had seemed fair. With hindsight, and bearing in mind that they had children, Beckman wondered whether she shouldn't have fought for a better deal.

She had sold her rented apartment in Guldheden many years ago. As she remembered it, she had given notice in happy times, without a second thought. Julia was growing inside her, and it was obvious that their growing family should live in the terraced house in Fiskebäck. The two-bed apartment she was now renting on Doktor Westrings gata felt cramped and dusty in comparison with Göran's house. She was no longer close to the harbour, no longer in an area filled with playgrounds, where people were comfortably well off — but not excessively so. Fiskebäck's little red and blue cubes, with their gardens and rockeries, were the picture of security and family life.

And now she was sitting in a sub-let, with most of her possessions either in storage or piled in boxes around her. The young girl from whom she was renting was a student in Kalmar, and wouldn't need the apartment again until the following January. Karin Beckman had no intention of staying that long. This was a very temporary solution. *One thing at a time* she told herself.

And Göran hadn't been in touch except to speak to the children.

Beckman was ashamed of how jealous she felt when she heard her eldest chatting quietly on the phone, even though she wanted nothing more than for the girls to have a good relationship with their father.

And it had been her decision to leave. But oh, how she wished she had *someone* to talk to like that, the unconditional love of another person, someone who didn't judge or condemn but merely understood.

Beckman was still worried that she might have made the wrong decision. That she would discover, too late, that that was just how life was: the nagging, the oppressive silences, the frustration at being misunderstood or not understood at all, both parties feeling hurt, the clumsy gestures towards reconciliation, the monotony when tenderness and friction were absent. These days she could hardly remember what she had hoped for from marriage. Perhaps she had imagined something like a parent's unconditional love, or the perfect echo of a twin soul. How else could she explain the roots of the discontent that had spread as the years went by?

No, she didn't want that toxic life back, but she wanted something in its place. Something more than this empty feeling.

"Mum . . ."

She was interrupted by Sigrid, who was only half-awake, and she realised she had been standing there frozen in mid-movement for some time.

The child exuded the delicious, familiar smell of sleep and baby soap. Beckman buried her nose in Sigrid's curls, which were damp from dreams. Her pyjama-clad body was soft and pliable; when the child had just woken up there was none of the stroppiness that normally characterised the age she had reached.

226

"You're up early, poppet," Beckman murmured into her curls. "Are you going to sit with Mummy for a while before you get dressed?"

Sigrid nodded thoughtfully, playing with her hair, which was still thin. As Beckman poured herself a cup of coffee, the child allowed herself to be picked up and she rubbed the sleep from her eyes with her adorable chubby fists. Then she spotted the mobile on the table and reached for it.

"No, poppet," Beckman said. "That's Mummy's work phone. It'll break if you play with it."

As usual she was amazed at the depth of resolve contained in her daughter's small body. She moved the phone out of reach, but retribution was as immediate as it was inevitable. Sigrid's scream made her eardrums quiver.

"I want it, I want it!"

Beckman took a deep breath. She was so tired it was as though a viscous substance were weighing down her veins.

"No, Sigrid! You can't have it!"

She tried to settle the child on her knee, keeping the cup of coffee out of reach as well. Beckman had been desperate for coffee, but as its aroma combined with the acrid smell of Sigrid's overnight nappy, her stomach turned. She pushed the cup to one side.

"You'll have to get down if you can't be good."

An attempt to remove the heavy nappy was met with a fresh barrage of protest. Sigrid was too old to sleep in a nappy, but every attempt to train her over the past year had failed miserably.

The kitchen clock showed that it was no longer as early as Beckman had thought. She would need to get Julia up straight away if she was going to get the children to nursery and pre-school in time; breakfast was served at eight o'clock on the dot. Woe betide anyone who was late for pre-school breakfast.

She went into the children's bedroom, which had a stale, unhealthy smell. Julia was lying with the pillow over her head.

"Come on now, Julia. We need to get a move on!"

After another frustrated glance at the clock, Beckman removed the nightdress from the limp body with a moderate amount of force and pulled on jeans and a top, while thanking her lucky stars that she had bathed the child the previous evening. When she was finally dressed, Julia mumbled something unintelligible, turned to face the wall and went back to sleep. Beckman could feel how hot the child was.

Her little sister was picking cuddly toys off the floor, more than she could carry; she whimpered in frustration when she dropped them.

One look was enough to make Sigrid scream again and clasp her wet nappy — that was staying on.

They were going to stay with their daddy at the weekend. Karin Beckman felt relieved, and this reaction bothered her.

Just as the cloakroom door at pre-school closed, Beckman's phone rang. As she retrieved it from her bag, she willed herself not to look over at the house she had lived in until just a few weeks ago. One missed call.

228

Shortly afterwards she picked up a voicemail from Bärneflod; his voice immediately dispelled all thoughts of the nursery wet-weather gear that might have been left at Göran's, and the dark clouds drifting over Fiskebäck.

"It looks as if there's been a breakthrough with your Danish guy. You're on your way in, I guess?"

"I'm on my way," she informed the voicemail.

With a sense of liberation, she abandoned her role as a parent.

CHAPTER
THIRTY-ONE

Gothenburg

"Höije?"

"He's in Varberg."

"What the fuck is he doing in Varberg?"

"He's at the spa. At some leadership conference."

When Beckman flopped into her chair, the inner circle was complete. Höije did not belong to that circle. Since their childish spat over Copenhagen, Tell had decided that it was necessary to cooperate with Höije so that his team could do the job as they saw fit. But Höije was not a sounding board for ideas and he certainly wasn't a friend.

Höije was a talker, a man who twisted words. Tell had always had a problem with that kind of man in his personal life and particularly in his job. For him, everything came down to gut feeling. Höije also had an unpleasant way of scrutinising the person he was talking to, as if he would love to crawl under their skin.

"Let's get started," said Tell.

Beckman rubbed her forehead. As she put on her reading glasses and looked through the material, she began to feel even more tired. Tell suspected that because she had to leave work in time to pick up her children, she felt driven to work furiously between eight and five, unlike some of her colleagues who had the luxury of greater flexibility; he also suspected that she often skipped breaks. He valued her commitment and competence, and made a mental note to tell her that.

"We've had a major breakthrough," he said. "Mads Torsen's fingerprints were among those found in the hallway of Rebecca Nykvist's house. Either we've been lucky, or else he's a complete klutz. He presumably put on his gloves in the hallway, but touched the door before that. We didn't find any other prints from him. We also know where Torsen is right now . . ."

"So why are we sitting here?"

"He's not likely to make a run for it. He's lying on Strömberg's table. Dead."

"Have you spoken to Strömberg?" asked Gonzales.

"Yes. Strangulation marks. Internal bleeding and a couple of cracked ribs. But the cause of death was a heroin overdose two to three days ago, and general poor health."

"I don't suppose he had any antiques on his person?"

"No antiques on him when he was found, Karlberg. He must have managed to sell the figure before he died, or he could have hidden it, for all I know."

"I was there." Gonzales poured himself a glass of water. "It looked as if someone had tried to beat him to death. He must have dragged himself to that bench through sheer willpower."

"Where was the bench?" asked Bärneflod.

"In Slottsskogen, hidden in a shrubbery near Plikta."

Tell looked at Beckman. "So now we know in principle that Torsen broke into Rebecca Nykvist and Henrik Samuelsson's house. But was he alone?"

"Have we checked the other fingerprints in the house against our records?"

Tell inhaled loudly. "No luck. Did you come up with anything else?"

"I took a couple of witness statements from people who were near the cathedral at the time of the initial attack on Torsen. Not much to go on so far, except that the attacker was dressed in dark clothing, and wasn't particularly tall or well built. Apart from that . . ." She went back to her papers. ". . . I'm just investigating a twenty-four-hour stay at the hostel in Stigberget, it's possible we might get something there. I'll come back to you on that. I've also been in touch with Kent in the drugs squad; he's asking his informers. He has no idea what Torsen might have been doing here, although he did know who Torsen was. I suppose the next logical step is to talk to our colleagues in Copenhagen."

"And Stena Line too, trains, planes, buses," said Tell. "He got here somehow. And if he had a friend, maybe that friend has gone home."

"That's a bit of a stretch," Bärneflod objected. "We don't even know for sure if Torsen had a sidekick. I think it's best if we speak to the Danes."

Tell shrugged. "Maybe. I've already spoken to Copenhagen; an Inspector Dragsted in their drugs squad has been keeping an eye on Torsen for quite some time. He seems to have a better idea of what Torsen's been up to than the man himself has. Had."

He leant back in his chair. "Dragsted is due in Malmö tomorrow evening on other police business. I'm meeting him there."

Tell's eyes and nose were itching. "Is everybody clear about what they're doing now?"

As the group dispersed, he caught Beckman's eye. "Could I have a word before you disappear?" he asked, attaching a picture of Torsen to the investigation whiteboard.

"No, I haven't got time right now."

He turned around in surprise. She had gone, leaving only the echo of her curt reply.

Tell had nodded off twice, even though it was a good film. When Seja tickled his neck for the second time, he headed to the bedroom. Once he was in bed, of course he couldn't get back to sleep. Scenes from *A Beautiful Mind* spooled through his head, accompanied by the squeaks Seja made as she changed position on the leather sofa.

He gave up.

"You're back!"

Seja moved up to let him lie down beside her, then laid her head on his shoulder. Christian yawned behind his hand, opened his eyes wide and tried to concentrate on John Nash's dizzying excursions into madness. He took another crisp, but regretted it as soon as the salty grease annihilated the fresh mint taste of toothpaste. He was working out a provisional schedule for the next day when Seja shifted to make room for his head on her knee. He had to put his legs up over the arm of the sofa to get comfortable; it really was too small.

"You're hot — do you have a temperature?" she asked, gently stroking his forehead.

Buy a new sofa, was the last thing he thought before his eyes closed. One that was big enough for both of them. He had had the same black leather sofa for twenty years.

By the morning his temperature had dropped, only to be replaced by a pounding headache that refused to go away, despite eleven hours' sleep, painkillers and a proper breakfast. A sore throat and the beginnings of a blocked nose didn't bode well for the afternoon's trip to Malmö. Tell thought of what the day had in store. He needed to fire off a few emails and make a couple of phone calls, including one to Alexandr Karpov about the photograph Beckman had found in Henrik Samuelsson's bedside cabinet.

He could just as easily work from home while he tried to decide if he was fit to go in.

Seja had left while he was still asleep. He knew she was intending to rise early to pick up her friend Hanna in Masthugget on the way out to Stenared; they were going walking in the forest or something like that. He felt stirrings of disappointment that she hadn't woken him up before she left, hadn't even written him a note.

Tell took his laptop over to the breakfast bar and emailed Renée, telling her that he would probably be in later. Then he opened and closed several messages asking him to contact Rebecca Nykvist. She wanted to know how the investigation was progressing; if they had any more leads. He deleted the lot; he had neither the time nor the energy to ring her. She would only get annoyed when he couldn't or wouldn't answer her questions.

Tell rubbed his eyes as he distractedly flicked through some papers Seja had left. Some kind of dissertation from the University of Gothenburg and several loose print-outs; he started when he saw the words Red List. She must have been researching something with a view to writing an article. Seja had a disturbing tendency to let his cases inspire her journalism, and this business of the Red List was something she'd picked up on in Copenhagen.

His first reaction was to feel slightly put out. They'd been through this before; sensitive police information was not to be toyed with. But he was glad that she was now at least being open about what she was doing, and that she wasn't writing about the actual murders.

He keyed in the dialling code for Denmark and the direct line to Alexandr Karpov's office, where an answering machine informed him that Karpov was not available to take his call.

He had better luck with the mobile number. Tell wasted no time on small talk when Karpov answered, and launched straight into an account of the incident at Holmström's Antiques, passing on Tony Svensén's description of the object in question.

"I'm going to send over a picture I'd like you to look at. It's a photograph of a necklace and a small sculpture. What I'm wondering is . . . There you go, I've sent it."

There was a click at the other end of the line. "Are you still there?"

"So what's your question?" Karpov said eventually, sounding stressed.

"What do you think the objects are?"

"Why don't you ask the expert you've already spoken to?"

"Because Svensén insisted that you were more familiar with the area these artefacts come from. An Assyriologist, I think he called you. He said that the clay figure definitely came from a museum in Iraq and is on the Red List — what does that mean?"

"That it's stolen."

"Go on."

Karpov sighed. "The Red List is compiled by an international group of twelve experts in the history of culture, who catalogued the artefacts lost during the American invasion of Iraq. When its museums were plundered."

"You might have mentioned this when my . . . my girlfriend and I saw you last?"

"Perhaps I did. The list was published via Interpol, and is monitored by the world's museums and serious antique dealers."

"And that system works?"

"To a certain extent," said Karpov. "Quite a lot has been recovered. But the area is still being plundered. Every day cultural treasures are dug up from graves in Iraq."

"OK. Have you looked at the picture?" Tell tried to control his impatience, tapping on his keyboard as he waited for Karpov to speak. "What do you think?"

"Just a moment." Karpov sounded uncomfortable. "So you're ringing me for . . . what shall I call it, a consultation? You're talking to me because I'm an expert in the field? Or because this has something to do with the murder inquiry?"

"Why else would I be bothering with it?"

"Is this an interrogation?" Karpov persisted.

"Call it a consultation if you like," said Tell. "Shall we carry on? Could you look at the picture, please?"

Karpov cleared his throat. "Well, let me see. First of all, I have to say that it's impossible to assess whether an object is genuine or not simply by looking at a picture. There's a host of fakes and copies on the market here in Denmark alone."

"But apart from that, what era are we talking about?"

"I would guess that the necklace could be from about six hundred BC, but the sculpture is older. Perhaps six thousand years old."

Six thousand years was definitely old. Tell had to struggle to regain his train of thought.

"So is it fair to say that there would be a certain amount of interest in this object?"

"Well . . . Of course people collect this sort of thing, and in some cases are willing to pay huge sums of money. If your expert is certain that this figure was stolen from a museum, perhaps he knows if it carries an inventory stamp? Thirteen to fourteen thousand artefacts were stolen from the museum in Baghdad after the invasion."

"Can you tell me more about the figure? Imagine you're talking to a five-year-old, please. I can see it looks like a person, at any rate."

"It's a woman. As you can see, she's holding a vase or some kind of vessel in front of her body. She's highly representative of the Uruk period."

"So you mean women were depicted in a particular way at that time?"

"And in that part of the world, yes, generally speaking. Present-day Iraq."

"Does the figure have a special meaning?"

"It could mean a number of things; we can't know for sure. But one interpretation is that female figurines were used to give strength to women at key times in their lives: puberty, marriage, pregnancy. The vessel and the water you can just make out flowing down over the skirt could indicate that it was used as an offering to the water goddess."

"Right."

Tell couldn't understand how Karpov could read so much into a scanned photograph of a battered lump of clay. He found it hard enough to tell which was the right way up.

"And the necklace?"

"That I think is Neo-Babylonian. You can see that it belonged to a rich person; it's probably gold underneath all that dirt. Could it have been dug up from the ground and stolen? It looks well made, the designs are embossed."

238

"What would it be worth?"

"It's impossible to put a value on it."

"I mean on the black market."

It was clear that Karpov was reluctant to answer. "It's impossible to say. The value is linked to collectors' tastes and opinions. And to availability. For example, an Assyrian relief was sold for around twelve million dollars at Christie's in London in 1994. But since the pillaging of this area began, supply has increased and prices have fallen. But, even so . . . And, of course, gold has an independent value. And then you have to take into account the aesthetic appeal, plus the fact that this is part of a country's cultural treasure."

"A hundred thousand?"

"I couldn't possibly say."

"Half a million?"

"As I said . . ."

"I understand."

Tell quickly consulted Google on Baghdad + stolen artefacts, which produced a long list of articles on the Iraq war.

"OK," he said eventually. "I'll be back in touch if we decide to look into this aspect of the case more closely."

"May I ask how these artefacts relate to your investigation?"

"I assume you will contact me if you think of anything which might be of interest to us."

Tell put the phone down and looked at the picture again. There was every chance this was a red herring. Henrik and Ann-Marie were archaeologists. They were interested in old things. The fact that Henrik had a photograph of two stolen antiques in a book in his bedside cabinet might have nothing whatsoever to do with the murders. But what about Mads Torsen's visit to the antiques dealer, and the fact that his fingerprints matched those found in Henrik and Rebecca's house?

The interconnections confused him. Could it all turn out to be a series of coincidences? Surely not.

Tell put a hand on the phone. He grabbed the receiver and quickly keyed in the number so he didn't have time to change his mind.

The answering machine.

Seja was incredibly hard-working once she got her teeth into a project. She was like a sponge, soaking up knowledge. And why work against one another when he could benefit from her skills? He had complete trust in her ability to absorb and interpret information, although he didn't always trust her ability to assess the risks involved.

"Hi, Seja, it's me. I realise you're busy at the moment, and as you know I'm off to Malmö later. And there's no great rush, but I wondered if you could email me some information? It's to do with the Iraqi Red List — I think that's what it's called. I want whatever you've found out about the artefacts, the thefts, any organisations involved, the black market. How the stolen artefacts are registered and catalogued, that kind of thing."

He pulled himself up. "If you have time and it's no trouble, of course. I just happened to notice that you'd already done some research."

CHAPTER
THIRTY-TWO

Gothenburg

Beckman was having a working lunch with an officer who had questioned witnesses to the attack on Mads Torsen.

They were sitting outside a café where tables and chairs were packed into a tiny space between the tall white walls of the buildings in the old part of town. It almost felt as though they were abroad; Mediterranean food on the tables, plenty of olive oil, espresso drunk from tiny cups made of thick white porcelain.

Beckman wolfed down half of her shellfish stew and suddenly felt terribly unwell. She had to rush inside to lean over a toilet and breathe hard for several minutes before venturing out again.

She had suspected beforehand that she wouldn't get much out of this meeting from a professional point of view. The attack on Torsen may have taken place in the city centre, but it had happened in a dark doorway. And how long did it take to knock someone out? The crime scene investigation showed that Torsen's head had been smashed against the stone wall. A couple of well-aimed kicks to the ribs, and the whole thing could have been over in a minute or so. And people saw so little, intervened so rarely.

Enquiries had been made in all the restaurants and shops overlooking the doorway, and in the surrounding streets, but to no avail. The antiques dealer had provided only a vague description of what had happened. The fact that the attacker had disappeared by the time Evert Holmström came out of his shop was confirmed by a man on paternity leave, who had parked his buggy outside the cathedral for a while. He had at least caught a glimpse of the drama; with the help of a sketch artist he might just be able to come up with a decent picture.

And the woman who had made the call could only remember that the man had been dressed in dark clothing and was quite slim, below average height and of a youthful build.

"I didn't dare go into the doorway," she had said. "Not even close. I just saw two figures moving around. But I could hear them, and it didn't sound pleasant."

Just as Beckman was saying goodbye to her colleague, Karlberg rang to tell her that the drugs squad had found out where Mads Torsen had been staying.

"You remember we had a receipt from a shop in Angered? Well, they started in the known places nearby, brought in a few guys who of course denied all knowledge but —"

"Yes?"

"But when they went back the second time they managed to wheedle it out of one guy that Torsen and a friend had been around the day before the break-in."

Beckman walked across and unlocked her car. "But we still don't have a name for his sidekick, do we?"

Karlberg was spinning it out. "No, the guy said he didn't know who Torsen's friend was. But the occupant of the place in Angered, Niklas Carlsson, is being brought in for questioning. Tell thought you and I could take that. It's probably the easiest way of getting a name."

"And we've got a few witness statements from the actual beating; we might be able to match those with what Carlsson tells us."

"Are you on your way in?"

"Yes. So what's the boss doing?"

"He was going to meet up with that Danish officer later, I think."

"OK, you make a start with Carlsson. I'll be there shortly."

Beckman switched off her phone. In the square outside the cathedral, two people were juggling with fire, although daylight ruined the effect somewhat. She noticed that several of those watching were eating ice cream, and within a couple of seconds she was craving something sweet. She stopped at a stall. It was as if her body was just one big greedy hole that had to be filled. She slurped a mouthful of the sweet ice cream and the cold hit her forehead. Exhaustion overwhelmed her once more.

Tears sprang to her eyes the second before she realised what it was she had been denying. She'd been here before. She didn't need to take a test: she was pregnant. It was like a bad joke.

She hadn't spoken to Göran for weeks.

CHAPTER
THIRTY-THREE

Gothenburg

Karlberg wasn't really the type to chat with girls at work. In fact, he wasn't the type to chat with girls full stop. He was far too ... shy? He quickly clicked through to the chat room. Just wanted to check what she'd replied.

Maybe not shy, exactly. A bit cowardly? That's what his cousin had said — it was a perfect way for cowards to meet. And, after all, he'd met his wife on the Internet. It was also good for people who needed a bit more time to work things out. When you were cowardly, it gave you plenty of time to decide how to phrase things, which meant that stammering and pauses could be avoided on the first date. By the time you eventually met up, you'd got to know a bit about each other's flaws and chosen to accept them.

But you have to be honest with what you say, his cousin had added in a serious tone of voice. Otherwise it won't lead anywhere. Karlberg had been embarrassed, mumbling that he wasn't about to start looking for female company in cyberspace, but if he should change his mind, he definitely wouldn't go making things up.

Footsteps in the corridor made him shut down the page, only to open it again when the clicking of high heels faded. Until Niklas Carlsson arrived, all he could do was wait.

"Do you like being a detective inspector?" Theresa P wondered. She had just told him she was a skincare therapist.

"Sadly, I'm only a detective sergeant," Karlberg wrote back. He wondered if he should put quotation marks around *only*, or if that might seem arrogant. Eventually he sent the message as it was.

It took a while for the response to arrive. Karlberg drummed his fingers on the desk in frustration. Should he write again, explaining the difference between an inspector and a sergeant? But why would she be interested — it would only serve to reinforce her view of him as a complete idiot.

He went back through their previous messages. Theresa P had written about herself and the salon where she worked. She had written an amusing description of a client — Karlberg grinned as he read it — but their conversations were serious too. She wrote about what she wanted from life, for example that she wanted to work less in the future in order to have more time to develop her knowledge of yoga and possibly open a teaching centre.

His own contributions seemed dry and uninspired; he didn't know how to be any different. And now he'd put her off, with his embarrassingly factual self-deprecation: "I'm only a detective sergeant". Get the violins out.

246

Karlberg shut down the page. Perhaps this Internet dating business wasn't for him; after all, the written word was not one of his strong points.

But no, he wasn't shy. He didn't really have a problem talking to girls. He got on well with his female colleagues. Over the years he'd had plenty of female friends. The only thing was that his relationships rarely progressed beyond friendship. He was the nice guy you could talk to, not the hot guy you wanted to go to bed with.

Karlberg could hear how gloomy he sounded when he answered the phone.

"Niklas Carlsson has arrived."

"Thanks."

He left his office for the interrogation rooms and an interview he had no desire to carry out on his own. But he couldn't shake off his train of thought. He had only had a long-term relationship with one woman. What had she seen in him at the beginning, before she started to think he was spineless and a walkover? He thought back ten years: her best friend had got together with his best friend, just as their friends were retreating from view, absorbed in careers or starting a family. Had they both just been left on the shelf? Would it take another lucky twist of fate for him to get together with another girl? Anyway, since he had passed the magic age of thirty several years ago, all the good ones were taken.

He went down in the lift, pulling on the jumper he had tied round his shoulders. He greeted the guard and entered the little room.

Karlberg didn't recognise Niklas Carlsson, although he knew the type. Baggy trousers and uncoordinated movements. Greasy hair tied back in a ponytail. A grin hovering on his lips. Karlberg knew that it would shortly give way to the sort of pathetic pleading that he always wished he could spare himself and the interviewee. Drugs robbed people of their dignity in so many ways.

"Detective Sergeant Andreas Karlberg."

"I'm saying nothing."

"You don't even know what I'm going to ask you."

"I'm saying nothing. About anything."

"I'm just looking for information, I'm not trying to catch you out."

"Are you deaf? I'm saying nothing. End of."

"OK."

Karlberg looked at Niklas Carlsson's hands as they tugged at his short denim jacket. His long, dirty nails left angry red marks when he scratched his wrists and throat. It was obvious they'd picked Carlsson up just at the right moment; in a few hours he would be a lot more talkative.

"You can go as soon as you talk," he said.

CHAPTER
THIRTY-FOUR

Malmo

The Violent Crimes team in Malmö had provided an office for Christian Tell and his Danish colleague as soon as he arrived, having made the journey from Gothenburg to Malmö in a record two hours.

"Was there anything special about Mads Torsen, or was he just like the rest of them?"

Inspector Dragsted nodded to indicate that he had understood the question.

"Yes and no. Twenty years ago he was a pretty successful burglar. Gold, among other things. He had a few guys working for him. I don't know exactly when he started; he hardly ever got caught, so a lot of what I say is based on assumptions. I don't think Torsen was completely stupid. He didn't really get caught until he started on the smack. He began to get more careless then, abandoned expensive targets for more typical junkie stuff. He got to be pretty miserable; in the beginning I remember thinking he was quite a character, if you know what I mean."

"So you've known him from the start?" Tell asked, letting Dragsted stay with Torsen for a while, even though it was really the other name that interested him

— the name Karlberg had announced in the voice of a delighted child. Rick Pedersen. According to Niklas Carlsson, Pedersen had come over from Copenhagen with Mads Torsen. After a certain amount of pressure from Karlberg and Beckman during the interview, Carlsson had said he thought Rick might possibly be short for Rikard.

"I was around back then but I was still green," Dragsted replied. "But so was Torsen; looking back now I'd say he was a snotty kid with delusions of grandeur. But he had a glint in his eye which he lost later on. When he became — how did you put it? — just like the rest of them. He kept on getting caught, dropping further and further down the pecking order. He's served a number of short sentences over the past ten years, mostly for breaking and entering and burglary. I think there was robbery too. And now . . . I heard a rumour that he'd been ill recently, maybe cancer, but I don't know if that's true." Dragsted shrugged. "Well, either way, he's dead now."

Tell nodded and tucked a plug of chewing tobacco under his top lip.

"I wanted to ask if you knew of a friend or associate of Torsen's; according to one of my colleagues his name is Pedersen. Rick or Rikard. Quite young, it would seem."

Dragsted shook his head.

"No . . . I can't say I recognise the name."

Tell's optimism fell like a stone. "He and Torsen came to Gothenburg."

"Did Torsen die of an overdose, by the way?"

250

"Yes. But he was badly beaten just before he died. It looks as if he was involved in something much bigger than breaking and entering."

"Like what?"

"Worst-case scenario, a double murder."

"Premeditated murder? Are you sure?"

"No. But certain factors are pointing in that direction."

Dragsted let out a low whistle. "Bloody hell. It wouldn't have surprised me if Torsen had killed somebody in the heat of the moment, he's always been a fiery bugger. But premeditated . . . Then again, why not? After all, he's lived his whole life in that world, so it's hardly surprising if he ended up damaged."

Once again he lapsed into deep thought.

"Pedersen, you say." He scratched his chin. "There's a . . . there's a woman. A working girl. Her name is Cilla Pedersen, the name doesn't ring any other bells."

Tell couldn't hide his disappointment. "I suppose Pedersen is a pretty common name?"

"Yes. But, then again, this is quite a small world."

Tell wasn't sure whether the other man meant the world in general, or the underworld in particular. He just wanted to go home to bed and sleep.

"Are you OK?" Evidently Tell looked as bad as he felt.

"More or less," Tell replied.

They stood up and Tell held out his hand, but his colleague didn't take it. "Just give me two minutes before you go."

He left the room, and Tell heard him making a phone call. Dragsted had been speaking a form of Danish which made considerable concessions to Swedish, much to Tell's relief, but now he was talking in the language Tell would never, ever understand.

It took a while. Tell rested his head on the palm of his hand and, having been offered water, swallowed a couple of painkillers. Just when he had decided not to wait any longer — it was getting late — Dragsted returned.

"Christian, listen. I checked out Cilla Pedersen. She's got a brother called Enrique Pedersen; he's younger than her, only twenty-two."

"Enrique Pedersen — have you got anything on him?"

"Not really, just a minor offence before he turned eighteen. But that's not to say he isn't in league with the big boys now."

Tell thought feverishly before nodding to Dragsted. "Is there any chance —"

"That we could help out? I don't see why not." He looked at Tell sympathetically. "How do you feel about coming back to Copenhagen with me now? I'm sure we can pick him up in no time."

Tell simply couldn't do it, he didn't have the strength.

"Could you try to pick Pedersen up tomorrow and give me a call? I can be back in a couple of hours."

CHAPTER
THIRTY-FIVE

Stenared

Seja was struggling up the slope on her bike. Perhaps it would help if she put gravel down. But, no, it would probably just get washed away in the November rains, turning into a muddy porridge that she would trail into the house.

The word *Solisinn* was inscribed on a white wooden archway above the gate leading to one of the cottages. It had an air of abandonment and neglect. Perhaps the owner had died, and none of the relatives were interested. The white shutters were rotting and a lace curtain covered the glass pane in the front door; the inside was completely shielded from view. The garden was overgrown, although it was obvious that once upon a time someone had looked after it well. There was an overgrown thicket of raspberry canes and something that might once have been a vegetable patch.

If you were in the garden you could easily believe that the forest went on forever, but it merely formed a horseshoe-shape around the plot. Beyond the trees there was a huge clearing, which was just beginning to grow again. Small signs of life, but something was definitely happening: birch and fir saplings among the low-growing blueberry bushes.

The garden at Solisinn was the starting point for the walk to the lake which Seja had marked out when she was relatively new to the area. She had marked it proudly with red paint, because Åke had insisted that the route was blocked for good, thanks to storms and fallen trees. It took an hour of climbing over logs and rocks, but it was worth it. No one ever visited the Stenared side of Älsjön, which was wild and beautiful. She had never seen a soul at the place where she went to swim. But she wasn't heading for the lake today.

Seja liked the warm breeze blowing through her hair. She allowed the bike to bounce through the hollows in the gravel track, not bothering to apply the brakes, enjoying the feeling of speed and allowing it to blow away at least some of her pent-up frustration.

Frustration about Christian, and now about Hanna too. Seja suddenly felt as though she had lost the ability to interact with other people.

What's the matter with me? Do I care too much about what people think?

She couldn't share the thoughts running through her head with anyone. But they were there, and they were very wearing. Brooding over petty irritations took up time and energy. And it annoyed her that she always ended up in the conciliatory role she recognised from her childhood, the one she had taken so that she would have someone to play with. She would always smile, tilt her head to one side and understand.

As Hanna had said, "It's so nice to talk to you, Seja, you understand. You let me get everything off my chest."

Seja had thought Hanna seemed tense earlier in the day; she was smoking more heavily than usual. She immediately started talking about the contact family she had finally applied for through social services.

"He's going to spend one whole weekend there every month, they live outside Alingsås. They're getting on a bit, she's a lovely woman who used to work in textiles. And the best thing is that they'll pick him up and bring him back. I said I didn't have a car or a driving licence and there was just no way I could do it. I mean, if I ended up trailing back and forth on the train it wouldn't be much of a rest for me, would it?"

Seja didn't understand. "A contact family — what are you talking about?"

"So Markus and I get some time apart. I mean, I spend all my time with him on my own and I told the social worker that sometimes I could just scream: *I want some me time!* She understood, she was fantastic."

"Well, of course it's hard being a single mum," Seja said evasively, and it was somewhere around that point that she slowly began to slip into the role she despised more than anything.

Was it because she really wanted to remind Hanna about Markus' biological father? He was desperate to get to know his son, but Hanna had shown him the door. Or did she want to point out that Hanna did have time to herself, every day when Markus was at nursery, since she was still signed off sick for spurious reasons?

Seja's fear of conflict manifested itself in strange ways. In certain situations she came across as strong and hard-nosed, dominant even. In others she was terrified of rocking the boat. Do you think I bloody well enjoy changing old folk's nappies? she wanted to burst out. Don't you think I suffer from stress and the early mornings? All those thousands of single mums who actually work full-time as cleaners, don't you think they suffer? They suffer, but they don't go to some half-soaked doctor whining about how difficult it all is. They don't get used to living in the half-light, trudging off to nursery in tracksuit bottoms then going back home to bed, sleeping until noon then spending the rest of the day surfing the net or sitting around drinking coffee with the other mums who are signed off sick, moaning about their hard lives: how misunderstood they are, how exhausting it is to . . .

You've got to stop thinking that way.

Seja slowed down after being forced to brake for a car which appeared incredibly quietly beyond the lilacs where the cycle track crossed a side road; she took a couple of deep breaths and tried to think things through.

I sometimes find life oppressive, she thought. I sometimes find it difficult to make ends meet. I'm anxious about my professional future. I'm worried that I might not make it as a journalist, that I might not get enough work to keep my head above water. Sometimes I wish I wasn't so isolated, I wish I could hand over the

256

responsibility for my life to someone else. And I'm sure that's why I get so bloody furious — yes, furious — with Hanna. Because she's just given up. And it doesn't even seem to bother her.

I'm displacing my unhappiness with my own fear of failure by transferring it to Hanna.

After Hanna had finally gone home, Seja had become hot with indignation. She was very fond of Hanna, but she found it difficult to listen to her friend going on about her life. She had suppressed her irritation, smiling and nodding even as a stale taste filled her mouth.

The conversation had taken a new turn. They had walked through the forest to the lake and gone for a swim, screaming in the cold water. Hanna had insisted she'd seen a water snake and panicked, which meant their spring dip had come to an abrupt end. They dried out on the flat rock, perfectly shaped for two resting bodies.

Seja had closed her eyes and reached out to pick little blueberry flowers, popping them in her mouth. They had a slightly acidic apple flavour, with just a hint of the sweetness to come. She took pleasure in the warm, silky smoothness of the rock and the friendship that had meant so much, and would mean so much in the future.

It was only when she had re-established contact with Hanna that Seja realised she had been lonely in the past, even when she was still with Martin. Most of their mutual friends had disappeared off the radar since the split. Martin had been the sociable one, after all, and

Seja . . . Seja had just been Martin's girlfriend. She liked the idea of an affinity with other people, but sometimes it was just that sometimes it felt like such bloody hard work.

But what do we really know about anyone else? Perhaps everybody felt the same from time to time. At least in Christian she had found the same existential loneliness. He had mentioned the experience of being in the middle of a social gathering and still feeling isolated — for a second the world shifted as one of the last gaps between them was bridged.

Seja had believed that the only thing that could fill the emptiness was a relationship with a man. But she had felt a new kind of closeness with Hanna. She had enjoyed the time they spent together, doing simple things. So now that the differences between them had created a sudden distance, she had wanted to be honest and find a way back to the uncomplicated friendship they had had. Instead, she had upset Hanna.

Suddenly she realised that her tongue was as rough as if she had just crossed a desert and her eyes were dry from the warm breeze in her face. She quickly ran into a small shop to grab a drink and buy a phone card. Afterwards, she pushed her bike slowly along the side of the road towards the local community centre at Bergumsgården; her mind was too restless and her legs too weary to cycle straight home.

The gates were open and a poster had been put up just inside: *Try our yoga classes.*

Find your inner peace.

Yes please, Seja thought. She couldn't help but smile. She wanted somebody to remind her that she was making a mountain out of a molehill; no relationship worth anything should be so fragile that it couldn't withstand honesty or a little friction.

Hanna had talked about how difficult it was to find someone to really talk to, unless you had plenty of money to pay for it.

"I think you'd feel better if you had a job and more structure in your everyday life," Seja had said, and when Hanna didn't seem to understand, she had continued, "I mean, mightn't these doctors who keep signing you off sick actually be doing you a disservice?"

Hanna had stood up and started drying her hair. The towel hid her expression, but Seja sensed a shift in her friend's mood.

"Those doctors who keep signing me off sick? You make them sound like charlatans —"

"No, that's not what I mean. I just mean that you're a clever woman. You could do anything, study anything, work as . . . Oh, I don't know. Do something fantastic with your life!"

"And I'm not doing that now? I'm doing nothing now, is that what you're saying?"

Seja tried to laugh away Hanna's outburst, but the laughter stuck in her throat.

"Come on, Hanna, it's as if you're deliberately trying to misunderstand me! Be honest, have you never thought about what you want to do with your life? How long are you thinking of being signed off on the sick?"

"For as long as I need to be. Until I'm ready to go out to work."

Hanna pulled on her skirt, half-turned away from Seja. It had suddenly turned chilly, as it does in May as soon as the sun disappears.

"What do you mean, ready?"

"I am intending . . ." She spoke slowly, like a schoolteacher, as she angrily brushed needles off her clothes. ". . . which is my right — to remain signed off until my doctor sees fit to discharge me."

"But you're not sick!" Everything Seja had been suppressing broke free, taking a detour around sympathy and good sense. "Those doctors are signing you off because you *say* you can't work! Because you *say* you can't cope with stress — who the hell can? You're just scared — but what are you scared of? Are you scared of failing? Because it's going to get more and more difficult the longer you spend at home. Soon you'll have completely bought into this idea that you're . . . incapable. And you're not!"

"Why the fuck does it bother you so much? Is that what life's all about, what you achieve, whether you have a good education or a good job, is that all that matters to you? If it is, then that's your problem, Seja. I'm doing other things with my life, I have a son and I'm a bloody good mother to him, let me tell you."

Seja could feel the weakness in her voice; she didn't know how she got the words out.

"But you've just denied Markus any contact with his father. And instead you're turning to strangers to give you a break."

"It's called a *contact family*." Once again, Hanna's articulation was exaggerated. "A lot of single parents have one. It is a right within our society, if you need it. I have no intention of being ashamed of the fact that . . . You don't have any children, Seja. I just don't understand how you can . . ."

She fell silent, and Seja shook her head disconsolately. "I really don't mean to judge you," she said.

"No."

"I just think it's such a shame. Such a waste for you to be hanging around at home thinking you can't cope. When you could be doing anything. You used to have dreams about what you wanted to do, back in the old days. I mean, this business of stress; studying or working isn't just stressful and hard work, it's good fun too! It's inspiring, it allows you to develop."

Hanna pulled on her trainers and pushed her towel and swimsuit into her rucksack. Then she dropped the bag between her feet.

"Yes, I had dreams. Some came true, and some didn't, same as everyone. And one of those dreams was that I wanted children."

"I don't remember that."

Seja suddenly realised that she was close to tears: fury and tears because every single thing she said was coming out wrong.

"I absolutely agree that you're a brilliant mum to Markus, but that's nothing to do with any of this. You can be a good mum and do loads of other things at the same time. Lots of parents manage it. And so do lots of single parents."

Hanna closed her eyes.

"I really don't know why we're having this conversation."

She pointed at Seja without saying anything else; Seja took the hint and quickly pulled on her clothes over her swimming costume as tears of frustration scalded the inside of her eyelids.

"You're taking everything I say the wrong way," she said quietly when she was dressed, her wet costume making her breasts and stomach itch.

Hanna didn't answer, she simply turned away and set off.

CHAPTER
THIRTY-SIX

Gothenburg

Michael Gonzales put his feet on the edge of his desk and pushed off, rolling his chair the short distance to the other side of the room. There was a bottle of tepid mineral water on the bookshelf, but nothing to open it with. He rested the cap on the corner of the desk and pulled down sharply. It left a little mark.

Tell was in Copenhagen; he'd virtually got home and set off again straight away. Paperwork was piling up. Gonzales and Karlberg had interviewed everyone who had any connection with the archaeology department: students, tutors, researchers. The majority appeared to know nothing, while others looked at them knowingly and told them what they already knew: that Henrik and Ann-Marie had been having an affair. That fact was shared in a half-whisper, mainly by other students. The small number of Ann-Marie's colleagues who knew what had been going on shook their erudite heads. They couldn't understand why Karpov had embarked on a relationship with a student, and one on the foundation course at that. She was well respected;

they had thought she was above that sort of behaviour.

At first Gonzales had been excited by the idea of peeking into the rarefied world of Olof Wijks gata, of charting the illicit relationships struck up behind its stone walls. But now he was tired of hearing the same thing over and over again. Some knew Henrik Samuelsson as a charming, intense, perhaps slightly arrogant know-it-all who liked getting into theoretical debates. Many thought he was inoffensive. The words *charming* and *committed* came easily to those who liked him. Gonzales found the workings of the female mind incomprehensible: on paper Henrik was a loser who could barely support himself. And yet he had obviously been popular with the ladies.

No one had a word to say against Ann-Marie. She was an expert in her field, inspiring, modest, blah blah.

Gonzales sighed. He flicked aimlessly through the reports, stopping at the transcript of Karlberg's interview with Marie Hjalmarsson. She had mentioned someone called Annelie Swerin, who had also been in Istanbul. Hjalmarsson had reluctantly talked about conflict within the group. Was it worth taking a closer look? According to the report, Swerin was working on a dig in India, but perhaps she was back now.

He checked the telephone lists and keyed in Swerin's number. Just as he put the receiver down, having gone through to voicemail, his phone rang.

"Gonzales speaking."

"Gonzales? I asked to be put through to Detective Inspector Christian Tell. I'm afraid I've misplaced his number."

Was it another Dane? Gonzales's mood lifted. "DI Tell isn't here; can I help you?"

"I don't really know."

"What is your name, and what's it about?"

"Forgive me. My name is Alexandr Karpov and I work at the Archaeological Institute in Copenhagen. I'd like to arrange a meeting with Inspector Tell . . ."

"I'm working on the same investigation," said Gonzales, turning to a clean page in his notepad. "If there's something you'd like to tell me I can pass it on. But I think Inspector Tell is actually in Copenhagen as we speak."

"Yes. But I'm at a seminar in London, at least for the next few hours."

Karpov seemed to hesitate. "Christian Tell spoke to me about my wife. My ex-wife Ann-Marie. And he talked about —"

"I'm aware that he spoke to you."

". . . about specific artefacts on the Red List." Karpov took a deep breath and exhaled as he spoke. "I think I'll have to call back."

"Please tell me what this is about."

"No. For personal reasons I would prefer to speak to Christian Tell face to face. But I can tell you that I know the murdered man, Henrik Samuelsson, had in his possession a stolen item which is probably extremely valuable. And . . ." Karpov took another deep breath. "And I know who knew he had it."

"And how did you know that?" Gonzales pressed the receiver to his ear. "Hello?"

"Because I was the one who told them. I told Knud Iversen and Dorte Sørbækk. My assistants."

Gonzales went over the conversation with Karpov in his head. He took out his notes from their recent briefings.

For some time Tell had been convinced of a missing link. Antiques. Danes. These apparently odd coincidences.

Gonzales stared in bewilderment at the paper in front of him. Sørbækk. Iversen.

He tried Tell's mobile. Even if Tell were mid-interview, he would prefer to hear the latest news, especially as he was in Copenhagen and could perhaps act on the information.

The person you are calling is not available.

What people like Mads Torsen and possibly Rick Pedersen had to do with this . . . gang of academic archaeologists was still a mystery to Gonzales. Tell was right, there was a missing link. Could Karpov's assistants be that link?

Gonzales spent half an hour ringing around Copenhagen police stations without understanding a fraction of what the receptionists said. The only thing he had grasped was that they couldn't help him to find a visitor, irrespective of whether this visitor was a detective inspector, and no matter how important the message might be.

Gonzales made an instant decision.

CHAPTER
THIRTY-SEVEN

Copenhagen

Pedersen hadn't been in the tiny room for long. He was still furious, a frame of mind at odds with his fey appearance. He was slightly built, with downy blonde hair. He wore a shabby suit several sizes too big, which made him look pathetic, like a little boy wearing daddy's suit for his first night out. His shoes also looked too big; they were brown and scruffy and didn't match the black suit. And then there were his white sports socks, which poked out every time he crossed his legs. His face was pale, narrow and pointed, with almost no sign of stubble.

His eyes were the only thing that gave him away; they were penetrating in their milky-blue intensity. Dark rings formed craters around them.

"He'll be a nasty piece of work in a few years — just look at those eyes," Tell said to Dragsted as they stood watching Pedersen through the glass.

"You're right there. He's one to watch. His sister's a bloody mess as well. But nicer. That one . . ." He waved in the direction of Pedersen, who was now rocking back and forth. "You don't know where you are with that one. Twenty-two years old, and on his way up."

"Have you spoken to him?"

"Barely. But he knows what this is about. You can see that. He's scared."

Enrique Pedersen grinned. He was trying to play the big man, but had ended up looking even more desperate. His eyes flitted constantly between Tell and Dragsted.

"This is Detective Inspector Tell. He's come over from Gothenburg, as I said."

"I'm a Danish citizen. He has no right to question me . . ."

"No, but I do," Dragsted snapped. "I'm the one questioning you. Inspector Tell will merely sit in on the interview, since we have discovered that you and Mads Torsen broke into a house in Gothenburg. There's no point denying it."

Tell nodded in agreement, even though Dragsted was stretching the truth.

"However," Tell went on quickly when it looked as if Pedersen was about to protest. "You might be able to help us if you just listen. The thing is, we know we're looking at something much bigger than a little break-in. I wouldn't have come all this way to hear about a little break-in, as I'm sure you're well aware."

Pedersen had pricked up his ears. He was tugging down his sleeves, which were already too long, presumably to hide the track marks on the back of his hand.

"So. We know that you're mixed up in this. The question is: do you know what you're mixed up in? Are you just an errand boy, or were you in on it from the start?"

Pedersen snorted, but continued to glare at the floor.

"How much money were you promised? How much did you and Torsen get for shooting Henrik Samuelsson and Ann-Marie Karpov?"

Pedersen looked up, obviously confused. "Shooting? I didn't . . . I haven't fucking shot anybody, I —"

"Yes?"

"I . . . I don't know about any shooting."

Tell shrugged. "You're the best lead we have in the case of a double murder in Gothenburg. A dozen clues lead straight to you and Torsen, via stolen goods worth . . . Well, it's impossible to say. Millions, perhaps. Do you know how much they're worth?"

"What the fuck? I don't know a fucking thing."

"Was it you who beat up Torsen before he died? He was found dead and he'd been badly beaten; you were the last person to see him alive. We can prove that."

"For fuck's sake, I didn't kill Torsen! If you go around saying that, I'll be dead in two days!"

"I'm a police officer. I don't spread gossip among junkies."

Pedersen pressed his hands against his bony knees, frantically shaking his head.

"I hit him. I was furious, I wouldn't have done it otherwise. I mean, the stuff was supposed to be in the house, loads of it. He must have taken it all himself! When I realised he was going to sell it, I . . . but I didn't kill him. I suppose he must have OD'd, he wasn't taking decent stuff, and there was something wrong with him. I didn't take the same stuff, because —"

"The same heroin?"

"Yes, but I took —"

"So you admit you were in Gothenburg with Torsen at the time of his death? It would be better for you if you did. We have several witnesses who can testify that you attacked him in a public place in Gothenburg. We have also taken his fingerprints from the house in which the burglary took place, and we know that he was not alone. What you need to tell us now is who was behind this."

"OK, yes. For fuck's sake! I went to Gothenburg with Torsen. It was just a job and we were supposed to look for some fucking . . . ornaments and stuff, I'd only seen a picture of them. Old things and gold. Cash in hand, and I don't know any more because Torsen wouldn't tell me a fucking thing."

"Sure."

"I didn't fucking shoot anyone, I didn't shoot this Samuelsson and I definitely didn't . . ."

His voice cracked and he swallowed before going on. "I didn't kill Torsen. He took a fucking overdose. That's all I can tell you."

In the cafeteria Dragsted introduced Tell to some of his colleagues. Tell was distracted and not in the mood for small talk.

"Could you possibly find me a computer? I'd like to check my messages."

270

Dragsted showed him to a computer and helped him to log in.

Dragsted had treated Enrique Pedersen like a hardened criminal. But his shell had buckled under a small amount of pressure; just below the surface he had seemed shocked and desperate. Scared. As if he had been lured into something on a false premise, only to discover too late that ... what? That shooting Samuelsson and Karpov was part of the deal?

If Samuelsson had indeed been in possession of extremely valuable artefacts, for reasons unknown, this might well have been the motive for the break-in. But the murders? Why not just take the stuff, go home, sell it on the black market and earn a bit of cash? After all, that must have been the idea from the start. Why go to the trouble of tracking down Samuelsson at Karpov's apartment and killing them both? Why take the risk? It was illogical. Tell contemplated the alternatives. Either one line of enquiry had nothing to do with the other or Henrik Samuelsson had some other link to Mads Torsen. Perhaps Torsen had got angry with Henrik and decided to put him out of action. Were they in on the same scam? Were they in a smuggling ring?

Tell switched on his phone and rang Gonzales for an update. He was surprised to find that his colleague was in the same building.

CHAPTER
THIRTY-EIGHT

Stenared

Seja was puzzled, but Christian's message had given her a boost nonetheless. She had gathered quite a lot of information on the illegal trade in artefacts of cultural importance. Whether this might lead to an article was as yet unclear, but if Christian could make use of what she had found out, that was fine by her.

She suspected the question might also have had a subtext: they should let bygones be bygones. He trusted her judgement. When she had written about the infamous Granith case eighteen months earlier, Christian had suggested that she had gone behind his back and exploited him after they'd got together.

With hindsight, the very fact that they had got together surprised her.

I just couldn't resist you, he had said. She was very happy about this temporary weakness — or perhaps you could call it a strength?

Seja went into the garden with her laptop. She had an hour to put together some material before she was due to pick up Hanna and her son at the bus stop. The incident by the lake hadn't been mentioned. After

Hanna's initial refusal to answer the phone, Seja had let the matter rest.

When they eventually spoke, Hanna had been a little short with her. Markus had started chattering in the background about going riding and sleeping over at Seja's, but Hanna suggested that Seja might not have time. Seja made it clear that she had all the time in the world. Her irritation hadn't gone away, but it no longer chafed.

We'll talk about it one day, she thought. I'll explain what I really meant. But their exchange hadn't exactly cured her of her fear of conflict.

The sound of snorting made her look up. She watched the horse rooting around among the tufts of grass and fir cones behind the stable. Even though she knew how much Lukas would enjoy grazing on the local farmer's extensive pasture, she was reluctant to move him. He made her feel safe.

But she really should move him.

"What do you think about that idea, Lukas?" she asked, kicking off her shoes under the garden table and resting her bare feet on the grass. She immediately felt a tickling sensation beneath the arch of her foot: an army of black ants on the march towards her larder.

The cat had spent the winter motionless at the bottom of the bird table, covered in a shower of seed husks, displaying the patience of a saint: one day surely a little bird would fall off. Perhaps it would forget to flap its wings, and it would be in his power. He would launch himself at the table, paw outstretched, causing a flurry of feathers. Very occasionally, he managed to catch one; he would play with the bird for a while before carrying the small dead body into the kitchen like a trophy.

The horse raised his head, registering her movements before going back to his grazing.

"We'll get you some company. When you come back after the summer, we'll get you a friend."

She was talking mostly to herself, trying to ease her guilty conscience after reading an article about the psychological stress horses could suffer if they were kept alone. She had rejected the idea of another horse; she didn't have enough space and she couldn't afford it. It would have to be a different animal, but she suspected that the cat didn't count.

"You can't get a sheep or a goat just so the horse won't be lonely, for God's sake," Christian had expressed his view in disbelief. "Anyway, the horse isn't completely stupid, is he? Surely he can see the difference between himself and a goat?"

"Of course. But it would still be company for him. Or do you think he'll refuse to go near a goat or a sheep?"

She knew he found it difficult to understand how she lived, but she didn't really think the odd medium-sized animal ought to make too much of a difference. Having Lukas meant she was already tied down.

She thought about ringing Christian, if only to check whether he had arrived safely in Copenhagen, but decided against it. Sometimes he seemed determined to misunderstand her. The silly quarrel they had had in Copenhagen had its basis in a significant issue, but that was the way things usually were with Christian. Constant guessing games, until he finally came out with the real problem in a burst of frustration. Christian found it very difficult not to interpret Seja's care and attention as some kind of implied demand on her part. No matter how often she told him that she asked nothing of him, nothing beyond his presence at that particular moment. She had never looked for promises about the future. Except in secret, when she was alone.

And yet she was sure he wanted her as much as she wanted him. They had found a safe harbour with one another, however odd that might sound, and in spite of their many differences.

They had changed the subject from animals quite quickly, but the idea had been born, and still lingered. Seja would have other matters to discuss with the farmer apart from summer grazing; for example whether he might have a sheep he was thinking of getting rid of. But not now. Now she was going to work.

She stretched and moved to a different chair, trying to find a spot where the light didn't create glare on the screen. In the end she gave up and took the laptop inside.

The kitchen looked dark. Pretty untidy too. She blinked away the sun-blindness. Cups filled with dark sediment cluttered the top of the wood-burning stove. She quickly washed them up and hung them up to dry on hooks above the sink.

She started to print out material relating to the Red List, which she had first heard of on her tour of

Glyptoteket with the Assyriologist Alexandr Karpov. She carried on Googling, reading information on Cultural Heritage Without Borders, an organisation formed in the wake of the Yugoslav war, following the systematic destruction of Bosnia-Herzegovina. She printed out an article by a member of the Swedish Museums Association:

Red List Can Save Cultural Heritage

Just imagine: Sweden is invaded by another country. Every single item is plundered from the Nordic Museum, the National Museum and the Historical Museum. Carl Larsson's paintings, Sergel's sculptures and medieval baptismal fonts are sold on the black market and taken out of Sweden. Part of our cultural heritage, our history, our identity and our future is gone for ever. How would that feel?

That was what had happened in Iraq. Over the course of a couple of days in mid-April 2003, archives, libraries and museums in Baghdad had been plundered and burnt. Seja read about the list of missing artefacts which had been compiled and saved the articles on her hard drive. She didn't know whether the information had any relevance to Christian's investigation. As usual, he hadn't told her very much.

CHAPTER
THIRTY-NINE

Gothenburg

Bärneflod would never have driven to Denmark in this heat on his own initiative. Motivating himself to go to work in the mornings was difficult enough. Particularly as his own car didn't have air-con; by the time he got halfway to work, he was stuck to the seat.

A few weeks remained before he could go on holiday. Ulla was due to start her leave in June — although how anyone could need a holiday when they only worked part-time was beyond him. Usually, this generated more work for him — Ulla didn't see her free time as a chance to do all the things she hadn't got round to. Instead she would wander round the garden in her new, gaudy orange sundress, which she insisted on calling a "maxi", making plans. Plans which involved him.

"Bengt, we've been talking about adding a veranda to the garage for years now. Don't you think it would be nice to get it done while you're off work?"

His idea of "nice" was to spend his holiday on a sun lounger on the perfectly acceptable veranda they already had, dressed in his sun hat and Bermuda shorts, with his feet up and a strong drink in his hand.

But there was no point believing that was ever going to happen. To make matters worse, his retirement was approaching at an alarming rate. He could hear Ulla already: "Now you've got all the time in the world to do exactly as you please. The garden's going to look lovely! And I saw a really daring solution for our hallway the other day . . ."

Bärneflod asked himself whether it might be more relaxing to carry on working for a couple more years, rather than retiring. At least in the office he had the chance to do the odd crossword when Tell wasn't in one of his moods.

No, if he was going to sweat his way down to Copenhagen, then it would have to be under orders and counted as overtime. He'd been in this game for a long time now, and he had learnt that you had to take responsibility for your own work-life balance. Otherwise, you were just asking to be exploited. If Bärneflod got the chance, he would have a chat with Gonzales. A kindly word of warning from an older colleague to a youngster.

According to Renée, Gonzales had taken off in a tearing hurry. Running after Tell, no doubt. Bärneflod wasn't happy about that. He didn't like the idea that Gonzales, who was still wet behind the ears, clearly thought he was entitled to the boss's attention. And, above all, Bärneflod didn't like the fact that he had no idea what was happening on the other side of Öresund. The information being shared with the rest of the team was so sparse they could already have arrested the suspect, for all he knew.

278

Bärneflod hadn't called Tell, but he didn't think that was his job. It was up to a team leader to communicate with his staff, and a lack of communication led to a vulnerable team. And as long as he heard *nada* from those hot-headed youngsters down in Copenhagen, he intended to work on the lines of enquiry he thought were worth pursuing. Rebecca Nykvist was one of them. In his opinion, nobody had looked carefully enough at Nykvist and her background. After all, she was the only one who had a decent motive up until now.

He had already found out that Henrik Samuelsson owed quite a lot of people money. The puzzling document found on his computer had indeed been a list of debts. Bärneflod would do the rounds of the people on that list, starting with those who had been most generous. Axel Donner, Henrik's fellow student and close friend, was one of them. Not that Bärneflod really believed that someone had murdered Samuelsson for a few thousand kronor, but it was possible that Donner might know why Henrik needed the money. What Henrik was mixed up in.

Bärneflod was standing on Mariagatan. Stupidly, he hadn't bothered to write down the address. He'd just glanced at it and thought he'd remember it, and now — gone. His memory wasn't what it used to be.

Still, no problem. Donner was an unusual name, and quite a few of the main doors seemed to be open.

Bärneflod couldn't understand why tenants of apartment blocks didn't insist that decent security systems were installed. Bärneflod was very glad he'd fitted a burglar alarm a few years ago; no bastard was going to come into his house and . . .

Ding!

Because several houses on his street had been . . .

Ding!

He had to jump out of the way of two lads cycling along the pavement. They even had the nerve to ring their bells at him. By the time he had prepared a few well-chosen words, they had pulled up outside Götas Bar. Fancied a cold one, no doubt, in the middle of the day.

Slackers.

He was boiling. He had told Ulla that this was a winter jacket, but she had maintained it was chilly in the shade and the wind. And, as usual, he had done as he was told, and dressed too warmly. Since their son had stopped listening to her nagging — and thank God for that, he was an adult after all — Ulla's ludicrous concern was directed at Bärneflod instead.

"Not a breath of wind," he muttered, glaring at the jokers who were just dismounting.

Axel Donner seemed surprised when he opened the door.

"Police."

"Right . . . what's this about?"

"Same as last time. Unless any more of your close friends have been murdered?"

Bärneflod cleared his throat pointedly when Donner didn't answer. "Well, aren't you going to invite me in?"

Donner stepped aside reluctantly, allowing Bärneflod into the small, sparsely furnished one-room apartment.

280

The bookcase was well filled, and there were piles of books on the floor, on a small dining table and on two shabby chairs. The only other items in the room were a mattress and a TV.

"Have you just moved in, or do you have something against furniture?"

"No . . . I can see why you'd think that." Donner gave a slightly embarrassed laugh and took a couple of quick steps over to the window. He watched a tram heading down Älvsborgsgatan towards Jaegerdorff. Bärneflod couldn't for the life of him understand the earlier assessment of this oddball: cooperative and a bit green.

"I've put some stuff in storage while I think about what to do next."

"Aren't you going to finish your education?"

Axel Donner was still half-turned away from him. The lad seemed depressed. Bärneflod looked around. This place really was miserable. In the corner the mattress lay on the floor with no sheets, just a checked blanket.

"Did you have to sell your things?" Bärneflod asked, more kindly this time. He hadn't forgotten what it was like to be a poverty-stricken student.

"I told you, I've put them in storage." There was a certain amount of anger in Donner's voice, but when Bärneflod looked him in the eye there was no sign of irritation. He ran a hand through his hair. "Possessions are overrated. We just consume and throw away; buy and throw away."

Bärneflod rolled his eyes as Axel Donner disappeared into the tiny kitchenette and started clattering around. What an arsehole. Out of curiosity — a virtue in any police officer — he peered into the closet to see if the idiot thought clothes were overrated too. Clearly he didn't. Several shirts and sweaters were arranged neatly on hangers, with trousers folded tidily on the top shelf. On the floor he saw a surprisingly modern laptop case next to an old chest, on top of which several more piles of books were balanced. As Donner was still busy in the kitchenette, Bärneflod glanced at the books. They were in English, a language he couldn't really understand.

"Are you looking for something?"

Bärneflod spun around. "No."

Axel Donner handed him a chipped glass containing something that looked and tasted like elderberry juice.

Bärneflod downed it in one.

"So, how can I help you?"

"Money," said Bärneflod, almost managing to suppress a belch. "I understand Henrik Samuelsson owed you money."

"That's correct."

"Why was that?"

"He needed to borrow cash, he didn't have any. I had some, so I lent it to him."

"Isn't that a bit odd?"

"In what way?"

"Well, Henrik Samuelsson had a well-paid partner and a house. You were alone and . . . not very well off."

Donner shrugged.

282

"I didn't ask him what he needed the money for. He was my friend, he needed my help. I gave it."

"He owed money to a lot of other people."

"I wasn't aware of that."

"Did Henrik have a drug problem?"

"Not as far as I know."

"Come on, you were his best mate. You'd know about something like that."

"In that case, no he didn't. Who says?"

"Come again?"

"Who says I was his best mate?"

"One thing I'm wondering, Axel . . . How long had you actually known Henrik? Did you get to know each other on the course, or before?"

"On the course."

"In the archaeology department?"

"The Department of Archaeology and Ancient Civilisations."

"I couldn't give a toss about its proper name."

"Fair enough."

"You're lying. But why?"

"I'm not lying, I just told you . . . the proper name. But OK, if you're asking where we met for the first time, it was . . ." He seemed to be thinking back. "A few years ago now. We were both doing a course in RE. No, hang on. We'd seen each other at Nefertiti."

"And what the fuck is that?"

"It's a jazz club."

"And you got acquainted?"

"Yes, you could say that."

"Started hanging out?"

Donner shook his head firmly. "No. We didn't hang out. But we ended up choosing some of the same modules, there was ... RE, social anthropology and —"

"When did you become friends?"

"When we started archaeology, I suppose."

"Isn't that a bit odd? That you kept choosing the same courses just by chance but still you didn't talk to each other?"

"That's not what I said. I said we didn't hang out together."

Bärneflod stared unashamedly at Axel Donner, who squirmed.

"What are you looking at?"

"You." He changed tack. "You're from the country, aren't you? From somewhere up north?"

"Is this an interrogation? If so, I have the right to remain silent."

Bärneflod let out a loud laugh.

"You're a funny bugger, make no mistake. I ask you questions about your dead friend, and you answer nice as pie. And then I start making small talk, and *that's* when you kick off!"

"I don't see why I have to talk to you about where I come from."

Bärneflod straightened up.

"Indeed you don't. You don't have to say a single bloody word to me. For the time being. But you are not leaving this place, not until I say: Now you can go. Until then, you are to be on hand, in case I or one of my colleagues wishes to bring you in for a more formal interview. And if that happens, my friend, you will have to answer all our questions."

Was the little bastard smirking? Yes, he was. He wasn't a fan of the police, Bärneflod had clocked that straightaway.

"Thanks for the drink."

CHAPTER
FORTY

Copenhagen

Gonzales was on his way back through the city after a bewilderingly short meeting with his boss. Tell's mood, upbeat and frazzled in equal measure, had proved infectious and Gonzales was now finding it extremely difficult to manoeuvre his car through the busy city centre streets.

The tip-off about Karpov's assistants had had the expected effect on Tell: he wanted to act on that lead immediately. He had given Gonzales a brief summary of his progress so far in the interview with Enrique Pedersen.

"He must have made contact with Mads Torsen through his older sister. She's well known to the police — she's been on the game for years. The question is, should we ask the police here to trace those links and any possible intermediaries so that we can get a full picture? That would leave us free to concentrate on Iversen and Sørbækk."

The colour in Tell's cheeks had risen with the heat and excitement. "We need to check out all known associates of Mads Torsen."

Gonzales agreed. "Karpov wanted to see you in person. I presume he wanted to explain why his assistants broke into Samuelsson's house."

"You mean, why they seem to have hired Torsen and Pedersen to break in, you mean?"

"Alexandr just said that his assistants knew that Samuelsson had valuable stolen goods at home."

Tell threw his arms wide. "I think we have to consider all the possibilities. Enrique Pedersen has confessed to the break-in, and said they were looking for specific objects, to order. He said he didn't know who they were working for, and that everything had gone through Torsen. I didn't have time to push him on this but, according to Karpov, Iversen and Sørbækk are most likely the masterminds."

"That's what I understood, but Karpov was fairly cryptic."

"And he's in London?"

Gonzales looked at his watch. "He's actually due back at Glyptoteket this afternoon. Any moment now, in fact."

"The alternative is to get Pedersen to confess to the murders. If he's guilty, that is. Or see if he can point us in the direction of the murderer," said Tell. "They were definitely in the house on Kungsladugåardsgatan; we've got proof."

"But as far as we know they weren't in the apartment on Linnégatan."

"No."

After a brief discussion they decided that Gonzales should drive over to Glyptoteket to catch up with Karpov's assistants.

The risk was that Iversen and Sørbækk might suspect something was wrong and do a runner, or jeopardise the investigation in some other way.

"Don't give much away at first, just talk to them about their professional relationship with Karpov," Tell decided. "You'll be on your own, after all. I'll talk to Dragsted about bringing them in for questioning later. That way we'll save time. I'll go back and talk to Pedersen again. Whoever finishes first joins the other. We'll keep in touch by phone."

Gonzales had nodded, his facial muscles twitching and a hurricane brewing in his stomach. He'd hit the big time. Just him and Tell in a critical situation. They would solve the case and return to Gothenburg triumphant. Gonzales was delighted with his decision to drive down to Copenhagen; it had thrown him right into the middle of things, side by side with Tell.

He could feel himself blushing at his own hubris. He was glad Tell couldn't read his mind.

There was no way of parking legally near Glyptoteket. Gonzales left his car on the pavement and hoped the Swedish police badge on his windscreen would act as a permit.

Gonzales didn't know whether Karpov's assistants would be prepared to talk to him. In fact, he had absolutely no idea how he was going to conduct the conversation.

Play it cool, Tell had said. Just check out the lie of the land. Did he mean Gonzales shouldn't let them know that the police were on their trail? But how the hell was he supposed to ask them about their involvement in this antiques business without giving the game away? It was impossible, surely.

288

The receptionist was unable to help him locate either Iversen or Sørbækk. However, one of the guards thought he knew where they worked, and fifteen minutes later Gonzales found himself outside the door of an underground room, in a wing of the museum closed to the public.

"Michael Gonzales, Gothenburg police. I'd like to ask you a few questions with regard to a case involving valuable stolen goods."

He thought it was a relatively innocuous introduction.

Knud Iversen was older than Gonzales had expected — perhaps the title "assistant" had misled him — and seemed to hesitate before stepping back to let Gonzales in. He was wearing black jeans and a short-sleeved pale-blue shirt. His face was large and square with a prominent hook nose and deep-set eyes; he was tanned, with unevenly coloured, acne-scarred skin.

The storeroom wasn't very big, and didn't look the way Gonzales had imagined. Broad shelves lined three of the walls from floor to ceiling and contained labelled cardboard boxes.

Iversen closed a drawer in the bank of filing cabinets propped against the other wall, as if he wanted to hide its contents from Gonzales. Then he stood motionless.

"Sit down." Gonzales pointed to a chair. "I believe you have a colleague, Dorte Sørbækk?"

"She's off sick today."

"OK."

Gonzales thought for a moment.

"We're investigating an incident which took place in Gothenburg on May 7th. I can't go into detail, but a number of clues lead to Glyptoteket and . . . other places in Copenhagen. We've been in touch with the Danish police."

"May 7th?"

At that moment they heard footsteps in the corridor. With a barely perceptible shift in his posture, Knud Iversen braced himself.

There was a hesitant knock at the door. Gonzales went to open it, but stopped and spun around when the man behind him shouted, "No! Wait!"

It was over in seconds. Gonzales had no time to react before Iversen was on his feet. The door opened and Iversen shoved past Karpov, who lost his balance and fell backwards in the confusion.

"What the . . ."

Gonzales came to his senses and made an impressive leap over the professor. Something crunched beneath his right shoe.

"Stop, you bastard!"

He was halfway up the stairs when a door slammed shut in front of him. It was locked.

"Open this fucking door! Give me . . ."

Karpov was whimpering; he groped for his glasses and found them broken by his side just as Gonzales snatched the pass hanging on a cord around his neck. When the door leading to the upper level opened, after long seconds of fiddling, the staircase was deserted.

"Fuck!"

Gonzales took the stairs up to the next door in a couple of long strides. He found himself in one of the exhibition halls. Having pushed a bewildered family to one side, he reached the foyer.

"Iversen!"

Gonzales stood panting on the steps in front of Dante Alighieri's statue, resting his hands on his knees.

If Gonzales had intended not to give the game away, he had failed miserably. But he had extracted a confession of sorts in less than five minutes; you could hardly interpret Iversen's behaviour in any other way.

Gonzales gradually became aware of the distant screams from the Tivoli theme park as the roller coaster rose and fell. He grabbed his mobile and rang Tell.

CHAPTER
FORTY-ONE

Copenhagen

Dorte Sørbækk didn't have time to have a cigarette, but if there was one thing she had learnt the hard way over the years, it was to take things slowly. Much better to compose herself and decide on her next move.

She sat by the window and came to the conclusion that there was no way out for her. She had walked into a trap, but she wasn't going to stand back and wait for the consequences.

Deep breaths.

Iversen's apartment had only two windows. One was in the room which looked onto Lundtoftegade, where people strolled along chatting, never thinking that someone could be sitting on the ground floor, by a window that was barely ajar, listening to what they said. If you sat there you were in direct contact with the outside world, with the sun-dappled pavements and the soles of people's shoes. Not much else was visible from where she sat, apart from tree trunks. Not like higher up in the building, where light flowed in freely and dark-green leaves muffled the noise of the traffic. And yet the room felt fresh. She usually sat in this alcove when she was feeling upbeat, seeking inspiration from other people's lives.

When she was feeling low she would sit in the kitchen, gazing out over the grubby courtyard, a patch of asphalt which the sun never reached. The narrow flowerbeds beside the frame for beating rugs had yielded nothing for years. Dead twigs protruded from the solid earth. Only the rats were alive. Rats so bold they hardly bothered to run away if you stepped over them. She found their slanting eyes so penetrating. Calculating, somehow; she was convinced that rats were intelligent, that they had been forced to develop intelligence to survive side by side with man. And the evil expression in their eyes was almost human.

It was cold, as always. The cold was what she hated most about Knud's apartment. Regardless of the temperature outside, the stairwell was cold, as were the tiny rooms. In the past they had never been able to afford wood for the stove, which was still the only source of heat; instead they had collected fallen branches in the park, loading them onto Knud's old Christiana bicycle. When developers renovated and rebuilt large parts of the area — there weren't many apartments like this one left now — she and Knud would clamber over barriers and take the waste timber, tumbling back down onto the pavements with their arms full of wood. Otherwise the gas hob was the best way of warming up red, frozen hands; they would gather round its straggling flame until their energy returned.

She clasped her hands tightly. Her mobile battery was low, and her charger was at home. Knud would soon be boarding the plane to Bangkok, Bastard. He'd booked his ticket in advance, just in case everything went wrong. There was no ticket for her. For the past week he had been tetchy and evasive — he would barely respond when she spoke. He had carried himself with a vague air of regret, which had become more and more obvious in his body language. Even though she didn't know the reason behind it, she was almost certain. He had blown her out.

If only she had the courage to ring Alexandr! To hear his voice telling her that he forgave her for this too.

She was ashamed; that was the only reason she had stayed away from work.

Dorte rested her head against the window frame. It was a double betrayal. Her eyes burnt: it was the only time Alexandr had come to *them* to ask for help. Dorte had been so happy that he trusted them — so often he was the one helping them, when the baggage of their pasts weighed them down and reason flew out of the window. Alexandr always allowed their outbursts to pass like a patient uncle, his dignity and wisdom eventually penetrating their fucked-up minds.

As she'd expected, Ann-Marie was the root of his trouble. It was clear that Alexandr still hadn't got over the divorce. That he still nurtured a hope that they might get back together. Dorte thought Alexandr would walk over coals for the sake of his ex-wife.

Knud had maintained that it was Alexandr who had first hinted at the break-in even though Dorte knew that wasn't true. Knud said the plan was simple: steal the immensely valuable artefacts Henrik Samuelsson was using to threaten and blackmail Ann-Marie. He insisted that it was a way of repaying the debt of gratitude they owed Alexandr. To take a risk and *defend* Ann-Marie would be the ultimate proof of loyalty.

As if Dorte were an idiot, unaware of the effect the smell of money had on Knud. He suddenly reverted to the man he used to be, his eyes revealing the evasiveness of old. There was a constant tension in his movements, the way he flexed his fists as he talked. It was a long time since she had seen him like this. He babbled as his enthusiasm grew: the plan was so clever, so simple! There would be no way of tracing them. And Alexandr need never even know.

He hired Mads Torsen, a face from the past. It would be a piece of cake for a man like him. Meanwhile, Knud and Dorte would make sure they had an alibi. It was risk-free and hardly even immoral: the artefacts were already stolen goods, after all. But Mads Torsen was crazy — the name sent shivers down Dorte's spine. Knud maintained Torsen was OK, that he was a man of his word.

But she'd been right. She realised that as soon as he got in touch and claimed they hadn't found anything in the house, well, just one little clay figure, which was crap — there were supposed to be between twenty-five and thirty figures, and gold.

Dorte remembered the look on Alexandr's face after Ann-Marie told him how desperate she was. Dorte had never seen him so agitated; Alexandr was their rock, calm and generous, while she and Knud were like children in adults' bodies, always in need of forgiveness.

She was weeping now because she had thrown away the only decent job she had ever had, and because she had betrayed a friend. Alexandr had taught her the job. He had ignored her background and given her more responsibility than she thought she deserved. Her post as Alexandr's assistant had been part of her rehab, a stepping stone to the world of work. She hadn't really believed that it would lead to a paid job, but if she had refused it she would have lost her benefits.

Dorte couldn't remember a specific moment when she had decided to stay and give it a go. She discovered to her surprise that she had a talent for planning and structure, unlike her employer. They joked that she was Alexandr Karpov's PA. They bonded, just like in some soppy film. At first they kept their distance. Dorte, the self-destructive, overgrown teenager whom everyone else dismissed as hopeless. Dressed in black, taciturn and sullen. Alexandr, the good, uncomplicated man. The man who sensed her ability, buried under layers of make-up and swearing, and didn't give up on it.

He expected her to deal with things right from the start, difficult things. Everyone else she had encountered had assumed she wouldn't be able to perform even the simplest tasks. She had been born into that frame of mind, after all, and she could play the role in her sleep.

When Alexandr's remit at the museum was extended, Dorte was given a permanent post. For the first time in her life she had a job, a salary she could live on. And when another post for an assistant came up, she'd suggested Knud. They had split up, but were still friends. He was clean back then, driven. He immediately started to learn more about the artefacts they handled. No, Knud wasn't stupid; Dorte would never have fallen for him if he had been. He was just easily influenced. Both of them were.

A tap was turned somewhere in the building and water surged through the pipes. If she took a taxi, would she get to the airport before the flight took off? She didn't have a ticket. What would she say to Knud if she found him? She didn't know. The words would probably drown in the thickness in her throat, and that would be his last image of her before he walked up the narrow steps to the plane: Dorte, a weeping mess.

She didn't want that.

There was also a risk that the police might be waiting for him at the airport, that they might have put out a call for him. It was just a matter of time. She wasn't registered at her home address, but it wouldn't take them long to find it, and then they'd be on her doorstep.

She had spent almost fifteen minutes smoking and gazing out of the window, but now she stubbed her cigarette out against the glass. It left a black mark surrounded by a misty patch of ash. The bag she had packed was in the hallway. She had to get going.

Alexandr couldn't help her any more, he would never be able to help her again. She must push the memories of the person she had become to one side, shoulder the old self-loathing like a familiar, well-fitting suit — as if it had been made for her. And she must keep moving. She slipped her bag over her shoulder and gritted her teeth. Yes, she would ring Knud. One last chat, for old times' sake. So he would know he hadn't broken her. Then she would set off.

CHAPTER
FORTY-TWO

Copenhagen

Gonzales had no intention of trying to find his way through a city which had begun to throb with evening crowds, aided only by a satnav he couldn't even understand. Not when his heart was thumping so hard against his chest. He hurled himself into a taxi: Lundtoftegade. It was in Nørrebro, on the other side of the canal, at the far end of the city centre.

"Step on it!" he said to the driver, the endorphins shooting through his blood like flashes of lightning. He forgot how nervous he was and, just for a while, he allowed himself to enjoy the moment, the heat, the excitement. To his left a local produce market slipped by, the stall-holders packing up for the evening, and a shabby archway leading into a park. Then a churchyard surrounded by an old, high wall, as if the people of Copenhagen were afraid of losing their dead. Gonzales recognised the ruins of the youth centre from a TV report.

He wondered whether Tell would come alone or whether he would bring back-up. Had Tell thought to bring his gun when he came down to interview Pedersen? Probably not. Gonzales was wearing his; he wasn't used to the feeling, it chafed against the side of his chest. Was he even allowed to carry his service weapon abroad? His mind was blank as the taxi pulled into a parking space twenty or so metres from Iversen's address.

Gonzales got out. There was no sign of Tell's car, nor a police car. But he had heard Tell barking out that order after Iversen did a runner: send a car there straightaway in case he's stupid enough to go home, and another to Dorte Sørbækk's address. They were both wanted, with immediate effect.

An overweight man pushed a trolley out of a grocer's on the other side of the street. Gonzales experienced a creeping sense of anti-climax when a black BMW screeched to a halt right in front of him. In the passenger seat next to Tell sat a tall, middle-aged man whom Gonzales assumed was their contact in Copenhagen CID.

"Evening." A quick handshake and then they ran towards number ten. Since Iversen's address was on the ground floor, Dragsted crouched down as he passed the window.

"Shit. It's locked."

They waited for two or three long minutes, then an elderly lady came out and they were in. They moved silently to the door marked Iversen and listened carefully. There was a thud.

"He's in there," Tell mouthed. "Gonzales, go outside. Watch the window, I don't want him getting out that way."

Gonzales nodded. "This might be a stupid question," he whispered, "but I'm just wondering whether —"

"Ssh!" Tell placed his ear against the door, rigid with tension. They heard footsteps inside, and an agitated voice. A woman's voice.

"Of course they're bloody well going to arrest me . . . That's not what this is about . . . Go outside . . . Wait there. You stupid bastard . . . Have a nice day."

She was standing in the hallway, just inside the door.

"I've got to hurry. I'm going now."

Ten seconds later, Dorte Søbækk walked straight into the arms of Tell and Dragsted. She'd confessed before they had even left the building.

CHAPTER
FORTY-THREE

Copenhagen

At Inspector Dragsted's station, Tell was taking in Dorte Sørbækk's bewildered expression.

"You work for Alexandr Karpov. I'm sure it hasn't escaped your attention that his ex-wife has been murdered, along with her boyfriend. Did you and Knud Iversen initially believe the artefacts were in her apartment? Or did Mads Torsen take it upon himself to kill them?"

Sørbækk's face was ghostly white. She shook her head slowly, over and over again, trying to get rid of what she had just heard.

"I haven't spoken to Alexandr about . . . he didn't say . . . He hasn't been in work and neither have I. I didn't . . . I didn't know they were dead."

Her head drooped between her shoulders and her body jerked. At first Tell thought she was crying, which she probably was, until the convulsions became more and more violent. Only when Dorte Sørbækk threw back her head, revealing a thin white foam at the corners of her mouth, did Tell move behind her, pulling her down onto the floor. She was wearing a tag on a chain under her sweater.

"She's having an epileptic fit," he shouted to Dragsted.

An hour later, Sørbækk was lying on a bed in another, smaller room. She had refused to let Dragsted call a doctor and had slept for fifty minutes.

They had just heard that Knud Iversen had been picked up at the airport, checking in for a flight to Bangkok, when Sørbækk asked to see Tell.

She was sitting up in bed with her back against the wall, her face pale and streaked with mascara, her eyes red from weeping.

"Thank you for coming back," she said as he closed the door behind him. "Are you going to talk to Alexandr now?"

"I will as soon as you and I are done here. You know you have the right to legal representation?"

"Yes. I just want to say that I haven't killed anyone. I didn't hire anyone to murder Henrik Samuelsson and Ann-Marie Karpov. I would never do such a thing. Please tell Alexandr that, if I'm not allowed to speak to him myself. Knud was planning to sell on the artefacts. But we're not murderers. You have to believe that."

"But there's one thing you can explain to me."

Dorte Sørbækk's fit felt like an eternity ago. Tell had sent for Karpov, who had just arrived at the police station. The interview with the professor would probably be Tell's last job before he handed over to the Copenhagen police.

"You said earlier that Alexandr came to you. That he was desperate. So was it Alexandr who wanted you to break into Henrik Samuelsson's house?"

"No." She pressed the palm of her hand against her forehead. "He was tired and fragile. Unhappy, stressed. He was worried about Ann-Marie; she had come to him in confidence and told him about that boyfriend of hers. The thing is . . . her boyfriend wanted to get rich by selling the stolen goods, and he was trying to drag Ann-Marie into it. She was panicking about her career, and about his behaviour too. He'd been threatening her — apparently he was determined to go public with their relationship, and . . . Well, Alexandr still loved her. He couldn't stand the thought of anything bad happening to her. But he would never have asked us to break the law."

"One more question." Tell could smell the cigarette smoke on her clothes. "Do you think Knud Iversen is capable of murder?"

Sørbækk opened her mouth but no sound came out. Eventually she said, "I don't think so. I don't like him, but I don't think he would ever kill anyone. And why would he murder those two people? Knud would never hurt Alexandr on purpose. And he was very careful to make sure he had an alibi for the night Torsen broke into the house."

"Yes, but that wasn't the same —"

". . . that was the whole point."

Tell contemplated the woman on the bed. It was going to take a lot more work before Sørbækk's testimony could be confirmed, and Iversen and

Sørbækk eliminated from the murder inquiry. But another interview with Pedersen, and one with Iversen, would hopefully verify parts of Dorte's story.

Tell was convinced she had told him the truth. Perhaps not about everything, but about the murders on Linnégatan. Suddenly his job seemed pointless, like trying to swim in a strong undertow.

Because as far as the murders were concerned, they were back to square one.

CHAPTER
FORTY-FOUR

Gothenburg

Karlberg was sitting in the police station yard, scratching at the paving stones with a stick next to a group of admin staff who were chatting and smoking away.

Beckman couldn't help cursing the fact that Karlberg just happened to be out here. She had taken this roundabout route from the toilets because she wanted to be alone. She didn't have the energy to talk.

But he was absorbed by the paving stones, and didn't appear to have noticed her. Beckman had her bag slung over her shoulder, burning against her hip, as if the contents were shining through for all to see. She was afraid that if Karlberg looked up he would immediately know what she had been up to in the toilets. And what the result had been.

She hadn't dared to do it at home. For some bizarre reason, she had thought it would be more difficult to get a negative — or in this case positive — result when she was alone. She had been wrong, of course. And she hadn't realised quite how hard it would be to see her colleagues behaving as though nothing had happened. Bärneflod in his office, absorbed in the paper, Karlberg sitting out here . . .

So it was official: she was pregnant. How many years had she worked as a member of the team? She couldn't remember off hand, but she knew that she and Göran had been in the process of breaking up for the past five or six years. She hadn't brought her private life into work — quite the opposite, in fact. Beckman had always drawn a veil over her chaotic home life. And yet still. People *knew*. People always realised more than you thought; they knew about the frequent trial separations, the rows, the way their children had been buffeted from hope to despair and back again. It was as though they could smell the shameful, shameful weakness that meant she always went back to Göran and his bloody house, because she just didn't have the courage to take that last step and start again from scratch.

But now she had done it. One day the strength had simply been there. She packed her things and the children's, answered an ad for a sub-let and hired a van. Göran helped to carry the boxes, his expression grim.

He stroked her cheek before she drove off to return the van. The sensation was like fingernails scraping down a blackboard, but she gritted her teeth.

Afterwards, she was surprised by the positive reaction of her friends. And it quickly became clear to Beckman that her colleagues had opinions on the matter too. Renée had given her a big hug when she had mentioned in passing that she was looking for somewhere permanent to live with her children.

"I'm so pleased, Karin," she had said, almost in tears. "Everything's going to be all right."

This enthusiasm bothered her, chipping away at her self-esteem. Perhaps it was because people assumed she was the victim. She wasn't a victim, not in relation to Göran nor in any other area of her life.

But, in spite of everything, she understood why people stayed in destructive relationships. Her marriage had been extremely destructive, even if Göran had never raised a hand to her, and the shame she felt was the same as that of a woman who has suffered physical abuse. She was ashamed at having settled for less, for not believing, deep down, that she was worth more than what she had ended up with.

But then again, there was that one evening. She and the children had driven over to Fiskebäck after nursery to fetch a toy which Sigrid insisted she absolutely must have, and Göran made spaghetti bolognese. The kids sat down to watch *Bolibompa* on TV and Göran opened a bottle of red — surely she could have one glass, even if she was driving. They talked as they hadn't talked for such a long time.

The kids were delighted that things were back to normal again, and after a few glasses of wine it was just like the old days for Beckman too. The way it had been long ago, before everything became tainted and toxic.

In the morning she was woken by the sound of Göran's heavy breathing. She was devastated.

So much for her newly won independence, her determination to put the turmoil behind her and think clearly for a change.

308

The divorce had just gone through; she was free, and now this. She had sensed it for a while. The nausea. The tiredness, the aching breasts, the cramp in her calves, the dizziness. And yet she had put off doing a test. And, of course, the longer she left it, the more difficult it would be to do anything about the problem. On a rational level, she couldn't keep this child. How would that work? She could only just cope as it was. Always late, always inadequate. Not to mention the thought of going through pregnancy again, alone, with two kids to look after. Hauling herself up three flights of stairs to their rented apartment with heavy bags of groceries and a huge belly. She was too old, over forty; the idea of waddling around work, her belly leading the way, almost made her blush.

"Beckman." Karlberg shaded his eyes with his hand. "Catching a few rays?"

"Yes."

"How are things?"

The secretaries gathered up their cigarette packets and lighters and went back inside.

"OK. I didn't notice you before. You don't smoke, do you?"

"No," Karlberg said in a surprised tone of voice, as if his smoking habits were common knowledge. "I just needed a bit of . . . Well, you know. A change of scene. A chance to gather my thoughts."

Beckman couldn't stay annoyed with Karlberg for long.

"I'm glad I'm not the only one with things on my mind."

Karlberg smiled and crossed his chino-clad legs. "No, you're definitely not. I went on a totally disastrous date the other day . . . It was . . . Well, it was a complete disaster, that's the only way to describe it."

Beckman couldn't help laughing; her laughter relieved the tension and Karlberg soon joined in.

"That does sound bad. What happened? Did you fall out over who should pay the bill?"

"It was one of those blind dates."

"A what?"

"A blind date. You know. On the Internet you can . . . Oh, fuck. I don't know why I'm telling you this."

Beckman pushed her sunglasses up onto her forehead. "No, come on. Sorry I laughed, it's just that I didn't even realise you were looking."

He shrugged. "Not seriously. But maybe we're always looking. One way or another."

"So tell me, what happened?"

Karlberg turned his head away, embarrassed. "She met a guy she knew at the restaurant."

"And?"

"She went home with him. After she'd left me waiting for over an hour."

He laughed again, harder this time. "Talk about a disaster."

"What a bitch."

He shrugged again. "Oh, I guess that's just how it is, but I'm not used to the meat market these days, or whatever you call it. And I'm not exactly a catch, or so it would seem."

310

Beckman gave Karlberg's wrist a quick squeeze. "That's rubbish, Andreas. You just happened to come across a rotten egg; they're always out there. Come on, let's get back to work."

As they stood up to go back inside, Tell rang on his way back from Copenhagen with the news that Karpov's assistants had been taken into custody. Sørbækk had admitted that she and Iversen had hired Torsen, who had conned them. He had contacted them after the break-in and insisted that he had found only one small clay statuette, in spite of the fact that there were supposed to be several, along with a quantity of gold jewellery.

As Beckman listened, she stopped dead. A vague idea formed at the back of her mind. She ended the call and ignored Karlberg's impatient questions, perching on the edge of the table and pressing her fingers to her temples. The sculpture Henrik had photographed next to the necklace, which they assumed he had planned to show to dealers, was clearly the only item the burglars had found. They had turned the entire house upside down. As soon as she and Tell had seen the devastation, Beckman had become convinced that the burglars had not found everything they were looking for. They had smashed open a stud wall upstairs. This wasn't a slapdash job. And she had searched the place herself after the formal police search, but had been unable to find a single nook or cranny that had been left untouched. But wait . . .

In a series of rapid images she saw a scene from that afternoon in her mind's eye. Rebecca Nykvist, spinning

311

around to face her on the chair at her desk in the study. The red hair, covering her face and the telephone receiver. The formal, professional tone of voice. The boiler: it hadn't been half as much trouble to instal as getting rid of it appeared to be.

She didn't know if the Danish junkies — or, for that matter, the crime scene investigation team — had somehow missed the boiler. She didn't know why they would have missed it. But suddenly she was certain: if anything was still hidden inside Rebecca Nykvist's house, then it was inside the boiler, which had been drained.

Henrik had found the perfect hiding place.

Forty-five minutes later, Beckman and Karlberg arrived at the house on Kungsladugårdsgatan. A van belonging to a company they had found on the Internet was parked on the cycle track. The engineers had already got out. Rebecca's voice could be heard all the way out on the street.

"I have absolutely no intention of letting strangers into my house without a search warrant! I couldn't give a toss if you're not the police, if you're doing a job at the request of the police, of if God the father himself sent you. I —"

"Rebecca!"

Beckman pushed her way past two confused young men dressed in overalls.

"Rebecca, you're absolutely right in principle, but getting a formal warrant will take time. You're welcome to ring my boss if you want to verify this."

Rebecca didn't look happy, and muttered something about a lawyer, but eventually gave in. She waved impatiently, as if to say that if they were going to do the job, then they might as well get on with it. She walked into the house cursing to herself.

Beckman nodded to the two men. One of them reversed the van up onto the lawn and they started to unload their tools. She wondered whether to go after Rebecca, or to oversee the opening up of the boiler. Hesitantly, she made her way down the cellar steps and found the narrow boiler room, cluttered along one side with cardboard boxes and a rail of winter clothes. In the corner was a kind of alcove, hidden from view by black plastic; she couldn't help being curious. As she pulled the plastic aside, she discovered what looked like an amateur darkroom, although there was also a stereo with headphones and loudspeakers.

Karlberg looked distinctly out of place in the boiler room.

The workmen were now wearing their heavy protective visors pushed up onto their foreheads, still unsure of their role but ready to follow orders.

"OK, so what exactly do you want us to do here?"

Karlberg attempted to look as if he knew what he was talking about. "Search it, check . . . er, anywhere that something could be hidden. Dismantle it if necessary."

"That's a hell of a job, mate."

"Drill it open then."

"What? The actual tank?"

"Yes, why not?"

The workman, who Beckman noticed was wearing black nail varnish, nodded and pulled the visor down over his eyes. He waved to them to leave the room, then suddenly stopped in mid-movement.

"Hang on," he said, turning back to Karlberg. "It's bolted at the top. If it's empty, someone might have sunk whatever it is you're looking for."

"As I said, check out every possibility."

"But what about the actual boiler?"

"What do you mean?"

"Well, if you're looking for something hidden, why don't you check inside the boiler first? Just inside the little door."

Karlberg desperately wanted to say that he wasn't completely stupid, it was just that he had a different system at home. "And where might that be?"

The man pushed up his visor and tapped on two small doors to the right of the enormous tank. "Here. And here."

"Do you think you can get them open today?"

He snorted. "They open like this."

Only now did Karlberg notice that the doors had handles. The top one opened creakily, revealing a pile of ash which might, at a pinch, be concealing something shapeless, but it seemed unlikely. Karlberg moved forward quickly; the workman naturally couldn't help peering inside.

"Thank you, we'll take it from here."

Beckman accompanied the engineers out to their van. When she got back to the darkness of the cellar a couple of minutes later, she saw that Karlberg was holding a soot-blackened bag.

"Is this what we were looking for?"

Beckman gulped. A dirty bag made of colourful fabric with a zip along the top; it didn't look like anything special. It looked like a gym bag. She took it, trying to keep her excitement under control. It was surprisingly heavy.

She and Karlberg slowly made their way up the cellar steps and out onto the lawn. There was something solemn about the occasion. She opened the bag and peered into it. She immediately recognised the necklace from Samuelsson's photograph. They breathed in the smell of old sand, metal and dust.

CHAPTER
FORTY-FIVE

Stenared

Seja dismissed the idea of riding into the village and tying Lukas up outside the library while she did her shopping. She had to keep her bohemian tendencies in check, otherwise she would become the village eccentric. Instead she decided to walk. She put on her well-worn trainers, shrugged her leather rucksack onto her back and ambled slowly down the hill. The gravelled section was dusty while the tarmac gave slightly beneath her feet, smelling of liquorice and petrol.

As always when she walked around the area, she became aware of the disparity between the world high up towards the forest and the pastel-coloured houses on the hill leading down to the main road. Even nature seemed to have been tamed here, with cypresses forming perfect ovals against the sky. Behind the perfectly clipped hedges surrounding a mint-green bungalow, a little girl in an orange swimsuit was jumping from a trampoline into an inflatable paddling pool. She popped up gasping for breath and waved.

Seja waved back and quickened her pace until she reached level ground and the bend by the farmer's house. She stopped at the side of the road and gazed out over the summer pasture. Beyond the cycle track, which had once been a railway line, the boxy former station building and the road to Gothenburg, the fields had been cut. The horses spent most of their time in the valleys formed by the river Lärje, which couldn't be seen from the road.

She spent a while trying to spot Lukas, but had to give up. She was disappointed. She'd only just moved him to the summer grazing, and it already felt desolate and empty up at the house.

The cycle track was lined with lupins and cow parsley, and later it would be possible to pick crab apples and sour cherries. Seja liked the overgrown hedgerows. Nobody bothered to look after the plants, nobody tried to tame them. She noticed that the surface of the track had changed from the muddy slop of early spring to a hardened moonscape.

Walking helped. She tried clearing her mind of trapped, unwelcome thoughts as she gazed down at her scruffy shoes.

It took so little for old doubts to surface once more. How could she imagine it would be possible to live in an old summer cottage without a shower and toilet? Surely it would be better to take the sensible option and buy the Melkerssons' house — but then how would she afford it? Down in the Glade she could live ridiculously cheaply and, at the moment, she did just enough shifts at the care home to make ends meet. She would need to rethink her lifestyle completely if she did accept their offer.

In her better moments, she liked to think that she had dealt with her wobbly self-confidence by making a decision about the way she wanted to live her life and seeing it through. By finding her place in the world.

And now there was Christian, on top of everything else. It was *his* incomprehensible mood swings that were slowly eroding the sense of security she had previously felt, awakening a fear that she never acknowledged because it would put further pressure on his vulnerabilities. And what were those vulnerabilities, a sharp little voice inside her wanted to know: was he afraid of being trapped in a cloying, cosy twosome, afraid of losing his freedom? Or was it the idea of living his life with her that scared him? They had agreed that their differences didn't matter — but what if they suddenly did?

She wasn't honest, that was one thing. She made a big point of treating his fears with equanimity, of being the stronger partner; she was the epitome of independence out there in her cottage in the forest, with her horse and her cat and her studies and her freelance work and her reluctance to accept help. She knew that. It was quite deliberate. It was a way of approaching the person she wanted to be. The person she thought she ought to be. A strategy for holding onto Christian — keeping him at arm's length in order to keep him close, adapting to his intimacy problems.

Suddenly she was furious. She had to be strong where he was weak; it was a role she had adopted because it seemed to be the only dynamic he could cope with. And yet her own vulnerability was ignored.

318

But Christian didn't know the extent to which his doubts affected her. When they first met, Seja had been living in the shadow of a recent break-up. She had been tied to a house in need of renovation, on an income consisting only of a student loan. On her way out of a period of debilitating confusion, she had chosen to turn things around completely. It was the only way to survive. Make the Glade a symbol of her own innate strength.

Christian had met a woman who was slowly building a life around herself; a self-sufficient, capable individual who attracted him. By falling in love with the woman she wanted to be, he had drawn out more of that integrity and independence. Now she was afraid that she was as emotionally dependent on Christian as she had been on Martin. That, if he left her, she would fall straight back down into the black hole she had only recently crawled out of. Relationships were strange.

But still, you know you're not going to die, she mumbled to herself as she walked past the school playground.

A group of people were standing outside the local museum chatting animatedly about things Seja couldn't quite hear. She walked past quickly, wishing she was back in the isolation of her garden. She didn't like crowds. When the 520 bus pulled into the stop outside the pre-school, she took a detour. Lyckåsvägen ran along the low stone walls of the community centre.

As long as the dependence wasn't practical or financial, she wasn't particularly disturbed by the idea of being dependent on another person — in theory, at

319

least. In fact, emotional dependence had to be the only real form of love. It was just so bloody risky.

This isn't good for me; she realised. It isn't good for me to be in a relationship with a man who isn't sure what he wants, whether he wants me or not. That's not what I need. This relationship is not what I need.

Seja nodded to the librarian. The place was empty apart from her.

"I'm looking for information on the Iraq war."

"Did you have anything more specific in mind?"

He turned the screen so that she could see the innumerable hits.

"Well . . ." She hesitated. "It's partly to do with thefts from museums. And I was thinking of writing something about what the country looks like today, maybe something to do with ethnic conflict. Or criminality in the post-war era. I could . . ."

The question made her think. What did she actually want to write about? Her article about the illegal trade in cultural treasures wasn't even half finished. She thought about what she had read so far. "Perhaps I could write something about the effect on civilians, especially on women?"

The librarian glanced at Seja before turning his attention back to the screen. "We do have a number of articles . . . quite a lot has been written about the political prelude to the war, if that's any use?"

He disappeared behind the shelves.

The library windows could have done with a good clean. Dust formed a spotty grey film against the light, making the ground outside look frosty. Windows covered in fly droppings brought back memories of her grandmother's barn in northern Finland. Seja had been there only once, when she was . . . six years old, perhaps. The ground had been grey and frozen, despite the fact that they had left Gothenburg in the warmth of late summer. Most things had been grey: grey tree trunks and grass nipped by the morning frost. Unpainted, windswept wooden buildings. The place where her mother's parents lived had been bathed in light; a tall, undisturbed pillar of light. The land of a thousand lakes. Her mother's land.

Her mother's longing for her homeland was restrained but still palpable. She didn't talk about it much; that was just the way she was. It was only when she became an adult that Seja realised how much her mother's homesickness had affected her upbringing.

Seja dreamed of a fairy-tale land, a thousand lakes, murmuring brooks and gilded bridges over water.

When Seja was very small, she used to curl up by her mother's side to listen to stories: the very name was magical, *The Land of a Thousand Lakes*. Perhaps even more so because her mother often seemed distant. Her mother had always had a great sense of empathy and understanding for those whose hearts were elsewhere.

The first and only time Seja visited her mother's farm, the family Saab behind her, she was disappointed. No gilded bridges, no silky-soft fairy-tale grass. Not even a single lake as far as the eye could see.

She found it upsetting now to think of how her mother's unspoken suffering had cast a cloud over her

321

childhood, and that the family had visited Finland only once as far as she could remember. As a child she had thought that the land of the lakes was at the end of the world, when in fact it was no more than a day's journey away. And her mother had chosen to be a martyr and to forgo visits home. She had chosen her exile.

Seja had never tried to share these thoughts with her mother. It became a vicious circle with Seja avenging her mother's silence with her own, when really she should have just spoken her mind: "Why couldn't you have chosen your life, Mum? Nothing good came of the sacrifices you made; you might as well have been happy."

Everything works out in the end, Seja thought. Perhaps that's why I've ended up in my little cottage. Why I've worked so hard to be able to choose my life. I've seen what happens when you don't make that choice. Maybe that's why I get so annoyed with Hanna; she daren't choose because she's afraid of failing.

Contact with her parents was now restricted to birthdays and the odd obligatory phone call. Those dutiful, clumsy pats on the head spoke of a series of betrayals. Betrayals that no one put into words. Seja would never be able to put them into words. After all, she had never wanted for anything, in material terms. She had kind, thoughtful parents who always did their best. But they had never given voice to their problems. And certainly not that Saturday morning when her mother wasn't sitting by the fan with her cigarette.

Seja suddenly had an idea. She took her notepad from her rucksack and wrote: *She had immediately realised that nothing was the same as usual when her father kept pacing to the window and looking down at the street.*

He'd waited until he thought Seja was asleep, but she wasn't asleep. In fact, she had buried her face in the pillow to avoid having to hear her father hide the anxiety in his voice — he didn't want people to gossip. Seja put her hands over her ears so she wouldn't have to hear Daddy's galloping heart. She didn't move until he fell asleep in front of the TV, then she crept out of bed and lay down beside him, head to toe.

The next morning, sitting on the kitchen worktop, she watched her father wander from room to room, listening to the reassuring things he was saying: Mum must be with some friend I've forgotten about. Or perhaps a friend we don't know about. Then, suddenly, he forgot that Seja was there and the words poured from his mouth, tumbling over one another, spilling forth his fears: "What's happened to her? What if she doesn't come back?"

He hid his face in his hands then, before becoming aware of Seja again, and trying to calm himself down. "There's nothing to worry about," he said. "She just needed a break. Sometimes grown-ups get tired. They just need a break."

Seja hunted for clues and searched among her mother's things. On the dressing table: eau de cologne and balls of cotton wool for removing her mascara. Boxes of different-coloured eye-shadow, although her mother used only blue. The tweezers she used to pluck out a single, stubborn hair on her chin. The jewellery box containing fake pearls and clip-on earrings.

The well-thumbed novels in Finnish were next to the bed, along with the knitted woollen jumpers that cleaned themselves and never needed washing. They exuded that Mummy-smell. Seja took one of the jumpers to bed when she started to realise that her mother might not come back. She slipped it inside a thin pillowcase because the wool was prickly and made her itch, but the smell came through. Mummy was dead or had disappeared, but the Mummy-smell remained. In a way it made sense. Mummy had gone to the land of the lakes and, suddenly, in her mind, the thousand lakes became the sky. Mummy became an angel of happiness. Seja did drawings of Mummy, the same subject but in different colours, and covered the walls of her room with them. They watched over her as she slept.

During the day, Seja and her father were united in silence; a stubborn determination to get through everyday life. Neither of them knew what else to do. Seja noticed that her father's face had grown set in silence because he didn't know how to talk to his child about the fact that her mother had chosen to leave them. In the evening, in front of the television, he would sometimes weep, in short, sudden bursts. There came a time when Seja's tears dried up. Sleep came even when she didn't think it would, whisking her away; she wanted to dream about the Mummy-country, but in the mornings she had no memory of whether she had dreamt or not.

On the seventh day, her mother reappeared at the door with rosy cheeks and a suitcase in her hand. Seja froze, her pen poised above the paper. She didn't remember what she had been writing, but she did remember the strange feeling of mute disappointment that had washed over her; she stared at her mother, then slid down from her chair and went to her room. She looked at the Mummy-angels in the land of the thousand lakes gazing down at her. The angels' eyes no longer had any life in them; they were just badly drawn circles with black dots for pupils, the drawings of a six year old, and she tore them all down. She meticulously ripped them into tiny pieces.

Sitting on the edge of Seja's bed, her mother explained that she had gone to her farm in Finland. She said that she had always intended to come back. That she just wanted to visit Granny and help out on the farm. That she had kept meaning to get in touch, but other things had got in the way.

She fell silent, then tried again; she said she hadn't been thinking straight because she was tired and sad and had convinced herself that nothing mattered. She said if the transport links hadn't been so bad, if the weather hadn't been so awful, she would have come back even sooner. Seja said nothing. Later that evening, her mother wept and Daddy asked Seja to forgive her; he said things weren't so bad after all, Mummy hadn't meant any harm, but Seja stuck her fingers in her ears and felt a devastating icy chill

325

spread through her body. Enough. She didn't want to hear any more.

The following morning, when she got up for breakfast, she found a trail of dolls and cuddly toys snaking across the kitchen worktop, from the little shelf where the telephone stood, all the way to the sink. Seja looked at every single one and established that they were new; she turned them upside down and saw that most of them still had the price ticket on. Some were from the Shell garage.

The librarian placed a pile of books on the table in front of her with a thud.

"Thanks." Seja opened the first book and had managed to read the first paragraph before he got back to his computer.

When Martin left, Seja recognised her reaction immediately: her heart seemed to miss several beats before exploding into a turmoil that was impossible to show or measure, while at the same time the icy chill spread like poison through her bloodstream, affecting every word and action. And yet it was simply impossible to let the pain show.

She closed her eyes. The dusty window panes were imprinted on her cornea.

That's exactly what I'm doing now, she realised. I'm pretending that it doesn't matter if Christian lets me down, if he doesn't have the courage to commit, to believe in us. And she was just waiting for the words to release their icy chill; the chill was her only coping mechanism. The only way to retain her pride.

They had decided to go away on a short break, and all she could think about was the extent to which she had *persuaded* Christian to go, against his will.

No, it was too difficult to get a grip on her thoughts.

She ran her hand over the closely-written pages and suddenly realised that it would be easy to carry on. Just a few more pages, then another one or two. If she continued, the text would pour over the pages until her story was told, not only in actions but in words. The story was splashing around inside her, unspoken, but it was definitely there. And it might not be remarkable, no more remarkable than anyone else's story, but it was hers, and she longed to write it without any demands or limitations. As a side project, at least.

After all, she wasn't the one who had a problem with words.

CHAPTER
FORTY-SIX

Gothenburg

Tell had finally managed to get a couple of hours' sleep as morning approached.

He might have to come back to Copenhagen in the near future, even if Dragsted and his team took on some of the workload. At the moment, however, he had other priorities. He had zigzagged along the motorway from Malmö to Gothenburg, stopping only to buy a hamburger which he shovelled down with one hand on the steering wheel. Some level of self-preservation made him let his mobile ring out, after he had checked each time that it wasn't Seja. She hadn't called, even though they hadn't yet made plans for their break.

He wished she had rung, even though they hadn't been apart for very long, and even though he hadn't called her and wouldn't have had time to talk, or barely even answer. He wasn't thinking logically.

The display showed three missed calls: he knew what Beckman and Karlberg had found in Rebecca Nykvist's empty boiler. In the bloody boiler! Beckman's inspired hunch, which had been brewing at the back of her mind since she heard Rebecca's phone call, then overshadowed by the drama with Mads Torsen, had been activated when she heard his brief summary of Dorte Sørbækk's confession. Just a couple of sentences, spoken at the right moment, had taken them to the end of one trail, although there was still work to be done.

While some pieces of the puzzle fell into place, others were snatched away, leaving a picture which was clearer in many ways, yet lacked the key points. Like a photograph with the wrong focus, where the figure in the foreground is obscured and the eye is drawn to the backdrop.

It all came down to jealousy, Tell concluded, replaying his interview with Alexandr Karpov in his head. Rebecca Nykvist's jealousy, and now Alexandr Karpov's. Although they had found different forms of expression.

Karpov had seemed so tormented by guilt that Tell had misinterpreted his responses during the first few minutes of their conversation, wanting to believe that Karpov was confessing to the murder of his ex-wife and her boyfriend.

"I never really believed she'd left me for good. Can you understand that? When you've lived together for all those years, when everything has got tangled up: love, work, friendship, I thought it was a whim." He gave a hollow laugh. "Presumptuous, I know, but now I realise I was just waiting for my chance to save the day, or at least to show her the safety net she would lose if we divorced."

"Are you saying that you did in fact hire your assistants to break into Ann-Marie's boyfriend's house?"

"Ann-Marie came to me in despair," he said. "I didn't know what to do."

His expression grew opaque, as though he was considering what he actually meant. "She was afraid. After I heard the fear in her voice I couldn't just stand back and do nothing."

"So did Ann-Marie ask you to arrange the break-in and theft?"

"No! She told me about the situation she'd ended up in. She didn't know what to do. Her relationship with this man had taken an unpleasant turn. She thought he was unpredictable and she'd tried to finish with him, but ... More and more people knew about or suspected their relationship and he was putting pressure on her to go public. He had everything to gain. Ann-Marie was afraid of her reputation being tarnished."

A touch of rancour that Tell hadn't noticed before had crept into Karpov's voice.

He clarified. "In order to be a good teacher, it's important to maintain a high level of integrity. Ann-Marie risked losing that integrity."

"But —"

"Henrik Samuelsson was planning to get rich by selling stolen goods from Baghdad. And he was stupid; he had these pipe dreams that would lead them both to destruction. Ann-Marie had tried to change his mind of course. If it all came out, her head would be on the block. She would lose everything: her job, her identity. Since a UN resolution was passed after the war, it's actually illegal to be in possession of artefacts

330

plundered from Iraq. When she tried to end the relationship, he got desperate and threatened to say they'd smuggled the items together."

"So when Henrik threatened to bring things to a head . . ."

"It wasn't an empty threat; he had firm intentions and told her all about his plan. He showed her the item he'd tried to have valued so she would realise he was serious; he'd hidden the rest somewhere. She panicked. She turned to me as you would turn to a friend. I just wished there was something I could do."

His voice broke and tears pooled in the bags beneath his eyes; he took off his glasses and wiped his face with his sleeve.

Tell gazed at him. "Alexandr. I have to ask: did you pay your assistant, Knud Iversen, to get rid of Henrik Samuelsson? For Ann-Marie's sake? Is that what happened? I realise you would never deliberately allow harm to come to Ann-Marie, but maybe something went wrong? Was the plan just to kill Samuelsson?"

Karpov opened and closed his mouth, his face a picture of astonishment.

"No," he said eventually.

No, thought Tell. "How did your assistants come to be working for you?"

"They were employed by the museum, not by me."

"But they worked for you?"

"Dorte came as a . . . Oh, what's it called? She was on some kind of work experience scheme. She had an internship for the first year and managed to make herself indispensable. When it was decided to increase the number of assistants, she suggested her boyfriend Knud. The posts were eventually made permanent."

"Dorte said that the fact she and Knud were allowed to stay on at Glyptoteket was largely down to your goodwill."

Karpov protested. "I couldn't have managed without them. My remit had expanded, and I became more reliant on practical help. Everyone deserves a second chance. And most of us get one. I was in a position to offer that chance, and it was my duty to do so."

He hesitated. "With hindsight, I can see that it was reckless and injudicious of me to speak to Knud and Dorte about Ann-Marie's problems but, believe me, it was never my intention that things should go this far."

"But, Alexandr," said Tell, wondering if he was right to say what he was thinking. "I believe you're protecting them now, just as you've protected them for over a week by not telling me about your suspicions. Dorte said you never asked them to steal the goods; that Knud went ahead behind your back. He hired two people to do the job — they would take all the risk. I don't suppose you were even aware of that?"

"No, no, but I was the one who sowed the seed," Karpov said firmly. "Without malicious intent, admittedly, but it's still my fault that things turned out as they did. I put the idea into their heads. I should have known they wouldn't be able to resist, besides which you have to remember that in their eyes, I'm an authority figure. I think they would do just about anything if I asked them. They were like . . . they are like . . . I won't say the son and daughter I never had, because that's a big thing to say. But if I don't say that, I don't really know what else to say."

"But you didn't ask them to do it. And that's the important thing right now."

CHAPTER
FORTY-SEVEN

The following day, when the team assembled in Tell's office, the mood was somewhat low. They had followed the wrong leads, and had gone down a blind alley. It felt as if they were starting again from scratch in the case of the Linnégatan murders.

Only Bärneflod seemed cheerful, uncharacteristically so.

"How the hell did you come up with that?"

It wasn't every day Beckman heard admiration in her colleague's voice.

"I heard Rebecca talking on the phone to a workman about getting rid of the broken boiler. Then everything just fell into place."

"Even so."

Karlberg waited as Bärneflod thumped Beckman encouragingly on the back.

"Henrik Samuelsson," he began tentatively; he didn't want to bring everyone down when an effort had been made to lift the mood. "He'd stolen these extremely valuable artefacts and stashed them away at home. Why didn't he sell them as soon as he got back from Istanbul? And why did he hide twenty-eight items inside the boiler and one behind the books in the bookcase?"

"One piece had to be easily accessible for valuations." Tell shook his head. "Henrik Samuelsson had no criminal record. He had no contacts in the underworld. People describe him as naive; it's not surprising he hadn't factored in how difficult it would be to sell hot stolen goods from a museum without getting caught. And no, he didn't necessarily steal them. In fact, I don't think that's very likely. He probably bought them at a knock-down price. They've most likely passed through several pairs of hands, but these artefacts *are* stolen property. I've been in touch with a Cecilia Lindgren, who is going to keep them safe at the Röhsska Museum for the time being. Can someone organise that, please? By the way, I presume nobody has a problem with the fact that I'm taking a few days' leave?"

"I can take the museum," said Karlberg. "Not that I'm particularly comfortable with the idea of carting around stolen property worth a million or so."

"Send a car. By the way, where's the stuff now?"

"In a safe here," said Gonzales.

Beckman took a sip of iced water. "But surely we're investigating —"

"The murders," Tell interjected. "I completely understand the frustration everyone here feels because our main line of inquiry so far has not led us anywhere. I feel exactly the same way. But that's just how it is. Apart from the action points I just mentioned, we are abandoning all inquiries in the case of the stolen goods, as long as there is no risk of any connection with the murders."

"And the Danish police are fully up to speed on this now?" asked Beckman. "Karpov, Pedersen, Sørbækk and Iversen. Our motley crew."

"We've said we'll keep in touch. But what do you all think? For the time being we are assuming that Sørbækk and Iversen have no link to the murders. We should have proof of that before too long. As things stand, we have no reason to doubt that Sørbækk was telling the whole truth when she confessed."

"In other words, all the key connections between the cases were pure coincidence, a theory that you refused to believe," said Bärneflod, throwing a screwed-up piece of paper into the bin.

Tell didn't respond.

"But the person who . . ." Karlberg began as he worked on a particularly complicated doodle in the margin of his notepad. "The person who actually links these coincidences is Alexandr Karpov, isn't that right?"

Silence fell around the table. Karlberg grew more animated. "How come he's never been our main suspect? He's the one with the textbook motive: jealousy. He has no alibi to speak of, he was at home in bed, alone. He's the link between all the key figures in the case. Is it because of his status, or because we regard him as honest and likeable?"

"His assistants swear that Karpov had nothing to do with the break-in at Henrik's house," Tell reminded him. "They're taking all the blame."

"But what about the murders?" Karlberg persisted.

"We've just established that the murders had nothing to do with the museum lot," said Bärneflod. "I'd actually like to make the same point about Rebecca Nykvist, if we're talking about motive and opportunity. She has no alibi either; she was at home alone. In which case, why did we let her go? I'll tell you why: because we were working on the vague theory that there was a link between the murders and the break-in. If we're thinking differently now, which we are, then surely Rebecca should be . . ."

"I hear you," Tell mumbled. "But we certainly haven't dismissed her. We've had her in mind and under surveillance all this time; it's just that she isn't behaving suspiciously. But you might still have a point, Bärneflod. Maybe we shifted our focus away from Rebecca a little too quickly. Karlberg, can you and Gonzales work on the Alexandr Karpov angle for a bit longer; Bärneflod, you take a look at Rebecca."

Tell chewed his lip absent-mindedly. "I'm going. But I want to be kept in the picture. I'm on email and I'll be back in a few days."

Beckman nudged him. "Off you go on holiday with Seja, and don't give us a second thought. Most of us can manage a couple of days without you."

Tell laughed politely. Out in the corridor Höije walked past. Tell didn't acknowledge him.

CHAPTER
FORTY-EIGHT

Falkenberg

They drove from Gothenburg to Falkenberg at first light to avoid the early summer traffic, with the husky voices of Mary Gauthier and Marianne Faithfull on the stereo.

When the engine fell silent on the drive of the B&B, they were rewarded by the first glimmer of morning sun breaking through the mist. They felt relaxed, glad they had decided to come away, even though they only had a few days. They couldn't check in yet; it was too early. Seja reached for Christian's hand and put her bare feet up on the dashboard. The dawn broke as a peculiar radio play reached its conclusion.

The veranda of the B&B jutted out over the water like a jetty. They could hear the lapping of waves from their room and had an unbroken view of the horizon. They went for a walk along the shore and Seja took a dip to freshen up after the journey. Christian shook his head — no chance.

The wind coming off the sea was chilly. The water tore and scratched at her skin; it had none of the smoothness of Älsjön, the lake back home. Seja leapt out, howling, in a shower of salty spray, fell into a sand dune and wrapped herself in a big towel. The sand was fine and soft and warm, it made her want to bury herself in it, just as she had on childhood holidays in Løkken, where they used to slide down the dunes between the dry tufts of grass.

They shared a bottle of white wine with lunch as they planned their afternoon; they wanted to visit two exhibitions. Christian felt like his father as he carefully marked the map.

"It doesn't matter if we get lost," said Seja. "That's when you find the best places."

He put the pen down. "We'll do whatever you want."

Seja took a deep breath and pushed aside her doubts about Christian and whether their relationship was what she needed, trying to revel in the moment. Only last week she had done a number of errands for the Melkerssons while their car was being repaired, so she didn't feel guilty about asking them to feed the cat and keep an eye on her cottage. And it was nice to get away; they were together in a beautiful place.

"It's difficult," she mumbled.

"Difficult? What's difficult?"

"Oh, nothing really," she said evasively. "It's just work. I wonder how things will turn out. What should I do — can I really carry on living in the cottage on my own? Will I have the courage and money to do what I want to do? I'm not likely to get a permanent job writing, that just doesn't happen. And sometimes I feel I'll go crazy touting myself around all the time."

"But you've always said you want to be independent. To be able to write about whatever you like. Don't give up on that. You had a fantastic response to those articles you did on the Granith family — though of course I must mention that you wouldn't have got to know them were it not for a certain someone . . ."

"No way. I found the dead body, then I stuck with the investigation and wrote the articles without any help from you."

"Don't remind me. But you could say that you got the scoop thanks to my incomprehensible naivety. That I was blinded by love. Among other things."

Seja took a sip of her wine and smiled. "I can't believe you're trying to take the credit for my only success."

"I'm joking. You know I think you're fantastic."

"Yeah, yeah, whatever . . ."

She twirled the glass absent-mindedly between the palms of her hands, apparently absorbed for a while in her anxiety about the future. He couldn't blame her. It was hard to succeed as a journalist; she wasn't twenty-one any more, and she had acquired a great many things to take care of, not least financially: the cottage, the stable, the animals, the car . . .

Even though he knew it was presumptuous, he couldn't help but feel a sense of responsibility towards her. If they did carry on seeing each other, then sooner or later the issue of living together would come up. What Seja had said in Copenhagen about the Melkerssons' house was doubtless only the beginning. The financial aspect certainly didn't put him off. But the little house in the forest frightened him. The stillness out there became silence, became emptiness and an anxiety-inducing malaise. He didn't know what he was prepared to do for the sake of love. It seemed to change from one day to the next.

"But then it's not easy to succeed at any dream, is it? And the idea of touting yourself around — well, that's part of every job, at one level or another. You just have to learn to handle it. It's a matter of self-esteem. People will never stop judging you; you just have to learn to do your best and not care so much about what they think."

"That's easy for you to say."

"Yes, but that's the way most men think. It's typical of women to adapt to how —"

"Stop, please. Let's not go all Men are from Mars, Women are from Venus! I'm sure you're right. But I just want to enjoy the moment. With you."

She held his gaze.

"We're so lucky."

Her fingers caressed his temple, then traced his hairline down his cheek to his jaw.

"So, what do you think?" she said. "Shall we spend the afternoon looking at art, or shall we order another bottle? We can look at the sea, get drunk and have an early night."

Christian grabbed her hand.

"Let's go up to our room now. We can go out later. And then we'll have all evening to drink wine."

He pulled her up from the chair.

The water slurped as it was sucked down the plughole. He lay there listening to Seja singing in the shower. He was tangled up in the bedclothes; he rolled over to the other side and yanked the damp sheet free.

Christian was also going to have a shower before they went out, but for the moment he was just glad he'd managed to stay awake. In certain respects the twelve-year age difference made itself felt. He wasn't thirty any more.

He glanced at the spines of the books on the bedside table; they were both about the war in Iraq. He flicked through them.

Seja emerged from the shower with a towel wound around her head instead of her body. "Have you read them?" she asked, gesturing towards the books.

"No, why would I have read them?"

"Because you're working on that case."

"That particular case is more or less closed. And these books are about the war in Iraq."

"It's all connected." She rummaged in her bag, hanging up her clothes in the wardrobe.

Christian was reading the back cover of one of the books. "Surely that's just a theory."

"An extremely well-founded theory, if so."

Seja pulled on her jeans and a top before going back into the bathroom. He watched her loop her wet hair into a knot in the doorway.

"So is this the kind of thing you're going to write about, then?" A bit louder, so that she would hear him.

"It's interesting. I'm thinking about it."

Christian hauled himself out of bed and pushed past her into the shower. The hot water woke him up. He was looking forward to a walk through the town.

"If you've finished, perhaps I could have a shave and clean my teeth?"

In the mirror her cheeks were flushed from the hot shower. She changed from her black top into a white one before deciding she was ready to go out.

"Will you be long?"

"I'm ready now. Ready to drink in the culture. But have a little patience, I need to check my messages first."

"Freak."

"Absolutely. And I need to get dressed. Do you want to wait for me downstairs?"

"I've got all the patience in the world when it comes to you."

She was just about to leave the room when she stopped. "Shall I tell you something? It comes back to what we were saying about my job."

"Sure, fire away."

"I've started writing something. No, two things actually. The first one is, as you suspected long ago, an article about smuggled cultural treasures, the ones you found in that house in Kungsladugaård. It's going to be an expanded news item with references to grave-robbing, among other things. I've spoken to two daily papers who will almost certainly take it."

She waited, probably to see how Christian would react.

"So why were you sitting there worrying about the future before? Things are going really well for you."

"Well, yes, but one piece doesn't make a future. Anyway, what I really wanted to tell you is that I've also started a slightly bigger project. Inspired by my mother and my grandmother. My mother's life when she was growing up in Finland, what happened when she moved to Sweden with Dad, and — I haven't got that far yet."

"Oh? Like a book? A sort of biography?"

"No, no. Not a biography. But the idea of a fictional account came out of my thoughts about . . . language. My mother's refusal to put things into words. I thought that instead of being angry with her, perhaps I should try to *give* her a language. After all, she was shaped by her grandmother and her upbringing."

Christian started buttoning his shirt. "You know, you've told me hardly anything about your parents."

She usually got annoyed when he asked. But this time she was the one who had brought it up.

"I know," Seja said pensively. "But that's a part of the problem. I've always been as inarticulate as my mother when I've tried to talk about her, as if the very thought of her made me unable to speak. Perhaps it was my way of adapting, I don't know. Just as my father has learnt to accept that everything is just *the way it is*. And I don't want to do that. I don't want to feel mute in any context; words are my thing, aren't they?"

She laughed. "At the risk of sounding pretentious, I'd like to relearn my mother tongue, literally. When I was little she sometimes used to tell me stories about when she was a child in Finland. I'd like to carry on where she left off. Fiction, but inspired by reality." She looked at Christian, her face tense with expectation, as if his opinion was of the utmost importance.

He chose his words carefully. "I think it sounds good. It's a good idea to sort things out with your parents before it's too late, because otherwise you'll regret it. And I also think it would help if you put your journalism to one side when it feels like hard work, and focus on something you feel really passionate about. It's important that you enjoy what you're doing. Otherwise you just can't hack it in the long term."

"Is that what you think? Do you find your job fun?"

Christian raised his eyebrows in response to her question, which clearly struck him as more or less absurd. Words such as fun and boring just didn't apply to his job. Eventually he smiled.

"I'm not talking about what *I* ought to do now. I'm talking about what *you* ought to do. It's not as though I've sorted things out with my parents either."

He laughed as she attempted to wrestle him down onto the bed. "Mind the shirt! It's new!"

She soon bounced back to her feet, gasping for breath. "It's a feel-good project. A turning-thirty-crisis project. I'm not saying I'm a writer, or that it will turn into a novel. But I know I've really missed writing, in my own way. Not as a journalist, but the way I've always done it: just writing what springs to mind."

"Don't justify it," said Christian. "Just go for it."

After she had gone downstairs, he logged on and scrolled through his emails. A message Renée had forwarded that morning caught his interest. He picked up the phone to ring the office just as Seja came into view in the front garden. She crouched down to examine something on the ground; he couldn't see what it was. He put the phone down, wrote a few lines to Karlberg and forwarded the message.

CHAPTER
FORTY-NINE

Gothenburg

The rain after the heat came as a relief. These days Rebecca Nykvist used Slottsskogen park almost as her own private garden. It lived and breathed as a perfect balance between man and nature. The extensive lawns provided open aspects and enclosures where it was often possible to catch a glimpse of fallow deer and elk. People were ridiculously afraid of getting slightly wet, reacting to the warm spring rain as if it were a vicious hailstorm, striking their cheeks like nails. The buggy mafia frantically packed away their blankets and plastic platefuls of half-eaten banana mash, their suddenly superfluous parasols and surprised, bawling offspring. Indifferent teenagers in front of Björngårdsvillan brushed dried grass off their backsides and headed off towards Linnéstaden or Majorna. Older couples looked up at the sky, their expressions irritated: was the weather trying to upset them personally?

Soon, Rebecca was alone. She tipped her head back, rolling her stiff neck until it felt soft and pliant. A pale rainbow arched above the tree-tops.

She had taken a half day's leave. Nobody said anything at work, of course they didn't. No doubt there had been plenty of talk when she came back to the office so soon after Henrik's death.

Sometimes Rebecca felt like a caricature of herself: even when her partner dies she doesn't cut herself some slack. She never takes any time off work.

The truth was that it helped her to stick to a daily routine. It gave her something else to think about when she was afraid that the agonising sense of loss would finish her off.

And the job itself had never really got to her emotionally, not even when she had been dealing with patients. If she let herself be affected by all the frustration she encountered, or mixed her own emotions with her relationships at work, she wouldn't last long. And, besides, she had no intention of addressing her colleagues' gossip.

No, she kept her distance, kept her sorrow to herself, and carried out the less than stimulating tasks she was given to a standard that was beyond reproach. Bided her time as she waited for some kind of closure.

Her troubles at work would soon blow over. This too shall pass, or whatever the phrase was. The same could not be said for her personal life. This bloody awful business with the police and the boiler and Henrik's . . .

Rebecca had come to realise the true extent of Henrik's double life. There had been parts of Henrik that she hadn't known at all. Could she have found a way in? Or was that just the kind of man Henrik was, a man with secrets? A man who was simply not to be trusted? Yet another one?

348

There was incontrovertible proof that he had hidden stolen goods in their cellar; Rebecca didn't know long they had been there. Henrik must have been conned into something he didn't understand — he was definitely naive — driven by the prospect of clearing his debts. And the fact that she had been constantly nagging him about money had no doubt played its part in his decision to get involved.

No. This wasn't her fault. She had unknowingly been exposed to mortal danger. She had lost her life partner and been accused of murder. But she had been released.

She saw him on the far side of the park. The path curved around the lawn and Axel Donner was walking under the trees, on his way up the hill that rose towards Säröleden. The constant hum of the traffic grew more noticeable as she got closer.

Had he sought shelter from the rain? He was facing the other way and hadn't noticed her yet. Rebecca was overcome by a sudden desire to follow him. Was she hoping he would give something away and, if so, what? Was he on his way to a secret meeting with a lover?

The first time she had joked about his friend being "in the closet", Henrik had been furious, saying her job had warped her world-view. Later, he had brought up the subject, making a joke of it. They had laughed together. Henrik admitted that Axel sometimes got a little clingy, and that he didn't seem to grasp the social norms of adult friendship: you don't have to be glued to the other person's side. It's OK to go out on your own. You don't walk around with a hurt expression on

349

your face. You give each other the freedom to explore other relationships.

In the midst of that refreshing laughter Rebecca forgot what "other relationships" might mean in Henrik's case. It was just so nice to laugh at Axel. To consolidate their sense of being on the same team, even though Henrik had immediately taken it back and insisted that Axel had definitely had women in the past — well, one at least. It was as though Henrik were defending not only Axel in the face of an imagined accusation, but also himself. Rebecca's good mood had quickly dissipated, to be replaced by irritation. She almost asked why he was being so defensive, but nothing annoyed Henrik more than when he thought she was analysing him. *I am not your bloody patient.*

She followed Axel Donner at a safe distance.

They hardly knew each other, even though Axel was supposed to be Henrik's closest friend. In a way, his taciturn, submissive demeanour had been a refreshing change. Henrik's narcissism sometimes embarrassed her, but that was just the way he was. He wasn't exactly subtle. The way he had introduced Rebecca to Axel as *my partner,* in passing and in a dismissive tone of voice, had aged her by a couple of decades in seconds.

Rebecca realised that she was thinking about Henrik and their relationship as if it still existed. Her heart skipped a beat. A black, gaping hole opened up at her feet before she briskly made a mental note to bring this up the next time she saw her therapist.

What *was* Axel doing under the trees? He walked onto the porch of a little red cottage with white eaves which looked out of place in the middle of the city. She watched as he tried the door. It was locked.

A twig snapped beneath Rebecca's feet and suddenly she realised she had been creeping around trying not to make any noise. She felt stupid as she backed away and hid behind a tree trunk. She stayed there until he set off again.

They had never actually been enemies, they just represented different aspects of Henrik's life. Rebecca's aversion to him stemmed from something as primitive as a territorial impulse. She was clever enough to realise that Axel had access to places within Henrik where she would never be allowed to set foot. That Axel knew the man Henrik was when Rebecca wasn't around.

At the beginning of their relationship, she had felt pride when other women responded flirtatiously to his banter and to the glint in his eye. Oh, how she wished things could have stayed like that for ever! Before the petty irritations of everyday life tarnished the unfettered desire that had brought them together. Before Henrik and his women — and it didn't matter whether they existed in real life, or just in her mind — dug a hole in her trust. Before — *Hey, presto!* — she was back in her dark place.

Back searching pockets and bags, checking messages. Spitting out accusations. Retreating with humiliating apologies.

Axel had colluded with Henrik over his sordid affair with Ann-Marie. The very thought of all the times Henrik had cycled off, allegedly to study at Axel's, or have a beer with Axel, made her face burn. On an impulse she decided to keep on walking, faster, to confront him about that telephone call. *Sorry, Rebecca. I don't know anything.*

Axel was down by the bridge now; he took a couple of tentative steps as though to reassure himself that it would hold. He then strode purposefully to its mid-point, where he stared down at the stream of speeding traffic.

He's thinking of jumping was her first reaction. She placed a hand on the railing.

A lorry drove past, drowning out her greeting. The exhaust fumes were suffocating.

"How are you?" she said eventually, and regretted it at once. The question should have been directed at her. She had lost her life partner. *She* should be the one standing on a bridge staring down at the Tarmac.

But she would never jump, and the thought made her soften. She was the strong one here, irrespective of what had happened; she had the dignity of a grieving person. Not a pathetic victim. She convinced herself that sorrow had given her crystal-clear vision. That the contours of the world around her were particularly sharp. Grief gave her the right to be frank. "You're not thinking of jumping, are you?"

His face was half turned away, his forearms resting on the railing.

"Here?" he said. "No."

"It's not high enough anyway," she said.

She wasn't sure whether her comment was an attempt at black humour, or merely factual.

"But the chances of getting run over are pretty good."

A smile flickered across his mouth but failed to reach his eyes. In those eyes she could see fear. *Is he afraid he's going to jump against his will?* she thought. *Or is he afraid of me?*

"How long had *you* known? About Henrik and Ann-Marie Karpov?"

Once again he leant over the abyss. "All along. Right from the start."

She nodded.

She'd thought about drawing a line under it all, moving away from her house and all the memories of mistrust within its walls. She could rebuild herself somewhere else. When she was advising others, she was usually dismissive of fresh starts. *Stay where you are and do better* was an attitude that guided other people out of crises. But the idea of starting all over again was so tempting.

CHAPTER
FIFTY

At night, he would have palpitations. Then he would go for a walk and calm down. For a long time, he had been a fragment of his former self. During that difficult year in the clinic — after Carla — he had even tried praying to the Father, unsure whether he meant his biological father or a father in heaven.

He had always struggled with the idea of faith. He was used to questioning things that could not be factually proven; he had been a student for a long time, if not a particularly successful one. But he had been brought up to believe that being a healthy person required a strong faith. You went to church because that was just what you did in the village. The image of his father came to him again, this time sitting in his pew wearing a pullover and tie. Callused hands that made the thick hymn book look so much smaller than it was. Across the aisle sat the woman his father used to meet. He would sit beside his parents, knowing that his father knew that he knew, that his mother knew that he knew that she knew, an endless cycle of humiliation. The humiliation was too much for him.

He was glad that his father hadn't set foot in the hospital, many years later, that he had chosen not to sully the memory further. That he had allowed his misunderstood son to retain a modicum of self-respect.

Because with Carla he *had* tried to do good. He had only wanted to talk to her, nothing more. To reach the woman who wanted to call herself his girlfriend; his plan involved mutual reflection and, of course, an element of punishment. The first missionaries had seen things in much the same way. They too found that the only way to chastise lost souls was to teach them the true faith, to suppress their sinful tendencies with appropriate punishment. Good is praised. Evil is punished. In schools these days, children were spared the consequences of their actions; another sign of the country's spinelessness. And it would be the country's downfall.

He had liked her, in the same contradictory way he liked Annelie. Behind Carla's self-destructiveness he had seen a frightened little girl — not unlike the boy he had once been. In many ways she too was a victim of the world; its vapours had wrapped themselves around her body in the form of the colours she smeared on her face, the vulgar clothes she wore to draw attention to her body. Peeling away layer after stinking layer would be like seeking out a diamond in a piece of blackened rock, then polishing it.

He had failed, not least because of his own inadequacy. He didn't have the courage of his convictions. Back then he too was like an unpolished stone. He wanted to do the right thing, but lacked the maturity, the understanding, the method or the means to achieve his goal. And she hadn't made it easy for him, after all. She had refused to listen, she hadn't been interested in the idea of reflecting on life. And he hadn't yet learnt to handle his anger, the fatal flaw that made him act without thinking, time and time again. He *had* acted without thinking.

In the confusion after he had let Carla go, the psychologist in the clinic had told him that the only way to move on was to forgive himself.

As time went on, he tried to regard the farce as a good father regards his offspring when they do wrong: with understanding. With a stern but amused tenderness.

He had felt compelled to hold on to Carla, since she refused to listen. Patiently waiting for a moment of insight, room for mutual understanding where she would see why he had had no choice but to deprive her of her freedom, just for a few days.

The lines scratched on the inside of his wardrobe door marked the number of days that had passed since he had left behind everything: Home and Church. His intended career, following in his father's footsteps. He would never be able to return to his former life. And yet he carried on counting the days. He had learnt one thing from Carla: his soul was divided, with competing impulses pulling him asunder.

But the liberation he had felt after he had cleared his house was indescribable. It made the possibility of forgiveness a reality. The road ahead may not be straight, but it was possible to start again.

CHAPTER
FIFTY-ONE

Gothenburg

Beckman regarded herself as a grounded, unsentimental person. She was familiar with every phase of pregnancy, and theoretically aware that the foetus was the size of a thumbnail, encased in layers of protective membranes, body and skin. There was no way that the movements she thought she could feel were the child in her belly.

She was always ravenous these days, and had shovelled down a tray of sausage and mash from a kiosk on her way from the station to Kungsladugårdsgatan; the fact that she was on the move might help her digestion. She was sitting on a bench by the paddling pool, which hadn't yet been filled, with her hand on her belly. The harbour wasn't far away, and a flock of screaming gulls circled above her head; one of them swooped into an open bin, grabbed a half-eaten tray of mash and took off again.

A woman in her forties sank down laboriously beside Beckman, her belly round and taut, a supporting hand at the bottom of her back. Beckman didn't realise she was grinning foolishly until the woman glanced back at her.

"Is it your first?" She pointed at Beckman's still flat stomach. "Your first child?"

Embarrassed, Beckman moved her hand away. "No, I've got two girls."

"Oh, how wonderful! I'd love to have a daughter, but of course I'll be just as happy if it's a boy."

"Is it your first?"

"Yes! At long last. I've been trying for years, and just when all the papers were in order for me to adopt, I fell pregnant. Apparently it happens all the time — your body relaxes and suddenly decides to cooperate."

"You must both be delighted."

"Yes. Well, I am. I'm on my own."

"Are you allowed to adopt as a single parent?" Beckman asked, then realised her question could be misinterpreted. "Sorry, I didn't mean it like that, it's fantastic. I just didn't know."

"It's fine. Yes, certain countries allow single people to adopt. But I was nearly too old."

Beckman quashed her impulse to ask the woman about her circumstances; perhaps she too had fallen pregnant by an ex-husband. But she realised it would be absurd to start asking questions. They didn't know each other. And even if this woman was in the habit of sharing her life story with all and sundry, Beckman certainly wasn't.

And yet the stranger's contented smile encouraged her. For the first time in months, the thought of an uncertain future didn't feel like a weight on her shoulders. It was foolish and impossible; inappropriate, even. But Beckman allowed herself to think irrationally, and the effect was liberating. She knew that feeling wouldn't last; of course she would go through with the abortion. But, for the time being, she turned her face up to the sun and closed her eyes.

The clock on Kungsladugård school was telling her it was high time she went back to the office. Tell was on holiday, the investigation had come to a halt, and she remembered that she had wanted to pick up the girls a bit earlier than usual. Drive out to Saltholmen, buy some Thai food and eat it on the rocks. Gaze at the sea. She couldn't remember when she'd last had the energy even to think about such exertions.

As she wished the other woman good luck, she realised that she really meant it. She felt a crazy, unexpected wave of happiness. She was delighted by that imagined movement, by the fact that she was a woman, she was strong; by all the strong, hard-working and competent women in the world. Suffused with this feeling she set off towards the car park. There would be no trip to Saltholmen today; she still had paperwork to do. You couldn't teach an old dog new tricks. Karin Beckman would behave as she always did: duty would come first.

CHAPTER
FIFTY-TWO

Stenared

Tell was secretly pleased about the rain that was bucketing down. Their short holiday would soon be over, so they might as well take it easy now they were back home. A lie-in, delicious food, a good film . . . but Seja was disappointed by the weather.

When he arrived at her cottage after a brief trip back to his apartment, he was astonished to find that she had suddenly acquired two sheep, which were now grazing behind the house. He was actually lost for words.

"I know what you're thinking, Christian," she said as soon as he reached the top of the slope. "I did it for Lukas, so that he doesn't feel so lonely."

"So where is he now?"

"Summer grazing. It's not good for horses to spend too much time on their own. And I've always thought I'd like sheep."

"Who the hell gets two sheep for the fun of it?"

"I do!"

This morning the ragged sheep were standing underneath Lukas' shelter, staring miserably at the rain.

As usual it had only taken a day or so before the thought of time off made Christian restless. It always did. Pacing between the living room and the kitchen he stared out at the rain, which was turning the ground in front of the stable into a muddy porridge where the well-trodden grass had grown sparse. If it carried on like this, the footbridge over the marsh would be submerged, and they would have to take the long way round to get to the car.

Seja accepted the fact that their holiday was being washed away. She even said it would be good for the plants. She made the best of the situation, drove down to the library in Olofstorp to borrow books, then curled up on the sofa to do some reading and writing.

Later, she put on her wet-weather gear and announced that she was going to visit Lukas; she asked Tell if he wanted to accompany her, but didn't seem particularly surprised when he declined.

Left alone in the little house he couldn't help but wonder. It was as if their moods were always at odds. He was contented when she was restless and vice versa.

They got to Haga at about two o'clock, and he suggested a stroll around the town. They stopped for a beer and ran across the square, where people waited gloomily in the shelter by the tram stop and the raindrops bounced off the cobbles. They ate fillet of pork with potato gratin, washed down with whisky and a bottle of red wine.

They chatted about ordinary things and had a nice time. And yet a familiar, unpleasant thought crossed his mind: *Is this how it's always going to be?* He had drunk far too much, which was why he dared to articulate this feeling now, in front of Seja.

It wasn't that he was unhappy with her, with life. Nothing was *wrong*. It was that he hadn't come to terms with the fact that they were settled, with the idea that *this is it*. As if the fact that this beautiful, intelligent woman actually wanted him was a trial by fire.

His gratitude was always at odds with his fear of being trapped.

He had blamed past girlfriends for not fitting in with his life, for not accepting him for who he was, for wanting to change him. But of course it had never really been about them. Deep down, he knew the problem stemmed from his own fears, and yet he just couldn't shake them off. He was set in his ways and the fact that Seja did not demand the same promises others had, made absolutely no difference to the way he thought.

In his mind, women wanted another half that fitted perfectly with their half, rather than a complete person. Seja had always been independent and did not need him to complete her. But still, that feeling of being irrevocably trapped loomed over their short holiday. A door was slowly closing. This was his last chance to make his voice heard and to change the way they were going.

"What are you thinking about?"

He relaxed and leant back in his chair.

"I'm thinking about this evening," he said.

Why can't I just come out with it? "About the rest of our lives," he added.

"How do you mean?"

He was skating on thin ice. He had to answer her somehow.

"I'm thinking that you and I are pretty similar. Well, I hope we are. What I mean is . . . I'd be happy to build that sauna for you. At the back of the house, like you said you wanted."

"You want to build me a sauna?"

"Well, have one built . . ."

"But I've never said —"

"No, I know you've never asked me to do it, but that's why I thought I'd like to do that for you . . ."

He hiccupped and suppressed a belch, then continued with what he thought was turning into quite a deep discussion.

"But what I *can't* say, in all honesty, is that I'll always . . . No, fuck it."

He let his head drop. "Seja. I'm forty-five years old. Every decent, serious relationship I've had has ended in . . . recriminations, bitter recriminations. Hmm. What I mean is I'm not even sure I want to. Maybe I haven't got married and started a family simply because I *don't want to*. Maybe I've subconsciously . . . wrecked —"

"What exactly are you trying to say?"

Tell realised he would regret every word as soon as he sobered up, and tried to backtrack. "I . . . Actually, I'm too drunk to talk about or even think about anything . . . remotely sensible. Shall we go home?"

He didn't wait for her answer, but got to his feet slightly unsteadily and went over to the bar to settle up. She stayed where she was, her arms firmly folded. He felt sorry for her, but it was true nonetheless: he was too drunk, too tired and too unsure of what it was he really wanted to say.

How could he get her to understand his feelings when he didn't understand them himself? Why was he trying so hard to destroy the first good thing that had happened to him in years?

They were walking through the park in silence when a shadow appeared behind them.

"Speed?"

The wary voice repeated its monosyllabic question, a little more boldly this time. A man in his twenties with cropped hair brushed against the sleeve of Tell's jacket; Seja was shocked when Tell spun around and pushed him up against a tree.

"Are you trying to sell me speed? Is that what you're trying to do?"

Seja grabbed hold of Tell's arms and pulled him back. "Stop it, what's the matter with you? Leave it!"

Tell wobbled and let go of the terrified dealer, with one final shove in the direction of Vasaplatsen. The lad took to his heels.

"I'll have that little bastard."

Tell managed the last few steps to his door, while Seja remained where she was. Perhaps she was considering going back to the cottage, leaving him alone in his pathetic drunken rage. He keyed in the security code, still aware of her in his peripheral vision.

She passed him on the stairs when he stopped to catch his breath.

"Yes, you're definitely too drunk to do any thinking."

They went for a walk in the Botanic Gardens the following day. Seja showed Tell the lily pond and the viewing points in Änggårsbergen. Raindrops were dripping from the leaves. Seja loved the smell of the wet ground, the feeling that the world was once again reborn and unspoilt. She loved the feeling of sinking into the earth. As long as her shoes were waterproof.

Tell's shoes were not waterproof, of course, so for him the best part of the outing was the French toast at the local pub in Änggården. He had insisted on that, even though Seja had proved almost as obstinate in her desire to have coffee in the pavilion at the Botanic Gardens.

They didn't mention the previous evening's performance. Tell was ashamed of himself, more because of his pathetic, alcohol-related sensitivity than because he might have upset her. As evening fell, his doubts about love began to seem foolish.

"You look so lovely, sitting there."

Seja didn't reply, just smiled to herself as she sat in the living-room window. And even though she reached out to squeeze his hand, it was only then, when she remained silent, that he suddenly felt afraid that he might have ruined everything. Had he given her the idea that their relationship wasn't strong enough, wasn't worth holding onto?

"It's been a good day," she said eventually. "I think I'm going to head home now. I'm tired and hungover and I'd like to get some work done tomorrow."

"You can sleep here; you said you were taking some time off."

"I need to catch up on my sleep."

He gave a short, humourless laugh as he followed her into the hallway.

"Oh, I see what you're doing. It's OK, maybe I made a fool of myself yesterday. I'll take my punishment. But I just want you to know that I didn't mean what came out."

"So what did you mean?"

"Well, I meant it at the time, and it's true that I do have a problem with the idea of lifelong commitment. But the problem's really me, the way I am in relationships. Things always go wrong, sooner or later."

"Have you finished talking about yourself?"

"What?"

She dropped her rucksack to her feet with a thud. "Have you finished talking about yourself and what *you* feel and what *you* think?"

Tell threw back his head and groaned.

"For fuck's sake! All my adult life women have told me I don't talk about my feelings . . . and now I'm trying, I'm fucking trying because I don't want to make the mistakes I've made in every single other relationship. I really want to make things work with you, Seja. But it's as if I've got —"

"Christian, forget what every other woman has told you. I'm not every woman. And the problem isn't that you're talking about your feelings, but that you're *only* talking about *your* feelings. You're talking about our future but you've left me out of the equation."

She tore the rubber band out of her hair, which fell like a mane over her shoulders, making her look even angrier.

"You with your fucking vague, self-satisfied guilt trip: just give it a rest! And you're so full of yourself . . . oh, I don't know. Do you have any idea how self-indulgent you're being? And another thing — I just don't know what you're making such a fuss about! What's the problem?"

Despite everything, he couldn't help laughing at his own self-indulgence. She was angry and confused, and he tried to straighten his face but it was too difficult, and now she was laughing too; she lowered her guard and she beamed, and there was nothing more beautiful than Seja when she beamed.

"Stay."

"No, I'm going. Not because of anything you've said, but because I've got loads to do at home. And we've been together for several days; I need to be alone."

Seja closed her eyes and sighed. "OK. It's because of something you did and said as well. Actually, because of everything you say and do."

Tell looked startled. "Go on . . ."

She started to button her denim jacket, her eyes fixed on a point just above his eyes and slowly shook her head. "You talk about marriage and children . . ."

"I do not!"

"You were certainly talking about marriage and children yesterday, and you always assume — we've talked about this before — that it's what I want. And you know what?"

He tried to talk but she waved away his words as if they were persistent flies.

"It doesn't matter. What I mean is that I love you, Christian. I don't *want* to be infected by your agonies over whether you're letting someone get too close, and I don't want to be embarrassed or ashamed because, God forbid, I might show my feelings. I'm so happy that we met. And I have never said I want to be with you *all the time*. But nor do I want to have to keep repeating that I *don't* want to be with you all the time. Nor can I promise — just like you! — that I'll love you for the rest of my life. There's no need to make that promise. But I don't want to live in some kind of atmosphere of doom and gloom, convinced that nothing ever lasts."

She shrugged on her rucksack and Tell felt an overwhelming urge to stop her from leaving, even though he knew he couldn't.

"I want to be with you," she went on, "but not at the expense of all the good things I had in my life before you came along. I want to keep all those. Just like you, I had a good life before I met you, although I did feel lonely sometimes. And I thought you and I could fill the empty space we used to have in our lives. We don't need to reorganise our lives or stifle ourselves, or encroach on one another just because we feel close to each other."

She tilted her head on one side, took a step towards him and touched his cheek. "It feels as if we've been through all this before."

"Do I have the right to reply?"

Seja sighed. "At the moment, I couldn't give a toss what you reply. There's something I've been wanting to say to you for quite some time. And it's difficult, so I want you to listen until I've finished."

He was afraid he could see tears in her eyes.

"It's not just your fault, your fears, your patterns of behaviour. I've also been afraid of destroying . . . the image of myself I've worked to create. Perhaps I thought that as long as I didn't mention it, there was still a chance that you *would* understand me if I just explained. That I'm not independent; on the contrary, I need lots of things. Attention, approval, security. I'm happy with my life, but I'm not content just to live in the present — although I know that's probably what I've given you to believe — or to settle for making no demands on you. I'm so tired of being strong because you're not, sometimes I just want to close my eyes and fall, knowing that someone will catch me, without anxiety, without hassle . . ."

She took a deep breath. "What I'm trying to say is that I don't think this relationship is good for me in the long run. I'm tired of arguments and misunderstandings. It's not enough."

"So you're dumping me?" he asked suspiciously, wishing his voice didn't sound quite so desperate. "I can't help feeling this is a punishment for yesterday."

"Dumping you? For God's sake, we're not sixteen! Shall I spell it out? I can't live with you. It would just make me unhappy."

Tell wanted to keep her there. He had a bad feeling: if she walks out that door now, she might never come back.

"And what can I do to stop you feeling like this? Or is it all too late?"

She shook her head. "Stop it, Christian. Don't lay everything at my feet, we can talk about it later."

Once the sounds of Seja's steps had faded, he let the door close. It was dark. Very little light came into the hallway. His back started to hurt from standing, so he crouched down while he thought about what to do next, overwhelmed by the idea that he was unbearably lost.

Perhaps he could watch a film. He hadn't read the newspaper yet.

He had absolutely no idea what to do next.

CHAPTER
FIFTY-THREE

Gothenburg

Annelie Swerin would miss Henrik. The fire within him, the naivety which was as endearing as it was infuriating. Henrik was a flirt, a gambler with an eye for the ladies, that was part of the deal, that was who he was. Annelie had chosen not to get involved in the issue of Henrik's love life. It was none of her business. She believed in love, whatever form it took.

Murdered. She couldn't take it in. Marie Hjalmarsson had been the first to tell her, the very evening Annelie got back from Bangalore. Her first emotion had been fear. That was only natural, Marie had said; you don't think that sort of thing could happen to someone you know, someone like you. Not the stuff you see in the papers and on *Crimewatch*: murder, torture, rape.

Annelie had thought she could detect melodrama in Marie's voice. The Marie she had a problem with came crawling out. The Marie who had once categorically condemned Annelie's relationship with David, as if Annelie's decision to embark upon a relationship with a married man had been a simple, well-thought-out choice. As if Annelie had never thought in terms of morality or female solidarity, as if the brief relationship hadn't torn her apart before she finally decided to give up and let him go back to his wife. Annelie had even left the country to put distance between them, and it had worked. Until now.

The trip had been a distraction; she wasn't sure it had changed how she felt deep down. Only a few hours after she had set foot in her apartment, after passing David's shop and glimpsing his wife inside, the old feelings of abandonment had threatened to resurface.

Then Marie had called.

Axel had been the last straw. Annelie just couldn't deal with his torment as well. He had turned up in the car park outside her apartment block shortly after she had got back. Since then she had seen him several times. Did he want to talk? They'd never spent time together alone before.

It was perfectly understandable that he was upset. Henrik was a close friend and she was perhaps one of the few people who understood how important he had been to Axel; so why was she so reluctant to go down and talk?

Seeing Axel reminded her of that night in Istanbul. Jefferson Airplane had been playing at full volume in the bar and he had sat very close to her, grabbed her hand across the table and squeezed it unbelievably hard; she didn't know why she hadn't stopped him.

Hesitantly, she slipped on her shoes and picked up her thin jacket. She needed to talk to someone, to David.

CHAPTER
FIFTY-FOUR

Gothenburg

That evening at the Nefertiti had been a meeting of minds. After the obligatory small talk, he and Henrik had discussed faith and the future of the universe — it was like a new language he hadn't completely mastered; he had stumbled, started again, gone round in circles, but Henrik had listened patiently. Taken it all in, thought it over . . . it was such a long time since he had talked to anyone, really.

They had been drunk, but that didn't matter, especially now.

Later that night, when he walked home to his empty apartment, along the desolate, echoing quayside, he had felt an immediate sense of loss. As if something he had hardly been aware of was suddenly missing, like an amputated limb. He knew he would do anything to resume the conversation where it had left off.

The four walls of his apartment closed in on him. For a while he felt a physical need to defend himself. Henrik's betrayal hurt. It reminded him of past betrayals, of his father, but he mustn't blaspheme. He mustn't sink below the surface. Hauling himself out had almost cost him his life.

For the first time in an eternity, he could see clearly. The first part of the journey had been long.

When he was on medication, his thoughts had been like the logs piled up by the stove back home in his village: predictable, uninspiring, or as tough as willow branches. He had noticed an immediate change when he stopped taking the tablets. Ideas crowded his brain, like a gang of schoolchildren with the bell still ringing in their ears, pushing and shoving to escape; the images in his head didn't always correspond with his inner voice and the words it used. More often than not the sentences were too long; it was impossible to follow them to the end. He noticed that there wasn't usually an end at all, in fact, apart from the obvious. Death. And that was only proper.

Time was running out now that she had come home. He had watched from a distance, staking out her window. The fact that she had seen him didn't matter, of course she had seen him. He wanted Annelie to see him, to respond to him just as she had done in Istanbul, only this time he was determined to be better prepared.

He was leaning on the wall with his back and the palms of his hands pressed against the warm bricks when she ran around the corner to the shop. She was glancing nervously around, looking but not seeing, blinded by anxiety. She could have looked at him and everything might have taken a different turn, but no, she was completely self-absorbed as she made her way to David's shop.

She yanked the door open as if her life depended on it. Her skirt ended halfway up her tanned thighs. He thought about how David must have undressed her with his eyes, unashamed, when she had been his mistress. How she must have begged for it, just as she had begged for attention in Istanbul. Duped him into talking. It was obvious that the trip to India hadn't brought her any kind of insight, or given her any more self-respect. On the contrary, she was running back to David.

What did she have to say to him?

The disintegration of his thoughts was accelerating. It was threatening the potency he had only just acquired.

All roads led back to Carla. But this time he was going to do the right thing and the circle would be complete.

"David!"

"Annelie?"

He walked around the counter and stood in front of her for a couple of seconds before his hand touched her upper arm, warm but hesitant. When he finally moved to hug her, she was the one who backed away. It made her feel stronger. "Leila?"

"She's not here. How have you been? You're so brown . . ."

He smiled without parting his lips, a melancholy smile which said all the things he couldn't bring himself to say: *I've missed you and I'm sorry that it has to be this way, that we had to make this choice, that we hurt each other.*

She looked down at her bare legs with their sun-bleached hairs and her feet, striped from the sandals she had worn most of the time in India; she bit her lip to stop tears from coming as she remembered that she had bought them in Istanbul and that Henrik had bought a very similar pair.

"Fine. I've missed you."

"Annelie, I —"

"I know, but you did ask. And I'm not fine at all, actually. Did you read about the murders?"

"On Linnégatan? Yes."

"I knew the man. Henrik, he was on the same course as me. I must have mentioned him, you might even have seen him around. And the woman was a tutor in our department."

"Oh my God . . . No, there were no details in the paper, it just said they'd been . . . Well, there's no point in going into all that now. Do you need someone to talk to?"

This time she couldn't hold back the tears. "You were the first person I thought of." She tried to pull herself together. David looked at her searchingly. "Is there something else? Sweetheart . . . How are you coping?"

Her fears suddenly seemed contrived, paranoid. She didn't answer him straightaway.

"I'll get through it." She shook her head slowly. "Of course it's horrible, I liked Henrik. And we used to hang out together, there were a few of us who . . . It's worse for the others than it is for me. His partner Rebecca. And Axel, his best friend — he was on our course too. He invested so much in Henrik, it was as if he didn't have anyone else, it was almost laughable sometimes . . . As if he only existed when Henrik was around. He seems so helpless, you know. I really do understand that he's completely devastated and confused. I mean, I really do feel sorry for him and . . ."

David nodded, broke in. "Stop, Annelie — you're in shock. You've come home to terrible news. I'd . . . I'd really like to say that I'm here for you, but you know I'd be lying if I made a promise like that. You know how things stand."

He pulled her towards him anyway, into his arms, stroking her back, smelling just the way he always did. She let the tears come, resting her cheek against his shoulder; all she wanted to do was to stay there, but because she knew that he would push her away at any second, she decided to get there first, in just a few seconds more . . .

He pushed her away gently. His voice was unsteady too. "Go and see a friend. Or go back to your parents for a while. Have a rest, let them look after you. And stop worrying about everybody else. You can't help Henrik's partner anyway, nor this Axel . . ."

"He sits outside my apartment."

It was too late to take it back.

"What did you say?"

Surprise and a shadow of doubt on David's face.

She took a deep breath. "He sits outside my apartment block looking up at my window. I've seen him several times."

"But what does he want?"

She shrugged, trying to feign nonchalance. "I don't know, like I said I think he's really upset about Henrik. I haven't wanted to go down and speak to him, because . . ."

In the silence that followed, her hands felt like lumps of lead, dragging her down towards the floor. He was waiting for her to carry on, to provide a clarification she wasn't sure she could give.

"I don't know. There was a kind of . . . desperation about him. I first noticed it on the trip to Istanbul, you remember that? A terrible loneliness — he's very quiet and a bit of an oddball, and . . . I got the feeling that his friendship with Henrik filled an enormous void, do you know what I mean?"

"And?" David said impatiently, unsympathetically, and she felt her face close down, felt herself clamming up because he didn't understand.

"And nothing. I'm just trying to work out why it feels peculiar. Now he hasn't got Henrik, he must be devastated."

"Hang on a minute," said David. "He's watching you? He sits and stares up at your window, but doesn't try to talk to you? That doesn't sound very healthy to me. Why the hell are you putting up with it?"

"So what do you think I should do?"

"Go to the police, of course."

"Oh, please . . ."

David waved his hand. "What? There's something the matter with this guy, he might be one of those stalkers who's decided to come after you instead, now Henrik's gone. If you don't do something right away you'll soon have him inside your apartment, and then you'll never get rid of him. What's the problem — I mean, you said you thought he was unpleasant?"

She sighed, tipped back her head and gazed up at a crack running across the ceiling. "No . . . Well, yes. Maybe a bit. I don't know what he wants. And there was something about his grip on reality when we were in Istanbul; it wasn't very stable. I'm sure he feels like shit, but I just can't carry someone else right now."

"And you're not even going to try, Annelie." David took her hands and looked into her eyes. "Go home now and call the police. Tell them exactly what's going on, that there's a man who won't leave you alone, that you don't want to talk to him and that you feel uncomfortable. What he's doing has to be illegal. The guy needs to have his card marked, if only for his own sake! And you don't owe him any particular loyalty, do you?"

"Well . . . only the loyalty we owe our friends."

"Friends don't creep around in the bushes without saying hello. No, the police will pick him up and speak to him. He might even be able to get some help. Trauma counselling, or whatever the hell it's called. Why do you always have to take the weight of the world on your shoulders?"

Annelie smiled instinctively as David placed his hand on her cheek, but suddenly she wanted neither his embrace nor his good advice.

"Now go and do what I said."

The doorbell alerted them to the arrival of a woman, followed by a man in an anorak.

"A packet of tobacco," the woman said hoarsely. "Lucky Strike and the evening paper please."

Annelie took the opportunity to back away towards the door. David made a vague gesture, his little finger to his lips and his thumb to his ear, call the police? Or did he mean that she should ring him? That they should keep in touch? As friends?

It was perhaps just as well that question remained unanswered. She realised that her unease had nothing to do with David, but that she had found no solace in him either. She would do better to rely on herself. Or a girlfriend. As soon as she got home, she would ring a friend. Ask her to stay over, cook a meal together and chat.

For the first time since her return from India, she had the feeling that there was water under the bridge between her and David. That in spite of everything, she was well on the way to putting the pain behind her.

She would run the final stretch back home.

Annelie and David had been standing in front of the counter for a long time, deep in a conversation.

He had taken up position a short distance away on the other side of the street. If he moved any closer to the glass wall of the shop they would see him, and he hadn't thought that far ahead. He screwed up his eyes so that he could make out their expressions; he was standing so close by now that he could see Annelie shaking her head, wiping tears from her eyes and cheeks.

Her body trembled in David Sevic's arms.

He moved closer, step by step. It had become a game: in the end he was so close to the glass that he felt like moving from the corner right up to the window and breathing on the glass. Writing his name: *Here I am*.

Was he really invisible?

David Sevic had his arms around Annelie, he was stroking her back, over and over again.

Gradually she relaxed.

But David didn't seem able to accept the hopelessness of his situation, to admit that he could do nothing to change his fate. It wasn't long before he pushed Annelie away and adopted an expression which suggested he wanted to find a solution, to take charge of the situation like a man. Was he going to ring the police? The shopkeeper waved his hand in a gesture that spoke more of agitation than resignation; it was just so typical of him! Now he was angry! Anger was his solution.

He suspected that Annelie had noticed him outside her window but was deliberately ignoring him. Did she feel hunted? Was she also thinking back to Istanbul?

When David let her go, Annelie slumped slightly, as if he had been holding her up.

He heard footsteps and the low murmur of conversation behind him. A couple walked past; they tied their dog to the lamp post outside the shop and went inside. David had to remind himself that he was working; he straightened up and moved behind the counter. Annelie backed away towards the door. As she stepped onto the pavement her former lover rang up a packet of tobacco and an evening paper on the till, put his little finger to his lips and his thumb to his ear as though he were on the telephone and nodded: I'll call you?

He slipped back around the corner and made himself even more invisible. His nails were digging into the palms of his hands.

It was so easy to give in to his impulses; he could already feel vague urges bubbling away inside him. He had done it before. David was suddenly a problem which had to be dealt with. Annelie wasn't going to disappear; he had no doubt he could make her understand.

She looked over her shoulder but didn't appear to notice him as she crossed Kabelgatan. She ran the final stretch back home.

He hadn't planned it in advance.

In the shop he surprised himself by asking David about Annelie. His approach was clumsy, and obviously David reacted. He must have meant for David to react! He *wanted* confirmation that Annelie had told David all about him!

"I know who you are and what you're up to," David said, his jaw tense. "Leave Annelie alone! Understand? I'm calling the police. We've just decided to call the police, so you'd better sling your hook. And don't come back."

By way of a warning, he placed his hand on a blue telephone next to the till.

We?

David was standing with his arms folded over his broad chest, it was a show of strength; like Father he was a big man, his gaze steady. Only his slightly parted lips and the tiniest twitch of a muscle in his face spoke of his fear.

"I'm calling the police."

"What makes you think you deserve to live?"

He placed his hand very gently on the gun he had stolen from his father a long time ago; it was hidden in a towel in his bag. "You're betraying your son and his mother. The boy is suffering, perhaps the mother takes her own suffering out on the boy. But what would you know? And what about Annelie? She's naive, she's not stupid but she is easily led. You have done your best to destroy her. I repeat, what makes you think you deserve to live, or that I will allow you to destroy my life?"

They were interrupted by another customer, a little girl who spent an age choosing sweets before counting out the exact money. Once again David had to pull himself together to serve her. Interrupting the conversation felt strange to both of them.

He had left the shop, crossed the road and gone up the hill where he knew he could watch the shop without being visible from it.

David hadn't said much, but what he had said was important. He turned the words over and over in his mind, tasted them: the order to leave Annelie alone, the threat that otherwise *we* would ring the police. A wave of nausea rose in his throat at the thought of *we*, of that evening in Istanbul when he opened up to her, lost control and told her about him and Henrik. How she had seen the real him, then made fun of it.

And in the end she had been afraid. Henrik had been sitting just next to them, it was crazy; it was as if he almost *wanted* Henrik to hear.

But Henrik had been so absorbed in Ann-Marie, he hadn't heard a thing.

He had never belonged. He got angry but calmed down in a couple of minutes. He sat there looking down at the shop: the man behind the counter, the girl's brown plaits, her white dress bobbing up and down, the door leading to the office at the back, then into the storeroom.

As soon as the girl had left the shop, he went back down the hill, quickly crossed the road and shot David with the gun he had kept hidden ever since his visit to England, ever since Carla. David had put back the jars of flying saucers, fizzy cola bottles and foam bananas and was just turning around, his hand reaching in vain for the telephone. There was nowhere to hide. It was easy, just like the last time. The bullet hit his temple. It didn't make much noise, you could easily imagine that nothing had happened. David didn't make any noise either, he didn't have time to scream or cry. Silently he doubled over and sank to the floor, then his top half fell to one side and it was almost as though he were stretching, as though he wanted to go comfortably into death.

There was no need to run. This time he didn't panic, even though he hadn't realised what he was about to do, nor did he feel that terrible exhaustion.

He wiped the gun, wrapped it in the towel and calmly left the shop.

CHAPTER
FIFTY-FIVE

Gothenburg

After the excitement of Copenhagen, Gonzales found it difficult to deal with the more mundane aspects of the investigation. The murders of Samuelsson and Karpov felt distant, particularly after the focus had shifted to the burglary. He wasn't in the right frame of mind.

He had gone through the newspapers as he always did, looking for smaller articles on the Linné murders, which been splashed across front pages before the blood was even dry. And now not a word. It really was yesterday's news.

He folded up the paper and tossed it away. The thought of backtracking to the point when Rebecca Nykvist was still the main suspect, back to Professor Alexandr Karpov or the gossiping students, held absolutely no appeal.

The Danish police were relaying information on a regular basis. As they expected, both Knud Iversen and Dorte Sørbækk had an alibi for the time of the murders.

And Tell was on holiday.

He tried Annelie Swerin's number again, almost out of habit, and was almost shocked to hear a human voice instead of an answering machine.

"Annelie Swerin."

"Michael Gonzales, police. I'd like to talk to you in connection with our ongoing inquiry into the murders of Ann-Marie Karpov and Henrik Samuelsson. This is purely a matter of routine; we're speaking to everyone who knew them. Could we arrange a time to meet as soon as possible?"

Höije appeared in the doorway.

"Excuse me a moment." Gonzales placed his hand over the mouthpiece.

Höije pointed down the corridor. "Could you come to my office when you have a moment?"

Gonzales nodded, suspecting that it wasn't really a question, and went back to Annelie Swerin, who had just returned from her dig. She didn't sound particularly surprised to hear from him, which led him to assume she had already been informed about the deaths, probably by one of her fellow students. She had actually been thinking of ringing the police herself, she said; she talked quickly and sounded a little on edge.

Höije was still standing in the doorway, which made Gonzales nervous, and he tripped over his words.

"I'll get someone to contact you as soon as possible."

To give himself something to do with his hands, and appear more efficient, he opened a Word document and started typing, nodding and making appropriate sounds of agreement.

"No, you mustn't feel stupid. Of course you don't have to put up with that sort of thing if it makes you uncomfortable."

Höije raised his eyebrows and Gonzales started to feel annoyed. What did the man actually want?

By the time he hung up, the boss had finally vacated the doorway. Gonzales headed for his office.

Höije was on the phone when Gonzales knocked, but waved him in.

"Yes, of course we'll consider all the options, yes, mm. Yes, that's our target, that's correct. But of course we must take into account . . . Yes, yes. I can definitely confirm that . . ."

Gonzales suddenly realised how tired he was, and that he was feeling slightly unwell. Perhaps the prawn salad he'd eaten last night had been off. He wondered how Höije would react if he bent over and threw up on his desk.

At that point Höije put the phone down.

"Michael."

He turned to face Gonzales, his fingers steepled beneath his chin. "I must applaud you for your efforts in Copenhagen."

"I didn't do much."

"How long have you been working here now? As part of the team?"

What the fuck is this all about?

"A couple of years, I think. Two. Just about."

Höije nodded thoughtfully. "And you're happy? In the team?"

"Yes?"

Gonzales wondered feverishly what Höije was getting at. He hadn't had many dealings with the new boss, but he didn't believe for a moment that this conversation was about his feelings. Nor did it seem as if Höije wanted an update on the investigation.

"You get on well with your colleagues?"

"I think we all complement each other very well."

He felt the urge to add a provocative "sir". The whole situation felt stressful. He was struck by the thought, perhaps unfairly, that a conversation like this would never have taken place under their former boss. Ann-Christine Östergren had been Gonzales' superior for just a year. That year had been enough for her to win his trust.

"And your superiors?"

Ah, so that was it. Gonzales stretched and adopted what he thought was a neutral expression. If Höije was after gossip, he'd come to the wrong person.

"Well, you haven't been in the post all that long, and we haven't had a great deal to do with each other, but so far —"

"I wasn't talking about myself, but about your immediate boss."

You think I don't know that?

"Tell?"

"Christian Tell, yes."

"It's fine."

"Fine?"

"Fine."

Höije seemed to be waiting for something more. Gonzales was waiting too — for him to carry on.

"You're . . . quite young to have got this far, to be where you are now."

"Yes."

"Part of this team."

"Quite."

"Hm. I can't make any promises, of course, but . . . from what I've seen so far, I think you could have a very promising career ahead of you."

Gonzales hadn't the faintest idea what he was supposed to say to that.

"I've always wanted to work in this team." *If there's something you want to say, let's have it.* "I've never wanted to do anything else."

Höije winked at Gonzales conspiratorially.

"Oh, come on, Michael. Don't tell me you've never toyed with the idea of promotion. And if you do, I won't believe you. Don't get me wrong, you're still new. We're talking about the future here."

Gonzales could feel his irritation growing. "I thought you were doing most of the talking."

Höije didn't return Gonzales's smile; instead he looked serious.

"In that case, now it's your turn to talk. According to what I've heard, from various people, I have the impression that Christian Tell can be . . ."

He fell silent, pretending to weigh his words carefully.

"Can be . . .?"

"Can be a little . . . unusual to work with. He likes to do his own thing."

Gonzales adopted a puzzled expression.

"I've heard he can be impulsive in a way that might negatively impact on team morale."

Höije removed his glasses and rubbed at a mark on the lens. "The quality of our work is largely dependent on teamwork. If a leader is unwilling to listen to the concerns of his colleagues —"

"Who — forgive me for interrupting — has this come from?"

"That's irrelevant. The main thing is that I know. And I want to hear what you think. You're relatively new, you haven't become institutionalised, you have a fresh pair of eyes and you can look at things in an objective, constructive way. My predecessor mentioned that —"

"Östergren had complete faith in Tell." Gonzales knew that his gaze was utterly steady. "And so do I. Besides which, I'm sure that the clear-up statistics prove that he's good at his job."

Höije pursed his lips; suddenly he didn't look half as conspiratorial.

"I wasn't talking about the clear-up statistics, I was talking about what Tell is like as a leader, and how you function as a team."

"Brilliantly."

The situation no longer felt uncomfortable; in fact, Gonzales wanted to prolong it, make it into a short film and post it on YouTube.

"As I said, we work very well as a team."

"Thank you, in that case I'm satisfied."

"No, *thank you*. Can I go now?"

Höije laughed sourly. "You can go whenever you like."

Gonzales made the victory sign at himself as he passed the mirror in the waiting room. Then he realised he really did feel sick.

CHAPTER
FIFTY-SIX

Gothenburg

As she looked around the corner shop, Karin Beckman decided that the owner must have been a stickler for detail. A place for everything and everything in its place, if you ignored the equipment the investigators had spread around. There was a little label under each item for sale and not a single one was crooked. The floor was polished to a high shine, except for the pool of blood in which the man lay. The very picture of life's fragility. He had been particular about his polished floor, but here he lay, and for what? A few hundred kronor?

Bärneflod put her thoughts into words in his own way as he fiddled with the buttons on the till. "What's happening to this country? Mark my words, we'll soon be in the same mess as America, where you can be stabbed for a crap pair of trainers. I remember when there used to be a code of honour, even for gangsters. You didn't shoot a guy for the day's takings, it just wasn't the done thing."

He brought his fist down on the uncooperative machine and was about to threaten it with further violence when Beckman bent down and found the button underneath.

"There. And keep your voice down. The family are still in the back."

The man's wife and son were in the room behind the shop. Beckman had made a fruitless attempt to persuade the family to go to hospital to see if they needed treatment for shock; the wife was on the verge of total collapse. The boy kept mechanically stroking her hair, his eyes frightened and full of tears as he took in the extent of her despair. He had lost his father. He swallowed. Over and over again. Beckman had seen it all before.

When the ambulance arrived, Beckman saw paramedics give the woman an injection, then she looked into the boy's desperate eyes one last time before the doors closed.

She went back inside to Bärneflod, who was waving a bundle of hundred-kronor notes in the air.

"I just don't get it! Look at this!"

"Perhaps they only took the bigger notes."

"There's a couple of thousand here — show me the thief who's too good to pocket that! Do you really think this was a robbery?"

Beckman put her hands in her pockets. The smell of blood seemed stronger now the body was gone.

"I don't know — it seems a bit odd. Have we got anything else on this place? Known association with gang activity?"

"Not as far as I know. Did you manage to get anything out of the woman?"

"No."

394

Bärneflod disappeared into the back room and spoke to one of the technicians, but she couldn't hear what they were saying. She let her gaze wander over the display of magazines: hardly anything but naked female bodies in degrading poses. One glossy was adorned with a picture of a pouting young woman with nothing but a big lollipop to cover her modesty.

She went outside to get some air. At first her legs seemed to move of their own accord, then she decided to go for a short walk. Not so long ago she had hardly known that this area existed. She set off at a fair pace towards a yellow brick building which turned out to be a care home, then along a track that snaked down the hill. After the second bend she was confronted by the roofs of Majorna: a high, recently built tower block in the foreground, with Gothenburg's trademark "governor's houses", imposing buildings set around courtyards, in the backdrop. Far away in the distance, toy cars sped across the Älvsborg Bridge towards the Sandarna area of the city. A mist was rolling in off the sea in spite of the fine weather. Or was it exhaust fumes?

Beckman turned, having established that the track went all the way down to Mariaplan, then marched back uphill until she could see the shop once more. Had the shooting been a spontaneous act? Surely the perpetrator must have checked out the area in advance, or at least known the lie of the land?

She scratched her hand as she grabbed a dry branch and pulled herself up onto the hill directly opposite the crime scene. Beer cans and sweet wrappers were strewn on the ground and there was certainly an excellent view into the shop. She would have a word with the crime scene technicians and ask them to take a look before they packed up; better safe than sorry.

A tiny drop of blood oozed from the scratch on the back of her hand. Beckman wiped it off on her jacket and looked up at the apartment blocks with their gleaming windows, then she slithered down the hill and went back into the shop.

Bärneflod had brought out a couple of files from the office behind the shop and was leafing through them. He made a note of a couple of names and telephone numbers. "I thought the owner's name was David Sevic?"

"It was."

"It says Josef Sevic here in the annual accounts."

"A relative, maybe?"

"Check it out."

"We've got a team meeting with the boss," said Beckman. "Soon."

"I thought Tell was on holiday."

"I meant Höije. He wants to discuss the Linnégatan case."

"Mm. I suppose he wants to make sure we're behaving ourselves." Bärneflod hated to be interrupted when he was in the middle of something.

"I'll go to the meeting," Beckman decided. "I can report on what we've found here and see if there's any new information. Then I'll come back. I'll leave you to go through the office in peace."

★ ★ ★

396

Shortly afterwards, Beckman nodded in Höije's direction and sank down next to Karlberg, who was looking lonely at the shabby conference table across from the boss.

"So where's Gonzales, then?"

"He went home, a stomach bug or something."

Höije pushed his glasses onto the top of his head and leant forward; he looked like a rugby player preparing for a scrum.

"Karlberg and I were talking about the murders on Linnégatan before you arrived. I suggest we change the subject and talk about this new case while it's still fresh in our minds. Karin, if you could give us a short summary, I'll suggest the allocation of tasks and you can pass that on to your colleagues when they return. When everybody knows what they're doing, you can get started. OK?"

They nodded in some confusion: was there any other way of doing things?

Beckman began. "It's a corner shop in Gråberget. The owner was one David Sevic. He was married with a ten-year-old son and he's been running the shop for about four years. According to his wife there were no known threats against him. He had no employees at the time of his death; his wife used to cover for him. A couple of students had worked there on and off in the past. The family lives on Södra Dragspelsgatan in Frölunda. It seems as if the business was in pretty good shape; the accounts were taken care of by a Josef Sevic and we've just identified him as David's older brother."

"Has he been informed of the death?"

"Not by us."

"Was he David's business partner?"

"No, I don't think so . . . I rang his work mobile, and his voicemail says he's caretaker at the Carl Johan church. Shall I go on?"

"Please."

"David Sevic was shot in the head in the shop. Nothing else of particular note. And that's more or less all I know at the moment."

"In the head?"

"Yes. Either at very close quarters or else we're dealing with an excellent shot."

"We don't know that yet," Höije interrupted. "Has a thorough investigation of the crime scene been carried out?"

"It's ongoing."

"And you've been there?"

"I left a little while ago. Bärneflod stayed behind. He might well have made a start on door-to-door enquiries."

"Good. In that case Karlberg will assist Bärneflod. Karin," *Isn't it just typical that he calls the men by their surname and me by my first name.* — "I'd like you to try to get hold of Sevic's brother. If you have time, check out David Sevic, then think about how we can proceed. Contact whoever's looking after his wife at the hospital and find out when we can speak to her."

"No problem."

"Good. And while Tell is on holiday, you report directly to me. That includes outside normal office hours."

★ ★ ★

It was almost evening. Beckman wasn't due back at the office; her report could wait until tomorrow and she didn't have the children. She was sitting on the steps of the Carl Johan church, getting her breath back after informing Josef Sevic of his brother's death. She hadn't done it alone, but these things were never easy. It was obvious that the brothers had been very close, but Josef Sevic knew of no threats to the family or the business.

"Some kind of protection racket?" Beckman ventured tentatively.

"Not as far as I know. Everything David did was above board. It must have been a meaningless, opportunistic . . . robbery?"

He buried his face in his hands when Beckman said that the police would need to talk to him again, as soon as he felt up to it, preferably tomorrow. He pulled himself together, the pain etched on his face, and got into the police car which would take him to the hospital and to his brother's son and wife.

The graphite-grey stone was soft to the touch. Beckman remembered how, as a child, she would count the fossils embedded in the steps of the church at home: snail shells or huge, grotesque wood lice.

She looked down at what she was wearing. Brown, low-heeled shoes, thin cotton trousers. The lace trim on the top under her sweater was just showing. She smiled without quite knowing why. The rush of happiness she had experienced when she talked to the pregnant woman by the paddling pool had faded, leaving a surprising feeling of acceptance: life really was very strange. Beckman had always been absolutely certain that we choose our own fate, but at the moment she was prepared to reconsider.

The traffic on Karl Johansgatan was beginning to ease. She walked along the narrow path around the church and the roar from the four lanes of traffic on Oscarsleden grew louder. She could see the water now: the Stena Line complex, one of the ships resting in the harbour like a white whale.

She was surprised that the church was open to the public and went inside. It was empty, her footsteps echoing as she walked up the aisle.

Karin Beckman had not walked towards an altar since she was a child at Sunday school. When she married Göran it had been a civil ceremony with four friends as witnesses — they had been very careful to keep it small and low-key. They went to Greece for two weeks instead of having a reception. She could hardly remember a thing about that trip. From time to time she regretted not getting married in church, since she was getting married anyway. Not having had the full works.

She tipped her head back and gazed at the paintings on the ceiling. The light in churches was always somehow ethereal, falling through high windows and capturing the drifting dust motes; licking its way along the ceiling as darkness fell. Beckman didn't have her glasses with her and couldn't make much out, but she could see many different colours, dull with age, merging in front of her. Was that the Last Supper? The rail on the balcony was covered in cherubs, just as the balcony in the church of her childhood had been strewn with winged infants. Beckman shuddered; she couldn't help thinking of the cherubs as dead children, children who had died and gone to heaven. Perhaps that wasn't exactly what she had learnt at Sunday school, which had been held on that very balcony above the rows of pews. She breathed in the smell of every Swedish church: paint and ancient bibles.

In spite of the fact that she had never been particularly religious, Beckman felt as if she had come home. Not that she necessarily welcomed the idea of coming home. She felt the security of the familiar, but also a growing sense of defiance, just as when she was a child but with no clear target.

She cleared her throat and the sound echoed off the stone walls. *I'm going to stay here for a while, but I'm not going to pray.* In her mind she lit a candle for the future.

CHAPTER
FIFTY-SEVEN

Gothenburg

Annelie had called a girlfriend and asked if she could stay over, claiming her encounter with David had left her feeling bereft; it wasn't really an excuse. It was good to talk about David, but she hadn't been able to talk about this business with Axel. She wouldn't have known where to start.

It was nice to hear her friend singing in the bathroom.

Annelie had finally decided to report the matter to the police, but they had got there first. She was surprised. The officer she spoke to was calm and authoritative, in spite of the fact that he sounded very young. Although his questions gave her no reason to feel that he was doubting her, she could hear herself downplaying what had happened.

It was as though she couldn't quite trust her instincts. She felt a pang of guilt as she heard herself listing vague accusations against Axel, and in the middle of it all she suddenly thought about Henrik and the way his enthusiasm had held together people who were essentially very different.

There was a cold, brief flash of light as yet another police car passed her building and disappeared, this one in less of a hurry than the first. What had happened to Henrik and Ann-Marie was still impossible to take in or understand. Now it looked as if something else had happened, and not very far away. She couldn't even begin to imagine what it might be: the police cars gathering, the silent ambulance that braked every time it hit a speed bump. But there was nothing she could do. After everything that had happened, it was entirely possible that she was making the business with Axel out to be more than it was.

But in Istanbul his eyes had terrified her, pinning her down. For a few moments she became an insect under his microscope, in his power.

"It's simple, you have to leave David alone." Axel had still been clutching her hand tightly. When she hadn't understood what he was talking about, he had tried to explain: "He makes you dirty, you make him dirty. He's betraying his family because of lust, just like those two over there. She means nothing to him, nothing at all. Henrik would never risk what he and I —"

"You and Henrik? Axel, you're mixing up —"

"I'm talking about our friendship. Nothing else."

"I —"

He stopped her again. "You and David have power, but you're abusing it. Do you understand? You're weak and self-centred and you're closing your eyes to the pain of others. Do you really want to be that kind of person?"

Annelie withdrew her hand. "What are you talking about?"

"You asked me for advice and it's simple: you must put everything behind you. Find a way back to your own moral compass and allow David to do the same. You and Ann-Marie and Henrik have to save yourselves while you can. If you can. I'm just trying to help."

He had gone on. He had started talking about his ex-girlfriend; Annelie remembered his words in fragments, crazy words from a crazy person, even if Henrik and Ann-Marie had brushed it all aside the next day when Axel was normal again, insisting he'd just had too much to drink. Nothing to worry about. Annelie was making a mountain out of a molehill. But they hadn't seen the look in his eyes.

CHAPTER
FIFTY-EIGHT

Axel had been reading his old notebooks. After his first proper meeting with Henrik, he had written: *He is intelligent, loyal, but untaught. There is hope.*

At first Henrik had been a project.

Henrik's standard response when he was asked to nail his colours to the mast was: "I believe in something. I believe in something greater than us, I just don't know what it is."

No indulgence was to be expected when it came to similar evasions. Loyalty was what he wanted from Henrik.

Many of the twists and turns in their friendship had been influenced by Axel's own confusion; he was the first to admit his weakness. At times he had found himself indolent and incapable, looking at things the wrong way. He had often doubted his project.

Henrik took me to his heart. After our first meeting I was caught fast. I, a weak-willed person who melts when someone really sees me.

That was exactly two years ago. From his own clumsy handwriting he could see that the words had been written under the influence of his medication. They might not have dulled his brain as so many other psychiatric drugs did, the ones he refused to take, but they had taken away his courage. *Foundation course in RE* — he had made a mental note of the course Henrik had been thinking of taking, even though they had both been drunk when they first spoke.

When the register was called on the first day, he recognised Henrik at once. The hesitation he felt on walking into the university building disappeared. Earlier he had questioned his motives, had almost felt stupid, but no longer.

He had raised his hand in greeting across the lecture room. Henrik looked puzzled at first, and then he knew.

When Henrik nodded in response, the world around them faded away. Henrik burnt with charisma, drawing people to him, indifferent to what anyone thought of him.

Culture and Society in Ancient Civilisations had come later. Ann-Marie Karpov had been wearing a black, sheer blouse through which you could see the outline of her bra. She was already flaunting herself in front of Henrik, even back then.

Henrik didn't notice Axel at first, but that didn't matter; he was nothing if not patient.

It happened a little way into the first term. They ended up in the university library and picked up the discussion where they had left it at the Nefertiti in the early hours of the morning. He had prepared his opening remarks very carefully, had talked about Christianity, Catholicism, the Swedish church and the mission church, and the conversation took unexpected, amusing turns. They got on well; this was a topic on which Axel felt completely at home and Henrik was impressed, that much was obvious. They missed a lecture because they couldn't tear themselves away from each other.

Henrik invited him for a drink and he drank again even though he hated the way alcohol affected him; however, if there was one thing at which he excelled, it was adapting to fit the perception of others. Before he knew it, he was someone. For a person on the run — which of course he was — it was balsam to a wounded soul. He didn't have to be himself, and he didn't have to be alone.

If it hadn't been for Ann-Marie Karpov, he would have been someone for ever.

Once Henrik fell for Ann-Marie, it was as though no one else existed. Ann-Marie sucked the nectar out of Henrik, the nectar that Axel himself would have dared to wish for. Henrik blossomed with Ann-Marie.

And Axel had become a nobody once more.

Ann-Marie had got in the way.

Rebecca had never troubled his hold. Axel soon became Henrik's confidant, gaining an insight into every corner of the couple's relationship. It was revolting and exciting at the same time. Henrik talked about their constant bickering. How rarely he and Rebecca were intimate, how she took away his freedom and exerted control. Sooner or later, Henrik would have broken free of Rebecca's chains, Axel was sure of it. All he needed to do was bide his time.

Yes. He'd got a lot of things wrong. Axel had been sure that the charming, slapdash boy was nothing but a persona, and he had deliberately let Henrik's constant flirting go unremarked. As a rule it involved young women, foolish enough to be impressed by knowledge and charisma. It all made perfect sense: Henrik's weak spot had been his vanity, the admiration of others his drug of choice — he had craved it. And yet in his stupidity Axel had been certain that Henrik would never overstep the mark and *act on it*.

Axel had revelled in the fact that he was the one who could see through his friend's disguise, recognising beneath the mask a person who was like him in many ways: a serious person, deep down, a man of morals.

Henrik's looks would soon disappear. In the years to come Axel would have been able to watch the bald moon on the back of Henrik's head gain new ground; Henrik would not have been able to play the attractive bohemian for much longer.

Axel would have swooped in. He had secretly longed to be the one who caressed Henrik's bald patch when no one else gave him a second look. There was nothing inappropriate in his fantasy. He wasn't like those men who had sex with one another; the very idea of being like them appalled him. What *he* had felt for Henrik was different. It was indestructible. Unattainable.

In the future, when all this was over, he could delete from his memories that part of the story where Henrik had crossed the line and had destroyed everything.

The taciturn but dedicated student, Axel Donner had found a good use for his outstanding ability to learn and to adapt. He had never revealed a hint of who he actually was.

He had wobbled on just one occasion: in Istanbul. He had been drawn along with the others, had filled his body with alcohol and, for a short time, he had allowed depravity to possess him. Minutes, perhaps fifteen or twenty, when he had been himself. Spoken in his own voice, seen his surroundings through his own eyes. But Henrik hadn't noticed a thing.

The only one who had noticed was Annelie; he regretted this, and yet he didn't. The uncontrollable need to talk had made him turn to Annelie when Henrik was caught up with Ann-Marie Karpov's viper tongue. At times he had been unable to suppress his sudden surges of hatred towards his tutor.

He had frightened Annelie; he couldn't remember exactly what had happened, but he had definitely lost control.

That was one of the reasons why he must go and see her now. To shut her up. The fear that he didn't have the necessary courage or perseverance had stopped him before. But no, there was nothing more he could do for Henrik now. Henrik had been dispatched. No point in grieving and remembering and thinking, even if he was thinking constantly.

He had failed with Carla too. But he would not allow the despair to take root inside him again. If he could just get Annelie to understand that she shouldn't tell all and sundry — as she had told David — about what had been said to her in confidence. If not, then perhaps there was no alternative. He would have to put her out of action as well. He hoped that wouldn't be necessary.

When Axel Donner looked back at Istanbul, he could begin to understand human frailty. It was tragic-comic, the way Annelie had boasted of her vulgar affair, trying to ennoble it by insisting that she and the married man were kindred spirits, when everyone around the table knew exactly what it came down to: flesh. Passion. But they had all been drunk, on alcohol and on Istanbul. They had all overstepped the mark in their own ways.

Annelie had made a big thing of the fact that she and Henrik got on so well. Any attempt to divert her attention had fallen flat, and Axel was angry and disappointed. Who was she, what was she? She was a nothing, just like him! It had infuriated him when she had openly, shamelessly, ridiculed the way he clung to Henrik. As if she thought she had seen through him.

But Annelie probably wasn't that close to very many people. She wasn't the type who gossiped or gave much away. That was one of the things he had liked about her.

CHAPTER
FIFTY-NINE

Gothenburg

His pale reflection shone in the mirror above the washbasin. Gonzales splashed away the worst of the morning's tiredness before collecting his file and diary and heading for the conference room. The only empty seat was directly in the sun. He went over and drew the blind before he sat down.

Höije stopped in the middle of a sentence, but Beckman got there first.

"So, how are you feeling?"

"Fine. It didn't last long. Prawns."

He had expected to see Tell at the meeting; he was supposed to be back from holiday and Gonzales thought he had glimpsed him in the car park earlier.

Höije carried on. "A man by the name of David Sevic has been murdered. I've put together a rough schedule which I'll go through with you at the end of this briefing. The investigation will run parallel with the Linné murders, which will remain our priority. I will continue as CIO until Tell returns from holiday, which he should have done today. Let's see if he turns up."

"I think you'll find that seat's mine," said Tell from behind Höije's back.

Höije half turned, awkwardly, and appeared to be weighing up his options. "I think I'll stay where I am," he said eventually.

"Why?"

"Curiosity."

"Fair enough."

Tell sat down at the other end of the table. "OK. I've had an excellent debrief on where we are. We'll be working on the new case. As far as the Linné murders are concerned, I would suggest that we continue looking into the background of both victims and talking to those known to them. We will continue to focus our attention on the archaeology department, but we'll also widen our scope."

Bärneflod waved his pen half-heartedly in the air. "Before we shift our focus from Henrik Samuelsson —"

"We're not shifting our focus from Henrik Samuelsson."

". . . I'd like to mention his friend. Axel Donner. He's the dodgiest character known to either of the victims. He has an alibi in the form of the phone call Rebecca made to him on the night in question, but that only lasted a few minutes. If you check the time of death and the distance between Donner's home and the crime scene, he could easily have done it."

"And —"

"I haven't finished, Gonzales. I had a chat with Donner. You can see he's depressed. He's got virtually no possessions, maybe ten or fifteen things: a grubby mattress, a table, the odd chair, a laptop, a few books and —"

"We don't need this level of detail," said Tell.

"I almost had the feeling he was ready to take off. And he freaked out completely when I asked him about his past, to the point where he just refused to answer. He seemed incredibly defensive."

"Has something happened?" asked Karlberg. "It's just that before he was really cooperative."

"He and Henrik followed the same freestanding courses at the university for several terms," Bärneflod continued. "Courses with a completely different theoretical content, I mean. It's as if they'd somehow planned to do everything together."

"Doesn't that indicate a strange attachment?" Beckman agreed.

"Perhaps they were in a relationship?" Karlberg ventured, but Tell shook his head.

"We've spoken to a lot of people who knew them, and there's nothing to suggest a homosexual relationship. Besides, Henrik was already having an affair with Ann-Marie. Although . . . No, that doesn't sound realistic."

He scratched his head and squinted at Gonzales. "Bärneflod, you were saying something about his apartment but I can't think what . . . Gonzales, what were you about to say?"

"I left a note on your desk when I had to go home, Bärneflod, about a call to Annelie Swerin. Do you remember her?"

"Absolutely," said Beckman. "She was mentioned early on, but we couldn't follow it up because she was away on a dig."

Bärneflod's expression remained unchanged, so Gonzales went on. "Anyway, I managed to get hold of her and I asked about her relationship with Samuelsson and Karpov. I don't know if this important, but she did mention, without prompting, that she thought Axel Donner was terribly upset about his best friend's death, that he'd been to see her or at least appeared to have been hanging around near her apartment ever since she'd got home, although she didn't really know why. She said his behaviour had overstepped the mark, and she almost felt as if he was stalking her. And then she told me a long, confused story about one evening on the trip to Turkey when he'd had too much to drink. Apparently he came out with all kinds of stuff and became slightly threatening. She was in the middle of a messy relationship with a married man and had told the others. Apparently this man ran a corner shop not far from where she lives; she'd started working there to earn a bit of extra money, and that's how they got together. She was finding it very difficult, but Axel Donner had something to say about the morality of —"

Beckman sat bolt upright. "A corner shop? Not far from where she lives? What the fuck . . . Has anybody got the list handy, the list of people we still have to contact? I thought . . . Doesn't she live on Gråberget?"

She quickly leafed through her own papers. "Do you remember the name of the married man, Gonzales?"

He looked at her in surprise. "I didn't ask."

"But don't you get it?" She was ready to carry on, but Tell stopped her in her tracks.

"Don't forget he's only just got here," he said, turning to Gonzales with exaggerated calm. "Listen up: a corner shop on Gråberget has been robbed. Or so we thought. A man was murdered — David Sevic."

Gonzales nodded; now he understood. "I'll check whether Annelie's married man was called David Sevic. But going back to what I was just saying: when they were in Istanbul, Annelie told Axel about this relationship. He was extremely judgemental. Then he turned and . . . She thought it almost seemed as if he was in love with Samuelsson. As if he thought they were in a relationship. She did sound a bit embarrassed when she said that."

"What did I say?" Karlberg exclaimed triumphantly.

"Anyway, she thought he sounded crazy, quite threatening as I said, then he started talking a load of rubbish about a . . . hang on, she had a name . . ."

He checked his file. "Here: Carla Burke, a girlfriend he'd had in England. He said he'd wanted to 'hold onto her until she understood'; Annelie thought the whole thing sounded weird."

"What do you mean, hold onto?" asked Tell. "Was he talking about kidnapping her?"

"She didn't mention that."

"For fuck's sake . . . Did he have a computer in his apartment, Bärneflod?"

"There was a laptop case — I didn't look inside it."

Tell turned to Karlberg, who was ready for action. "Start a search on this Carla — an international search. And everything you can find on Axel Donner. Check the net as well. Google Carla . . . what was her name again?"

"Carla Burke."

"Check if there's anything related to kidnapping, that kind of thing. It might have been picked up by the press."

Tell took off his jacket and loosened his tie. "What else?"

Gonzales looked at his boss, his expression tense. He was excited, but concerned that he hadn't seen the significance of the information himself.

"That's about it. Oh, she also said Axel had talked about military discipline. The thing is, she said he'd been sitting in the courtyard of her apartment block looking up at her window. She kind of sounded as if it wasn't really all that serious, because after all they knew each other well, and . . . I thought he probably fancied her and didn't quite know where to draw the line, that's what it sounded like, not . . ."

"Karlberg!" Tell let out a deafening shout down the corridor. "Check . . . whatever the fuck they're called. Military academies, paratroopers, that sort of thing."

He didn't wait for a response. "Bärneflod, you're with Karlberg once we've finished here, looking for anything that might back up our hypothesis. I'll go to Donner's apartment."

"You mean the hypothesis that Axel Donner is our killer?" Beckman clarified.

"Yes, because you know what else has occurred to me? That computer you saw, Bärneflod. It could have been stolen from Linnégatan; Ann-Marie Karpov's laptop disappeared and it still hasn't turned up. Several of the people we've spoken to have said that Donner was fanatically opposed to computers, so it's obviously not his, is it?"

Beckman agreed. "That would also explain how the murderer got into the apartment without damaging the door. They let Axel Donner in, of course they did. But *why* did he take the computer?"

"To hide the evidence, maybe?" Tell suggested. "Maybe he's afraid that something he sent to Ann-Marie will come to light?" He drummed his fingers impatiently on the table. "Call Annelie Swerin and see how she is. I'll pick you up when I'm leaving, just give me two minutes. We'll take a radio car so we can bring someone in to force the door if it comes to that."

Höije shook his head firmly.

"You mean when you go to see Donner? You want me to come with you to bring him in?" Beckman asked.

Höije tried to interrupt by raising his index finger in the air, but Tell pretended not to notice.

"We'll have the bastard in no time," said Tell, despite the fact that his stomach was looping the loop.

Beckman left the room.

"Tell," Höije said eventually. "If you strongly suspect or have proof that this Axel Donner is our man, then you are definitely not to go there alone without a plan. You know perfectly well that this is a job for the specialists."

Tell got to his feet, drawing out every movement.

"No, I don't have any proof. The only thing I *know* is that some people think he's behaving oddly and is confused, and that he has a computer even though he hates computers. And I'm not going alone. I'm taking Beckman with me."

"I can't back you up if . . . No strong suspicions or proof means no smashing down doors. That's just the way it is. You are not to take any risks. And — one more thing before you go."

"Yes? Or no, for God's sake! I don't have time right now." Tell backed towards the door, his expression apologetic. "I'll see you when we get back."

"So how long are you going to be angry with me?"

"I'm not ang —"

"But isn't this some kind of fucking childish protest?" Höije exclaimed. "Bloody hell!"

Höije was so frustrated he almost looked astonished. The sight of him made Tell want to laugh out loud, even though he felt anything but cheerful.

"I know," he said from the doorway. "Not much longer."

CHAPTER
SIXTY

Gothenburg

He was perspiring heavily as he made his way up Gråberget; it was hot even though it was still early. Axel passed the road the police had cordoned off leading to the corner shop: David's Deli and General Store. David's Lies and Empty Promises.

The previous day he had seen the policeman out of the corner of his eye, the one who had encroached upon his person and his home; the fat slob with his teasing insinuations. The watery, insouciant, peering eyes; he'd seen eyes like that before, on the pigs at home. Nor had he forgotten how they squealed when they were slaughtered. The policeman had looked up. Axel had bent his head and hurried past.

He took the path over the hill to avoid meeting anyone. Lingered a while in the silence, feeling his concentration improve. Through the trees he could just see the peach façade of Annelie's apartment block.

He was carrying everything he needed in a plastic bag.

He suspected that she had started locking her door after seeing him in the car park. She rarely went out; she had had a girlfriend staying over. That had simply meant that he had to wait. There was no point in getting agitated.

Axel convinced himself that he was doing what he could to deal with the situation. He could do no more.

CHAPTER
SIXTY-ONE

Gothenburg

Her neighbour was lying on the grass in front of the building, a vision of summer with her sun-lounger, baby buggy and radio. No doubt she thought it was important to seize the day. The early summer weather was unreliable.

A magazine was propped on her knee, the glossy pages reflecting the sunlight.

Annelie kept on ending up here, ready to hide behind the curtain, staring out at the street. The care home was a colossus; it looked as though it was clinging to the hillside on the twisting, turning road. In the other direction, heading down the hill, at least the aspect was wide and open.

If he came that way she would be ready.

Annelie backed away from the window slowly, then went into the bathroom and emptied her bladder for the fourth time in an hour. She grimaced as the feeble trickle splashed against the toilet bowl. The urinary tract infection, which the previous evening had been a bearable nuisance, had worsened during the night. Now she was pissing acid again. That was one of the burdens she had to bear in life, a tendency to these infections.

Even though she avoided sitting on cold surfaces. *Sit on a cushion!* She had heard that at home for as long as she could remember.

When the phone in her hand rang she jumped; the sound was somehow magnified, bouncing off the tiled walls.

"Hello?"

"Annelie Swerin?"

"Yes?"

"My name is Karin Beckman, I'm with the police. I just wanted to check if everything's OK?"

Annelie managed to fasten her trousers and went into the hallway.

"Thanks for ringing. I think I'm OK, I've had a friend staying. It just feels a bit funny now she's gone home, that's all."

"You haven't seen Axel Donner since you spoke to my colleague? You can't see him outside your apartment at the moment?"

"No, no. No . . . It's just a feeling, really, that he's going to come back."

If you want them to help you, you'll have to be honest. It was nice to hear a voice in her ear and she wanted to keep this woman on the line as long as possible.

"I realise you might think this sounds a bit airy-fairy and not that important, but he —"

"Listen to me, Annelie," Beckman broke in. "I haven't got time to talk right now, but I have to tell you that we will be arresting Axel when we find him, and that won't take long. Just stay where you are. Don't leave your apartment and don't let anyone in until we get there. You've got my number, haven't you? Call me immediately if anything happens, anything at all."

Annelie pushed the stale air out of her lungs with difficulty. She shivered as she closed her eyes: the shock of hearing her thoughts spoken out loud. Above all, she felt a vague relief at being taken seriously. She wasn't crazy or paranoid. The fear Axel Donner evoked in her was real, as was the glimmer of insanity that had flashed straight into her eyes when his mask had slipped. Afterwards she had felt compelled to rationalise it away, to laugh off what had happened.

When she thought about how he had sat there on a bollard in the car park, his body rigid as he stared up at her window, she wanted to scream. The very thought of what she had suppressed but should have realised at the time: he had murdered Henrik and Ann-Marie!

Were they going to arrest him on suspicion of murder?

She thought back to the police cars she had seen speeding past. She didn't know what they had meant, but she had a bad feeling. And the silent ambulance earlier on, just down the road . . .

She whimpered. The street door slammed shut; she padded quickly over to the spy-hole and peered out onto the landing. Everything looked as it should: there was no one on the stairs. Her neighbour's door was closed, the shoe rack full of Wellingtons and trainers.

A second later, everything went dark. It was as if the light had gone out, even though the stairwell had been lit only by daylight. Then there was a scraping noise and the light came back, a fleeting shadow at the bottom of her field of vision, and the picture was intact once more.

She was hurled backwards by her reaction, her heart somersaulting in her chest; she ran back to the window. The sun-lounger was empty; she grabbed the phone.

"Marie, hello? It's Annelie, from next door. Please could you check the stairwell for me? See if there's anyone there? Please?"

"Er . . . hang on a minute."

Through the spy-hole Annelie saw the door opposite open, then her neighbour appeared, looking puzzled. *She thinks I'm crazy.*

"Hello?"

Her neighbour went back inside.

"No, there's no one there."

An optical illusion. Annelie thanked her and swallowed; she had to pull herself together. "I don't suppose you fancy coming round for a coffee?"

They didn't know each other that well. "It's just . . . I don't want to be alone."

Her neighbour hesitated, unsurprisingly. "No, I can't — Eskil's asleep. But you can always come round here if you like."

She could hardly call the police because she'd seen a shadow through the spy-hole; that would be like crying wolf. And when the wolf did come, nobody would dash to her rescue.

She would have to find another solution; she couldn't stay in the apartment without losing her mind. Whatever was happening outside, she couldn't stay here alone. Nor could she go out, not even to catch the tram. Not with Axel skulking around.

She caught sight of her pale reflection in the mirror, wiped away tears she didn't know she'd cried. I've got to pull myself together, she thought. For God's sake, pull yourself together, Annelie.

She was just as frightened when the phone rang again. As her hand hovered over the receiver, she forced her breathing to slow. It was the police, she told herself, nothing to worry about. It was her mother, it was a friend. She needed to hear a human voice, a voice that would talk sense into her, because the state she was in at the moment was beyond all . . .

It wasn't the police. It was little Sara. As soon as Annelie registered this, she realised it had been quite some time since she had been in touch with everyday reality. It was a palpable relief to experience feelings of guilt at having forgotten her five-year-old niece's birthday.

Annelie's voice held. Every word she spoke took her further away from fear as reality hauled her ashore. She slipped back into her life, recognised the sound of her own voice.

"Oh, Sara, I'm so sorry I didn't ring you earlier on! I meant to sing to you over the phone, but one or two strange things have been happening lately. Happy birthday for yesterday!"

The present she had bought in Bangalore was wrapped, but it was still lying on the bookcase. How could she have let go of what was important, forgotten Sara's birthday?

A noise. What was that outside? Annelie peered through the spyhole again, close to tears and with a lump in her throat, but the stairwell looked the same as it always did.

"I haven't sent your present because I was going to ask your mum if we could all meet up at Granny and Granddad's, maybe later on today." A white lie which suddenly became the truth. Could she ask her dad to come and pick her up? Would the police drive her to Varberg, or at least to the central station? Did she dare to take a taxi?

"Then I can give you your present."

Annelie's sister and her family lived in Varberg, not far from their parents.

"And I could get to see you as well! But maybe you're doing something else today?"

"No, we're going to Granny and Granddad's, me and Mummy and Daddy and Oscar. If you're going too we'll see you there. We're leaving in an hour."

In the background she could hear Sara's little brother and the sounds of a children's TV programme, or a CD. *The wheels on the bus go round and round, round and round . . .*

Annelie breathed calmly from her abdomen, feeling the muscles around her eyes relax.

"That would be fun! See you later, then."

The thought of sitting in her parents' living room, far away from Gothenburg and Axel, David and everything else, filled her with relief. They would sing a belated *Happy Birthday* to Sara, whose cheeks would be flushed with excitement. Then she would rip the tissue

426

paper from the handmade drawing book and colouring pencils Aunt Annelie had bought on yet another of her trips.

Annelie would avoid the usual questions about her love life, her course and plans to get a job — anything to do with her life, really. But she would feel normal, safe and good.

She picked up the phone; she would ring her neighbour and say that she had decided to come over for coffee after all, she couldn't cope with being on her own, but then it occurred to her that normal social convention would simply be to knock on the door, since they had only just spoken. And from there, she could call Karin Beckman. She could ask about Axel's arrest, find out what they suspected, put forward her own evidence. And she would ring her parents and arrange how to get to Varberg before evening fell.

Just as long as she didn't have to be on her own any more.

She quickly threw some clothes into a suitcase. Her keys were on a hook in the key cupboard, exactly where they were supposed to be. She didn't bother turning off the light in the hallway; she just pushed the handle down carefully, opened the door as slowly as she could and lifted her suitcase over the step. The landing was empty and silent.

She was leaving, she was leaving; it was like a mantra.

She would ring the police from her neighbour's.

And she knew she would be able to stay with her parents for as long as she wanted.

She stood in the doorway, the keys in her hand — she was just checking that her wallet was in her bag — when someone's body weight thrust her into the door. Because she was leaning forward slightly, the door hit her head and it really was very strange how associations managed to flash through her head as it exploded with pain. When she'd lived in London, her French roommate had taught her to hold her keys between her fingers like a knuckle-duster when she walked alone at night.

Annelie didn't have time to turn her keys into a knuckle-duster; she dropped them, felt her knees give way and fell over her suitcase. She was shoved back into the hallway and the door closed behind brown shoes and grey trouser legs.

CHAPTER
SIXTY-TWO

Gothenburg

The pavements of Mariaplan were crowded outside Axel Donner's building, distracting Tell. His energy levels were flagging and he almost wished he had gone through his plan in more detail before he and Beckman took off. He could have covered his own back by letting Höije determine how to proceed.

For a moment he questioned his judgement, and his attitude to Höije: had he been thrown off-balance by everything that had happened with Seja?

She hadn't been in touch. He had gone over their last conversation forty times, searching like an imbecile for clues that would lead him in the right direction. He had loathed every second since the door closed behind her. Now he was displacing his frustration by taking action at work, and perhaps he had acted with undue haste.

He and Beckman had crept along the flowerbed right next to the wall so that they couldn't be seen from the windows of Donner's apartment. He heard a child's voice in the stairwell as he pushed the door slightly ajar. There was no leeway if anything went wrong. Although he no longer believed they would find Axel Donner in his apartment, it was still the first place they had to look.

They let the woman and child go out before they went up to Donner's door; the stairwell was silent and empty. He could hear Beckman breathing quietly behind him as he knocked, waited and knocked again. Having got this far, Tell had to admit that he had already made a decision of sorts, against his better judgement. If they'd taken a back-up team with them, the door would have been open in no time and everything would have been a whole lot safer.

Beckman signed a question: should she go back to the car and fetch some tools to break open . . .?

Tell shook his head without looking at her.

The door offered little resistance, but Tell was out of practice; he had to put all of his strength behind his right shoulder. One last well-aimed kick and the lock shattered. The door opened, revealing scratched floorboards and very little else.

He suppressed a whimper as he moved his painful shoulder in a reflex action which brought the hand holding his gun up past his face. It smelled of gunpowder, even though it was a long time since it had been fired.

They could clearly see the apartment's one room and kitchen. Beckman kicked open the bathroom door while Tell headed for the wardrobe. A few clothes, a pile of books and a laptop. Just as they'd expected.

Without putting down his gun, he pulled the laptop out of its case. "We'll take the books and the computer with us. Do you think he's gone for good?"

"Maybe."

Beckman had the feeling Axel Donner wasn't planning on coming back.

Tell opened up the laptop and let out a whistle. "Just as I thought — it's Karpov's!" He groaned. "Fuck! It was him all along! How the hell —"

"Come on," Beckman said, trying to remain positive and keep a cool head. "We had no reason to suspect him more than anyone else. Right, let's start thinking. Where's he gone? If we put out a call, he's not likely to get very far. And we think he's lapsed into some form of psychosis, don't we? He committed the murders on Linnégatan while in full possession of his senses — you know how peculiar a killer's reasoning can be — but now he's lost the plot."

"But what about David Sevic? Was that really Donner as well?"

"I think so. His motive for killing Henrik and Ann-Marie certainly wasn't rational by normal standards, but for him there was a logic behind it. Presumably they had upset him somehow. But now he doesn't need a motive, he's just following the voices in his head. David Sevic got in the way."

"It could be linked to his affair with Annelie Swerin."

"That's what I mean."

"We'd better put her apartment block under surveillance." Tell asked for a patrol car to be sent to Swerin's address, while Beckman crouched down and started flicking through Donner's books. She groaned and half stood up as she felt a stabbing pain in her side.

They were mostly reference books, related to his studies. There was also a battered notebook full of his handwriting.

Beckman tried to interpret the densely written squiggles, concentrating on the names she recognised — Henrik, Ann-Marie, Annelie and David. Annelie was the only one still alive. She read about what Annelie had heard and done and thought and realised in Istanbul.

"Listen . . ." She hesitated for a second, her breathing rapid as she keyed in Annelie's number. There was no answer.

Why was there no answer?

Her lunch came back up into her throat and she gasped for breath as a sharp, ice-cold claw raked at her belly. The fingers holding the notebook whitened.

"Get some back-up sent over to Kabelgatan. We need to get round to Annelie Swerin's place as soon as possible. It looks as if things are more serious than we first thought." Tell was already in the stairwell and his answer sounded hollow and muffled.

Beckman took a couple of steps before the ice in her pelvis suddenly surged up through her stomach and into her head via her throat; she staggered towards the outside door. Something's not right, she thought, she wasn't going to be able to go to Gråberget with Tell. She needed to go home. A weight was pressing down through her belly, and the scarf she had tied around her hips earlier to support her aching stomach began to tighten, slowly at first, like an iron band. Then she felt a sudden jerk. A piece of barbed wire ripped through her womb. For a couple of seconds she disappeared; when she came back, she was on the floor. The back of her skirt was wet.

It had happened so quickly, she thought illogically. I would have expected it to hurt more. She felt a stabbing pain in her side as she got to her feet, grabbing hold of her gun, which had slipped from her hands and slid across the floor. Blood was trickling between her thighs, a macabre stain against the pale fabric of her skirt.

Her mobile buzzed. Tell was wondering where she was, no doubt; she could hear him shouting impatiently from outside the building.

Beckman didn't have the strength to protest as he raced inside and caught sight of her, a quizzical expression on his face as he took in her blood-soaked clothes and the smears on the floor.

"I'm having a miscarriage."

She still couldn't look at him as he rang for an ambulance, ignoring her feeble protests about needing to take her car home.

"David Sevic's shop is almost opposite Annelie Swerin's apartment block," she said as he helped her out into the street with a clumsy arm around her, his face creased with anxiety.

Tell didn't reply, he just stared anxiously at the roundabout.

"The ambulance will be here in two minutes. I'll wait until then."

"No, you go," she said. "I'll be fine."

★ ★ ★

He pulled up at the same time as the patrol car and raised a hand in greeting. It was Marklund, an older officer he knew well, along with a younger colleague he hadn't worked with before.

The back-up hadn't arrived.

Once inside the building he stopped them from going up the stairs; he tipped his head back and listened. There wasn't a sound from the third floor, but the stone walls were probably very effective at shutting the residents in and keeping the world out.

Tell had phoned Annelie since leaving Donner's apartment, but there was no response, and he didn't know what that meant.

"The woman's name is Annelie," he whispered as they crept up the stairs. Marklund was completely focused. "The guy we're after is Axel Donner. About thirty-five, knows how to use a gun. If he's here, we can assume he's stark raving mad."

The younger officer, Nilsson, suddenly looked ill. He was staring at his raised gun instead of looking for a possible threat. He had probably never had to use his gun before, not for real, away from the safety of the police-training facility.

Tell noticed the spy-hole in Swerin's door and pressed himself against the wall so that he couldn't be seen. He nudged the letterbox open and listened. There were faint sounds, but they could have been coming from a television, from another apartment. He thought he could hear a voice, a whimpering . . . muffled. By a gag? He listened again . . . Yes, maybe.

434

He gently pushed down the handle just to check that it was locked. There was a risk that Annelie Swerin was behind the door along with Axel. Her life might be in danger, even more so if he shouted into the flat. They could wait for back-up, but that would take time. Time they couldn't necessarily afford.

Tell stepped aside, making room for Marklund.

It probably didn't take very long to break the lock, but it would be a long time before Nilsson forgot how time ceased to exist both before and after, metamorphosed into just a few trembling seconds or minutes of action. He was pretty new to all this, used to hearing *theoretically* and *hypothetically*. In the real world, you could make a series of decisions that would turn out to be right only with hindsight. Or you could make the wrong decisions, with devastating consequences. An impossibly short space of time, which was also somehow endless, and only these few seconds mattered.

She was kneeling on the floor with her hands tied behind her back, gagged and blindfolded. The apartment was in darkness, with the blinds drawn and blankets covering the windows. One single candle was burning on the windowsill, making the shadows in the room flicker.

Tell became aware of laboured, wheezing breathing. He was at her side in a second, ripping the tape off her face and pulling the wet stocking out of her mouth. She threw up over his hands and a heart-rending sob welled

435

up in her throat. There was only one other room and that must be beyond the kitchen.

"Take her outside," he said to Nilsson, who immediately helped Annelie Swerin to her feet and out onto the stairwell.

Tell turned to Marklund. "You take the living room."

A book lay open on the kitchen table, along with a pile of notes. A small television was on, the volume low; was that what he had heard from outside? The bedroom door was ajar, but all he could see was a dressing gown that had been dropped just inside, and the corner of a bed.

Tell pulled one of the blankets from the window. He opened the door between the kitchen and living room wide so that he could see in all directions, then kicked open the bedroom door. A bed, a desk, a walk-in wardrobe. He tore the clothes off their hangers and peered into the darkness, groping along the wall for a light switch.

Once he had established that the wardrobe was empty, he lowered his gun for the first time since they had entered the apartment. Axel Donner had left Annelie; had he changed his mind?

Tell walked back into the living room just as the candle flame sucked in a corner of the curtain. He barely had time to react before the flames reached the ceiling.

"Bloody hell!"

Marklund came to the rescue; he threw a blanket over the fire, then got out of the way as Tell beat the same blanket against the burning curtain, but it wasn't enough. The acrid smoke made him cough and his hands were smarting as he hurled one of the sofa cushions at the window, smothering the flames. Annelie Swerin came into view on the street below. No doubt she was yelling, but it looked as though she was miming, pointing up at the window. She was alone; he couldn't see any sign of Nilsson.

She'll call the fire brigade, thought Tell. He spun around as he heard a thud.

A second later, the door of the linen cupboard at the other end of the room flew open. As if in slow motion, Tell saw Axel Donner grab hold of Marklund, pressing his gun against his neck, and a feeling of unreality swept over him. The last few minutes flashed before his eyes. *How the fuck had he fitted in the cupboard?* Annelie managing not to choke on her own vomit, the fire.

An eternity had passed since they entered the apartment, and yet it was just a few short minutes. And now the barrel of the gun was pressing into the loose skin beneath Marklund's chin, his face deathly pale and his eyes teary as he wondered if this was how his police career was going to end.

Tell had had the same thought a couple times himself.

"Drop the gun," Donner hissed, his eyes ablaze. "Drop it."

Tell bent down slowly, placed the gun on the floor in front of him and kicked it away. He raised his hands in the air.

"OK, Axel, I've dropped the gun. Now you let go of Christer Marklund."

He said Marklund's name in order to make him seem human in Donner's mind, but they were probably beyond any form of communication by now.

Donner buried the barrel deeper into Marklund's skin.

"Move away from the door."

Tell moved away, hands in the air, and Donner backed towards the hallway using Marklund as a shield. When he reached the landing, he aimed a sharp blow at Marklund's temple and kicked the back of his knees hard, sending him crashing head-first into the hall mirror. He landed on the floor in a cascade of broken glass. Donner hurled himself down the stairs.

Tell jumped over Marklund and was halfway down the stairs when he heard Donner crash into Nilsson, who was ready and waiting. Nilsson used all his strength to knock the gun out of Donner's hand and slam him against the wall. Taken by surprise, with Nilsson's gun pressed against his stomach, Donner was no longer a threat.

Tell just managed to make out the young officer's trembling words, which would be quoted for years in the department: "Not one more step, you fucking scumbag!"

Donner shuddered, leant forward and breathed very close to Nilsson's face.

The back-up team screeched to a halt outside.

438

CHAPTER
SIXTY-THREE

Gothenburg

As Tell walked up the stairs to his apartment — the lift was out of order yet again — his shirt sleeves were sticking to the blistered skin on his hands and wrists, but now a blessed, cooling evening breeze was blowing through the rooms. Tell had opened all the windows wide, and it provided welcome relief.

When he had thrown his stinking clothes in the bin and showered away the worst of the soot, he realised that he had come off lightly from their incursion into Annelie Swerin's apartment: his skin was red, blistered and sore, but would soon heal. He rummaged in the bathroom cabinet and found an old tube of ointment and a roll of gauze bandage; that would have to do.

Bärneflod had taken over when he left to go home, since Beckman was off sick. That was fine. Donner was in custody and they had his gun, which would match the bullets retrieved from all three victims: Henrik Samuelsson, Ann-Marie Karpov and David Sevic.

Donner hadn't formally confessed to the murders, but he had been talking about them, and you could tell from how he looked that he had lost all grasp on reality. He might well be sectioned. Tell had already heard the *experts' initial hypotheses, concepts such as the terrorising and destructive superego. Heightened impulses. Inadequate defence mechanisms. Lack of sublimation. Lack of empathetic ego functions. Inflexible but split superego.*

Those who had known Donner before his illness took over had described him as taciturn and odd. But he was no longer short of something to say. Dropping the façade of normality had opened the floodgates. He kept arguing with himself, veering between self-loathing and illusions of omnipotence. If anyone could bear to listen to him, they might eventually find explanations of sorts for what he had done.

Tell had no intention of listening to him. As soon as incontrovertible proof was on his desk, his job would be done. And yet he couldn't help being fascinated.

"Is it possible to understand someone like that?"

He couldn't ask Beckman, who was usually on hand to answer his questions about the more obscure corners of the human psyche. Tell sat down to go through the material Karlberg had put together.

A number of years ago, during a trip abroad, Axel Donner had had a relationship with a twenty-three-year-old Englishwoman, Carla Burke. He had been held on suspicion of depriving Burke of her freedom, of making illegal threats, and of actual bodily harm. The fact that he had not been found guilty was largely due to Carla Burke's own testimony. She had stubbornly insisted that a stranger wearing gloves had broken into her house immediately after Donner had left, and had dragged her down to the cellar. Everything she said contradicted the relatively insubstantial evidence against Donner.

They hadn't been able to pin anything on him, despite repeated interviews where it was put to Burke that she was protecting her ex-boyfriend because she was afraid of him.

Tell had tried looking up the case on the Internet. He found a couple of articles from British newspapers and a short interview with Carla Burke, plus a picture of her holding her hand up in front of her face. After four days imprisoned in the cellar, she had been rescued by a workman who was insulating a wall on the ground floor.

The image of Annelie Swerin, on her knees with her hands tied behind her back, came into his mind. He shuddered. If they'd arrived any later, Annelie Swerin could well have been dead.

The next article was about Carla Burke having married the workman who had saved her life.

He shut down the computer and headed straight for bed, without turning on the television.

CHAPTER
SIXTY-FOUR

Gothenburg

The following morning, Höije managed to arrange a long overdue chat with Tell. He spelled out their respective areas of responsibility, and where the exact demarcations lay. With the more pressing aspects of the Donner case behind him, Tell could afford to sit back and listen. There was nothing noteworthy or unreasonable in Höije's words, apart from the fact that he was couching the blindingly obvious in the most pretentious terms possible.

"We'll get there in the end," Höije concluded. "We simply have to ensure that we respect each other's professional roles. I can tolerate you pushing the boundaries from time to time, if you can tolerate the fact that I'll have to intervene now and again."

"I can indeed."

"Good. And we'll soon be able to put this case behind us."

"Yes."

They were interrupted by a text message from Gonzales, which said that he and Karlberg and a couple of crime scene technicians were at a house in

442

Pennygången in Högsbo. There had been a stabbing and they needed Tell to come over.

Tell remembered that Beckman lived not far away.

He drove towards Majorna with mixed feelings. He didn't want to think about the blood, about how his colleague had avoided looking him in the eye as if she was ashamed. At the time he hadn't been able to . . . it would have been impossible to take the time to . . . do what? Go home with her, console her, ask all the right questions. Miscarriage — the word didn't sit comfortably in his mouth. And he hadn't even known that Beckman was pregnant.

They didn't have that kind of relationship. They were colleagues. But something had happened when they had worked together closely the previous year, when their former boss Ann-Christine Östergren had told them she was suffering from an incurable and aggressive form of cancer. Their mutual fear had brought Tell and Beckman closer, and at times they had acted almost like friends.

He usually preferred to mind his own business, as did Beckman; she demanded openness and honesty from those around her, while at the same time shielding her own life from public view, terrified of revealing that she needed anyone.

But he was her boss. It was his duty to make sure she was all right.

Tell found Beckman's address on a street of interchangeable three-storey apartment blocks. He parked on the street and went inside. The window in the stairwell looked old and draughty. On the second floor he found a piece of paper stuck to a door: K. Beckman.

She answered his knock almost immediately, wearing a blue shirt over a pair of trousers. He felt relieved; stupidly, he had expected to see her in the bloodstained clothes. He was also relieved that she looked cheery and didn't seem particularly surprised to see him.

"Come in," she said. "What have you done to your hands?"

Tell waved his bandaged hand dismissively. "I'll tell you some other time."

He followed her into a small, lime-green galley kitchen. Before he had the chance to ask about the miscarriage and the fact that she had moved out of her family home after ten years of marriage, she asked him to tell her about the Donner case.

Tell gratefully took the ball and ran with it. "He's definitely our man. He's babbling away, and a whole load of people can't wait to interpret what he's coming out with."

"Aren't you curious?"

"About what?"

"Who he is and why he did it?"

"Not any more, to be perfectly honest. Are you?"

"I am. I think just *wanting* to understand broken people who do desperate things makes the job easier."

She was talking quickly, her voice tense. "For me, anyway. It protects me against burn-out. It stops me being so cynical."

"I didn't mean —"

"No, sorry, I know." Beckman fell silent and shook her head, embarrassed, as if she'd been caught out. She changed the subject: "And what was the story behind Ann-Marie's computer? Was there anything on it to explain why Donner took it?"

"Well, there was a message sent from an anonymous Hotmail address just before the murders, telling her to leave Henrik alone otherwise their affair would become common knowledge."

They sat in silence for a while. "I just meant that now he's safely behind bars, he can't cause any more trouble," Tell said eventually. "There are explanations for everything. Victims become perpetrators and all that jazz. A story behind every crime. But that's not something we need to worry about."

"A violent, verbally abusive father who had some kind of affair. An isolated, rural environment. A small community heavily influenced by old-fashioned values."

Beckman smiled wanly at his surprise and leant back against the draining board before she went on.

"His kidnapping of Carla Burke and his breakdown led to short-term psychiatric care. He was eventually deemed to have made a good recovery and fled to Gothenburg, where he met Henrik. Perhaps their relationship was a sexualisation of his desire for his father? Henrik became the father figure who accepted him at last, a father who accepted him as he was and made him feel valued."

Tell's bewilderment was obvious. "Sorry to interrupt, but how the hell do you know all this?"

445

She smiled. "I had a quick look at Axel's notebook just before . . . before I had the miscarriage. But mostly I've filled in the gaps with my own interpretations. Just for the sake of it."

"Feel free to carry on."

"When Axel became aware that he was expendable — when Henrik fell in love with Ann-Marie, and was therefore 'unfaithful', just as his father had been — his feelings changed from hero worship to contempt. Axel couldn't bear the betrayal; it reminded him of how his father had betrayed him. His anger at Henrik became mixed up with suppressed rage towards his father, perhaps Henrik might even have triggered forbidden homosexual impulses, how should I know? At any rate, Henrik had to go. Henrik, and everything else that reminded Donner of his past disappointments."

Tell was silent for a moment, then he burst out laughing. "You're good at this stuff, you really are. But what about David Sevic?"

"Aha." Beckman nodded eagerly. "I think Axel identified himself with Sevic's son. According to Annelie, he was totally opposed to infidelity, possibly as a result of his own experience. As far as Annelie is concerned, she was also a rival for Henrik's attention, and I think Axel believed she had seen through his facade in Istanbul. Plus David almost certainly knew more than was comfortable. He was Annelie's confidant, after all."

"Although I've got a feeling that Axel liked Annelie," Tell said. "He didn't kill her, even though he had the chance. He imprisoned her, but why? So that he could

446

talk to her. He wanted to explain himself, perhaps he even wanted her for himself. And that's why he killed Sevic. Is that possible?"

Beckman looked at him thoughtfully. "Well . . . I think you're right in one respect. Axel Donner was a lonely person who'd invested deep emotions in this small group of students. When he was around them, he became someone. He couldn't cope with the feeling of being excluded. And he was afraid of change. He wanted things to stay the way they were, but he didn't know how."

"I'm lost for words," said Tell.

"It's just speculation."

He shook his head, but then his smile slowly faded and he looked at his shoes.

Beckman knew why he had come, and she also knew he hadn't a clue what to say.

"I lost the baby," she said softly. "I'd just got used to the idea that maybe I was going to have another child, but now it's gone."

Tell still didn't know what to say.

"But . . . I'm beginning to look at it pragmatically. It was for the best, I think."

Tell nodded uncertainly and leaned against the stained kitchen table, which wobbled.

"I'm renting the place furnished," she said, pointing at the table. "Most of my furniture is still at Göran's. There's no point fetching it until I've found an apartment, or a house." She laughed. "So where should I settle? Do I let him keep the bookcase? Questions you don't really consider when you start wondering whether

you have the courage to leave a doomed relationship —
or whether you have the courage to stay."

Tell waited. Beckman had hardly said a word about
her marriage, not really, although he had read between
the lines and gathered that it had been stormy.

"By the end, I really wanted him to hit me, just
once," she said suddenly, waving away Tell's awkward
protests. "Yes, Tell, today you're just going to have to
deal with the fact that I can't do small talk . . . I
provoked him to make him lose his temper. If he hit me
it would mean a definitive end. I would have won and
he would have lost. That would have made it easier to
go, but he never did."

She rubbed her forehead with the palm of her hand.

"Recently, I was just trying to get at him in every
possible way. Telling him how unhappy he made me,
how disappointed I was, how our life was so different
from what he'd promised. I wanted to reclaim ten years
of my life, and the only way I could do that was if he
admitted it had all been his fault."

"But you made your mind up in the end?"

"It's strange, I don't remember when . . . But I do
have a crystal-clear memory of the moment I decided
to live my life with Göran. There's no point in talking
about that now, of course, but I remember exactly what
he meant to me and how I . . . I don't really understand
it myself. Perhaps the Göran I thought I knew never
existed. Perhaps he existed only in my head. Then
suddenly, one day, it just dawned on me. I was fighting
tooth and nail to get close to him, pleading and
whining, offering compromises, then screaming insults

at him. I was trying to get as close as I thought I wanted to be, ought to be with my life partner. Otherwise why would we call it a life partner?"

"And the more you fought, the more he pulled away, I suppose?"

Suddenly the whole thing seemed embarrassingly obvious to her. "Of course. And to make it even more complicated, I think a part of me was also frightened of closeness."

She ignored Tell's confusion.

"This pattern, I mean. On a subconscious level I shared the responsibility for forming it. Because I didn't have the courage to be close to someone either, to be vulnerable in that way."

"But is that what you have to do?" Tell asked with a hint of panic.

Beckman had long since passed the boundaries of what Tell could relate to, but her words affected him nonetheless.

"Of course. That's what real love is. Sooner or later, you have to make that choice, unless you want it to slip through your fingers."

He looked down at his hands, his expression troubled, and Beckman sighed.

"I don't know . . . I just don't know any more. Maybe I've never really known what I wanted, and that's why I've never had the courage to fully commit. To anything."

"That's just not true. You're one of the most competent police officers I have ever worked with."

"I know I'm good at my job." Beckman moved over to the window and stood with her back to him. "I was in such a panic when I found out I was pregnant. It was a mistake, a one-off with Göran weeks ago. I could see only obstacles and demands, I thought it would be embarrassing; that I would just look pathetic."

She turned around to face him. A single tear crept down the side of her nose; apart from that she was quite composed.

"Then everything changed and it all fell into place: me and Göran. Our genes, our history, joined together in this child. I was completely absorbed by that way of thinking, blinded. Do you understand? This sudden change of heart, and then I didn't get to keep it. I didn't get to keep the child or the strength that came with it. The wonderful feeling that everything, even the impossible, is possible. That it's possible to say goodbye to cynicism, to stop sneering when people say things like *love conquers all*. It was real for a little while. This new child. And everything else seemed unimportant."

She wiped her eyes, then went over to the sink, poured a glass of water and drank it in one.

Tell undid his top button. He wanted to get out of here. He wasn't used to this sort of talk. He was the wrong man in the wrong place, and he was no use to Beckman. He could see only himself in what she said, himself and Seja and all their problems. Whatever those were.

Beckman's words simply reflected his own questions. Would the exact moment come when he knew he

450

wanted to spend his life with Seja? Deep down, did he really want to share his life with another person?

He was far from sure about his ability to make such a commitment.

He had been nervous around Seja in the beginning. But, at the same time, he had been afraid; he felt the cowardice that had been his constant companion for such a long time.

Seja was on his mind, but Beckman was standing in front of him; she jumped as if she had felt a sudden stab of pain and placed one hand on the side of her stomach. He got up to help.

"Shouldn't you be lying down?"

She held up her hands as a shield, protecting herself from his distracted concern.

"No, it's OK. It's not that painful any more."

Tell remained standing, his arms hanging awkwardly at his sides.

"I'm sorry I can't be more help. I've . . . been distracted ever since we brought in Axel Donner, the whole circus. Everything that happened, there was a fire in the apartment, it was all so quick, yet it seemed to be in slow motion . . . You know how it feels sometimes. It's as if I'm drifting up in the air and I can't get back down to earth. I've got a sense of unreality that just won't go away."

"There's nothing you can do," she said after a short pause. "Nothing more than you've already done. You came to see if I was all right. I know you find these things difficult, and that makes your visit all the more touching. But I'm fine, don't you worry. I'll get through this, even if I've had to make a lot of adjustments lately. I'm looking forward to picking up where I left off, to building something new, something good."

When she moved into the hallway, he took it as an indication that she wanted to be alone.

"Every coin has a reverse side. That's been very clear to me lately, particularly over this past week. Even if you don't see the positive side until much later."

For a moment his hand rested on the door handle. "Sometimes I just wish that I was a bit better at seeing the silver lining sooner. It would save a lot of unnecessary suffering."

"True."

Beckman smiled slowly and Tell smiled back; he came down to earth with a sudden growing understanding. He was back.

"Thanks for coming, Tell. I'm off work for the next week. Then I'll be back."

Tell walked through the courtyard and out onto the street; he had the feeling that Beckman was watching him from the kitchen window. He didn't get his phone out until he reached Slottsskogsgatan.

He would have preferred to see her face to face, but he was still pleased when Seja answered.

"I just wanted to say that I love you. Very much."

As he ended the call, he realised that, oddly enough, he hadn't heard her reply, and yet his body felt warm and soft.

He pulled off the bandage and threw it in a bin.

He had heard a child in the background, which meant that her friend Hanna was there with her son. He made a decision: to Pennygången for a quick check on the situation, then back home to throw a few things in a bag. He could definitely be in Stenared by five.

CHAPTER
SIXTY-FIVE

Gothenburg

Valand was abuzz. Trams were screeching and rattling as they rounded the corner from Kungsportsavenyn to Vasagatan, and the taxis right behind them revved impatiently. Shoppers emerging from the Pressbyrå mini-market stepped straight out into the cycle lane and cyclists rang their bells amidst the in-line skaters and strollers. Röhsska Museum stood calm and solid, like a colossus in the midst of the chaos.

Karlberg felt foolish, sitting in the passenger seat of an armoured car transporting priceless treasures. Cecilia Lindgren was waiting on Teatergatan, a back door leading into the museum standing wide open behind her.

"Welcome at last," she said when Karlberg had retrieved the unassuming bag from the back seat. "You're leaving it in safe hands."

"I'm just glad to get rid of it, to be honest. Sorry it took so long, a few other things came up. But now . . ."

Lindgren took the bag with both hands, her lips slightly parted. She was wearing a short knitted skirt which looked as if it might be rather warm for this time of year, and bright rose-patterned tights. Karlberg

454

glanced down at her legs and suppressed a smile. The first drops of rain began to fall from a darkening sky.

"Would you like to come in while I take a look at these?"

"Er . . . yes. Thank you, that would be interesting."

"Rain again! Whatever happened to the nice weather?"

Their footsteps echoed off the walls, which carried within them the smell of dust from stone and fabric, and which had remained cool even in the early summer heat. *Hence the knitted skirt and tights.* Karlberg felt as if knowledge from every epoch had settled within these walls, in the air which every visitor breathed, which Cecilia Lindgren breathed . . .

"I'm working on a project at the moment," she said as they walked. "I'm studying the museum's artefacts from the Middle East. We can go along to the office I'm using in a little while, but first I'd like to show you the architecture exhibition room. It contains a lion and dragon from Babylon. Here we are."

"I'm not sure . . ."

She led Karlberg to the centre of the room. Only then did he see what she meant. Each side of the opening leading to the foyer was adorned with a huge relief made up of glazed tiles.

"Impressive," was all he could muster.

"They certainly are. I wanted you to get an idea of what . . ." She gestured towards the cloth bag. The reverence with which she was looking at the reliefs was remarkable given that she must have seen them countless times.

"They were found during German archaeological digs, and they are the only examples of Babylonian culture we have in Sweden. Do you know much about Babylon?"

"Er . . . I vaguely remember from my RE lessons that they built a tower reaching up into the sky."

"About two hours' drive from Baghdad, across the desert, is what is called the cradle of civilisation. Many Sumerian towns were located there; the best known is Babylon, with its notorious tower of Babel. At least according to the Bible it became a symbol of hubris, avarice and materialism; the Babylonians tried to construct a tower which would reach all the way up to God, and He punished them by confusing their languages. These reliefs come from a hill that was the centre of the city."

She pointed to the pictures. "There would have been sixty lions on either side. The dragon — the animal sacred to the gods Marduk and Nabo — comes from the gate itself."

Karlberg nodded, trying to summon up the same enthusiasm as Cecilia Lindgren. The lion's mouth was wide open, its tail high in the air; a depiction of strength. The dragon had the head and tail of a snake, but the front legs of a lion and the hind legs of a bird of prey.

With Karlberg trailing behind her, Cecilia Lindgren headed back through the foyer. They entered a room which wasn't particularly large, but the high ceiling gave an impression of space. She offered Karlberg a chair by a window looking out over a rain-soaked

Vasagatan. She spread a cloth over a table next to him then, with infinite care, she unwrapped twenty-nine artefacts from the padded cloth and arranged them in a straight line from one side of the table to the other: two necklaces, earrings and hair slides, a dozen or so clay figures, two bowls and a number of seals.

Karlberg was certainly curious, yet he couldn't take his eyes off the expression on Cecilia Lindgren's face. It almost embarrassed him; he felt as if he ought to leave the room and give her the privacy the occasion demanded.

"Some of the jewellery is just incredible," she said eventually. "The style is actually quite similar to the pieces that were dug up in Nimrud. Not quite as showy, perhaps, but still, if they were cleaned so that you could see they were gold . . . Have you heard of the Treasures of Nimrud?"

"No . . ."

"Sixty-five kilos of gold, silver and precious stones in the form of jewellery, bowls and goblets was discovered beneath a palace in the city of Nimrud in northern Iraq. The jewellery was worn by three historically important queens and symbolised their power over Iraq. It was thought that these artefacts had been stolen during the invasion, but they were later found in a bank vault where they had been placed for safe-keeping. I think these items date from approximately the same period, perhaps six to eight hundred years BC. Have you noticed the gold leaves decorating the necklace and these two bracelets? Such precise work!"

"And the other items?"

"Well . . . they're a bit of a mixed bag," she said after some hesitation. "Some are probably considerably older than the ones I showed you before. I would guess that the representations of women and animals are approximately seven thousand years old."

She held up a fragment of clay which didn't look like anything remotely recognisable to Karlberg. He thought he might just be able to distinguish the outline of a pair of narrowing eyes.

"A pair of eyes is widely thought to be a symbolic representation of a god. Otherwise I would say that most of these figures were meant to somehow glorify the ruler, or they had religious or symbolic significance. They would have played a role in rituals of praying to or appeasing the gods, to influence nature, to prevent unforeseen disasters . . . Or to drive out evil; we think bowls like these, inscribed with religious quotations and spiritual invocations, would be placed in the corner of a room, or buried under the threshold of the house, to capture demons and other creatures."

She showed him something that looked like a small stamp. "Can you see IM marked on the seals? And on a number of the figures. Iraq Museum."

"Our contact at Glyptoteket in Copenhagen, Alexandr —"

"Alexandr Karpov, yes. He's more of an expert in this field than I am."

". . . said this had something to do with the war in Iraq."

"Oh yes?"

"So these objects come from Iraq?"

"If I mentioned the Land Between Two Rivers, what would you say?" When she smiled, her laughter lines reached all the way to her temples. "And if I said Mesopotamia?"

"I wouldn't say very much at all."

She laughed. "What I mean is that these items come from the place we now call Iraq — and its neighbouring countries. Some of them are from the Iraq Museum, as I said. Some might have been stolen — from graves, for example. Which makes them even more interesting in a way: nobody has had the opportunity to analyse them yet. So, do you know anything about the war in Iraq?"

"Yes, of course. Sort of. Well, only what's been on the news, really."

"OK, so perhaps you know that on the night American soldiers entered Baghdad, Iraq's national museum was plundered; this was an event of world importance. There were pictures from the cradle of human civilisation and the dawn of science. The origins of writing, mathematics, astronomy . . . The innermost rooms of the museum were emptied. Things were smashed to pieces, stolen."

"And sold?"

Cecilia Lindgren nodded. "The suspicion is that those responsible were linked to the illegal international art trade. It took two days to empty the museum, and another day or so before the first artefacts turned up on the Internet."

She folded her arms over her chest, her fingers digging into her upper arms.

"May I ask how all this ended up in the hands of the police?"

"It's a very long story. But our theory is that one particular individual bought these items on a trip."

"A trip where?"

"He was in Istanbul a while ago."

"Not impossible. Hmm. At any rate, it's fantastic that they've been found; let's just hope that —"

"What are you doing now?" Karlberg heard himself say, and could have bitten his tongue a second later. *Timing, it was all about timing.* And his was usually terrible.

Cecilia Lindgren did indeed look surprised.

"What do you mean by now?"

"I just think what you're doing is really interesting — *Oh no, inane flattery, it's getting worse and worse.* — and I wondered if you'd like to join me for some lunch . . . so that we can carry on chatting about what happened when the museum was plundered?"

"OK, if you hang on a minute, I'll just get my coat. Good job it's waterproof."

To Karlberg's inexpressible surprise, this beautiful woman was smiling at him.

CHAPTER
SIXTY-SIX

Gothenburg

Sitting outside the Marmalade Café, Rebecca Nykvist was just finishing a letter to Henrik's parents. It had ended up as a brief but conciliatory account of their relationship, which had been more good than bad, in spite of everything. She hoped that was true.

After tucking the letter into her handbag, she listened in to the conversations around her. They were all about trivial things. Rebecca envied these people for their ordinary lives so much that it hurt. She wrapped her hands around the scalding glass of tea and watched her palms turn crimson. Her skin was burning.

A man came out of the Co-op with a newspaper and made his way clumsily across the tramlines. He glanced over the tables and their eyes met.

"Anyone sitting here?"

Grateful for the illusion of company, she moved over and indicated that the man was welcome to sit down. He spread *Göteborgsposten* over his half of the table. Rebecca dared to lean her head back at an angle and glance across at Axel Donner's apartment, its two dark windows reflecting the light.

After she had handed an application for sick leave to her boss, she had felt drawn to Mariaplan. She knew perfectly well that she couldn't change anything by sitting where she now sat, or even by standing in the stairwell outside the door that still bore the name A. Donner. Or if she reached out and touched the door. She wouldn't lose her feeling of terror. And Axel wouldn't be there. She would have liked to talk to him, but he had no doubt been charged with murder by now.

Rebecca had phoned the police switchboard and been informed that the inspector was unavailable and his colleague was off sick. She tried again, her mobile pressed to her ear: Christian Tell was still unavailable.

Her tea was cooling fast and she lost interest in it. She fiddled with her phone, wanting to talk to anyone who could throw some light on what had happened between her and Axel on the bridge.

She closed her eyes and went over it again: his agonised expression. It had been like staring straight into her own deepest pain. Her envy. And their exchange had been over so quickly that afterwards she wasn't even sure it had happened. They had shared an involuntary, incomprehensible moment of intimacy. It is often said that when a person is drowning, his life flashes before his eyes; she remembered the very first time she had seen Axel and Henrik together, joined in their own secret little club and, as usual, she had felt like a piece of ice. The feeling reminded her of when she was upset as a little girl. But then she had swallowed hard and decided to become untouchable. She had become conscientious and so strong that she never needed anyone, and this had worked terrifyingly well.

She had intended to confront Axel with the accusation that he had known about Henrik's infidelity all along, with his fucking lack of honour and basic human courage. She had wanted to take her anger out on him. But instead, standing there on the bridge, he looked so small, and she just wanted to give him a hug. She had no experience of that emotion; afterwards she had linked it to other situations where she had been exposed, thinking of sex or clichéd notions of kindred spirits, but what she had actually looked directly in the eye was her own smallness. Her old jealousy, reflected in Axel Donner's jealousy.

It was strange. The hatred she felt for him was so strong. And yet: the sight of him before her, slowly turning to face her. The glimpse of the abyss. The extent to which his love for Henrik had been sexually charged or unrequited was irrelevant; it had been real to him. Just as hers was real, regardless of her inadequacies. Regardless of her inability to trust, her deep-seated suspicion of unconditional love; regardless of her constant, corrosive self-esteem problems.

The man on the other side of the table apologised for taking up so much space.

"No problem," she mumbled.

The difference was that Axel Donner was mad, and she wasn't.

She wasn't mad.

Rebecca stood up and went out onto Mariagatan, where a packed number 11 tram was rumbling its way up Sannabacken en route to Saltholmen. She cut across the noisy area around the paddling pool — they'd filled it up so early this year! — got generously splashed with water and continued along the King's Walls with her skirt sticking to her legs.

When she turned into Kungsladugårdsgatan, there was very little traffic; summer was ready and waiting to begin.

She could see the red door in the distance.

CHAPTER
SIXTY-SEVEN

Stenared

Seja couldn't hear what they were talking about, just that the conversation concerned the dung heap and the wheelbarrow.

The man in the leather trousers was being prevented from helping with the unwieldy barrow as the boy, who looked as if he knew what he was doing even if it was hard work, pushed it towards its destination next to the garden shed. The boy showed him the back of the house, the shower hose over the wooden plinths and the rusty iron shelf housing soap and shampoo. Then the front, with its outdoor kitchen under a projecting fibreglass roof, varnished yellow shelves above the sink, lined with glass jars and dried herbs from the garden; he pointed to the sheep, Nebuchadnezzar and Ishtar — even if he had been extremely doubtful about the names.

They headed into the stable. Earlier on, Markus had helped Seja to grease the harness, and the delicious smell of warm saddle grease was still in the air. The men's voices died away as the stable door closed; all she could hear now were wasps buzzing.

Hanna strolled across the grass and flopped down next to Seja under the sour cherry tree — it was too warm to sit in the sun. The early summer heat was infused with the smell of the conifers, but the lawn had regained its fresh green colour after days of torrential rain. It was alive with activity: ants on their daily procession towards the kitchen to build nests in the sugar and hot chocolate powder, bees — Seja had already trodden on one of them with her bare foot — and shiny beetles scuttling over the soil. The fruit bushes would soon be weighed down with bunches of black, red and white currants.

The sight of it all brought a lump to Seja's throat. She was proud of herself and of the choices she had made; proud that she had found a place of her own in the world. She had been feeling sad, upset about Christian's passivity and the uncertainty surrounding their relationship, but a recent telephone call had given her fresh hope.

She felt alive. And she was writing; several articles on grave-robbing and the smuggling of cultural artefacts, but on other topics too.

Hanna pointed to the stable door. "He's happy."

"Markus or Peter?"

"Markus, of course."

Seja nodded. "And what about you?"

Hanna gave a wry smile. "I feel good. For the moment."

They fell silent. Hanna folded the hem of her dress back over her thigh and absent-mindedly rubbed the angry red mark above her knee which was slowly turning blue. She had fallen off her horse in the summer pasture that morning. The first and only time in her life she had tried riding bareback, and she had sworn never to do that again. Regardless of how much her son might nag her.

Markus was becoming quite a good rider, even though he was only small; he loved looking after Lukas.

Seja enjoyed having visitors in the house, preferably the kind who looked after themselves and made their own entertainment. She had nothing against coexisting with another person for a couple of days, as long as the silences were easy.

Today they had Markus' father Peter with them. While she was showering that morning, Seja had been dragged back into the house by the urgent ringing of the phone: "We're coming over, and Peter's coming with us!" Hanna babbled. "We've just picked him up from the station, Markus is spending the day with him and I don't want to leave them on their own, but I don't want to hang out with Peter all day either!"

Seja had no choice but to agree.

Peter was sticking close to Markus; he didn't seem particularly interested in making friends with Seja, or reviving the flame that had gone out between him and Hanna some years ago. Perhaps that had surprised Hanna at first; if so, she was hardly likely to admit it.

But Markus had certainly been glowing all day. Down at the summer grazing he had had the opportunity to show off his skills when he caught Lukas, tacked him up, mounted, then trotted back and forth in front of his shyly applauding daddy, who was dressed from head to foot in leather, complete with boots, in honour of the hot weather.

Hanna snorted loudly at something in the magazine she had open on her lap. On an impulse, Seja leant forward and squeezed Hanna's tanned knee.

"I'm so proud of you, Hanna. I really am."

It was true. Seja knew how difficult it was for her to put aside her anger at Peter's betrayal.

The aroma drifting out from the kitchen suggested that the food would be ready soon. Seja got up and went inside to fetch plates. When Åke rang to say that he and Kristina had put their plans to move on ice, she clamped the phone between her shoulder and her ear and said she was very pleased they would still be living nearby. She also said she hoped the offer to sell her their house would still stand in the future, and would they like to come over for something to eat? Right now, because it was almost ready.

She was just spreading a white cloth over the table when an unmistakable clinking sound coming down the slope made her turn around.

"Christian!"

He was carrying a sports bag over his shoulder and four bags from the off-licence in his hand.

"Do you need help carrying all that?"

"No, but I might need some help drinking it!"

He put everything down before kissing her for longer than he ever had before, his eyes firmly locked on hers.

"Are you thinking of moving in?" she joked, pointing to his bulging bag.

"If that's OK with you."

468

"I thought the forest gave you panic attacks." With a smile she took a carrier bag in each hand.

"It does, but you don't. I suppose I can cope with a few pine needles in the bed."

"Thanks for ringing earlier. It made me very happy."

"I'm the one who should be thanking you."

Christian held her gaze until he was sure she had understood. He could hear voices coming from the stable. They would talk later, when there was time and they were alone. About what had been, and about what was to come. And, no doubt, she would be the one who did most of the talking, after he had explained why he was standing in her garden with the bag.

"If I've made it hard for you to adapt . . ."

He couldn't find the words to tell Seja how wrong she was. He asked nothing of her, not in terms of who she was. But they had just got past all that it's-not-you-it's-me stuff.

"I'm just so bloody glad you want to be with me," he said. "Nothing else matters. I need you too. I thought you understood that."

They were a "we" now.

"In any case, I'm sick and tired of both the city and my job; I can just imagine spending the whole weekend lying in a hammock with a couple of beers."

"Hammock? I thought you were building me a sauna?"

"Don't tease me. Don't tease me just because you're cleverer than me."

"You're not wrong there."

"And more beautiful."

He uncorked a bottle of red wine just as Hanna came round the corner of the house.

"Hi."

Christian handed her a glass of wine before turning to Markus and Peter, who were just emerging from the stable with dusty grey hands and faces.

The two men shook hands.

Seja couldn't help laughing at what they must have looked like; Detective Inspector Christian Tell, who had come straight from work and hadn't had time to change out of his smart trousers and tie, but had just shoved some things into a sports bag and headed out into the back of beyond to hang out with a former punk turned counter-urbanisation freak.

And he fitted right in. When Åke Melkersson appeared through the trees with Kristina following behind, it was Christian who served the drinks.

They ate as the evening drew in. Christian, Peter and Hanna shared a cigar, Kristina looked as if she was falling asleep on her husband's shoulder, and Åke was soon immersed in the tangled thicket of his childhood memories. There was a girlfriend who ran amok — Hanna thought that was hysterically funny — a mad mother-in-law and a part-time job selling ice creams door to door. During the lulls in conversation they could hear deer moving quietly through the edge of the forest.

Seja tipped her head back and gazed at the tops of the fir trees, outlined against the sky.

Later she would light citronella candles to keep away the mosquitoes in the deepening darkness.

470

Afterword

While working on *Babylon*, I have encountered a number of people who have been a great help to me in different ways. I would like to take this opportunity to thank just some of these: Staffan Lundén, who is an archaeologist at Museion, the University of Gothenburg and Gotland University. Gerd Brantlid, head of the investigation unit with the Gothenburg police. Beata Kjellberg, psychotherapist and tutor at the Institute of Psychotherapy in Gothenburg, and Per Dahlström, curator at the Röhsska Museum.

I would also like to thank Carin, Rolf, Irene and, of course, Åsa and Katarina at Wahlström & Widstrand. Last, but not least, I want to sing the praises of my family for all their stalwart support and involvement in the sometimes difficult and disorganised creative process which culminated in *Babylon*.

In this book I have chosen to write about archaeological finds and cultural treasures, among other things. I have learned more about the subject through reading, visits to museums and conversations with experts. However, as always, the basis of my writing remains my imagination — happily an author's principal task. Any "errors" which may have crept into the narrative are therefore my own, and any resemblance to actual persons is entirely coincidental.

Camilla Ceder

The Shadow Girls

Henning Mankell

Tea-Bag, a young African girl, has fled a refugee camp in Spain for the promise of a new life in Sweden. Tania has made a long and dangerous journey to escape the horrors of human trafficking. Leyla has come with her family from Iran. All of them are facing challenges in their new home.

Meanwhile, celebrated poet Jesper Humlin is looking for inspiration. Harried by his mother and girlfriend, misunderstood by his publisher and tormented by his stockbroker, Jesper needs a new perspective on life. A chance encounter with Tea-Bag leads him into the shadow world of the immigrant experience in Sweden. Initially he sees the girls purely as material for his next work, but soon discovers they have very different ideas.

ISBN 978-0-7531-9206-1 (hb)
ISBN 978-0-7531-9207-8 (pb)

The Blinded Man

Arne Dahl

Now a major BBC TV series

Two of Sweden's most powerful businessmen have been murdered. In the face of mounting panic amongst the financial elite, a task force has been created to catch the culprit before he kills again. To his surprise, Detective Paul Hjelm, currently under investigation for misconduct after shooting a man who took an immigration officer hostage, is summoned to join the team. But the killer has left no clues — even removing the bullets from the crime scenes — and Hjelm and his new teammates face a daunting challenge if they are to uncover the connection between the murdered men and identify any potential victims before he strikes again.

ISBN 978-0-7531-9194-1 (hb)
ISBN 978-0-7531-9195-8 (pb)

You
ww
Plea
Ove

Is fé
ww
Mun
50c